"An intricate and compelling new tale from one of the great
original voices of fantasy. Full of fascinating ideas, engaging
characters and magic."
ADRIAN TCHAIKOVSKY

"*Talonsister* is wonderfully rich and inventive, it takes familiar
things and places to make them new and interesting and the tone is
perfectly balanced. I hugely enjoyed it."

TALONSISTER

JEN WILLIAMS

TITAN BOOKS

Talonsister
Print edition ISBN: 9781803364353
E-book edition ISBN: 9781803364360

Published by Titan Books
A division of Titan Publishing Group Ltd.
144 Southwark Street, London SE1 0UP
www.titanbooks.com

First Titan edition: September 2023
10 9 8 7 6 5 4 3 2 1

A CIP catalogue record for this title is available
from the British Library.

Printed and bound by CPI (UK) Ltd, Croydon, CR0 4YY.

For Marty – into the Wild Wood we go!

PART ONE

THE LIP TO THE LICH-WAY

PROLOGUE

In our beginning there is yenlin, the slow forming within the shell.
Those who are yenlin are the responsibility of all. At the time of
yenlin, the unhatched is neither talon clan nor claw, and cannot
be held on bond-oath or attached to a feud.

The Griffin Creed, as written
on the Silver Death Peak by
Fionovar the Red

T he scent of blood was threaded through the sky like a red
ribbon; slippery and quick, but unmistakable.

Flayn tossed his head towards T'vor to see if his partner
had noticed it, but T'vor was already folding his wings, his long sleek
head bent towards the ground. They were on the very edge of official
griffin territory here; the mountains had become foothills, and the
human territory of Brittletain lay to the south, although most griffins
preferred not to acknowledge that name at all. Directly below was a
clear patch of ground, bare save for grass, snow, a handful of trees.
T'vor landed with a shuddering thump, scattering dirt and snow, and
Flayn dropped down neatly next to him.

'Blood,' said T'vor, unnecessarily.

Flayn let his beak hang open for a minute, tasting the air on his
tongue. It was an unusually warm day in the deep winter, and he
could smell many things at once: pine needles, snow melt, lichen, the

sharp scent of T'vor himself. And over and under it all, blood, and also violence. He snapped his beak shut.

'Human,' he said. 'And...'

He stopped as a shriek rent the air around them. T'vor took an indignant step back, while Flayn felt all the feathers on his neck stand on end. The noise was piercing and shrill, awful. Belatedly, he realised that something was moving on the very edge of the clearing. He had missed it initially because it was so close to the ground – only the smallest prey or inedible things were so close to the dirt – and now he padded over to it, T'vor close at his shoulder.

'What is it?'

At first he took it to be a bundle of something, perhaps of the clothes that humans liked to press around themselves, but looking closer he saw that it had a small, round face, soft and bare, and tiny clasping hands. The hole in the middle of the face was wide, the eyes scrunched up with the power of its call.

'It's a cub,' he said. He lifted his head and looked around. Humans didn't usually let their cubs out alone, especially not ones this small, but he could see nothing else moving in the dripping forest. 'The smallest human.'

'It is yenlin?' T'vor dipped his head down to the snow and quickly wiped his beak across it, first one side and then the other, cleaning it and making it shine, black like old river ice. 'We'll take it back for T'rook. She is long enough out of yenlin to eat hot meat.' Seeing Flayn hesitate, he snorted with impatience. 'Hurry up, it is noisy. I tire of it. Pull it in half and we shall each take back a piece. Then you shall not be the favourite with her, as you usually are. Or eat it now, if you must. Just make it quiet.'

The shrieking seemed to double in volume, as if the cub knew what they were talking about. Flayn settled his paw on the thing's chest, easing out his claws slowly, and to his surprise the cub took hold of his claw with one fist, almost as though it were trying to push him away, or greet him. It would be a good treat on a winter's day like this, a quick hot beakful of blood and flesh, a few rubbery organs. The bones wouldn't be up to much, not in a thing this small, but they would add to the texture. Instead, Flayn leaned down to look more closely at its furious face, and then addressed it carefully in the dialect of Brittletain.

'Are you lost?'

T'vor squawked with amusement. 'As well ask the cow if it enjoys the sun before you eat it.'

'It's strange, though.' Flayn looked around again, at the dark trees and the dirt. Where T'vor hadn't scuffed it with his talons, he could see that the snow was marked with prints – the footprints of humans larger than the yenlin cub on the ground. 'Human cubs are not normally left alone in the cold. And the smell of blood does not come from it. Where are the humans that laid it? Are they dead nearby?'

This had T'vor's attention. A human cub might make a good meal for their hatchling, but a pair of humans would represent a significant amount of meat for all of them. The big black griffin lowered his head and opened his beak, scenting the area around them, and after a moment he stepped into the line of trees, beyond the screaming yenlin cub. Flayn watched as T'vor stamped around for a time, his partner's blue scaly legs quickly becoming flecked with mud and pine needles, until he came to a halt and began scratching at a particular patch of earth.

'Something half buried here,' T'vor said shortly.

By the time Flayn reached him, he had dragged something out of the mud and was preening at his long flight feathers, oily black under the dappled forest light. It was the head of an adult human, a male, the skin on its face a yellowish-green. There were clods of mud in the black hair that sprouted from the top of its head and the bottom half of its face.

'It's dead?'

T'vor snapped his beak together derisively. 'Humans usually keep their heads attached, Flayn. Here, look, is the rest of the body.'

Flayn came closer until he too was standing over the dead thing. Blood had turned the earth around it a deeper, meatier black. It certainly smelled dead, but it also smelled wrong.

'One of us did this?' asked Flayn.

This time, T'vor did not snort. Instead he seemed troubled by the question. 'From the wounds, yes. Talon or claw, human bodies fall apart before both. But from the smell...'

'From the smell, not us. And why leave it intact? We would have eaten it.' Flayn dipped his head and tore open the dead human's lower half; he buried his beak in the guts, letting the smell overwhelm him. Behind them, the yenlin had grown quieter, making small hiccupping noises of weariness. There was the good, rich scent of human blood, awakening his hunger as it always did, but underneath and over that was another, colder scent, something that smelled deeply wrong. He pulled his head away and snapped his beak a few times, trying to place what it was, but clarity danced just out of reach. Oddly, it made him think of the Bone Fall, the high and lonely place that griffins went to when they felt the ache of their last days. It made him afraid.

'I don't like it,' he said eventually. 'I cannot smell a poison, but even so, I don't think we should eat it.'

T'vor shook out his coat and feathers in irritation, sending a brilliant cascade of water droplets to patter against the foliage.

'Fine. I will trust your word, *forvyn*.'

Flayn lifted his head, surprised. T'vor usually only called him 'beloved wise one' in jest, but there was no trace of his usual affectionate teasing this time. The strangeness of the human corpse had clearly gotten to him, too.

'We'll find other game, T'vor.'

'And we can at least eat the yenlin. Or save it for T'rook.' He turned away and moved back to the edge of the clearing, lowering his powerful beak to the tiny wriggling shape on the ground.

'Wait.'

'What now?'

'I don't think we should eat that, either.' Flayn went and stood over the cub, already feeling foolish. 'I think we should take it back, let it grow a little, see if we can learn more. Whatever killed that human, I feel like it is a danger to us.'

For a long moment T'vor said nothing, his great yellow eyes narrowed in confusion. 'You want us to... look after it? In our own nest?'

'T'vor, many times we've listened to my instincts, and it has kept us flying, hasn't it? We need to know more about what happened here. And besides, it's yenlin.' He looked away, too aware this particular argument was nonsense. 'Yenlin is the responsibility of all.'

'Listen to yourself! This is a human cub, some featherless, ground-stuck meat bag. It is not worthy of dirtying our nest, unless our daughter is eating it. Too soon I called you *forvyn* – you know as well as I do that we remember very little from the time of yenlin, and I doubt that humans, with their tiny soft brains, are any different. This thing can grow and it can become more troublesome, but it will never teach us anything.'

'I don't believe that's true.' When T'vor began to turn away in disgust, Flayn butted his shoulder with his head. 'We can stand here arguing about it while we lose the light, or we can skip to the part where you let me have my way, as you always do.'

'Ha!'

'I have a feeling about this, T'vor. A strong one. I swear it on my bones.'

'Hmm.' T'vor shook out his feathers again. Bones were a serious matter, not to be sworn on lightly, and Flayn could see him weakening. 'Well, *you* can feed it. And you'll have to explain to Queen Fellvyn why we are keeping food alive in our nest. It is not hygienic.'

They flew back with the wailing bundle clutched carefully between T'vor's powerful talons. On the way Flayn spotted a small herd of mountain goats creeping cautiously up the sheer side of Silver Death Peak, and without slowing them down he snapped up a couple of the rangy animals, breaking their necks quickly and efficiently, so that they would have something to eat that night at least. The Silver Death was one of several mountains that punctuated the hazy border between griffin territory – known to them as Yelvynia – and the many scattered settlements of the ground-stuck humans. These lands were strictly forbidden to those prey animals; any foolish enough to venture near the mountains and get caught were killed without trial or discourse, and their stripped, severed heads were left on the southernmost foothills as a warning. Humans, it seemed, did not learn lessons quickly or well, since the southern foothills were awash with ancient skulls, turned white and yellow with the freezing winters and bleaching sun.

A griffin bringing one over the mountains personally was unheard of, and Flayn had no real idea of how the clans would react. Most likely there would be demands the thing be killed immediately, yenlin or no, or if they were really unlucky, someone would decide it was a grievous insult to Great T'vyn the Trickster himself, and they would be driven out of their nest to avoid bringing a curse on them – all three of them, including T'rook, who was too small yet even to fly.

'The queen may not even bother with exile,' said T'vor, as if he knew exactly what Flayn were thinking. 'She could simply tear our throats out for this.'

'I do not think she will,' said Flayn. In truth, he wasn't sure at all, but Queen Fellvyn was claw clan too, like him, and he thought there was a chance she would listen. 'T'vor, this creature is fate-tied to us, and perhaps to all griffin.'

'Nonsense. What are you, a witch-seer now?'

'I feel it in my bones.'

T'vor made a growling noise in the back of his throat, and they flew back the rest of the way in silence, the bundle still clutched carefully in T'vor's talons. When they reached their own nest-pit, T'rook lifted her head and squawked at them, her feathers still a sticky downy fluff, her eyes not quite fully open.

'She is too small to understand yet,' said T'vor. His harsh voice was softer than it normally was. 'Flayn, she may eat this thing anyway, regardless of your supposed fate-ties.'

'She might,' conceded Flayn. 'And then you can tell me I was wrong about everything.'

Yet when T'vor placed the human cub into the nest-pit with T'rook, the hatchling sniffed at it, then tugged at the material it was wrapped in, as though trying to understand what it was. After a moment, she folded her wings away – bony crumpled things as yet – and curled up next to the wriggling bundle. The human yenlin, which had freed one of its own smooth limbs during the flight, reached out and touched T'rook's downy head. For the first time it seemed calm, its small eyes closing.

'Well,' said Flayn. 'Would you look at that?'

1

SIXTEEN YEARS LATER

The tavern was busy, but Leven had no trouble weaving her way to the front of the crowd. When she got to the bar, a foaming tankard of The Lip's best ale was placed in front of her.

'No Herald will pay for a drink in my lifetime.' The barkeep did not quite meet her eyes, as if embarrassed by his own emotion. Further along the bar, several men and women were nodding furiously at his words, and a murmur rose up all around that *a Herald was in the bar*. A short woman to Leven's right placed a hand on her bare forearm, where the silvery-blue ore-lines traced intricate patterns across her skin.

'You are the pride of the Starlight Imperium,' said the woman. 'When you've finished that, girl, come and tell me. You won't go thirsty tonight.'

'Stars bless you.' Leven grinned and picked up the tankard. She nodded to the barkeep. 'Another one of these, if you'd be so kind?'

She made her way back to their table through the attentive crowd. Foro had chosen to sit right at the front, where the bar was open to the outside, the wooden shutters rolled back to reveal the spectacular views beyond. The Lip, as its name suggested, sat at the very top of the vast crater that was the city of Stratum, and its patrons could look out across a teeming landscape bathed in clean golden sunshine. Leven spared it a quick glance as she set their drinks on the scratched table. Right at the very bottom a lake glittered as blue as the sky, and it was just possible to see boats down there, white sails as tiny as the half-moons on her fingernails.

'It's true what they told us, Foro,' she said as she sat down. 'We never have to put our hands in our pockets for a drink again. One look at the ore-lines and they're falling over themselves to provide. I think this lot would buy us dinner too, if we wanted.'

Foro did not have his ore-lines on display. Despite the heat of the afternoon, he was wearing a thick hooded cloak, and he wore long sleeves over his burly arms. Even his hands, which bore blue circles of the Titan ore on their palms and on their backs, were covered with fingerless gloves. He glanced bleakly at the tankard of ale, then looked away.

'Aye.'

'The war is over, and we're living the high life.' Leven took a sip of her ale. 'Fuck me, that's good stuff. Do you remember some of the swill we drank on campaign? No more of that Unblessed toilet water they called wine, and no more of that brutal stuff Nines used to brew up through his socks. Do you remember that? More than once I lost all the feeling in my feet after a night of drinking his brew.'

Foro drew himself up, taking hold of the tankard and turning it in his hands. Around them, Leven was still very aware of the men and women watching their table. It had been almost three months since their company of Heralds had returned to the capital of the Imperium, and the novelty of their existence had yet to wear off.

'Have you seen Nines lately?' asked Foro eventually.

She shook her head. 'He said he was going to find a wife, buy some land, settle down. Last I heard he was very enthusiastically looking for a wife in a number of taverns. Have you? Seen him?'

Foro didn't answer. Instead he took a large gulp of his ale, the hood on his cloak falling back slightly to reveal his weathered, ore-lined face. To Leven's surprise, he did not look well at all. There were dark circles under his eyes, almost like bruises, and his cheeks were gaunt.

As he put the tankard back on the table, she noticed that his fingers had a slight tremble.

'Do you remember what they promised us, Leven? Glory, gold, our names written in the stars. For every Unblessed nation brought into the warm bosom of the Imperium, our names would live for another age. Remember all that?'

'Yeah.' Said out loud, it sounded a little ludicrous, but it was what they had been told, all of them, over and over. 'Sure.'

'Our names, to live on. But what does that mean? I don't even know my name. You don't know yours, either.'

'Foro...'

'Yeah, yeah, I know the numbers we were *given*. But what's your real name, Leven?'

'Is that supposed to be a joke?'

He leaned forward, meeting her eyes for the first time. He looked haunted.

'A joke. Maybe that's what the whole thing is.'

'Foro.' Leven lowered her voice. She didn't want the rest of the tavern to see them arguing. 'What's wrong? I don't hear from you for weeks, and then you want to go for a drink, and *then* you've got the hump. Has something happened? Something I should know about?'

He looked away from her, placing his hands flat against the table. Leven had the idea that he knew they were shaking and he didn't want her to see it.

'I've been having... dreams. Except they're happening in the middle of the day. Visions of places that, as far as I know, I've never visited. Seeing faces of people I've never met.'

'You're readjusting, that's all. It's been... I mean, eight years of war, Foro.' She forced out a laugh. 'A few bad dreams are to be expected.'

For a long moment he didn't say anything at all. Around them the tavern was full of people talking loudly, and beyond the wide open window the dim roar of Stratum was a constant pressure on the ears.

'They feel like memories, Leven. I think they *are* memories. Glimpses of my life before the ore-lines took all that away from me. And every time, it's like being knocked sideways. I'm having blackouts, and when I come back for a little while I don't know who or where I am.' Foro turned to look at her then, and she sat back from the table a little, alarmed by the glassy fear in his eyes. 'We all saw some terrible things during the campaign, yet I've never been as afraid as I am now. It's like my idea of who I am is falling apart.'

'Perhaps you're coming down with a fever. Stars only know what you could have brought back from the Unblessed lands. Have you been to a healer?'

But Foro was shaking his head. 'Do you remember the last battle coming out of Lamabet, that green river that cut through the mountains? What we did on the banks there?'

'Oh come on, I don't want to talk about that.' Leven swallowed the rest of her ale in one gulp and looked around the bar. She wanted to be somewhere else. 'It's over. Let's drink until we fall down, then roll ourselves downhill to a livelier tavern. That's what we're supposed to be doing now, not reliving past glories like we're ancient old gaffers.'

'Past glories?' Foro shook his head. 'Maybe you don't remember the green river, then.'

'Of course I bloody remember it.'

She didn't want to, though. The last remnants of the Unblessed Lamabet armies had been retreating, fleeing from the scene of their last clash with the forces of the Imperium, towards lands in the north that might still conceivably be safe. Many of them had been wounded, and quite a few were being carried by their fellow soldiers, but there were still enough viable enemy combatants – according to Boss, anyway – to make it worth tracking them. It had been a cold, wet day, the river running high and fast, and the smell of water had been everywhere, strong and mineral, a thick taste at the back of Leven's throat. From their vantage point on the cliffs overlooking the river, the Heralds had watched the men and women passing below with a patience that was edging into indolence. Leven remembered that the enemy's steel helmets had gleamed like new coins, the dust and the blood driven from them by the rain.

'It was a slaughter,' said Foro. 'I know you remember that.'

Leven shook her head. She wanted another drink, something stronger. Despite the bright clean sunshine of the Imperium pouring in through the windows, she felt cold. It was as if he'd brought back the chill of the green river just by talking about it.

'Have a drink and fucking cheer up, will you?'

They had lined up along the cliff edges, Boss shouting them to their places. Below them, one or two Lamabetian lookouts had spotted what was looking down on them, and it was possible to hear them calling orders too, their voices floating up from below like the calls of frightened birds. There had been laughter along their line – they were so close to the end of this war, everything seemed too easy now – but at the time Leven had felt an uncomfortable tightness in her gut. The enemy were retreating. They were injured. They were no real threat to the forces of the Imperium.

But when Boss had given the order, she had stepped up to the edge of the cliff like everyone else, and as she leapt into the yawning space beyond it, she had summoned her wings with the same shout of joy she always did. They had snapped into existence at her shoulders, like clear shards of lethal blue glass, and then she was swooping down, her focus on the scattering troops below, and if she'd had any regrets when she cut down the first of them, she couldn't remember them now. There was no space for regrets on the battlefield; the battlefield was for survival, blood, and the glory of Titan strength at your fingertips.

'Half of them drowned,' said Foro quietly, as if he could picture the parade of grisly images currently marching through her mind. 'After we hunted them across their own country for months, they were so terrified that half of them ran into that river, even though it was swollen with rain and they were wearing heavy armour. We barely had to do anything.'

'Yeah, I was there too. I remember pulling their bodies out of the water.' She took a breath and tugged one hand quickly through her hair, making it stand up in messy corkscrews. 'So what has that got to do with anything, Foro? What does any of it have to do with your... dreams?'

'I always knew that being a Herald was a chance for me to make a new life, even if I couldn't remember why I had abandoned my old life in the first place. But now... I think of what we did in Lamabet, and I wonder if it was an honourable way to live after all. Pieces of who I was are returning and it frightens me. What if I've always been a butcher, Leven? What if my whole life has been about spilling blood?'

'Foro, the past doesn't matter,' she said, too quickly. 'What's done is done. We are the Imperium's *champions*. That's what matters.' She felt annoyed with Foro. All her pleasure at their heroes' welcome was being chased away by his gloomy mood. 'Listen, recovering your memories could be a good thing.' She tried to make a joke of it. 'Could be that you're the lost prince of some newly Blessed country, about to come into a huge inheritance. Right?'

'You can laugh, Leven, but people who volunteer to have their memories wiped away are not running from riches and happiness.' Foro shook his head. A cloud passed over the sun, and the light shining on his face dimmed for a moment. 'I am remembering pain, Leven. Shame, and violence, and terrible mistakes. What if you find out who you were, and you end up wishing you never knew?'

'That is ridiculous. You are flinching at shadows. Do you want me to take you to a healer? You have picked up a fever, that's all.'

He shook his head. He seemed less angry and more bewildered. 'I am a man with no name and a history soaked in blood and cruelty, Leven. I only know I can't go on like this.'

Leven tried to remember which Heralds she had seen recently. In the months following their discharge most of them had left Stratum, heading for the lush lands directly south, intending to buy land and start building new lives. A few, like her and Foro, had stayed in the city, enjoying the sense of being around a large number of people you didn't have to kill. They had kept in touch, at least at first, but it had been a while since she'd seen any of them. She had, in fact, been thrilled to get Foro's message to meet up – without her brothers-in-arms she had been starting to feel alarmingly lonely.

'Don't you think it's strange that they've let us go at all?' said Foro.

'What do you mean?'

'The Imperium's greatest weapon.' Foro smiled sourly. 'We've presented them with the majority of the Unblessed lands on a silver plate, yet we're allowed to just walk away, and settle wherever we would like? No more fighting for the empress – just a cosy retirement.'

'We did our eight years, Foro.' Leven looked down at the metallic lines etched into the skin of her forearm. 'That has always been the agreement. They've just kept to their word, that's all. And they can always make more of us.'

'So they just give up their sharpest blade, to keep their word? When the Titan ore they use to give us powers is so rare, so valuable? Does that sound like the Imperium to you?'

Leven sighed. '*We* are the Imperium, Foro. Their chosen few, taking the light of the stars to the Unblessed lands.'

Foro snorted. 'Stars' arses, you sound like Boss.'

Leven scowled. To her own dismay, she was beginning to feel angry with Foro. Why did he have to question everything? Wasn't it enough to just take what you were given and be grateful for it? Asking difficult questions only caused problems. She lifted her hands in defeat. 'Foro, I don't know, do I? I'm just a soldier. I just go where they tell me, except I don't anymore. We don't have to think about the Imperium or its ambitions ever again if we don't want to.'

'My friend.' Foro leaned over and briefly clasped her shoulder. 'Believe it or not, I didn't ask you to come here just so that I could bitch and whine at you. I want you to be careful—'

At that moment, a giant shape stepped in front of the window, casting their table into shadow. Leven glanced up, annoyed at this interruption, to see an enormous man beaming down at them. He looked to be a warrior from the south, his chest bare and his forearms crisscrossed with scars, and his long yellow hair was braided into plaits. Once he saw that he had their attention, he smiled all the wider, revealing one tooth chiselled into a point. Belatedly Leven realised that there was a group of smaller people standing just to one side of him, wearing a variety of nervous expressions.

'Small woman.' He had a thick accent, marking out his origins as even further south than Leven had initially thought. 'My friends, they tell me you are strong. That you could beat me in an arm wrestle. I have seen many things, small woman, but none as strange as this. So I would like to see it.'

'That woman is a Herald, and you will show her some respect!' Leven didn't see the owner of the voice, but they were clearly agitated, and on the back of the outburst she could hear an undercurrent of angry muttering.

'It's alright!' Leven held up one hand. Next to her, Foro had bent back over his drink. 'You don't want to fight me, friend.'

The warrior seemed positively delighted by this response. He pushed his braids back over his shoulders, as if to better show off his muscles, and gestured to her grandly.

'But you are small woman. They tell me that because of your silly tattoos you are very strong. It is impossible.'

Leven didn't entirely blame him for this assumption. He was at least a head taller than her, and she was slim, wiry even. She had a handful of scars here and there, but nothing unusual for a soldier of the Imperium, and while her arms showed some evidence of muscle, there were cooks in the army with biceps bigger than hers. She was not, by any stretch of the imagination, an imposing figure. She stood up, pushing her chair back.

'My friend, not only could I beat you in an arm-wrestling match, I could pick you up and throw you out this window.'

In the end, Leven settled for picking the man up – much to his bellowed surprise – and, holding him up over her head, doing several circuits of The Lip. When the cheering and the shouting had died down and she had deposited the warrior back on a stool, she found that the grateful citizens of the Imperium had been queuing up at the bar to buy her even more drinks; there was a whole line of them, from glass beakers of wine to foaming tankards of ale to a tall green drink she had never seen before. She stood for a moment, bemusedly taking it in, while the southern warrior ordered in even more. When he was finished, he turned back to her, his face rather redder than it had been.

'So you have shown me the impossible, small woman. It would be a great honour in my life if you would show me a little more?'

'I think you've had enough excitement for one day, don't you, big man? I don't want to do you a mischief.' Leven looked back over the bustling seats to the table where she had left Foro. His seat was empty. She plucked up one of the small glasses from the bar and downed its contents. 'But you'll finish the rest of these off for me, won't you? There's someone I need to see.'

2

'Thank you for seeing me so quickly, sir.'

'Anything for our brave Heralds. Such a victory you've brought to us, Blessed Eleven – the Unblessed lands have finally been brought into the fold. All the ones that truly matter, anyway, and I'm sure that with the Imperium changing the lives of thousands across the sea, even the barbarians of Brittletain will eventually warm to us.' Imperator Justinia was an older woman with warm, weathered skin, her dark eyes lined in black and her hair oiled so that it fell in ringlets the colour of old, tarnished gold. The smile she gave Leven was warm enough, but the rolls of parchment on her desk and the presence of an Envoy at her shoulder suggested that the Herald could have picked a better time to come calling on her old employers. The Envoy was a tall handsome man with warm brown skin, a neat beard framing a mouth that was carefully free of smiles, and he wore loose, dark clothes, the only hint towards his station the solid silver pin in the black scarf at his throat; it was in the shape of a stylised comet, a chip of emerald glinting at its heart. The Envoy – whom Leven vaguely recognised on sight – kept his hands behind his back and his eyes on Leven.

'It's about Foro.' At the Imperator's blank expression, she carried on. 'Blessed Forty, sir. He hasn't been feeling well, and I think he needs help.'

'Ah.' Imperator Justinia glanced down at the notes in front of her, as if there might be answers there. 'He is... poorly?'

'Yes, sir. We don't have access to the army's healers now, you see, now that we are officially discharged—'

'You were paid your victory bonus, were you not?' Justinia cut in. She picked up a sheet of parchment and nodded at it, a small smile on her lips. 'Yes, I see you were. A sizeable sum, I should say.'

'Ye-es that's true, sir, but I'm concerned that—'

'There are healers in Stratum, are there not?' Justinia turned slightly to the Envoy, who nodded. 'Good ones, I believe. Where would you say the best healers in Stratum are, Envoy Kaeto?'

'The Street of Bonesaws,' he replied instantly, his voice smooth and quiet. 'There are healers with flashier premises of course, but if you're looking for real practical experience, I would point you in that direction, Herald.'

'There you are then,' said Justinia brightly. 'I'm so glad we could help you today, Blessed Eleven.'

'Forgive me, Imperator, I don't think you understand.' Leven cleared her throat, looking around the room for inspiration. It was a small gilded box, the walls covered in lacquered wood panels, while a narrow channel in the floor housed a constantly flowing stream of perfumed water; it ran around all the buildings of the Imperial Concourse. It was disorientating, a thousand leagues away from the concerns of soldiers, from men and women who went to sleep at night with blood drying under their fingernails. 'Whatever's wrong with Foro, he believes it's a consequence of being a Herald, and, well, I don't think a healer from the Street of Bonesaws is going to be able to deal with that.'

A flicker of annoyance passed over Justinia's face. Envoy Kaeto remained as impassive as ever.

'What is wrong with him, exactly?' asked Justinia.

Leven shifted on the spot. They hadn't asked her to sit down. 'He's having... he called them waking dreams.' She didn't see Envoy Kaeto move, but now he seemed to be watching her much more closely. All at once, coming to speak to the Imperium Office directly didn't seem like such a brilliant idea after all. 'Look, it doesn't sound like a normal illness to me. You know what we are, what the Heralds are. We're tough to knock down. I've seen Foro fight all day and all night without pausing to eat or rest, and now this same man looks ten years older. Is there anything you can do for him, sir? Perhaps he could speak to Gynid Tyleigh directly. Sir.'

There was a moment of silence then, filled with the gentle trickle of the narrow waterway.

'Speaking to the Imperial Bone Crafter herself is out of the question,' said Imperator Justinia eventually. 'But you are right. The empress values every man and woman who fights for the Blessed Imperium, but none more so than our star-touched Heralds.' She said it smoothly and without much emotion; Leven had the impression it was something she had said before, perhaps many times. 'We will have healers dispatched to your friend Foro, and he will be given the very highest levels of care. You can be sure of it, Blessed Eleven.'

'Thank you, sir.'

'You may leave.'

Leven bowed quickly, and turned her back on them, glad to get out of the gilded room. As she left, she was certain she could feel the eyes of the Imperator and the Envoy boring into the back of her head.

———

Envoy Kaeto watched the young woman leave, making a note to himself to look back over her official files. All of the Heralds were known to be 'unusual characters' – they were, after all, men and women who had known nothing but war – but even so, he doubted that many of them would come all the way to the Imperium offices to tell Imperator Justinia that she hadn't been doing her job properly. Leven was the youngest of the Heralds, and one of the least imposing; not especially tall, not especially bulky. She had worn her dark brown hair short during the war, but since they had been discharged she had let it grow, so that her untidy brown waves now framed her face. She had clear grey eyes, and the silvery-blue patterns of the ore-lines stood out starkly against her tanned skin – and there was a look, a stubbornness about her jawline, that was oddly familiar... Yes, he would have to check the records again.

Next to him, Imperator Justinia sighed noisily.

'These soldier scum are an endless pain in my arsehole.'

'Yes, Imperator.'

'And she had the cheek to say "you know what we are"! Yes, I know what you are – a sorry collection of thieves and murderers who were given a second chance by our merciful empress!'

'Not all of them were murderers, Imperator.'

'Yes, well. That hardly matters now, does it?' Justinia poked at the pieces of parchment on her desk as though they had done her a personal injury. 'What news do you have on our other problem, Envoy?'

He inclined his head slightly and moved to stand in front of the desk. 'As I understand it, the work is slow, and dangerous...'

Justinia tutted loudly.

'And everything must be conducted in the utmost secrecy, which means the boats must be manned by our people, the ports must be bribed not to look too closely at our cargo, and the wagons have to travel a long way, over dangerous ground. Nowhere Unblessed, but even so, the risk is still considerable. And,' he paused, uncertain how his next portion of information would be received, 'I fear we must keep the numbers of people involved as low as possible, or keep our bribes extremely high. There is no predicting the level of outrage if any part of the Imperium's business is revealed.'

'Of course,' said Justinia, her tone bitter. 'The Titans must remain untouchable.'

'It's inconvenient, but it's worth remembering how many cultures and nations the Imperium encompasses,' said Kaeto. He wasn't quite able to resist delicately hammering the point home. 'The Titans are considered sacred all over Enonah, Imperator. Even the denizens of Stratum consider them to be the most starblessed of all creatures –

they gave us history, stories, the first sparks of alchemy. They gave us language. They are the gods that walked among us.'

'Yes, yes. I'm quite aware.' There was a small golden plate of dried fruits on her desk, and Justinia began poking about amongst the small brown pieces. She was looking for dried sweet-apple, her favourite; it was Kaeto's job to know that sweet-apple was her favourite, in case he should ever need to poison her. 'And this Foro. I suppose you know where to find him?'

'I do, Imperator.'

'Then I suggest you get on with it.'

'It is not my place to question your orders...'

Justinia laughed. She found a piece of sweet-apple and munched on it with satisfaction for some moments. 'What is the place of an Envoy, exactly? Who can guess?' She waved a hand at him dismissively. 'Go on. Say what you want to say, Kaeto – I know you'll say it anyway.'

'The Heralds must be dealt with carefully.' He let that hang in the air for a moment. He knew that Justinia had certain opinions on this; had watched from a dark space on an interior balcony as she had spoken to the empress herself, her face closed and furious. 'The empress understands that they are heroes to the people of the Imperium, celebrated everywhere her starlight touches.'

'And I *don't* understand. Is that what you're saying?'

'I am just here to remind you of the delicacy of the situation. The agreement was...' He paused, trying to think how to phrase it. 'It was agreed that for the Heralds to all die at once would be too suspicious, invite too many questions. We have to be careful.'

'Celestinia has been cloistered inside her palaces for years. She doesn't know what real people are like anymore, Kaeto.' Justinia looked up at him, her dark eyes shining. 'The people will forget about the Blessed Heralds soon enough – as soon as some other war or wedding comes along to distract them, and those are always just around the corner. And meanwhile, we have cut loose these dangerous men and women to roam freely. Carrying the secrets of the Imperium with them. Blessed Forty believes that his illness is related to his Herald magic, and has gone as far as to talk to another Herald about it. He has become a danger to us, and he's dying anyway, Kaeto.' She lowered her voice. 'We should have ended the problem months ago, but Celestinia wouldn't hear of it. Now we shall have to deal with each one as they deteriorate. And who gets their hands dirty now? You and I, Kaeto.'

Your hands will remain spotless, thought Kaeto, *as they always do.*

'And what of Blessed Eleven?'

'Oh, let her get on with it. She too will get distracted soon enough, or she'll find some young farmer to marry, or she'll sicken and die like her friend. I'm not as bloodthirsty as you make me out to be, Envoy. Until she starts to actively cause us trouble, I am happy to let this particular little bird fly away.'

———

When Kaeto was dismissed, he left Justinia with her as yet unpoisoned dried fruits and retreated to his own rooms, hidden away in one of the upper corners of the Imperium offices. It was a space he had worked for years to cultivate; far enough away from the main hub to be quiet; enough space for his records – all written in his own version of the Envoy cypher; and close enough to the Tower of the Voice that he could intercept messages coming and going faster than anyone else. Belise, his assistant, greeted him at the door, her eyebrows raised.

'Anything I should know about, chief?'

'The Imperator is a fool, the Herald problem isn't going away, and my afternoon is ruined. Any surprises there?'

'Not as such, chief, no.'

Kaeto stopped to look down at the girl. He had picked her up off the street when she was eleven, a sharp-eyed street rat with more sense than he usually saw in children of her ilk, but not quite enough sense not to attempt to pickpocket an Envoy on official Imperium business. Two years later and his impulse had proved a wise one:

Belise was smart, loyal, devious and entirely unfazed by the darker portions of his work.

'I'll need my grey work kit laid out for me as quickly as possible. And here,' he dropped a small bag of candies into her hand, 'the Imperator doesn't lock her treat drawer.'

He was rewarded with a quick flash of a grin, and then Belise was gone, back into the small locked room that smelled vaguely of chemicals. Trusting her to prepare what he needed, Kaeto went to his desk and unlocked a compartment built into its underside. From there he withdrew a slim leather folder, filled with pieces of ragged parchment, some old and yellowed, others still crisp and covered in dark, rich inks. He pulled a few items out and spread them on the table.

It occurred to him that Blessed Eleven would be very interested to see some of the information he had gathered here. She struck him as the curious sort, and these slim pieces of parchment were the only remaining evidence that the Heralds had had lives before Gynid Tyleigh had etched her lines of Titan ore across their bodies. The Herald known as Foro, for example, had once been an overseer in a gladiator complex in Unblessed Caucasore. It had been his job to take the prisoners given to him by the country's army and turn them into people who could fight for the entertainment of Caucasore's aristocracy – one of life's delicious little ironies. He had by all reports been a brute of a man, and those who entered the training grounds were more likely to die – beaten to death, starved, or torn apart by wild animals – than make it to the arena. And then when Caucasore had been absorbed into the Imperium, Foro had fought against them for a while, one of the most vicious captains in their militia. This apparent loyalty, however, hadn't stopped him taking the opportunity to become part of the Herald programme when the alternative was to die an honourable death next to his soldiers. The man known as Carlen Forgathers had happily switched sides when he saw that the tide was changing. Not that he knew anything about it now, of course.

Kaeto was just frowning over this information when Belise came back into the room and laid his tool belt on the desk in front of him. Her jaw was working rhythmically on one of the toffees he had given her.

'Thank you, Belise. I hope you didn't put that in your mouth in the Workroom? No food, no drink, and gloves at all times, remember?'

She rolled her eyes at him and then nodded at the folder.

'What's that about then?'

Few people would dare to ask what the Imperium's master spy was reading, but it was one of the reasons he kept her around.

'Just secrets and forgotten things.'

'It's *always* secrets and forgotten things.'

'Yes.' He paused, flicking through the documents in the leather folder a second time. There should have been a complete record of the former lives of each Herald, yet curiously Blessed Eleven did not seem to have one. Absently, he reached up and unclipped his silver Envoy badge, placing it carefully on his desk. Tugging out his scarf, he pulled it up and over the back of his head to make a hood. 'Secrets and forgotten things are what we live for, in our dark little world.'

'Yes, chief.' He could sense her resisting the urge to roll her eyes again.

'I have to go out.' Standing up, he swept the folder and its documents back into the hidden portion of his desk and slammed it shut, before wagging a finger at her. 'Don't eat all those sweets in one go, you'll get a stomach ache.'

'*Pft*. You want me to shout up the coach?'

'No, I'll go out the back way.' He picked up the grey toolkit belt and tied it around his waist, making sure to cover it with his long dark shirt afterwards. Through the narrow windows he could see that the sun was well on its way down, and Stratum was slowly being doused in shadows and oily lamplight. 'I'll want your help when I come back. Prepare the wet room.'

She grimaced at that, but as he was going out the door he noticed her slipping another toffee into her mouth. There wasn't much that could ruin Belise's appetite – she'd spent too long hungry on the streets for that.

———

Kaeto was gone for no more than a couple of hours. Foro had been renting a room in a boarding house on the Second Ring. It was a well-appointed place with large, ornate windows, standing open in the stuffy evening air – all the better for a quick shot with a poisoned bolt. The key to killing a Herald – something the armies of the Unblessed never quite seemed to grasp – was to do it from a distance, and to do it very quietly.

When the Envoy arrived back at the Imperium Concourse, he took one of the quiet back entrances and allowed a small team of staff to take the body, carefully hidden in an unremarkable travel chest, up to his rooms. There was a shaft in the back with a system of pulleys specifically designed to quickly move heavy, unpleasant things. When he arrived, Belise was already poking at the heavily laden sack.

'You could have taken him out of the city,' she said. 'Dumped him in a river. Don't see why you had to bring him back here at all.'

Kaeto pulled his hood back and made for the small clay pot by the hearth. One of Belise's jobs was to keep it full of fresh tea. He poured himself a large cup and doused its heat with a thick slug of milk before taking a sip. It needed honey.

'This particular corpse is property of the Imperium.' When she just raised her eyebrows at that, he continued. 'When we made the Heralds – when Imperial Bone Crafter Tyleigh, dreadful creature that she is, made the Heralds – they essentially signed over their bodies and lives to the Imperium. What are the ore-lines made of, Belise?'

'The bones of Titans,' she replied instantly. 'Long-dead ones.'

'Yes. And how many Titans are left in the world?'

'Just the griffins,' she said, her voice taking on a slightly bored tone. 'In northern Brittletain. And there's that one who's still alive in the south, the giant bear one. But that's just one.'

'The Druidahnon, yes, although how much longer he will live we do not know.' He put the tea cup down. 'All the other Titan races – the wyverns, the great krakens of the eastern sea, the huge god-boar of the south, the giants, the unicorns, the firebirds – all died out hundreds and hundreds of years ago. The bones of a Titan are special. They are strange, magical. Heavier than normal bones.'

'I *know* all this,' protested Belise. She had gone back to picking at the bag. 'If you're going to drone on I'd rather go into the wet room.'

'You know it all, yet apparently you haven't *thought* about it. The remains of Titans are incredibly ancient and extremely hard to find, so the Imperium spent a great deal of coin sourcing enough bones to make the Titan ore Tyleigh needed. Ore-lines, then, are incredibly valuable – imagine if your body were lined with gold. Imagine if your bones were gilded with it.'

'I would be very heavy,' said Belise.

Kaeto ignored this. 'And it's more than that. Tyleigh's methods are closely guarded secrets. Enemies of the Imperium might believe that they can learn her secrets by examining the body of a Herald. They can't, but there's no reason we should let them try.'

'What's to stop the Heralds selling themselves to some Unblessed country now that we've let them loose?'

'Technically? Nothing, except loyalty to the Imperium, and the small fact that after around eight or nine years the magic that Tyleigh grafted onto their skin begins to degrade, leading to confusion, a resurgence of their previous memories and personality, and eventually, death.'

'Ah.'

'Imperator Justinia would prefer that we deal with all the Heralds as we have dealt with Foro here – kill them all now, remove the risk of losing our secrets or their loyalty, and invest ourselves in the next generation of Heralds. But to do so would be heavy-handed.'

'And it would be as popular as a cold bag of sick with the Imperium's citizens,' added Belise. 'They are the people's champions. It'd be like killing the empress's children, if she had any.'

'Quite.'

'So.' Belise stopped nudging the linen sack with the toe of her boot and looked up at him. 'Are we going to strip all the ore-lines from this man's body now? Can we even do that? Is the stuff reusable?'

Kaeto sighed. The girl liked to pretend the fool, but she had an infuriating habit of getting to the heart of the matter with one fatal stab.

'No. We're going to cut his body up into pieces and dispose of them as we always do, because now that the man is dead, the magic is dead.'

'Then what was the point of any of it?'

'The point is, child, that Blessed Forty was a soldier of the Imperium, and if anyone is going to murder him and desecrate his body, it will be us and not our enemies. He deserves that much at least.'

'It doesn't seem like much gratitude to me, for eight years of fighting and killing.'

Kaeto looked away from the girl. 'In the end, Belise, the secrets of the Imperium are worth more than any one man's life, and it is our duty to do as we're told.'

Belise seemed mostly satisfied with that answer. Kaeto downed the rest of his tea and set the cup back down on the work table.

'Now. Did you lay out the bone saws?'

3

T'vyn the Trickster plucked the moon from the night sky and cast it down into the Last Lake to become an egg. From this, Fionovar the Red came forth, and Yelvynia became 'the place where wisdom is hatched'.

Extract from the further histories
of Yelvynia, written on the Silver
Death Peak by an unknown griffin

'You're hogging the liver, and it's the best bit!'

Ynis ground her teeth against the tough meat, half determined to bite off another chunk before she gave it to her sister, but the organ flesh was rubbery and difficult to get a purchase on. Instead, she swallowed a mouthful of hot, salty blood and passed the liver to T'rook, who snapped it from her fingers with one darting movement of her beak.

'Cut it up for me, then,' she said, rubbing her bloodied hands on the grass. The carcass of the goat was a few feet away from them, its chest and stomach open to the blue sky. 'I'm starving.'

'I will slice it into delicate slithers, the better to suit your tiny human throat,' said T'rook mockingly, but in a few seconds Ynis had several long strips of purple offal in her lap, and she ate them up greedily. For a little while they sat in companionable silence, eating their way through their lunch while a handful of white clouds scudded overhead. They were in the lowest valley of Yelvynia, and it was one of the first properly warm days of spring. Ice had melted on most of the small streams that ran across the valley floor like veins in a leaf, and the first wildflowers were nodding their heads all around, a speckling of white, yellow, pink and orange. Ynis finished all but one of her strips of liver, pushing the last inside the flat leather bag she had tied around her waist. The bag was one of her most prized possessions, the result of an entire summer's experimentation with the human processes of skinning and tanning. T'vor and Flayn had always encouraged her interest in human crafts and customs, had even brought her home various artefacts found on the bodies of humans who had explored too far. Her fathers then had borne the process with quiet patience, but T'rook had complained endlessly, about the smell and the waste of food and the general indignity of it all, only letting it go when Ynis had presented her with a little leather band to wear around her leg. T'rook was partial to presents.

'We should get moving.'

'I suppose so.' T'rook stood up and unfurled her wings, chasing away the flies attempting to land on the goat corpse. Still not quite fully grown, her feathers edged from warm brown to an oily black, the smaller downy feathers on her chest and belly speckled with dots of grey and cream. Her eyes were golden, like yellow leaves in autumn, and her legs and taloned feet were covered in tough, blueish skin. 'I don't want to be flying under the moon if I can help it.'

'Coward.'

'*Pft.* What would you know about flying in the dark, *featherless egg*? These lower valleys all look the same in the moonlight. We'd get lost.'

'If I had my own wings nothing would stop me flying,' said Ynis, with feeling. 'I would live in the sky. Nothing would chase me from it. Not ever.'

'Perhaps it is good you do not have them then,' said T'rook dryly. 'No one can live in the clouds.'

Ynis rolled her eyes, recognising one of their fathers' favourite phrases – usually deployed when Ynis had spent a day exploring beyond the borders for human artefacts, or attempting to combine foods with other foods, or even make them hot; a concept the griffins found quite unsettling.

'You do more talking than you do flying, T'rook. Let's get back up there.'

Ynis stood up, eager to be back in the sky. She went to T'rook, who bent long enough for her to get a purchase on her shoulder feathers, and then they were up, pelting into the blue, the heavy ground dropping away behind them. *I would stay up here forever if I could,* thought Ynis. It was a small, fierce, private dream, one she warmed herself with when all else was cold and dark. *It's freedom, to be able to fly like this.*

Up above the valley the warmth of the spring sun drained away, turning Ynis's bare arms bumpy with gooseflesh, but she didn't mind – if anything she yearned for it, this cold battering silence that only ever belonged to the many-coloured sky. Ahead of them the ground dropped away, revealing a deep crevasse and a series of old nests burrowed deep into the rock.

'Hoy!'

They were not alone in the sky. A pair of young griffins, both bigger than T'rook, barrelled towards them, calling aggressive battle shrieks as they came. Beneath Ynis's hands, T'rook grew tense.

'Just stay low,' she said, all her usual mockery vanished. 'Perhaps they didn't see you yet.'

But Ynis could already tell it was too late. One of the griffins, a talon-clan brute with feathers the colour of blood, was shouting 'egg' and 'stink'. T'rook had decided to try and ignore them, continuing to fly straight as if they weren't there, but the smaller of the pair flew up and under, nearly knocking them from the sky. T'rook cawed with anger, swiping at them with her blue talons, but they moved easily out of the way.

'What do you want?' Ynis sat up on her sister's back, already angrier than she could say.

'The yenlin speaks!' cried the red one in mock surprise. His companion, a smaller white and grey griffin with heavy grey paws and an elaborate crest of silver feathers at the back of her head, snapped her beak aggressively. 'You have eaten messily, talon-clan – you have a big piece of food still on your back.'

T'rook dropped away from them towards a patch of rocky ground, but they reappeared instantly, chasing up behind her tail like they were on the hunt. When they landed they were laughing, and Ynis felt a hot panicky hand grasp at her heart. This was going to end badly.

'There is food on your back, talon-clan, but it smells too bad to eat. It must have gone off years ago.' This was from the smaller griffin, a female with blue eyes.

'Very clever!' shouted Ynis. 'Great T'vyn himself clearly blessed you with brains – it's a shame they were the brains of a weasel!'

'My sister was raised in Yelvynia, same as you,' said T'rook, her voice uncharacteristically quiet. 'Queen Fellvyn herself granted permission. Think on that before you cause us trouble.'

The big red griffin shook his head. 'You hide behind the protection of someone else? Perhaps you are no griffin either, little one. Perhaps the human yenlin fed on your *yost* as you slept in the nest together, and now you are little more than a *bird*, covered in human stench.'

T'rook hissed, but Ynis was already climbing down from her sister's back. She had taken the claw-knife from her belt and was holding it in front of her.

'Look!' cried the white griffin. 'It has bared its claws!' The two of them laughed together. Ynis swallowed down her fury.

'If I had talons like my sister, you would be bleeding your last in the dust.'

The red griffin laughed heartily at this. 'What are you, human egg? A claw or a talon? Or is it nothing?'

'Come closer and I will show you, weasel brain,' said Ynis.

'You should leave us be now.' T'rook shook out her wings and fluffed up her throat feathers, trying to look bigger than she was.

Ynis could hear the anxiety in her voice. 'We have fathers. Do you think they will just hide their heads under their wings if you hurt us?'

'We should eat this one,' said the white griffin. 'We'd be doing them a favour. And we are hungry.'

The white griffin darted forward, her black beak open wide enough that Ynis could see her purple tongue, but Ynis moved faster, ducking away and scrambling up onto the griffin's back. The white griffin squawked with rage, but Ynis was out of range of her beak. It was a mistake griffins often made with her – she was smaller, faster, and her hands meant she could climb to places they didn't expect.

'Get off of me! You are making me stink!' The white griffin began to beat her wings, half rising off the ground. Her big red partner seemed bemused, taking an unsteady step backwards. Ynis took hold of the largest feathers on the white griffin's crest in one fist, and with the other she ripped her knife along the place where the hollow quills sank into skin. There was an awful tearing, popping noise, and abruptly she had a handful of loose silver feathers. She caught a glimpse of crimson blood, torn skin, and then the griffin was shrieking, bucking her off. Ynis hit the ground with a thump but was back on her feet instantly. It wouldn't do to bare the back of her neck to these griffins, even for a second.

'Get back on!' cried T'rook. 'Now!'

She jumped onto her sister's back just in time. The white griffin was screaming with rage and throwing her head back and forth, not quite able to see what Ynis had done. The big red griffin seemed in shock, as if he couldn't understand why there were droplets of bright crimson blood on his partner's snow-white feathers.

T'rook flew up again, as fast as she could, before sweeping back down to fly as low to the ground as possible; if they went straight up into the blue sky, they'd be an easy target.

'What did you do that for?' she hissed.

'You know why! She was about to bite my arms off.'

'There is always trouble with you,' said T'rook, bitterly. 'Those two will not forget this, Ynis, and we'll both have to pay for those silver feathers at some point.'

Ynis looked down at the feathers still grasped in her fist. There was a thick piece of bloody grey skin still attached, but they were very beautiful, even so. She shook them until the piece of skin fell off.

'Are they coming after us?'

Ynis turned, one hand still buried in T'rook's shoulder feathers. There was no sign of the enemy griffins in the sky, but she was sure she could see movement on the ground, even so. Not for the first time she wished for the eyesight of her sister, able to spot a fish the size of Ynis's smallest finger whilst up amongst the clouds.

'I... I'm not sure.'

'Never mind. Look. The cliffs are here.'

Below them, the ground fell away to reveal a great chasm in the earth. At the very bottom was a wide, shallow river, lively with rocks and rapids, but directly opposite were a series of dark holes in the cliff, burrowed directly into the rock.

'Hide in those,' said Ynis. 'But go further down. They'll expect us to fly into the first one we see.'

T'rook did as she suggested, slowing down and flying lower, moving west along the cliff face. In the end she chose a tunnel entrance that was half hidden with vines and straggly bushes, flying in neatly and landing just beyond the narrow rim of light that illuminated the entrance. She fluffed up her feathers again and Ynis climbed off hastily.

'We should wait here for a bit.' She sat back on her haunches and plucked jerkily at her wing feathers. With a stab of guilt, Ynis realised her sister was both exhausted and genuinely frightened. She looked down at the feathers in her hands, and then hurriedly stuffed them into her leather bag. The blood on her hands had dried, griffin blood now indistinguishable from goat's blood.

'I'm sorry,' she said quietly. 'I don't know why I did that.'

'You did it because they intended to eat you,' said T'rook, a little testily, in Ynis's opinion.

'I made things worse.' Ynis rubbed her hands down the front of her tunic. She had made it herself, a ratty thing of leather and scavenged human fabric, covered in a layer of brown, black and grey feathers scrounged from her sister and fathers. All at once, it seemed like a stupid thing: a desperate attempt to look like something she wasn't; to be griffin, to be *yost* – to be something she could never be. To her own disgust, she felt her cheeks grow red with shame. *Another stupid human reaction.* Being sorrowful and ashamed wasn't the griffin way. 'We'll wait here for a bit longer, just in case they're still looking for us.'

'That white stone-licker won't be in the mood for fighting anyway.'

Ynis smiled reluctantly – she recognised when her sister was trying to humour her.

'Sorry,' she said again. 'If I were a real griffin, we wouldn't get into trouble like this. I wish...' She looked down at her hands, so delicate and strange in comparison to her sister's beautiful talons. 'I hate being human.'

'You are what you are,' said T'rook. In the gloom of the cave, her eyes flashed a burnished gold. 'You cannot change it. You will always be my sister.'

Ynis turned her head away a little, so that T'rook would not see her wet eyes.

'And you will always be mine.'

They waited in the cave until T'rook got bored, which didn't take long, and poked their heads cautiously out of the tunnel entrance. There was no movement anywhere close by save for the lazy hovering of bees and a handful of white birds nesting in the cliffs opposite.

'They called me a *bird*,' said T'rook, her voice dripping with disgust. 'I should have scalped them myself for that alone.'

'I do not think they will insult us again,' said Ynis, although when she looked at the dried blood on her hands, she wondered what price they would pay for winning such a fight. 'Come on. Let's go home.'

4

If you want more information about the Titan races, you could do
worse than to look over Gynid Tyleigh's notes on the matter. There
can hardly be anyone still alive that knows more than she does. And
yes, you will have to speak to her directly to access them, there is no
getting around it. This isn't the sort of information the Imperium
leaves lying around in a library.

Extract from the memos of
Envoy Kaeto, to a lower-
ranking colleague

The night was calm and still, the lights and the noise of Stratum left behind them. Kaeto travelled on his own horse, while Belise sat atop a pony borrowed from the Imperium Office stables. They were on the long straight road to the Indigo Sky Palace, and to either side of it stretched a largely featureless landscape of tall grass and the occasional wizened olive tree.

'All I'm saying is,' Belise piped up from behind him, 'all I'm saying is, this is a long way to go just to sit around outside waiting for you to have your chat, is all.'

'You will not have to sit outside, Belise,' Kaeto replied. His eyes were on the softly mounded shapes in the distance, and the great glass dome at the heart of them that was the empress's beloved observatory. 'You will be permitted to wait in an antechamber. How many scruffy children from the Fifth Ring get to sit in an antechamber in the Indigo Sky Palace, do you imagine?'

'Oh it's a *huge* honour.' Kaeto stifled a smile at the girl's tone. Sarcasm was bone-deep with Belise. 'I'm just not sure what the point of it is. It'd be much more interesting to be able to see the empress myself. I'll be quiet. Just sit in a corner. You know I can be quiet when I need to be, chief.'

'Hmm. That's debatable. However, it doesn't matter either way. Empress Celestinia is… uncomfortable around children. It's better if she's not distracted.'

Belise snorted at that. She didn't really consider herself a child. Not like other children, anyway. After all, she had a *job*.

'Tell me, Belise, why is the area around the Indigo Sky Palace so quiet?'

The girl sighed. Kaeto let his horse drop back a little, so that they were riding side by side.

'Come on. This is an easy question.'

Belise leaned forward and scratched her pony behind the ears. 'It's because of the great lenses in the palace, isn't it. The empress likes to look at the stars, and if there were people around here, with their houses and lamps and fires and such, the night would be harder to see.'

'That's right,' said Kaeto softly. 'There used to be a town here, I would say, oh, ten years before you were born, Belise. A thriving little place, a spillage from the lip of Stratum, but doing well for itself, until the empress decided that she wished to build an observatory some distance from the city. It would need to be a quiet place, no noise, no lights. And so the whole town was crumbled to dust, its people turfed out of their homes. They were left to wander the roads, their possessions in carts or just clutched in their arms.'

Belise turned to look at him. It was dark on the road, with only the blessed starlight and moonlight to illuminate them, but he saw the sheen of interest in her eyes clearly enough.

'It sounds like you don't think that was a good idea, chief.'

'Judgement is not one of our duties, Belise. But there is always something to be learnt, if you are watching closely. You can learn as much from the things that are missing as you can from what's in front of your nose.' He gestured around at the empty plain. It was just possible to make out a small broken house, the roof half fallen through. 'Witness the might of the Imperium.'

When they reached the palace, Belise went with the horse and her pony to see that they were looked after properly in the stables, and Kaeto made his way into the vast, echoing space. The Indigo Sky Palace had only a skeleton staff, just enough people to ensure that it was clean and welcoming, and that the empress had everything she needed. The guards on the observatory door knew him well. He stepped through into the huge circular hall at the heart of the palace, and stood for a moment just taking it in. The walls were of deep blue marble, and on top of that shining surface the constellations had been painted in gold. In the centre of the room was the huge contraption of brass that pointed up at the glass ceiling; it was through this that the empress looked at the Blessed stars, bathing in the light of the Imperium's most gloried ancestors.

He cleared his throat. 'Your Luminance, I have come as you requested.'

His voice sounded small in the vast room, but after a few seconds of silence there was a whirring sound from the brass contraption, several of the huge cogs on its outside moved in unison, and a narrow door in the back of it popped open. Kaeto saw a small, slippered foot exit carefully, as though uncertain of the reception it might receive, and then following it came the diminutive figure of Empress Celestinia. She was short – if they stood together, he knew, the top of her shining head could come no further than the bottom of his ribcage – and if seen from a distance it was almost possible to mistake her for a slightly portly child. But then she would glance up, turning her moon-like face towards yours, and the illusion would be lost. Her hair was a dark gold, oiled and combed daily, and set into long braids like ropes, and her eyes were wide and slightly bulbous, as though she were permanently surprised. She was wearing a silk house-gown, a deep dark blue to match the walls, and across her forehead there was a slim band of gold dotted with tiny pink crystals. Under her arm, there was the doll – Kaeto glanced at it once, then fixed his gaze at her feet, just to be safe.

'Envoy,' she said. Her voice had a slight whistle to it, like an exhausted kettle. 'Our ancestors are bright tonight, as they have been all month. I can barely leave the lenses, lest I miss something.'

'That is good to hear, your Luminance. The Master of Glass I sent you from Blessed Gäul has made improvements?'

'He has!' Celestinia beamed. 'What a keen eye he has. I didn't think they knew much about glass in Gäul but I am glad to be proven wrong, for once.' She squeezed the doll under her arm and bent her cheek down to it briefly. 'Come, let's sit. I have been cooped up in the observatory for hours.'

They left the observatory hall and emerged onto a long, wide balcony area. Here, the empress's servants had already prepared a table for them. It was covered with fruits and small pastries, and a huge steaming urn of something that smelled like herbal tea. It was, Kaeto reckoned, around four or five hours before dawn, but the empress had long kept unsociable hours and the staff of the Indigo Sky Palace knew to have a meal ready at any hour of the night or day. The empress tucked her doll into one of the seats – there was a stack of cushions on the chair, so that it may sit properly at the table – and seated herself facing out across the plains. Kaeto, after a nod from her, seated himself.

The empress picked a sugar-dusted plum off a plate and began to cut it into delicate slices.

'Tell me,' she said, shortly.

Kaeto cleared his throat. 'The first company of Heralds were retired around three months ago, your Luminance. A number of them have left Stratum, to start new lives in the Blessed lands to the south. A few remain in the city.'

'Any problems so far?'

Belatedly Kaeto realised he had managed to sit himself opposite the doll. Against his will his eyes were drawn to its small, shining face – the thing had head, hands and feet made of white clay, varnished and painted with an expression that Kaeto always thought of as shifty. Its loose fabric body was draped in black silk and lace.

'Only what we expected, your Luminance,' he continued. 'Some illness, some weakening. Others have not experienced any changes at all. Yet.'

The empress took a slither of plum and placed it on her tongue. For a handful of seconds they sat together in silence. Somewhere within the palace, a door closed with a bang. Kaeto wondered how Belise was getting on in the waiting room, and whether she'd caused trouble for any of the servants yet.

'And?'

Kaeto held in a sigh. 'One of the Heralds, known as Blessed Forty, was deteriorating faster than the others. It was the Imperator Justinia's decision that he be... removed from the equation early.'

The empress's thin pink lips twisted into a brief, sour smile.

'It was her decision, was it? Be careful, Envoy. Sometimes your tone says more than your words.'

'Apologies, your Luminance.'

'That woman insists on pushing back, doesn't she?' The empress reached out and tugged at the doll's lace, making it sit a little straighter. 'She cannot see an order of mine without seeking to tweak it. I wanted the Heralds to be left alone as much as possible. After all they have done for the Imperium, it is the least we can give them. And yet, having said that...' She touched her tiny, wizened fingers to the doll's face, as though she wished to smother it. 'Perhaps a merciful death is the wiser option.'

'Your Luminance, as I have said before, if all of our freshly retired Heralds met a sudden end, well, it would—'

'Give rise to questions, yes, I know. Besides, this is not what I wanted to talk to you about today, Envoy.'

Kaeto sat up a little straighter. Many of the higher ranking citizens of the Imperium, including Imperator Justinia, thought the empress to be insane – or at least no longer able to grasp the finer points of running a sprawling empire like the Imperium. Kaeto knew this was not accurate. She was a woman with intense focus and strange passions, and perhaps that was the only way to stay sane in a job like hers. When she spoke, he listened.

'Do you know Gynid Tyleigh well, Envoy Kaeto?'

'I'm not sure that anyone does, your Luminance. She's something of an enigma even to the Imperium. I have done some tasks connected to her work over the years and helped to locate the resources she needed. We have spoken, once or twice.'

'And what is your opinion of the Imperium's chief bone crafter and alchemist?' When Kaeto did not reply immediately, she waved a fork at him. 'You may speak as you see fit.'

'She is a terrifyingly clever woman. She understands magic, and the Titans, better than anyone under the Blessed stars. She is also extremely single-minded. Ambitious, certainly.'

'You would trust her judgement?'

'On the question of Heralds, Titans and ore-magic? Absolutely. On compassion, fairness, fashion, art, food, or any one of a hundred other subjects? Certainly not.'

The empress chuckled dryly. 'I suppose that will do. Because Tyleigh has convinced herself that she may have located a new source of ancient Titan bones, far to the north-east of Stratum.'

'A *new* source?' Kaeto leaned forward. 'What does that mean? I thought we had assured ourselves that the Imperium owns the vast majority of Titan remains at this point. Save for whatever Brittletain is hoarding.'

'That is what we thought. But Tyleigh thinks these bones may be...' The empress took a long, wheezing breath. 'Well, she believes they are the remains of an as-yet-unknown Titan.'

Kaeto sat back, blinking. 'A new Titan?'

'It's a remarkable thought, isn't it? These new remains, Gynid believes, could have entirely different properties to the bones we have in our possession. They could lead to Heralds who live longer than their current paltry lifespan. Heralds with different powers, perhaps. This is what she tells us.'

'That is remarkable.'

'Isn't it just? If what she believes is correct, it would also mean that our current little project...' Celestinia let her words trail off. She reached for a silver sugar bowl and began spooning small white heaps of the stuff into her glass.

'We'd have no more need of it,' finished Kaeto.

'I know you have always objected to our actions in Yelvynia.' The empress took a delicate glass decanter and poured a clear liquid into her glass, dissolving the sugar. The smell of strong alcohol drifted across the table. 'I believe the words you used were "outrageously risky" and "near suicidal".'

'And I stand by those words,' said Kaeto. 'It's dangerous to the life and limb of our operatives, and dangerous to the reputation of the Imperium, if word of it were ever to get out. What are these remains then? And where are they?'

'I'm glad you are so interested.' Celestinia took a sip from her glass. 'You will be travelling with Tyleigh. It will be your job, as it was before, to source for her anything she needs, and to remove any barriers she may face. Do you understand?'

Kaeto held himself very still. The last thing he wanted to do was spend any time with Gynid Tyleigh, or travel to the Unblessed east, but Envoys did not get to choose the missions the empress gave them. Even so, he couldn't quite stop himself from an unwise question.

'Have I done something to offend, your Luminance? Have I been unsatisfactory in some way?'

The empress gave a short, sharp bark of laughter. She shuffled down from her chair, and plucked the doll up off its seat. 'Is she really so awful, Kaeto? I have heard rumours of course, but if even you are moved to obvious dislike she must truly be a character. You leave by the next eye-moon. If I were you, I'd go to her rooms in Stratum and find out what she needs – and perhaps start practising biting your tongue.' She ducked her head and placed a kiss on the doll's shining cheek. 'Come, sister, the stars are waiting for us.'

5

Rather than the lethal blades or the wings they can summon, the true secret of the Heralds' success is their speed. The Titan augments do not last indefinitely, after all – half an hour, perhaps, if you are lucky – and when your time is up the wings and the blades vanish, and the Herald is left in need of rest (this means that Titan powers are not practical for travel, for example. Get halfway across the sea on Titan wings, you'll find yourself getting wetter than you would like). Therefore every battle must be fought quickly, with devastating might and superior planning, in order to crush the enemy as swiftly as possible. 'Visit your fury upon them like a summer storm' was one of the instructions in Gynid Tyleigh's initial notes for the soldiers. Who would have thought that creature could have such poetry in her?

Extract from Envoy Kaeto's
private notes

I t was late, and Leven had had too much to drink. Halfway up the stairs to her lodgings she slumped against the wall, the world around her tipping back and forth queasily. The novelty of being bought drinks in every tavern had yet to wear off, but she suspected that by the morning – when she'd likely be spewing her guts into a basin – she might feel rather differently about the whole thing.

'Are you alright there?' A voice floated up from the landing below. Leven waved an arm in its direction and mumbled at the wall.

'Fine! I'm fine, just great!' She waved again. 'Just regrouping. With my legs.'

There was the sound of footsteps as the concerned citizen moved away again. From below it was possible to hear the general hubbub of the tavern, still going strong now that its guest of honour had left, and someone had even started picking out some notes on the knackered old piano. It seemed she had left just in time.

Straightening up as best she could, she took a few more steps, leaning heavily against the wall. She considered summoning her Herald wings and flying the rest of the way, but even in her inebriated state she knew that was a bad idea; the staircase was narrow, and she'd probably just end up punching out the wall that was at that moment her very best friend in all the world.

Leven had almost made it to her door when the ground appeared to drop out from under her, and for a second or so she was somewhere else; somewhere dark. There was snow, and the ground was uneven with dirt and stones. A freezing wind blew across her back, making her grit her teeth.

'What?'

She blinked, and she was on her hands and knees in the corridor, her room just a few feet away. The snow had gone, the pitiless moonlight had vanished. Instead the corridor was warm, stuffy even. The smell of wood polish was in her nostrils.

All at once, she no longer felt quite so drunk. Leven got carefully back on her feet.

'What just happened?'

She took the last few steps to her room, got safely through the door and it happened again: the warmth and safety of her lodgings dropped away and she was in a freezing shadowy darkness. She was small and cold and weak, and terrified of something. She turned around, trying to get some sense of where she was – there were trees, she could see that much, and terrible dark spaces between the trees. Something, she was sure, was watching her from those dark spaces; something that wished her great harm. Taking a step backwards, she felt the soft *crump* of snow under her boot, and then there was another, stranger noise – a soft clicking, a little like a key turning in a lock, but over and over again. *Click. Clack. Click. Clack.* Gradually, the sounds grew quicker, and for reasons she didn't understand this scared her more than the dark, more than the freezing cold seeping up through her feet. She had enough time for one confused thought – *I should have run when I had the chance* – and then she was in her room at the tavern again, sprawled across the bed.

'Stars' arses...'

Leven sat up and rubbed her eyes, trying to smooth away the unsettling images. She looked around, trying to anchor herself to the normality of the room. She had been staying at the Blessed Brew tavern for a few weeks, and she had made herself at home; as much as she could, anyway, given that she had few belongings of her own. Her dirty clothes were slung over a chair, the enamelled basin was still thick with soap suds from that morning, and there were used plates and cups on most surfaces. She dug her fingers into the thick blanket that covered her bed. Everything looked normal.

'Whatever it was that I was drinking... I think I should avoid that in future.' She spoke to the empty room, hoping that the sound of her own voice would cheer her, but instead it only reminded her of all the people who were not there. After eight years of travelling with the same group of soldiers, solitude was unnerving. 'I didn't have enough to eat today, that's all.'

But she thought of Foro, and the things he had told her that day in The Lip; about nightmares, and memories resurfacing. And she hadn't heard from him in weeks.

She stood up and moved cautiously over to the table where there was a large jug of water and a heavy drinking glass. She picked up the jug and took a few big mouthfuls of the water, trying to wash some of the booze out of her system, but it was oddly difficult to hold the jug for long, and when she put it back down, her hands were trembling.

She held them up in front of her, glaring at the silvery-blue ore-lines that traced their way across her palms.

'Alright,' she said, her voice low. 'What the fuck is happening to me?'

The next morning was about as rough as Leven had expected, but she forced herself out of bed and out into the streets. It was a viciously bright and loud day, and she kept her head down, letting her hair fall in front of her face – she was in no mood for fans. Foro was staying in a large boarding house on the Second Ring, a rough and ready sort of place with lots of rooms crammed into three overpopulated floors. He could afford better, but he was a cautious man, aware that the money they'd received on leaving the army would not last forever. Leven went directly to the office at the front of the building and found a small, harassed-looking man behind a desk. His fingers were stained a chalky pink from the red weed tobacco he stank of, and he looked at Leven as though she were a long and familiar nuisance in his life.

'Oh, another Herald,' he said, although now he was looking over her shoulder. 'Just what I need.'

'He's in, is he? Foro? I need to see him.'

'Here? I wish he were bloody here. Rudeness, is what it is. Pure and simple.'

'What?'

'He left two weeks ago,' he said, finally meeting her eye. 'Must have snuck out in the night, because I didn't see him.'

'What do you mean, he's gone?'

The little man raised his eyebrows at that. 'Do you have extra meanings for the word "gone", young lady?' She opened her mouth to reply, but he carried on. 'He cleared out, took all his stuff with him, no word to me or any of the staff, just like that.'

'He left without settling his bill?'

The little man's eyes slid away again. 'Well no, he left a neat pile of coins there, on the table, just exactly what was due, but that's not the point, is it? If I'd known he'd vacated, I could have had my lad in there, cleaning up for a new tenant. Instead it sat empty a whole day and a night and half the morning before I realised. It lost me a whole day's earnings, is what.'

Leven blinked, trying to gather her thoughts.

'Well? Is there anything else you want? I am a busy man.'

'No.' Leven took a slow breath. Part of her was entertaining the thought of reaching over the desk and pulling the little man out of his den by his hair. 'Just… did he say anything to you at all before he left? Anything strange?'

The innkeeper shook his head slightly. 'They didn't pick the smartest citizens to be Heralds, did they? Are you listening to me, girl? He said nothing to me.'

Leven left, walking out onto the busy streets with the beginnings of a thumping headache. Foro had gone, taking everything with him – no word to the innkeeper, and no word to her. Was that really so strange? Foro, like all the Heralds, was the captain of his own ship now. He could do what he liked. He didn't have to tell anyone.

And yet.

Everything about it made her uneasy.

He'd probably had enough of that little tit downstairs, she told herself. *Taken his custom elsewhere.*

She was just passing through an alleyway she knew to be a shortcut when the shadowy warmth of the narrow passage faded, and a cold wind cut across her shoulders, sending a blade of ice down her neck. Leven looked up, and instead of the solid brickwork of the alleyway she saw tall dark trees, their trunks bloated and mottled with fungi.

'Not again…'

There was snow and soil under her boots, and just ahead, there was a set of ruins, something hewn from dark, crumbling stone. And as she looked at it, she had the strangest sensation; the feeling that she had been there before, many times. She knew that just behind that wall there was a ditch, littered with rocks, and beyond that, a well that was rimmed with ice. She was afraid of the well – it echoed strangely at night.

'Where *am* I?'

There was a piercing cry from overhead, and she looked up to see a sky the colour of a robin's egg, and a dark shape moving across it.

'A griffin?'

The huge beast turned in the sky, as if it had heard her, and she caught a glimpse of its silvery-grey eye as it sought her out. And then the thing was diving down, crashing through the canopy of the trees...

Leven shuddered violently and awoke to find herself crumpled on the floor of the alleyway. A figure stood at the entrance, looking down at her with concern, but as she moved the man seemed to think better of his curiosity and hurried off. She got to her feet, dusting herself down carefully. Her hands were trembling.

A griffin. None of it made any sense. The ruined building in the woods was nothing like any of the places they had travelled during their eight years of service, and yet she had known it, and known it well. And the griffin...

'The griffin means it had to have been Brittletain.' The one nation the Imperium had repeatedly failed to invade; the one nation that the Heralds had never even got close to. Standing in the warm alleyway, she shuddered, the memory of the icy woods still breathing down her neck. *How is that possible?*

6

The forest was bracing itself for something.

Cillian could feel it through the tips of his fingers. The lively green fizz that was the living presence of the Wild Wood and everything it contained was strangely expectant, on edge. He found that he kept looking at the shadows, as though a shape might emerge at any second.

'Do you feel that?' he murmured.

The older Druin crouching a few feet away amongst the undergrowth glanced at him and furrowed his brow. The morning light filtering through the trees overhead lay dappled against the man's horns, which were long and swept back from his head – a black goat's horns.

'You can't miss it,' insisted Cillian. 'It's all around.'

'Will you be quiet?' Aeden snapped, his voice rising a little. 'We'll lose her otherwise.'

Cillian bit down a reply, and instead moved through the thick undergrowth to position himself closer to the Path. From this vantage point he was able to see the Dunohi they were tracking; her vast shape shimmered at the edge of the beaten earth, her wide antlers tangling with the tree branches above. Leaves fluttered gently to the ground around her, and that in itself was a worry – usually the forest souls moved through the Wild Wood as less than a breeze, touching nothing, only encouraging growth. The great beast moved, the long bare skull that served as a face turning slightly as though listening to something.

Cillian took a few more steps forward, pausing to pull a twig from his own curling horns.

'Cillian,' hissed Aeden. 'You are getting too close.'

'She knows me,' he hissed back. 'Let me speak to her.'

'You're an idiot. Speaking to the Dunohi is for your elders only, as well you know.'

'We need to know what's wrong.' Cillian turned to look at Aeden. 'Isn't the fastest way to ask?'

'If any asking needs doing, it won't be you that does it,' snapped Aeden.

The Dunohi did not appear to be aware of them at all. She came out onto the Path, her stance uncertain. Cillian knew this forest soul well, had seen her moving around the woods of the region for years. She was tall, even for one of the Dunohi – at least twelve feet, including her antlers – and her huge shoulders were covered in shaggy green moss and trailing ivy. Her body was wiry and spare; muscles formed of thick bark and pale wood fibres that stood out clearly in the intermittent morning sunshine, and her knees bent backwards, like the rear legs of a deer. Her head was formed of a huge, long skull, like that of a moose, and it had been bleached a stark yellow-white by time. Between her gaping jaws, things moved; worms, beetles, other tiny crawling things.

'She looks nervous.' Cillian made note of the trailing ivy that hung from the forest soul's great arched back; the leaves that brushed the floor were yellowed and shrivelled. 'I'm telling you, they can sense something. We should ask what it is.'

The Dunohi rarely came so close to the paths humans followed. They preferred to be out in the untouched deep of the Wildest Wood, where the ground was permanently lost under a tangle of undergrowth and decaying foliage. It was the Druin's job to keep the Paths clear, and to make sure that all was well with the forest souls. Most of Cillian's Druin brothers and sisters spent their time on the Paths, doing small bits of maintenance or guiding any travellers who needed to pass through the Wild Wood, but Cillian yearned to explore the places unseen by human eyes.

'Move back.' Aeden had edged close to where Cillian crouched. 'If we leave her be, she'll wander back on her own.'

Cillian shook his head slightly. It was clearer than ever now that something was wrong with the Dunohi. She was stepping back and forth, shaking her long bony head, as though she had something stuck in her antlers that she wanted removing.

'I have to speak to her,' he said. 'Something is troubling her.'

'No! You don't have the experience, Cillian.' Aeden grabbed the back of his cloak and yanked it. 'You run the risk of making it angry, or... or going thrawn. Is that what you want?'

Cillian turned back to him and tersely pulled his cloak away from the other man. 'Don't be daft. This is what we're trained for, isn't it?'

'Our primary duties are sharing minds with the life of the Wild Wood, and keeping the Paths open,' Aeden said primly. 'Communicating with the Dunohi would be an upper-level duty, Cillian, not for the likes of you. Or the likes of me, for that matter.'

'Leave me to do it if you like. I'm better off on my own.'

'You would speak to me so? I am your elder, you sapling idiot...'

Aeden muttered a few more expletives but Cillian had already turned away, stepping boldly out onto the packed earth of the Path. The forest soul turned her skull-face towards him, clearly aware of his presence. Cillian held his hands up, showing that they were empty.

'Dunohi, tree-walker, forest soul. What is wrong?' He spoke softly, and as he did so he opened up his own awareness of the forest's green inner life. The tingling he had felt before in his fingertips spread up his arms and across his chest; the feeling of life and growth all around became a tart green taste on his tongue. And there was decay too, the gentle rot and letting-go of the dead leaves under his feet. All of that was as it should be, but when he turned his focus towards the Dunohi, there was a discordance. It was a narrow, slippery thing, but it was there, he was sure of it. 'Dunohi, we are the children of the Druidahnon. Share your pain with me.'

DEATH. The voice crashed around his head without needing to go through his ears. Cillian winced, but kept himself very still. The Dunohi was looking at him directly, regarding him through her empty eye sockets. MURDER.

The forest soul shook herself all over, sending another shower of dead leaves fluttering onto the ground, and then she dropped her head, lowering her antlers towards him. Despite himself, Cillian took an awkward step backwards, a flash of embarrassment turning his cheeks hot – *if I get torn to pieces by a charging Dunohi, Aeden will be telling this story for years* – but instead of flinging herself at him and perhaps pulling his guts into strings between her flat, yellow teeth, the forest soul dug her huge antlers into the packed earth of the Path. She surged forward, and dirt flew up in great clumps, stones and turf and roots coming up as easily as a knife through butter. She charged across the Path, tearing a deep trench through it, and then she crashed off into the trees on the other side, quickly becoming nothing more than a shadow again. Cillian stood where he was, for the moment too surprised to move. His heart was hammering in his chest.

'What was that?' said Aeden, who had appeared at his side again now that the danger had passed. 'She's destroyed the Path,' he added, unnecessarily.

Cillian walked over to the trench, which was a good four or five feet deep. He had never seen a forest spirit behave that way, and he could still hear her words echoing in his head. The Dunohi had been angry, but about what he couldn't have said. Murder? Who had been murdered? And what would that have to do with the forest souls? They had little to no interest in human affairs.

'We'll have to get a team out here to repair the Path,' said Aeden. 'And you'll be lucky if you see any of the Paths again.'

'What?'

'We will go back now,' Aeden said shortly. 'And you can explain yourself.'

'What are you talking about?'

Aeden exhaled through his nostrils, briefly looking very goat-like indeed. 'You provoked her! You *demanded* the attention of a forest soul, and this is the result. This is why we don't let the newly-horned practise the higher Druin talents...'

'I have had my horns for years!'

Aeden gestured at the broken Path. 'If Kirka has any sense, she will have your horns cut off for this arrogance. You are half a step from thrawn, and you know it.'

'I—'

'Enough. We will head back now, and as we travel the Paths you will think about who is the Master Druin here and who is the sapling whose horns have barely had time to curl. I do not want to hear any more from you. *Share your pain with me*, indeed.'

They left, Aeden opening the first Path, his every step stiff with rage, but Cillian turned back to look again into the trees. He could feel her there still, watching.

The Wild Wood was afraid. And angry.

7

L even found Boss in one of the Imperator's gardens, a series of green spaces in the First Ring set aside for the Imperium's military staff. As usual, she was easy enough to spot; despite their recent retirement, Boss still wore her famous gold-plated breast plate and pauldrons, and her pale hair, loose across her shoulders, shone as brightly as the metal under the late-morning sunshine. She was talking to an officious-looking young man with a satchel full of documents over his shoulder.

'Boss!'

The golden woman turned, smiling, and nodded a greeting to Leven. She muttered something to the young man, who passed her a handful of documents from his satchel and hurried off.

'Leven, what brings you here? Had enough of celebrating?'

'I wanted to ask you about something, sir.'

Boss nodded absently. She was paging through the papers, looking closely at the inky scribblings. Leven could see maps, too, places far to the south of Stratum; the Imperium's next campaign, no doubt. Although their legion of Heralds had been officially retired, Boss had offered to stay on, and the Imperator jumped at the chance to keep her – or so it was said. Boss had been their leader over the last eight years of war, and had proven herself ruthless, efficient, and the possessor of a keen tactical mind. Boss was a sword too good to throw away after all, it seemed. Leven thought about what Foro had said, about why the Imperium would let them go.

She forced a smile onto her face and tried to put it out of her head.

'Have you seen Foro lately? When I last spoke to him, he was ill, and when I went to his lodgings, the dreadful oik running the place said he'd left in the night a fortnight ago.'

Boss lifted her gaze from the pages, her blue eyes finally settling on Leven's face. Being looked at by Boss was like being skewered by the thinnest silver lance; it was so sharp you could barely feel it, yet you were held firmly in place. She was also strikingly beautiful, was even famous for it, across the Imperium. As far as Leven could tell, she was in her early fifties now, and her hair was as golden as it had ever been, her cheekbones as sharp as the first day Leven had seen her, a slim figure waiting in the heat of the training grounds. There was a statue of Boss in the central plaza of Stratum, a space reserved for the most star-touched heroes.

'Foro,' Boss said softly. 'You spoke to the Imperator about him, didn't you?'

'I did.' Leven glanced away from the icy blue gaze. 'He's not well. I'm worried about him.'

'Worried?' Boss smiled gently. The morning was heating up rapidly, but the older woman's face remained entirely free of sweat, despite the heavy armour she wore. 'About that old reprobate? He's tough, Leven, perhaps the toughest of all of us. I'm sure he'll turn up eventually.'

'I don't know...' Somewhere across the gardens, music was playing, some old Imperial tune. 'Did Justinia say anything to you about it, sir?'

Boss tipped her head to one side slightly, and Leven was forcibly reminded of the Boss she had known in battle; her dewy skin spattered with the blood of the Unblessed, her mouth open and distorted with a scream of rage; her gleaming blue Titan wings slicing through heads, limbs, torsos. The statue in the plaza depicted Boss standing with her face tipped up, calmly gazing at the stars – the contrast to the reality made Leven dizzy.

'Blessed Eleven, you have been discharged. Do you know what that means?'

'Of course, sir, I just—'

'Listen.' Boss folded her papers and tucked them under one arm. With the other, she took hold of Leven's elbow and squeezed it. When she spoke, her voice was soft. 'I will only say this to you once, Leven, so perhaps you could take this as my final order to you. Let Foro go. Leave Stratum and make your own life. Eight years is such a short time for a young woman like you — it's time to find a new path.' When Leven didn't respond, her voice became a low hiss. 'Get out of Stratum now, you idiot, before it's too late.'

Boss dropped her arm and turned away, a smile back on her beautiful face, just as though they were two friends catching up. Leven watched her old commander walk away, a cold feeling in her chest. Had she just been threatened by someone she practically thought of as family?

As if in answer, the ore-lines on her hands burned and prickled.

8

To be griffin is to be yost. The hunt, the flight, the responsibility of the yenlin; these are the roots of griffin, the essence of yost. Yost is the heart of what we are.

The Griffin Creed, as written
on the Silver Death Peak by
Fionovar the Red

'There they are!'

Ynis shrank back, pressing herself closer to her sister's neck. They had arrived back in Yelvynia just as night was falling, and hadn't even made it back to their fathers' nest before they were shouted down by a small group of griffins coming directly from Queen Fellvyn's sanctum. Beneath her, T'rook gave an indignant squawk as a huge, pearly-coloured griffin flew up in front of them, maroon talons brought up as if to tear her sister's throat out.

'That's enough!' That was the queen herself. She turned a huge golden eye on the pair of them, then just as quickly turned away. Ynis had seen the look many times before: disgust, embarrassment, irritation. She forced herself to sit up straight on T'rook's back, and glare back at their accusers.

'This is them, my queen,' the pearly griffin was shouting. 'These are the ones who attacked my daughter, mutilated her! Tore the very feathers from her head!'

'That's a lie!' Ynis shouted back. 'She attacked us first! Her and the other big idiot she was flying with!'

'So you admit that there was a fight,' said Queen Fellvyn. When Ynis made to open her mouth, she snapped at her. 'Be quiet, human. We will go to the speaking circle now, and you will not speak again until I permit it. Someone, go and fetch their fathers. I'm sure they will want to see this.'

The speaking circle was a clear space of white rock with a raised wall of grey rock around it; over the centuries the griffins of Yelvynia had scratched a great interlocking tapestry into the wall, depicting their conflicts and resolutions with pictures of themselves triumphant, alongside snatches of cloud-poetry. Griffins with a dispute or even a blood feud went to the speaking circle to put their arguments to the test or, in less enlightened times, to fight until one was left bleeding in the dust. When they got there, Ynis was distressed to see their fathers were already standing on the stones, watching their arrival. Flayn was sitting, his big paws crossed in front of him, while T'vor was standing, his muscles taut; he looked ready to rip out someone's feathers himself.

As soon as they had landed, T'vor was with them, putting the bulk of his body between them and the pearly griffin. With her was another, Ynis noticed, a male talon-clan griffin with deep russet feathers. This one was staying quiet, watching from over the other's shoulders, but something about him made her deeply uneasy. He had to be the father of the red-feathered griffin who had tried to knock them from the sky. Queen Fellvyn looked, as she often did, exasperated, and she darted a quick peck at the shoulder of the pearly-coloured griffin.

'T'bre, you will calm down or I will drag you out of this ring myself. The same goes for you, T'vor. Now, what happened?'

Everyone began shouting at once. Queen Fellvyn spread her wings wide and screeched, a terrible piercing sound that made Ynis cover her ears with her hands. The griffins all took a step back, turning their heads from it.

'Enough, you bunch of stone-lickers! I could be hunting now and instead I am dealing with more nonsense brought about by the human yenlin.'

'Queen Fellvyn, with respect.' Flayn was standing now, the fur at his neck standing up in agitation. 'We do not even know what happened yet.'

The queen muttered at that but nodded to the pearly-coloured griffin. 'Very well. Tell us, then, T'bre.'

'These two set upon my daughter and her friend as they were out hunting. The human creature used its dirty limbs to climb all over her, soiling her feathers with its prey-stench, before tearing out her beautiful crest feathers with its broken claw.' T'bre sniffed, and swept her beak back and forth over her chest feathers; the movement of a griffin in distress. 'She is mutilated, her beautiful crest ruined forever. I demand justice!'

'That's not true!' Ynis burst out again. She stood up on her sister's back. Surrounded by fully grown griffins, she felt tiny. 'They attacked us! They called us names—'

'They threatened to eat my sister,' added T'rook, 'and for that alone I should have gutted them both!'

'Be quiet!' bellowed the queen. 'The speaking circle is not a place for children to air their petty rivalries.'

'Why are we bloody here then?' cried Ynis.

Flayn pushed her gently with his head, and muttered, 'Be quiet for me now, little one. We need to get her on our side.' He stepped away from them, into the centre of the circle. He spread out his wings and briefly touched his forehead to the ground, the traditional behaviour of one who is about to speak in the circle, and his sudden formality seemed to calm the crowd. He raised his voice and spoke clearly, and directly, to the queen. 'My flock-kin, what a strange world it would be if hatchlings did not fight, or squabble over hunting lands. Have we not all grown up with scars earned in childhood? My queen is right – the speaking circle is not for the disagreements of hatchlings, so why are we here?'

'We are here, Flayn, because your human pet has disfigured my girl,' snapped T'bre. 'She has lost her crest! It may never grow back.'

The larger, russet-feathered griffin stepped forward then. His voice was quiet, and almost as reasonable as Flayn's.

'And what an insult, to be injured this way by a human,' he said. 'You are right, Flayn, scars earned in playful tussles with other hatchlings are nothing to become upset about. But that creature is not a hatchling – it is prey. And you have brought it here. You have enabled it to insult us, year after year after year. When will this folly end?'

'It will end when I rip your throat out, T'yorne.' This was T'vor, shoving his way past his husband into the centre of the circle. 'Come here now and settle it with me, you mewling yenlin.'

Queen Fellvyn shook her head. 'Oh, how I am sick of you all.' She rounded on Flayn, her shining beak catching the moonlight. 'I said to you when you brought it here, did I not, that it would cause trouble? And if that happened, that you would have to deal with it yourself?'

'Yes, my queen, I do remember that. And if it is as our daughters say? That they were attacked by these other griffins?' said Flayn. 'Is it not every griffin's right to defend themselves?'

'So we have a griffin's word against that of a prey creature?' put in the big red griffin. 'It hardly seems we have to think about it at all, in that case.'

'I was there too!' said T'rook. Ynis's sister was quivering all over with a combination of rage and fright. Ynis put her hands into her neck feathers, breathing in their woody scent. *How has everything gone so wrong so fast?* 'What of my word?'

'What I should do,' said the queen, 'is have the lot of you torn to pieces and fed to the worms.' She turned and settled her golden gaze on Ynis. 'Human child, is it as they say? Did you cut the crest feathers from that griffin?'

Ynis felt cold. She thought of the bright silvery feathers in her bag, just inches from her fingers. Without wanting to, she glanced at her father, Flayn, and she saw the pain and the hope in his eyes. *He wants it to not be true*, she thought, her heart sinking low into her stomach. *He wants me to say it's all a lie. But I can't.*

Something of this must have shown on her face, because she saw her father's expression change, ever so slightly. Stiffly, Ynis reached into her bag and pulled out the feathers. There was a gasp of shock from the pearly-coloured griffin, and a low noise of amusement from the red brute's father.

'Do you see what it is?' said T'yorne gently. 'It keeps trophies of us. No doubt one day it will skin us and wear our skins, as it does with its fellow prey animals.'

'My queen.' Flayn's voice was no longer quite so assured or calm. 'My queen, please let me remind you of the fact that we have sheltered Ynis for sixteen years, that she knows no other family than ours, and loves no one better than her griffin flock-kin. Let me remind you of the new arts she has shown us, and the clever things her paws have created. These things have been beneficial to us, and to Yelvynia.'

Queen Fellvyn sighed noisily. For a few moments, no one spoke at all. Ynis put her arms around her sister's neck, and looked at her fathers standing together in the speaking circle. This, she knew, could be the end for all of them. If the queen ordered that she be killed, her fathers would not submit without a fight and they were vastly outnumbered.

Ynis hugged her sister once, and then slid down from her back to stand on the bare stone. She squared her shoulders and looked up at the adult griffins gathered around them.

'I will go away,' she said, trying to keep her voice steady. 'I will leave Yelvynia and find somewhere on the edges of our world to live.'

'No!' cried Flayn and T'rook together.

'Be quiet,' said Queen Fellvyn. She took a few steps towards Ynis and leaned her great head down so that she could peer more closely at the girl. 'You would exile yourself, child?'

Ynis nodded. Every muscle in her body was thrumming with emotion, but she kept herself still. 'I will not bring any more shame upon my fathers.'

'This is nonsense,' spat T'vor. He flexed his talons, scoring deep scratch marks in the stone. 'Our daughter brings shame on no one!'

'No, the girl speaks truly,' said the queen thoughtfully. 'Perhaps you have managed to instil some yost in her after all, despite her human weaknesses. Ynis, you will leave central Yelvynia, but I give you leave to find a home on the outskirts. You will keep yourself out of griffin affairs, but those who wish to can visit you.' When Flayn and T'vor began to speak up at this, Fellvyn snapped her beak at them. 'I have spoken!'

'Then I will go with her,' said T'rook. 'You can't stop me!'

'Queen Fellvyn, please.' Flayn turned to the queen again, his head held low in supplication. '*Please.* I know my daughters, they will not be separated. Is this truly a just punishment for a childhood scrap? The loss of both our children?'

The queen turned her head away, but when she spoke again her voice was soft, almost as though she genuinely regretted her words. 'You brought this on yourselves, my friends, by bringing it back here in the first place, all those years ago. A wingless thing cannot live with us for long.'

9

The port was thrumming with people, so many that Leven was transfixed. Now that it was time to go, she felt seized with a sudden reluctance.

'Blessed Eleven, if you are sailing with us to Brittletain, it's time to board.' The Nost woman, who had introduced herself as Captain Elisa-Glory, was watching her warily. She spoke with a strong northern lilt, which made Leven think she was one of the rare Nostia born not on board a ship, but on their distant and secret islands to the north. 'We have to go with the tide if we want to make our timings, and well, you are just one passenger, my love.'

The captain gestured to the last barrels being rolled up the boarding ramp. The crew were working swiftly to secure them in the hold, and even as Leven watched they disappeared, one by one.

'I will not hold you up any longer.' Yet still she couldn't bring herself to move.

'Do you wish to sail, or not?' The captain raised an eyebrow at her. 'I have to tell you, the crew are quite exercised about the idea of having a Herald on board. Unless you'd rather stay on dry ground for now?'

Leven looked around the port one more time. Everywhere she looked, people were starting out on journeys to new places, perhaps ready to start new lives, or discover new things about themselves. From here, this busy edge of a newly Blessed country, she could sail to Brittletain and perhaps discover some things about herself. She knew, as everyone did, that the world's last Titans lived to the north of Brittletain. If her life before the ore-lines had involved griffins, it stood to reason that she had to have lived it in Brittletain – as little sense as it made to her. And yet, the temptation to go back to Stratum and forget the whole thing was persistent, a tugging deep in her stomach that made her long for rest, uncomplicated days, and a few more weeks of free drinks in every tavern.

'You look like a woman with a lot on her mind.'

Leven smiled reluctantly. 'It took me days to fly here,' she said. 'You'd think I could have used that time to make my mind up.' She didn't mention that it had actually taken her much longer than usual – every other day she had been stricken with visions of the snowy woods again, visions that left her confused and weak.

The captain was still watching her crew. As she spoke, she fiddled with a brass charm that hung from her belt. It was in the shape of one of the great krakens that had once filled the seas of Enonah. 'You can only fly for short periods. Is that right?'

'If we don't take regular rests, we fall straight out of the sky. The magic that keeps us up there uses too much energy.'

'I had heard this.' The captain turned to her as the last of the barrels disappeared into the hold. 'Blessed Eleven, every day you had a chance to turn around and fly back to Stratum, but you didn't. Even though it cost you to do it, you flew across the lands between Sans Rosen and your capital city, made it all the way here to have this conversation with me now. Whatever it is that you seek in Brittletain, you know in your heart that it is important. Too important to ignore, perhaps.' The captain's serious expression broke into a grin. 'But what do I know of Herald business? I simply do not wish to miss out on your coin.'

Further down the boardwalk, a crate of fat melons fell from a stall, scattering yellow and green fruits across the salt-encrusted boards. Leven watched as the stall's owner went running after them, shouting at sailors and merchants to get out of her way. She was thinking of Foro, who had had many questions, and no answers. She was thinking of Boss, who had made it clear that to remain in Stratum was dangerous. If there *were* any answers to be had, they had to be in Brittletain, where the griffins guarded their secrets and made their nests on the mountain peaks.

Besides which, what real reason did she have to stay? Her days were her own now. And she had never sailed aboard a Nost vessel.

'You know, Captain, the *Faded Glory* is such a beautiful ship, it would be a shame to travel all this way only to miss seeing her sail in deeper waters.'

The captain smiled at that piece of flattery, and together they walked up the plank. The crew scurried around them, as busy as ants, and very soon Leven found herself standing on the deck as the *Faded Glory* made her sedate way out of Sans Rosen port. The busy coastal town drifted away, accompanied by the calls and whistles of the Nost crew. When it finally vanished from view, Leven made herself turn and look out across the sea. Somewhere out there, beyond the steely blue waters, the island of Brittletain was waiting. For better or for worse, she had taken her first step on a new path.

An hour or so later, when the continent had dropped behind them entirely, and Leven had done a few circuits of the *Faded Glory*'s deck, Captain Elisa appeared next to her again. She seemed a different person on board, Leven realised; more vital somehow, and less approachable. She wore a golden scarf wrapped around her head, hiding her tightly curled black hair.

'Blessed Eleven, I hope you don't mind, but now we are on our way, I need to ask you a few questions.'

'Ask away.' Leven noticed that there were a couple of crew members standing just behind the captain, as if they expected trouble. One of them, a young lad with freckles, was holding a small white bird close to his chest. Leven suppressed a smile. What did they expect to do against a Herald of the Imperium, exactly? Sea shanty her to death?

As if reading her mind, Captain Elisa pursed her lips slightly. 'I wondered if you would perhaps share a few more details regarding your business in Brittletain.'

'Do you enquire after the business of all your passengers, Captain?'

The small group behind her shifted uneasily, but Captain Elisa stood her ground.

'Only those passengers who are living weapons, if you'll forgive the bluntness. The Nost prize our neutrality – it's how we keep bread in our galleys and wind in our sails. We take no sides. Now, whose side would I appear to be supporting if I delivered, to Londus, one of the prized Heralds of the Imperium? Your two nations do not have the happiest history.'

'Brittletain has turned away the Imperium's hand of friendship many times, if that's what you mean, Captain.'

'I mean that your people have attempted to invade them several times.'

'Not recently,' said Leven. 'And not the Heralds.'

The wind picked up, making the ends of the captain's gold scarf fly up around her head like streamers. 'For my ship to drop you on the coast of Brittletain with no warning – that would be, and I don't believe I am overstating this, an act of war. Now, we are very happy to transport you, Blessed Eleven. Very happy indeed!' She flashed Leven a quick, sharp smile, like a friendly stab in the ribs. 'This will be a story that jumps from ship to ship, no doubt, and if there's one thing that pleases a Nost captain, it's to hear the name of her ship on the lips of every tavern-goer from Caucasore to Blessed Averly. However...' She smoothed her silk wrap with one hand. 'I have a duty of care to warn the port we are approaching.'

Leven nodded. The bird being carried by the freckled boy was a messenger bird, then. And what did it matter? Her skin was covered with silver-blue ore-lines; it wasn't as though she could avoid being recognised for what she was.

'I see your point. The truth is...' There was no way she could explain the truth to this woman. 'I don't have an official reason for going. Call it a whim. I want to see these last Titans – I want to see the place where the griffins fly, for myself. You can tell them that, and I suppose if I get there and I'm turned away by a lot of angry Britons with spears, I will pay for passage back again, or wherever you are going next.'

The captain nodded once, her face carefully neutral. She turned to the boy with the bird and nodded, and he scurried away to send the message. The rest of the group, content that the Herald in their midst wasn't about to go on a rampage, went back to their usual duties. When they had gone, the captain turned back to her, some of the formality in her stance seeping away into the deck.

'Sightseeing? I know you did not fly all the way from Stratum because you long to see the Wild Wood of Brittletain.'

'Why did you wait until I was on board and in the middle of the sea before you asked me?'

'I didn't want to scare you off. Or provoke a fight in a port, where you could happily destroy my ship and think nothing of it. Out here,' she gestured to the expanse of blue sea that surrounded them, 'hopefully you'll be less than keen to destroy your transportation. Your wings might not be able to carry you all the way back to shore.'

'Do you really think Heralds so dangerous? You make it sound like I am an unpredictable brute.'

There was a flurry of calls from overhead, and a freshly unveiled sail snapped in the wind. The captain, Leven noticed, was looking at her oddly.

'Blessed Eleven, how many nations did you march through on behalf of the Imperium?'

'Five.' She did not have to think about the number. When you'd spent eight years of your life on a project, the details stayed with you.

'Five newly Blessed countries, brought into the warm embrace of the Imperium.' The captain nodded, her eyes on the deck.

'The Nost have business all around the continent, and beyond,' she said. 'Much of the time we provide transport to those who wish to explore new lands, or those who are fleeing an oncoming disaster.' She lifted her eyes to look at Leven directly, and a lot of the warmth that had been there before had cooled into something else. Something much chillier. 'You and your fellow Heralds have provided the Nost with a lot of work over the last few years. And the men and women fleeing your *blessed* occupation call you much worse than unpredictable brutes.'

'Oh. I see.' Leven cleared her throat. Not for the first time, she missed having her Herald brothers and sisters at her back. 'Maybe the people who run from a fight are exactly the sort of people who would turn down the Imperium's gifts. I'll try to keep my more violent urges under control while I'm on board, Captain.'

She left the captain where she was and walked back to the guardrail with as much dignity as she could muster. Travelling to an island that hated the Imperium more than any other did not seem like such a wise decision after all. What was she expecting from the rulers of Brittletain? A warm welcome and an explanation to mysteries she barely understood herself?

Standing with the sea crashing and rushing below her, she thought again of Boss's warning, the older woman's fingers digging into her arm.

What have I thrown myself into here?

10

The centre of Druin life was Dosraiche, the last great Mother Oak planted by the Druidahnon himself when he was just a cub. Cillian had grown up amongst its gargantuan roots, but even now it never failed to take his breath away. The vast oak tree stood hundreds of feet taller than every other tree in the Wild Wood, and within its enormous trunk it held an entire world – or at least, so it had always seemed to him. Over centuries the Druin had carved out their great cathedral from its soft white heartwood and Dosraiche – always so much more than a simple tree – had continued to grow around them. Now, as he and Aeden appeared on one of the Paths that led to the great oak city, the place was as busy as it ever was. Windows glittered with lights from within the grey-green bark; men and women with all manner of horns sprouting from their heads streamed in and out of the many entrances burrowed into Dosraiche's roots; a complex system of ropes and pulleys lifted wicker baskets to the upper branches, while jackdaws and magpies and ravens flew from the special bird-flues that had been built into the trunk of the tree, a steady flicker of black and white overhead. This was the permanent home of the Druin council, but it was also where the youngest initiates learned how to navigate the Paths of the Wild Wood, how to speak to the flora and fauna within it, and, crucially, how to keep control of themselves when the green power that was the Wild Wood coursed through their blood.

Inside, the place was illuminated with thousands of candles, clusters of them clinging to the creamy heartwood like strange, pale fungi. Somewhere in one of the rooms at the top of the many spiral staircases, someone was playing a set of pipes, while on any available perch clusters of jackdaws waited, adding their own clatter to the tune.

Aeden turned to him, his cheeks still pink with annoyance.

'You, wait here. I'll have to make my report to Elder Kirka first but I'm sure she'll want to have words with you after what I have to say.'

The older Druin stalked off towards one of the staircases. The place was crowded with other Druin, waiting in the central hall to receive orders, or just catching up with each other. There were peat fires burning in the many hearths, sending up thick twirls of pungent smoke to slip through the hidden gaps in Dosraiche's cavernous trunk. Cillian wandered towards the message wall. Here, jackdaws and other tamed birds waited to be given messages, usually written on tiny scraps of vellum and strapped to their legs. The birds waited in small alcoves, like a huge meandering honeycomb carved into the interior of the tree-city. Most of the alcoves were empty, their birds out on errands.

Cillian sighed. Even the splendour of Dosraiche couldn't soothe him today. His mind kept returning to the broken Path, the way the Dunohi had thrust her wide antlers into the earth, tearing it up like it was nothing; like that Path hadn't been there for hundreds of years, trodden by the feet of thousands of passing humans. Most of all he couldn't stop thinking of the discordance he had felt in the soul of the forest – a discordance that Aeden had not picked up on.

There was a squeak from above his head, and he looked up to see a young jackdaw peering down at him from one of the alcoves.

'Hello,' said Cillian.

The jackdaw squeaked again, quite insistently this time, and Cillian found himself digging around in his pockets for anything a bird might find edible. He came up with a handful of inkwort seed – a handy snack for long days walking the Paths – and as soon as he had it flat in his hand the small jackdaw flew down and perched on his arm. The bird turned its head to peer at him through one silvery eye.

'You're welcome to it,' said Cillian. 'I might not be back on the Paths again for a while, anyway. They'll have me copying the texts or sweeping the floors. Mopping up your droppings. If Aeden has anything to say about it.'

The jackdaw gave a soft caw at that, as though it had personally met Aeden and thought him exactly the sort to give out menial punishments. The bird hopped along his forearm and dug an enthusiastic beak into the palm of his hand.

'Ow,' said Cillian, although quite absently. He was questing towards the bird's presence, trying to get a sense of its inner life, but the animal was a curious blank. Or, almost blank – the warmth of all warm-blooded creatures was there, like the feeling of sunlight resting on your skin, but he could not get a sense of anything clearer. *Oh well*, thought Cillian. *She's a friendly enough creature.*

The bird had stabbed almost all the seed out of his hand when Cillian heard a soft sigh behind him. He turned to see Aeden standing with Elder Kirka.

'You were supposed to wait where I told you to,' said Aeden. The older Druin turned slightly to Kirka. 'You see? Even simple instructions.'

Kirka sighed again. She was one of the Druin elders, a tall, gracious woman with white hair she cut close to her head. Her horns were graceful spirals sprouting from her temples. The look she turned on Cillian was a tired one.

'I thought you had forgotten about me,' said Cillian. 'No such luck, I suppose.' The little jackdaw left his hand – now bare of seeds – and hopped up to rest on his shoulder.

'Cillian.' Kirka glanced once at the bird, then away. 'Come with me, please.'

He followed the pair of them up one of the elegant wooden staircases until they arrived at Kirka's own meditation cell. Like all of them it was simple: a clean, warm room that smelled of sap, filled with light from a diamond-shaped window. There was a thick embroidered rug on the floor, on which Kirka sat, her legs crossed. After a moment, she gestured to Cillian to do the same. Aeden went and stood by the window, his arms folded over his chest. Cillian felt his heart sink. He really was about to get an official dressing down from an elder.

'Cillian. You are a gifted ranger,' Kirka began. 'A *very* gifted ranger...' Aeden muttered under his breath. 'But you must listen to the instructions of your leader when you are out in the Wild Wood. It is dangerous out there, and today's incident only proved that. The Dunohi are unpredictable.'

'I've said before that I prefer to walk the Paths alone,' Cillian replied. 'I can hear the forest more clearly that way.'

'You see what he says? The arrogance of it,' put in Aeden. 'He thinks he has nothing to learn from any of us.'

'I didn't say that,' said Cillian. 'And that's not important, anyway. Did he tell you what we saw? The Dunohi destroyed part of the Path. The Wild Wood is angry about something. Or afraid. I can't tell. She said... she spoke of murder. And death.'

Kirka looked at him steadily.

'Aeden says this happened because you provoked the forest soul.'

'What?' Cillian shook his head, causing the jackdaw to squawk in his ear. 'I did nothing of the sort. You have to listen to me, Elder Kirka. There's something wrong, something bigger. The Dunohi can feel it, and they're worried.'

'Nonsense,' scoffed Aeden. He turned away, his mouth creased with sour amusement. 'A sapling is barely even capable of talking to the Dunohi, let alone interpreting what it says. He's just trying to cover up his own mistake.'

'I'm telling you the truth! I felt it. Aeden wants to blame it on me because, I don't know, probably because he hates any Druin with more talent than him.'

'Green Man take you!' Aeden glowered at him. 'You think you know better than us?'

'Alright, Aeden, alright.' Kirka looked down at her hands where they were folded in her lap. She wore a crimson cloak over her soft green tunic, pinned in place with a sprig of mistletoe: the mark of a Druin elder. 'Cillian, do you know why communication with the Dunohi is something reserved for elder Druin alone?'

Cillian didn't reply. He knew where this was going. He was glad for the warm presence of the jackdaw on his shoulder.

'Cillian, the bond the Druin have with the Wild Wood is held in a very delicate balance,' Kirka continued. 'When you are bonded to the Wood, what are the two most important gifts you are given? The two principal powers of the Druin?'

He sighed. 'To share minds with the flora and fauna of the Wild Wood. We listen with their ears, see with their eyes. And we are given the knowledge of the secret Paths through the Wild Wood, so that we can open and close the ways through.'

Kirka smiled. 'It's a conversation. A balance. We can feel their minds, we can share thoughts, we can even communicate – with the small creatures of the forest: birds, beetles, mice, squirrels... and the larger animals: the foxes and the deer, the wolves and the bears. Everything that lives in the Wild Wood.'

'I know all this. The youngest initiates know this.'

Kirka continued as if he hadn't spoken. 'What we don't do is force our minds on them. We do not command, and we don't force the connection...'

'And I haven't!' Cillian shot an angry glance at Aeden, who was looking smug by the window. 'What has he told you? Has he suggested I'm... I am not going thrawn, if that's what he's accused me of. Do my horns look blue to you?'

'You demanded to speak to one of the forest souls, Cillian, you disobeyed Aeden's instructions, and when you made this connection—' she held up a hand to stop his protest, 'whether it was forced or not, it upset the Dunohi and caused it to behave bizarrely. That is only half a step away from thrawn.'

'That's nonsense.' Cillian ran a hand over his cheek, feeling the rasp of stubble there. Behind Kirka, Aeden rolled his eyes. 'I respect the connection, and the Wild Wood. It's my whole life! I would never...'

'Do you know why we're so careful about going thrawn, Cillian?'

'I know the stories,' he said quickly. 'I *know* the risks.'

Kirka leaned away from him, stretching out her back. 'Some years ago, there was a Druin woman called Echni. She was, like you, a very talented ranger – she knew the Paths instinctively, and she felt all the Wild Wood's many moods. She spent much of her time out there, on the Paths, talking with animals, sharing their lives and their pains. She was hugely curious, was Echni. Wanted to know everything, to understand everything.'

'I know the story of Echni,' Cillian said quietly.

'Her biggest fascination was with the Dunohi. She would track them for days, reaching out to them, trying to read them the same way she did squirrels and rabbits and deer and birds. When they wouldn't respond in the same way, she began to... force it. Echni was remarkably strong-willed, Cillian, and she broke them eventually. Corrupted them. She painted her horns so we would not see the blue discolouration. Three Dunohi were at her constant beck and call before anyone noticed what was wrong, and when we tried to remove her from the Wild Wood, the forest souls attacked us, killing four of our Druin rangers.'

Cillian knew the story well – all the young initiates did. It was one of the first warnings they received when they started their training.

'Our pact with the Wild Wood is a very delicate balance,' Kirka continued. 'And the Dunohi themselves are unpredictable. Which is why communication with them – which we only ever do when it's desperately needed – is left to the most experienced Druin. Talking to them requires finesse. If you are not careful, a conflict with the Dunohi can lead to injury, to death. And even a severing of our entire relationship with the Wild Wood.'

Cillian looked down at the rug, focusing on the embroidered vines and flowers.

'I am sorry,' he said.

Kirka nodded briskly, as though glad to be done with the conversation. 'Good. The Path will be fixed in the next few days, no harm done. Just be careful in the future. Going thrawn is... no joke. Now. This is not why I wanted to talk to you, anyway.'

Aeden stood up straighter.

'What?'

Kirka ignored him.

'The Druidahnon wishes to speak with you, Cillian.'

'He... he does?'

'Asked for you by name.' Kirka looked up and met his eyes. He thought she looked worried. 'Was most insistent about it. So you'd better get on the road, Cillian, and before the moon is up, if you can.'

'What could be so urgent?'

'And what could the Druin-Father want with him?' put in Aeden, his voice pitched a little higher than normal. There were two pink marks on the tops of his cheeks, Cillian was pleased to note. 'A ranger who won't do as he's told!'

'Aeden.' Kirka rubbed a speck of dirt off of her cheek. 'Please listen to yourself. The order of Druin is a clan of priests and warriors and rangers, not a... not a finishing school for young ladies.'

Cillian stood up. He felt as though he'd narrowly escaped a punishment only to be thrown down some other uncertain path.

'What happened to her? To Echni?' he asked. 'I've heard the story so many times, but no one ever talks about what happened after the other Druin were killed.'

'Her horns were sawn off,' Kirka said shortly. 'And she was exiled from the Druin order for life.' She cleared her throat. 'Why are you still here? Get moving.'

11

So much of Brittletain remains shrouded in mystery. The Imperium has been attempting to take the island for centuries, but that in itself is not so mysterious; the island lies across a band of sea that is well known for its treacherous sea life and unpredictable weather. Any army of the Imperium that makes it across that must then charge a heavily armoured coast, lined with warriors that have no interest in mercy or diplomacy. The queens of Brittletain, it is said, bathe each newly born prince and princess in the blood of an enemy, so that they will never balk at the sight of it. No, more interesting to me are the secrets of Brittletain's forests, and specifically, the order of the Druin. These freakish horned men and women are the ones tasked with maintaining the paths through the heavily wooded island, and they do this through the management of so-called 'forest souls'. About these, we know virtually nothing at all, save a few intriguing legends.

Excerpt from *The Lore of the Deep
Forest: An Examination of the
Myths and Facts of Brittletain*

C illian made his way south along the Paths, before catching one of the smaller carts leaving for Londus. He sat in the back with several barrels of pickled chestnuts and crates of barley wine. The driver had offered him a seat up front, almost bowing as he did so, but Cillian didn't have the energy for making conversation with the man, so he had told him he intended to use the journey time to meditate. Meditation was always a useful excuse for avoiding small talk: the people of Brittletain did not understand the point of it, but were largely happy to consign it to a list of things the Druin did that no one really understood.

Half an hour or so into the journey, his small jackdaw friend appeared, alighting on top of a crate of barley wine and giving one of the corks a hopeful peck. Cillian pulled the last of the inkwort seed from an inner pocket and spread it on the boards next to him.

'Inkwort would be a good name for a jackdaw, don't you think?' He reached out for her mind again and felt only a general friendliness. 'If we're going to be spending time together, it would be nice to have something to call you.'

The jackdaw peered at him with one pale eye, then set to pecking up the tasty little seeds.

'Inkwort it is.'

A few hours later, he was woken by the cart driver giving his shoulder a brisk shake.

'There you are, son. Meditating real deep, were you?'

'Yes,' Cillian sat up, rubbing a hand over his face. The jackdaw had snuck herself into a gap between the sacks, and now she opened one sleepy eye to look at him. 'Yes, thank you. Are we here?'

He climbed out of the cart and stepped down onto a cobbled path, followed a moment later by Inkwort. The Druidahnon lived within a huge enclosure on the outskirts of Londus; a kind of massive walled garden, shrouded from the road by a crowd of ancient oak and elm. The carter had stopped at one of the gates, which was lit with several hanging oil lamps. The man was clearly keen to get on his way again, yet when Cillian tried to press a coin into his hands, he looked embarrassed.

'Not that I don't appreciate it, you understand, but I wondered if you could have a word with Bluebell here instead. She ain't been right for the last few weeks, and I'd consider it a great kindness if you could give me some clue, as it were.'

Cillian made his way to the front of the cart. Bluebell was one of the shaggy little ponies that were bred all over Brittletain. She had a thick mane of brown hair hanging half in her eyes. Cillian swept it back and placed his hands on the velvety place beneath her eyes.

At once, he could sense her lively mind, friendly and warm and also, curiously, pleased with herself. He frowned slightly, gently chasing after the reason for that satisfaction, letting the question pass from his mind to her mind... then drew his hands away, smiling.

'She's pregnant, that's all,' he said.

'Oh, well, bless your horns, son.' The carter patted the pony's rump affectionately. 'And what have you been up to, aye, Bluebell?'

Cillian left the man at the gate and made his way down the cobbled path that led to the main building. It was a huge, sprawling thing of red and grey brick, with several meandering towers for the Druidahnon's attendants, and an enormous hall in the centre. As he reached the entrance, he was met by a sturdy woman with broad shoulders and thick red hair. She looked him up and down once, shrugged, and gestured for him to follow.

As he stepped over the threshold, Inkwort flew up and away again, disappearing into the night, and Cillian felt a pang of sadness.

'Do you know why I've been summoned?'

'He has his little funny moods, don't he,' the attendant said, not looking at him. She wore a thick woven jerkin, the sigil of the Titan bear stitched across the back. 'You lot, you're always off in the forests, aren't you? Not here to see all of his little moods. Just a few months of his company you get, then off you go, down the Paths.'

'I trained for a year,' said Cillian, half under his breath.

'Be thankful,' carried on the woman, 'that he doesn't have you here every other day, running around after the Court of Bears. Oh no, that's what we're for, isn't it. Your work is too important, I suppose.'

'It's the work the Druidahnon gave us,' he said, a little louder this time.

'*Hmph*. Good luck to you, that's all I can say.'

They paused still some distance from the Great Hall. The area just outside was known as the Court of Bears, and although the bears that lived there were largely docile and took little notice of the humans that passed back and forth through their territory, it was never a good idea to rush through without thinking and looking carefully. There were three bears in the undergrowth, two brown bears sitting together, seemingly half asleep, and one big black bear prowling the foundation stones of the Great Hall. Next to the Druidahnon himself they looked tiny, even smaller than cubs, but Cillian knew that they would have paws the size of tree stumps. As gently as breathing, he reached out to them along the green connection that held all of the Wild Wood together, and felt their quiet minds like beacons that had banked down to embers. They watched, and they were curious, but they were not threatened.

'It's safe,' he said to the attendant, who glared at him.

'*I* know it's safe,' she said. 'I know when it's safe and when it's not safe better than anyone. Bloody goat-heads, telling me my job...'

They walked slowly across the Court of the Bears, and she left him at the door to the Great Hall.

It was a human-sized door, one that gave no clue as to the enormous Titan dwelling beyond it. Cillian knocked, feeling vaguely foolish, and after a moment, a huge shaggy bear head thrust itself through an opening in the wall some ten feet above him. The eyes of the Druidahnon glittered in the lamp light, and then he drew back inside.

'Come in then, young Cillianos! Don't just stand there with your dick in your hand!'

Cillian took a slow breath and opened the door. The inside of the hall was very much like still being outside; the floor was carpeted with thick grass, and small trees sprouted here and there. The only real differences were the towering walls, and the deep, vaulted ceiling, crisscrossed with several huge wooden beams, from which hung a number of impossibly heavy-looking chandeliers. There were gaps in the walls, near the ceiling, which the Druidahnon liked to hang his head out of occasionally. The wall furthest from the human door was non-existent — it was through this space that the Druidahnon came and went, and humans were expressly forbidden from using it. Aside from being a matter of courtesy, they ran the risk of getting accidentally squashed by a vast paw.

'My lord?' Cillian stepped inside. He had spent a lot of time with the Druidahnon in the past, both as part of his training and in service, yet the sight of the great old Titan never ceased to be extraordinary. He stood at around thirty feet tall, a huge old bear with a squarish head, his fur a mixture of black and brown. His long muzzle was crisscrossed with old white scars, and each of the claws on his massive paws were as long as Cillian's forearms. The old bear wore a kind of crown, woven from branches that still grew leaves, flowers and fruit, and when a drop of slather fell from his jaws, a new flower sprouted from the ground. It was the Druidahnon's habit to walk around on his back legs, like a man, although now he sat and hunched over, his intelligent brown eyes narrowed.

'*There* you are,' he said, as though he had been waiting for Cillian for days. 'The horns are coming in well, aren't they? They suit you, as I knew they would. How are you feeling since your joining, Cillian?'

'Good, my lord.' Cillian touched his fingers to the ridged horn sprouting from his left temple. It had been a good seven years since his official joining to the forest, and he now barely remembered what it was like not to have horns, but the Druidahnon, as ancient as he was, had a strange and somewhat unconventional relationship with time. It was quite usual for him to ask about events that were long in the past as though they had happened that morning. 'The joining was everything I had hoped for. More, even.'

'You look a little scrawnier than I would like. Eating enough, are you? It's not good for Druin to forget to eat because your heads are all caught up with roots and sap and birds and what have you.' The Druidahnon lumbered back to his feet. 'Walk with me a little way, Cillian. It is nearly dawn, do you see?'

Cillian did as he was asked, being sure to keep some distance from the bear's thundering step. At the far end of the Great Hall, the garden stood like a picture framed in stone, the first silvery-lilac light of dawn gilding the edges of every plant and tree. There was another of the Druidahnon's bear attendants out there, snuffling through the undergrowth.

'My lord.' Cillian paused, cleared his throat. 'My impression was that your message was urgent. Did you need me for something?'

'I've read over some of the elders' reports, Cillian, and they say that you are a good ranger. No surprise there! Rarely have I seen a human more cut out for the calling than you. I'm surprised you weren't born with horns on.'

'Thank you, my lord.' Cillian stood with his arms behind his back, feeling a mixture of pride, embarrassment and irritation. It wouldn't be entirely out of character for the Druidahnon to summon him for a casual chat, which was in its own way a great honour, but already Cillian felt anxious to return to the heart of the Wild Wood.

'But the reports also say, my young friend, that you do not work well with the rest of the order.'

Cillian shook his head slightly. Could Kirka and Aeden have sent a message before they had even spoken to him? Had they suggested to the Druidahnon that he was turning thrawn? 'I'm better as a solitary ranger, my lord. I've always said that, but the order...' He cleared his throat. 'They don't listen to me. What can I say?'

'Hmm.' The giant old bear leaned against one of the walls, where a series of thick wooden posts jutted out. He rubbed a shoulder blade against one, grunting with satisfaction. 'You think you should live a solitary life, out on the Paths? No company but your own, is that what you think?'

'Truthfully, my lord, I can think of nothing better,' said Cillian. He thought of Aeden snapping at him, and he grimaced. 'I serve the Wild Wood better alone.'

'Do you remember when you came to the order, Cillian?'

'A little.' In truth, Cillian had barely any memories of his life before the order. He had lived with his mother on the edge of the Wild Wood, and then she became ill, coughing into a scrap of linen until it was dotted, then soaked, with blood. There his memories grew very hazy, until he remembered passing into Dosraiche, a tall woman with horns holding his small hand in hers. He had been around four years old. 'It felt like coming home, my lord.'

'We don't take all orphans, as you know, Cillianos, but there was something about you. Sap in your veins rather than blood, that is what I remember thinking. But it can be a hard way to grow up. Encouraging this *greenness* in you... perhaps I did you a disservice without knowing.'

'No, my lord,' Cillian said with feeling. 'The Wild Wood is my home. I don't need other people. I am sorry if this disappoints you in some way, but it is true.'

'You know the story of Echni?'

Cillian bit down on a sigh.

'I do, my lord, but I promise you, I am not trying to bend the Dunohi to my will, I just wanted to know—'

'She also was not good with people,' continued the Druidahnon. 'She wanted to know *things*, not people. And so to her, people became things, and then, less important than things.'

'You knew her, my lord?' Cillian didn't know why it had never occurred to him before, but the Druidahnon was older than the Druin order; of course he had seen every part of their history. Even the shameful bits.

'Oh yes. I was there when they decided to banish her, and when they took her horns.' The great bear shook his head gravely. 'She never did understand what she had done wrong, that one. Not an ounce of regret. When they took the bone saw to her head she screamed and hollered and cursed us all. Such fury couldn't continue to be connected to the Wild Wood. The consequences would have been... they would have been terrible.'

Cillian felt a flush of shame and anger colour his cheeks. Kirka and Aeden had made the Druidahnon consider him in the same terms as Echni, when he had only ever acted out of concern for the Wild Wood.

'I swear on the Green Man himself, my lord, all I want is to be the best ranger I can be. If I were left to walk the Paths and speak to the Dunohi alone, it would be better for everyone.'

'It was easier, when my people lived,' said the Druidahnon. His deep, gravelly bear voice had taken on a wistful tone. 'We were the natural conduit between the forest and your people. We spoke to the Dunohi as easily as I am speaking to you now, and they saw us as neighbours, friends even. It was a small thing then, to convince the forest souls to stay away from the Paths, to let the men and women of Brittletain move through their territory. But then...'

He trailed off. The rest of Brittletain's bear Titans had died away many hundreds of years ago, fading back into the forests and disappearing. No one alive now knew why, save for the Druidahnon, and he did not speak of it.

'You gave us the order of Druin,' said Cillian. 'People who could continue to be the link between the forest and the human settlements. It has been your great work, my lord.'

'Hmmm.' The Druidahnon sounded dissatisfied, even melancholy. 'I have always thought myself quite wise, you see.' He grunted. 'The wisest of my kind. I am the only one still here after all, aren't I? And yet...' The old bear shook himself. Cillian felt the disturbance in the air like a sudden hot breeze. Small, crawling things dropped from the Druidahnon's jaws. Cillian watched them wriggle away into the grass. 'Cillian, Queen Broudicca has sent a message to us.'

'What?' Cillian blinked, wrongfooted by the change in subject. 'I mean, she has, my lord?'

'Indeed. She has had advance warning of a very interesting visitor to the shores of Brittletain. An emissary from the Imperium, no less.'

Cillian frowned. The Imperium summoned images of war, of power, of people he did not wish to meet. 'What do they want?'

'That is the question, isn't it? An interesting one. According to Queen Broudicca's limited knowledge, this visitor wishes to, for want of a better description, explore our island nation. They wish to see the griffins in the north – to see these last Titans.' The Druidahnon chuckled rather dryly at this. 'I am not impressive enough for the Imperium, you see.'

'This person cannot seriously expect a warm welcome?'

'Perhaps not, but that is exactly what they will get. Queen Broudicca wishes for the Druin order to provide a guide for this visitor, one that will transport them safely to the north, and the edge of Yelvynia.'

Cillian grasped where the conversation was going. He tried not to let his feelings show on his face.

'No,' he said.

'And you will be that guide, Cillian.'

'You can't be serious.' He took a breath, half laughing. 'Me? Showing some rich idiot from the Imperium around the Wild Wood? I...' He bit down on several more remarks. 'My lord, forgive me, but that doesn't seem like a good idea at all. I know nothing about dealing with these people!'

'You know very little about dealing with *people* at all,' said the Druidahnon. He leaned his head down to meet Cillian, so close that the Druin could see the bees buzzing lazily around his garland crown. 'You are not a tree, or an animal, Cillianos. You need to remember that.'

'I...' For a long moment, Cillian was lost for words. No part of what was happening made any sense to him. 'Please, my lord, the order is full of Druin who would be better suited to such a task. Pretty much anyone else, in fact.'

'No, no, you are quite wrong there, I am afraid. It must be you.' Already the dawn light was stronger, picking out the coppery flecks in his fur, and the light seemed to pool in his eyes like liquid fire. *He looks sad*, thought Cillian. *This isn't just some whim of his.*

'My lord.' Cillian felt cold. He missed the company of the small jackdaw. 'Have you *seen* something?' He spoke quietly, afraid that saying it too loudly would make it inevitable.

The Druidahnon looked at him in silence for a long time, long enough that Cillian began to feel like he'd forgotten the human was there at all; that instead his gaze was directed inward, at some distant point in the past that was long lost to him. Eventually though, the spell was broken, and the old bear lifted himself up, so high that he nearly dislodged one of the chandeliers.

'Yes. The horns, they suit you, boy,' he said, already turning away to the garden. 'Go to Londus, Cillian. The queen is expecting you.'

12

L even ate dinner in the galley with the portion of the crew who weren't currently on a watch. It felt strange to be in such a group of people and to be a stranger. If she tuned out their words she could almost believe she were with the Heralds again – both groups were rough and ready, hardened by the sea or by battle. Yet there was no sense of welcome or camaraderie here. Instead, she sat on a bench by herself, in a pool of silence with tension in its depths. No one tried to make conversation with her, and the few times she attempted to make eye contact with someone they either looked away or glared back, challenging her to make something of it. She felt uneasy, and it was making her ore-lines itch.

Eat your dinner, she told herself. *Who cares what the Nost think, anyway? It's easy to sneer at soldiers when your ships keep you far away from every war.*

The soup, at least, was good: spiced broth with tomatoes, herbs and pieces of oily fish that tasted like the sea. Travelling across the Unblessed lands she had eaten plenty of dubious meals, and if they let her into Brittletain, there was no knowing what she might be forced to eat over the next few weeks—

A sudden, pointed silence made the hairs on the back of her neck stand up. Leven turned on the bench in time to see a wiry man approaching her with a dagger in one hand and an intent expression on his face. The men and women on the other benches had gone quiet, and a couple had half stood up, yet none of them, Leven couldn't help but notice, were trying to stop him.

'Hey!' She hopped up from the bench, both hands held out in front of her. 'Is this a joke?'

'You are a *butcher*!' The wiry man advanced, the dagger now held at head height. Buttery light from the lamps slid along the blade. 'You and all your lot. And I won't have you poisoning the decks of the *Faded Glory*.'

'This is ridiculous.' Leven edged away. Still no one was making a move to stop him. 'You know what I am, little man. I could gut you in seconds.'

He didn't appear to hear her. His lips twisted into a snarl, and to Leven's surprise, she saw that his eyes were wet.

'Never thought I'd get the chance to see one of you up close,' he said, muttering into his chest. 'And now here you are. It's got to mean something. The gods want me to avenge them.'

'Stars' arses.' Leven found herself backed into the bench. Her initial confusion had boiled away into anger, and the Titan power coiled under her skin, urging her to summon it. Her wings in this low-ceilinged space would cause a blood bath, but what of it? They had attacked her. They had brought this on themselves. 'So be it, you idiot. I hope you've made peace with those gods, because—'

'Stop that!' The captain was on the wooden stairs, her face a picture of cold fury. 'Stand down, both of you!'

The wiry man flinched as if he'd been slapped, and two burly crew members nearby belatedly took hold of him. The dagger clattered to the floor.

'No!' he cried, trying to pull away from them. 'This is my chance, let me go!'

Captain Elisa moved to one side of the stairs so that the men could pass her. 'Put Gray in the brig,' she said. 'And take him some lunch.'

There was a chorus of protest as the wiry man was dragged back out onto the deck, but the captain held up her hand.

'He won't be there for long,' she said shortly. 'He just needs to cool off.'

'Is this how your passengers are usually treated, Captain?' Leven could hear the indignation in her own voice, and somehow that made everything worse; even to her own ears she sounded like some whining Imperial lord. 'Stabbed in the back while eating their dinner?'

'Come,' the captain gestured to the stairs again, 'we will talk in my cabin.'

'I hope your crew will save me some of that soup. Although I get the sense I am not the most popular passenger you've ever had.'

The captain nodded wearily and poured a tawny liquid into two short, fat goblets. The cabin was a cosy nook hidden under the forecastle, with three leaded windows looking out onto a sea the colour of beaten steel. There was a sturdy table covered in maps, which were weighted down by a solid lump of purple crystal, and a small brazier in the corner provided a welcome blast of heat. The smell of salt water was especially strong in the small space.

'I did warn you, Blessed Eleven. Here, drink that. It's the brandy I keep for anyone foolish enough to fall overboard.'

'As long as I can be sure it isn't poisoned,' said Leven, although she picked up the glass and took a gulp anyway.

'Gray is a recent recruit. We picked him up on the shores of Lativia. You know it?'

'Blessed Lativia. We were there for six months or so.'

'I'm sure Gray would prefer you not call it that. To him, the coming of the Imperium – the coming of you, the Heralds, specifically – was the end of his old life. Two brothers and a father, killed in your war.'

Leven took another gulp of brandy, looking away from the captain this time. 'If Blessed Lativia hadn't resisted the blessings of the Imperium, then that man's family would still be alive.'

Captain Elisa said nothing for a long moment. Outside, it was possible to hear the calls of sea birds and the endless rush of the ocean.

'Do you truly believe such a thing?' she said eventually. 'The Imperium as a protecting father, taking lesser nations under its protection? Forgive me, Blessed Eleven, but I had thought you sharper than that.'

Leven put the empty glass down on the map table with a little more force than she intended.

'We were always a blunt instrument, rather than the sharpest.' She forced a smile on her face, trying to make it into a joke. 'I don't want trouble with your crew. Or with anyone. I'm not a Herald anymore. What I did – what we did – is in the past now. People need to get over it and move on.'

The captain narrowed her eyes. 'Easy enough to say when it was your boot on other people's throats. You might think you can simply shed the identity of a Herald and everything that comes with it, but you should know that the past often has a habit of coming back to bite you on the arse.'

Leven looked away.

'I would like to retire to my own quarters now, if it's all the same to you.'

Brittletain slipped into sight a few hours after dawn the next day. Leven went up onto the deck and stood at the forecastle watching it come into focus. It was a beautiful, clear day, and at first the island was a thin line of white, and then as they drew closer, Leven saw that they were sailing towards tall, chalky cliffs. Sea birds of all types were crying overhead.

'It's not the friendliest coast, is it?' she said to the captain. 'Where can you even come ashore?'

'The great port of Londus-on-Sea is just east of here,' said the captain. 'But I thought you might like to see these cliffs. They are quite famous among those of us that spend our lives on the sea.'

As they drew closer, Leven saw that there was something poking out of the cliff, some huge shape hanging suspended there. Eventually, the shapes and blurs resolved themselves into a huge, monstrous skeleton, trapped in the chalk. The bones were a dark, bluish black, and they appeared to make up an animal around twenty feet tall, from feet to head. The skull was turned to its side, its jaws slightly open, so that Leven could see the dark circle of one eye socket and long, vicious-looking canines.

'Now *that*,' said the captain, 'is a Titan. One of the Great Bears who used to populate Brittletain. Can you imagine, beasts so large?'

'It must be worth a fortune,' said Leven. 'Why doesn't the ruler of Brittletain dig it out and sell it?'

Captain Elisa sniffed. 'Spoken like a true citizen of the Imperium. To the people of Brittletain, the bones of the Titans are more than trinkets to be sold. This is the old bear Magog, and he is sacred to the Britons. And it shows a certain amount of power, doesn't it? Leaving something so valuable on display like that. Queen Broudicca is no fool. But I imagine you shall find that out yourself, shortly.'

'The queen?' Leven looked at the Nost woman, although it was hard to drag her eyes from the Titan skeleton snarling from the cliffs. 'I'm just here to see the country, to see this mysterious place for myself. Why should the queen have anything to do with it?'

Captain Elisa said nothing to that. Instead she went back onto the main deck to shout more orders to her crew, and soon enough the ship was bearing to the east again, following the line of the coast. Another messenger bird left the ship. The cliffs, which Leven saw held a thick band of forest at their top, eventually gave away to flatter, rockier land, which then itself became a series of swampy marshlands. Here and there Leven spotted tall, lonely stone towers poking out of the marshes, some of which had strange green lights winking from their windows. Leven thought she could see things moving in the marsh, tall things with long, thin legs, but the marshes were oddly difficult to look at; a shimmering haze gradually rose as the day grew warmer, and Leven couldn't be sure of anything she saw there. As a Herald she had seen many places across the continent, Blessed and Unblessed, but this small corner of Brittletain had already proven to be stranger than all of them.

In a couple of hours the marshes had faded away to be replaced with a more reassuring grassland, and then the *Faded Glory* was turning into a wide estuary. Sunlight bounced from the water, and then just ahead of them a city seemed to spring out of nowhere. The river was busy with ships and barges, and in the distance, there was a huge bridge with great arches underneath for ships to pass through. The harbour they turned into bristled with stone and wood buildings, and thin lines of grey, white and black smoke trailed up into the blue sky. For Leven, who had spent so many months in Stratum, it looked a small enough place, yet there was an energy and a vitality about it that was startling.

'There you go, look.' Captain Elisa was at her elbow again. 'There's your welcoming party.'

Leven narrowed her eyes in the direction the captain was pointing and was taken aback to see a jetty crowded with people, all apparently watching the *Faded Glory* as she eased her way into port. The crowd was varied, but at the front, Leven could not help but notice that there was a line of men and women in armour, with halberds held at their sides. At a quick glance she would have guessed around fifty, maybe more. In the centre of the crowd was a chariot, its sides covered with what looked like dark blue velvet embroidered with gold. Two women stood within it, dressed in bright silks. They had blue paint on their faces and they were watching the ship closely.

'What is all this?'

Captain Elisa raised her eyebrows. She looked pleased – Leven suspected it wasn't often that the *Faded Glory* received such a welcome.

'Queen Broudicca is a canny woman. I imagine she wants to hear the reasons for your visit in person. You see those two women there?' She pointed to the richly bedecked chariot. 'Those are two of her daughters. You will have quite the escort to her palace. Will you take some advice from me, Blessed Eleven?'

'It looks like I'm in desperate need of it.'

'Queen Broudicca was once a northern queen. Twenty years ago Londus was already an extremely prosperous kingdom, and this city – Londus-on-Sea – was growing ever larger with trade from the continent. Broudicca came down through Brittletain with her army, following the sacred Paths through the Wild Wood until she came to Londus, and then she massacred most of the city. Burned it to the ground. All what you see here is less than twenty years old, built on the smoking remains of another queen's city. Broudicca saw it, took it, made it her own. And she hasn't left since. Her old kingdom in the north, Galabroc, is now ruled over by her daughter Ceni, who she proclaimed a queen – a queen who will forever be loyal to Broudicca. All of which makes her the most powerful ruler in Brittletain.'

'I see.' Leven was still watching the crowd at the port. There was a lot of shouting going on now, and she couldn't quite discern whether they were welcoming her or calling for her blood. 'What am I supposed to do with this knowledge?'

'Just know that you are not dealing with some provincial backwater here, or some warlord ruling over four households and a pig. Queen Broudicca is clever, ruthless and extremely ambitious. Don't underestimate her, Blessed Eleven.'

Ropes were being thrown, and the anchor lowered. Leven watched as the crew brought out the plank to disembark. She had thought to find answers in Brittletain; had assumed that she would be allowed to find them in her own time, without any interference from the Imperium, or Boss, or any of the other figures that usually had a say in how she spent her time. Yet, it seemed, she was walking straight into a new court, one that she had no knowledge of, and one that owed her nothing. It seemed, in short, a lot more dangerous than she had imagined.

When it came time for her to walk down the gangplank, she pulled her untidy hair back into a short tail, smoothed down her shirt, and plastered a nonchalant smile on her face.

13

I've said it before and I'll say it again – the woman is unhinged. Have you actually been in her workshop? I suppose not. Easier for you to all sit up here and pretend it's not going on, but those of us who are forced to work with her – you know that she won't refer to me by my title? Not a bit of it. She sees me as some sort of lackey, someone to do the heavy lifting or the unpleasant tasks. And there are plenty of those. She has no scruples, not a single one. I am hardly known for being a soft and sentimental type as I'm sure you know, but even I have to balk at the experiments she is doing down in that pit. I won't do it. I won't be a party to it. Find some other fool.

Transcript of an interview with acclaimed surgeon
Krem Lexis on his time working with the Imperial
Bone Crafter and Alchemist Gynid Tyleigh

'Don't touch anything while we're in there. I know you'll be tempted.'

'Is she really so bad?'

Kaeto paused with his hand on the door. He and Belise were stood outside Gynid Tyleigh's underground workshop, a huge, low-ceilinged space hidden below Stratum. The tunnel that led to it was well maintained, and lit with oil lamps at regular intervals along the walls. The place smelled of sand, and heat, with a deeper, more unpleasant smell beneath it that Kaeto could not quite place; chemicals of some sort. They were directly underneath one of the great plazas in the very centre of the city, and every now and then it was possible to hear a rumble as some cart or carriage passed overhead.

'As a loyal citizen of the Imperium, Belise, I feel that I cannot offer an opinion on her relative badness.' He pushed open the door. 'But I can advise that much of what you might see in here will be dangerous, and if you feel like sticking any of it in your pockets, you may lose your pockets. And your fingers.'

They stepped through into a huge circular room built from red brick. In every direction there were workbenches, tall iron cauldrons, racks of shelves heaving with instruments and bottled chemicals. In the centre there was a collection of apparatus that looked rather like the inside of a blacksmith's shop, and just above it there were several carefully cut holes in the ceiling; Kaeto knew that these led out to a concealed chimney, somewhere in the chaos of Stratum above. There were a few silent figures moving about the workshop: Tyleigh's assistants, their heads down and intent on their work.

'Come on, I see her. Let's get this over with.'

Tyleigh herself was standing by a stack of cases, rooting through an open one as if she had lost something. As always, Kaeto was struck by the sparseness of the woman. She was wiry, from the thatch of brown hair half hidden beneath the thick blue headband she habitually wore across her forehead, to the taut muscles in her forearms and her shoulders. Her face was thin and pointed – it made him think of a fox, often – and her clothes were always an afterthought. Whichever holey jumper was on the floor at the time of dressing, a white leather apron that looked like it had never seen soap. As they approached, she spared him a quick glance over the top of her spectacles.

'Oh. It's you, is it?'

'Good afternoon, Crafter Tyleigh. I'm here to see if there's anything you need.'

'Are you now? Well.' She picked up a stack of books from the case and dumped them on a low table behind her. 'You could get me some help that hasn't had its brain boiled. YOU!' She turned away from them slightly, bellowing at a hooded shape that was just scampering into sight. 'Did I say pack *these* books? Did I fuckery. Get them out of here and fetch the ones I wanted in the first place.'

The hooded figure moved over to the case, its head bowed.

'If you want extra help, Tyleigh, you only have to ask for it.'

The woman gave a short exhalation of breath. 'And have a bunch of the Imperium's best muscle brains getting their mitts all over my work? Aye, thank you very much, but I'll stick with these idiots; at least I don't have to see their faces. So, the empress has you keeping an eye on me, does she? Can't trust that one as far as you can spit her. Dolls,' she added darkly. 'I ask you? *Dolls.*'

'I'm here to help, Tyleigh, as always. Perhaps you could tell me a little about where our expedition is bound? Then I might be better able to prepare.'

'Like I have the time to lead you through it,' she said, but she dropped the book she was holding and led them over to a desk. This was covered in parchment and maps, most of them inky with Tyleigh's narrow, spidery handwriting. 'Here, then, the Unblessed east.' She pulled one of the maps towards her, scattering notes and a handful of wood shavings. Kaeto recognised the map – it showed the easternmost provinces of the Imperium, and, beyond that, a stretch of land they officially knew very little about. Three countries that shared borders, and each with a coast on the edge of the Sea of the New Moon. 'Here,' she jabbed a finger at the country that sat the furthest north, 'Unblessed Houraki. Complicated place, lots of warring aristocracy squabbling for power – no problems with that sort of thing in the Imperium, of course.' She gave a short, dry bark of laughter. 'There is a place in Houraki that is forbidden to all – travellers, natives, even their ruling elite. No one is officially allowed to step foot in it. They call it the Black City, which is an overly dramatic name if you ask me, but there you go.' She pointed out a shaded region in the south-eastern portion of the country. 'It's widely believed to be cursed, which is a good rumour to spread if you have something valuable you don't want anyone else getting a look at.'

Tyleigh stalked off from the desk to approach a set of shelves. When she returned, she had another piece of parchment in her hand. She passed it to Kaeto. It appeared to be a very old drawing; on it, Kaeto could see three humanoid figures with animal heads – a bear, an eagle and a horse with long, spiralled horns sprouting from its forehead. They stood before a much larger humanoid figure, which stood with its arms raised and clothed in flame. Its head was a snarling, twisted thing; it made Kaeto think of the vicious biting lizards he sometimes saw for sale in Stratum's more disreputable markets. Kaeto gave the parchment to Belise, who peered at it intently.

'This is a piece from a larger book about Hourakian history – a book that has taken me years to find, since their written history has some very large gaps. You see here this term, *Othanim*? I've never seen it elsewhere.' She tapped the word with one finger. It was written in red ink that looked a little like blood. 'It strongly suggests that there once existed another Titan species, these Othanim, that we know nothing about. You see this creature's lizard head? It is my belief that the so-called Black City contains the remains of this unknown Titan.' Tyleigh took her spectacles off and rubbed the lenses with a grimy sleeve. 'I think the Othanim may have been human-shaped.'

Kaeto frowned. 'That they have been given human bodies in this image means nothing. The Druidahnon, and the rest of the giant bears of Brittletain, were bear-shaped. As the unicorn Titans had four legs like a horse. This is just… artistic licence.'

The look Tyleigh threw him then made him glad she wasn't holding any weapons.

'Do you take me for an idiot, Envoy? This one picture is merely the culmination of a decade of research. No, I am positive that these forgotten Titans were the only truly humanoid variety, and finding their remains is crucial. One of the biggest difficulties with the Titan ore, and grafting it onto humans, is that it remembers its old shape, which leads, eventually, to a painful disintegration after eight years or so—' She shook her head and thrust her spectacles back on her face. 'Why am I telling you this? As if you'd understand any of it. The point is, we have to go there, and retrieve the Othanim remains.'

'Unblessed Houraki? What is the Imperium's relationship with this place? Friendly, I assume, if we're crossing their borders?'

'Relationship? As far as I know, we don't have one. This isn't some bloody diplomatic mission, Envoy. If it was, I wouldn't be taking a backstabber like you, would I?'

Kaeto composed his face. He did not bother asking if the empress knew that they would essentially be stealing from an Unblessed state. Of course she would know.

'I see,' he said. 'So we will travel to this forbidden area, this Black City. Do you have an idea where your remains are to be located? We may need to—'

At that moment there was a commotion beside them. Belise had been poking at one of the shelves and a rain of inkstones clattered onto the floor.

'What the bloody hell do you think you're playing at?' shouted Tyleigh.

'Forgive the child, she has an overly curious mind,' said Kaeto, laying a hand heavily on Belise's shoulder and steering her towards the door. 'I'll get her out of your way now, Crafter Tyleigh, and I will begin preparations for our journey.'

'Huh. If you are bringing the brat, see that you keep her out of my way,' sneered Tyleigh. She was already turning back to her crates and books. 'Bloody children. I've no bloody use for them.'

'That was less than wise, Belise.'

They were back out in the dizzying sunshine of the centre of Stratum. Kaeto felt uneasy; what had been an unpleasant job had formed itself into a new constellation of difficulty. A forbidden stretch of land in an Unblessed country, a potential new Titan, the risk of war.

'There was a lot of interesting stuff on that shelf. You didn't say anything about not looking,' said Belise. 'Just not touching.'

Kaeto sighed. 'Did you even stick to that rule?'

Belise pulled a small inkstone out of her pocket and shrugged. 'She had loads. She won't miss it.'

'Listen.' Kaeto took the girl by the shoulders, made her look up into his face. 'When we are travelling with Crafter Tyleigh, you must keep out of her way. I am not joking here. She is a hard-hearted woman, with no affection or kindness for children. *Especially* not for children. Do you understand?'

Belise was frowning. 'What did she do?'

Kaeto straightened up and sighed. He thought of the Imperium's project in the west, and of the Herald he had so recently killed. Perhaps if this mission with Tyleigh was successful, that might put a stop to at least one flavour of the Imperium's cruelty.

'Never you mind,' he said. 'Come on, my fellow backstabber, let's go and sharpen our knives.'

14

'I knew Fionovar the Red of course, although he was already ancient by then, only a hundred years or so from his final journey to the Bone Fall and I myself little more than a cub. He was wise and boisterous, full of a fierce joy, although the slow dwindling of his people had wounded him greatly. Once, the griffins could be found in every part of Enonah, the most numerous of all Titans, but their mistrust of humans drove them from the open lands until they could only find peace in the cold northern reaches of this island.'

Extract from 'A Conversation with the
Druidahnon' by Druin Elder Hazel

'You don't have to do this.'

'If you say that one more time, sister, I will pull your guts out and leave them here on the snow.'

Ynis nodded once, accepting the point. They were some distance from the centre of Yelvynia, having flown for days, and they had stopped under a thick thatch of trees to find some shelter. It was snowing again, and getting darker by the minute, so Ynis got out her fire-making tools from her satchel and got to work gathering as many dry twigs and leaves as she could. Under the trees at least, the earth was bare of snow.

'I could do that,' said T'rook, after she had been watching Ynis fiddle with the flint for some minutes. 'Faster than you.'

'There aren't any rocks around for you to scratch,' Ynis said. 'There, look, it's going now.' It was a skill their fathers had insisted Ynis learn, along with other human ways of doing things – bathing, making clothes to keep warm and cups of clay to keep berries or water – things her hands could do that their talons and paws could not. Sometimes she wondered if they had done this because they knew that one day she would be cast out of Yelvynia and forced to return to the human world.

A tiny flame licked into existence amongst the twigs. Ynis sat by it a moment longer, feeding it leaves and making it grow, shielding it from any sudden gusts of wind. Eventually it was burning merrily, and the warmth against her face was very welcome. She held her hands out to it and bit her lip fiercely to stop from crying. The need to cry had come upon her in waves lately, leaving her feeling raw and exposed. It was a stupid human weakness. You did not see griffins wailing and sobbing. T'rook came over to the fire and curled up next to it, her wings folded neatly along her back.

'How much farther do you think we should go?' she asked, her voice uncharacteristically quiet.

'We are far enough, I think.' Ynis rubbed a hand down her face quickly, hoping her sister hadn't seen her tears. 'We just have to find somewhere we want to stay.'

'Somewhere with rabbits,' said T'rook. They were her favourite thing to hunt. 'Fat ones.'

'Yeah,' said Ynis. She went and sat next to her sister, leaning against her flank. The warmth and the feathers were comforting. 'Somewhere we can build our own nest. We'll make it just how we want it. No one can tell us what to do.'

They fell into a silence. Ynis could hear the odd soft *flumph* as snow fell from the branches around them. Their parting from their fathers had been hard. The queen had forbidden Flayn and T'vor from escorting them to a new home, saying *we are not so numerous that we can afford to lose two fully grown males, and I know very well that you would likely disobey me and stay with your children.* Flayn had argued, and T'vor had threatened violence, and so in the end they had accompanied them to the edge of the wide valley. *We'll find you again,* T'vor had said. *Your scent is as well known to me as my own, my yenlin.* Kind words from T'vor had almost been too much for Ynis, and as they flew away from their fathers, she had pressed her face to the back of T'rook's neck, hoping that her tears would melt away in the wind.

All because I am what I am, she thought bitterly. *All because I am human and cannot fly.*

The next day they flew in a kind of circle, looking around for a place that might become their home, but the land seemed especially bare beyond the trees. They saw no rabbits, no animals at all, so that night when they made their fire they went to sleep hungry. On the second day, they flew a little further out, and in the distance they saw unfamiliar mountains, hazy and purple in the day, looming patches of darkness at night.

'What are those?' asked T'rook.

'They must be the northernmost mountains, the ones at the very edge of the world,' said Ynis. Looking at them made her uneasy, and when T'rook spoke again she remembered why.

'That means that the Bone Fall is somewhere ahead of us,' she said. 'We'll have to stop searching soon, unless we want to dig our new nest-pit in a graveyard.'

That night when they settled around their fire, T'rook went to sleep quickly, tucking her head under her wing as soon as they were settled. She was, Ynis reasoned, exhausted – it was on her griffin sister to carry her everywhere they went, and although she had grown up doing it, it was an extra burden when they were already cold and hungry much of the time. She decided to let her sister sleep as long as she could, only waking her up to take over the watch when she absolutely had to. To keep awake, she chewed on a small piece of dried meat from her pack and took out her whittling knife. The tiny blade was one of her favourite finds, scavenged from an old human camp on the very edge of Yelvynia. The humans themselves had ventured too close to griffin territory, and their skulls were little more than fragments of yellowed bone dusting the foothills. Humans were stupid, but she admired their metals – the whittling knife was as sharp as a talon and almost as strong.

She awoke with a start in the dead of night, the blade on the ground by her foot. A noise had woken her, she was sure of it, but the knowledge of where it had come from or what it might have sounded like was already retreating with her uneasy dreams. T'rook was still sound asleep, and the fire was down to its embers, casting their tiny makeshift camp into a grotto of amber shadows. She snatched up her knife and got to her feet.

'Who's there?'

The night was not entirely still. Wind moved through the trees around them, and there was a scuttling and a scratching from all the small prey animals hidden in the foliage. The snow had stopped, but the woods were full of the sounds of dripping water as the frozen places melted again. Ynis walked beyond their fire and approached the darker, thicker trees. She felt sure the noise had come from that direction.

'Speak if you are there,' she said, raising her voice a little. 'You might not think it, but I have claws too.'

The dark mass of branches and leaves shivered and rocked. At first Ynis thought it had to be the wind, but then the branches seemed to convulse, and a dead griffin face thrust through the leaves, empty eye sockets glaring.

Ynis leapt back, knife raised. A spirit of the dead!

The creature emerged from the branches, more blue-black bones revealing themselves in the light of the fire. There was a rattling, dry noise, and its beak fell open.

'What are you doing in this sacred place, human?' The dead griffin dropped to the floor heavily. Ynis felt the impact through her feet.

Behind her, Ynis heard T'rook give a startled squawk. The commotion had woken her up. 'We're just looking for a place to stay, that's all.' She held the whittling knife higher, wishing it were larger. 'Leave us be. We're not doing you any harm, but I could be persuaded.'

The dead griffin laughed. 'Harm me? And how will you do that?'

'A spirit of the Bone Fall,' hissed T'rook. 'We have to go. Now! Get on my shoulders, sister.'

'Spirit of the Bone Fall? You are not far wrong.' The creature came forward so that the dim orange light of the fire revealed a greater solidity to it. Ynis saw thickly furred paws, long flight feathers with an oily cast to them. Belatedly she realised that the griffin was wearing a larger griffin's skull over its own face, and other bones were worn across its shoulders and down over its wings, like a macabre shawl. The dry clacking noise she had heard was the sound of a string of backbones knocking together; these ran down the griffin's back like a broken necklace.

'You are not dead at all,' she said, feeling her face flush pink even as she said it. 'You are just wearing bones.'

'How observant. Sisters, are you? A strange pair of sisters – one talon clan, one human clan.'

Slowly, Ynis lowered the knife. She had never been called human clan before. The griffins of Yelvynia preferred to call her 'prey animal' or 'ground-stuck featherless yenlin'. Now that her eyes had adjusted to the low light, she could see that the griffin had fine black and red feathers, and black fur across her heavily muscled legs. She was claw clan, like their father Flayn.

'You don't seem very worried about it.'

The strange griffin tipped her head. 'I am an Edge Walker. I have seen stranger things, child.'

'An Edge Walker?' T'rook shook out her feathers. 'That's just a story.'

'What?' Ynis looked at her sister, who, to her surprise, looked away. 'What story? I've never heard of it.'

'The other griffins talk about it sometimes.' T'rook pressed her beak to her chest in embarrassment. 'But they won't talk about it. In front of you.'

Ynis felt her cheeks grow hot with shame. 'And you didn't tell me?'

'It's stupid anyway,' said T'rook. 'A story for hatchlings.'

'How gratifying to stand here and watch you debate my existence,' added the strange griffin. 'What are you two doing all the way out here?'

'We are travelling,' said Ynis. 'Looking for a new home.'

'So far from Yelvynia?'

'We don't like it there,' said T'rook. 'So we have decided to roost elsewhere.'

'You are practically yenlin,' said the griffin, although not in an unkindly tone. 'What is the truth? You cannot lie to an Edge Walker.'

'It is none of your business!' said T'rook hotly.

'We have been exiled,' said Ynis, ignoring the look her sister shot her. For some reason she couldn't quite name, she felt that they could trust the griffin with bones on her face. 'We can't stay in Yelvynia.'

The strange griffin said nothing for a long moment, and then she nodded, as though she had expected that answer.

'Very well. You will have to come with me, I think. It is not safe to be here alone, in this forest.'

'We're not going anywhere. You are a strange griffin!' T'rook dug her talons into the dirt, as if expecting the Edge Walker to pick her up and carry her. 'Why should we go with you?'

'My name is Brocken. Does that help? Now we are not strangers. Follow me, and I will take you somewhere safer.'

'Brocken?' Ynis put her knife away in her bag. 'That is an odd name for a griffin.'

'The Edge Walkers are not like the rest of you. We have different names.'

'And what is so dangerous about this place?' asked T'rook. 'We are not freshly hatched. We can fight!'

The griffin called Brocken turned away, as though expecting to see the danger lurking in the spaces between the trees.

'I cannot tell you, for I do not know myself, but the lands around the Bone Fall are not safe for griffins these days. Come on, before I change my mind and leave you here to starve.'

—————

They flew up above the trees again, T'rook grumbling about how she'd been perfectly happy asleep. The night sky was lively – Ynis saw streaks of light across the dark, stars falling, or hurrying on their way somewhere else. The land below was covered in thick forest, but it thinned out again as they approached the distant mountains – huge absences in the dark – and then the light of dawn began to seep in from the east, revealing a landscape of jagged hills and fast-running rivers. Brocken flew on ahead of them, her huge black and red wings spread wide. As the night eased into morning, they could see more and more of the mysterious Edge Walker, and Ynis soon realised that she must be one of the biggest griffins she had ever seen. In the growing sunlight the red of her feathers had turned a deep, fiery chestnut, striking against the white and green ice below, and the pads of her huge paws were scuffed and scarred in places. The bone armour she wore was held together with long pieces of dark twine, and the bones themselves were a dark, shiny blue. Ynis had never seen griffin bones before.

'What is an Edge Walker?' she said, leaning down to speak into T'rook's tufted ear.

'I told you, it is a stupid story for yenlin,' said T'rook. Ynis gave her shoulder feathers a sharp tug, and her sister huffed. 'They are the griffins that tend to the Bone Fall. And the dead. They keep watch over them and even...'

'What?'

'It does not matter, it's not true. Not that part anyway. You know what the Bone Fall is, yes?'

'It's where we go to die. Or where our bodies are taken when our yost is gone.'

'Yes. The Edge Walkers keep watch over our ancestors. But they are strange. We do not like to talk about them.'

'Why not?'

'We just don't.'

Ahead of them, Brocken gave a long, eerie call, and it was answered by several floating up from below. The land in front of them was gradually rising, becoming a long jagged line of rocks and ice, and on that line she could see tall, spindly towers, made of branches and griffin-spit. But before they got there, Brocken called to them again, and they followed her down towards a still, blue lake. There was a huge platform of ice in the middle of it, glittering white and gold in the first light of dawn, and on it Ynis could see a small gathering of griffins. Like Brocken, they all wore griffin bones. Several lifted their heads to watch them land, but then, as Ynis was climbing down from T'rook's back, a number of them took wing and were quickly lost in the sky. Ynis pressed her lips into a thin line, deciding to pretend she had not noticed.

'What is this, Brocken?' A griffin with grey feathers edging into black towards his neck turned to meet them. 'Visitors?'

'Why have you brought us a child and her prey?' asked another.

'They say they are sisters,' Brocken said, and the others did not seem particularly troubled by this information. Instead they peered at Ynis and T'rook with open interest. One or two opened their beaks, tasting their scent on the wind. 'I thought it interesting enough to show you, Scree.'

'Even so,' answered the grey griffin, 'they should not be in this sacred place, Brocken.' This griffin, Ynis noticed, had more elaborate bone armour than the others; long cords of spine bones fell from the skull he wore like a headdress, and there were feathers of many colours woven through them and stuck to the skull with griffin-spit. It made him look fearsome, and important.

'Wait, look at the human clan's paws.' Brocken dipped her head towards Ynis. 'Yenlin, show them your paws. Hold them up, now.'

Ynis took a step backwards, but T'rook pushed in front of her.

'Leave her alone. We didn't come here to be mocked. I don't care who you are!'

Brocken clicked her tongue inside her beak, puffing up the feathers around her neck again – it made her look even larger and more formidable.

'Just do it!'

'It's alright, T'rook.' Ynis held out her arms, trying to keep them steady. The icy cold of the glacier had worked its way through the leather and fur of her boots and her feet were rapidly turning numb. She held up her hands and spread her fingers wide.

'Do you see?' said Brocken to the other griffins. 'The tiny claws they have. She is sent to us, I think, on a summer wind.'

'Will it do it though?' asked the griffin called Scree. 'We cannot trust a prey animal.'

'Can I do what?' Ynis dropped her hands back to her sides. 'Just bloody ask me, I am standing right here.'

Scree crept forward over the ice, his long talons sinking easily into the rock-hard surface. He reached the sisters and bent his head over them. Behind him, the other griffins had drawn together, their heads close, as if discussing something.

'Our witch-seer is injured,' he said, speaking slowly as if he thought they would not comprehend normal speech. 'The wound is small, but now full of poison, and our healing has failed. Without help, she will die, very soon.'

'We do not fear death. We are Edge Walkers,' put in Brocken. 'But our witch-seer is the wisest of us. To lose her would be to lose a great portion of what we are.'

Scree shot the other griffin a sharp look, as though she had said too much, before turning back to the sisters. 'You will heal our leader now, with your small claws.'

'What?' Ynis stuck her hands under her armpits. Everything was going numb. 'What are you talking about? I am not a healer.'

'You have the small claws,' said Brocken, as though this were the most reasonable thing in the world. 'You have been sent to us for this very purpose.'

Ynis found herself half laughing. Her breath turned to white clouds, and she looked around her, hoping for some obvious escape route, but to the east and west there were only more glaciers, and ahead of them, the frozen wall of the Bone Fall. 'My small claws have nothing to do with it. I wouldn't even know where to start.'

'You will do it,' said Scree, simply enough. 'Or we will feed you to her instead. Either way, you will be useful.'

15

A hundred loyal men and women, their memories erased and their dedication to the Imperium absolute. Their bodies are inscribed with the power of the Titans, and none will stand in their way.

Extract from the commencement address
of the Imperium's so-called 'Great Tour'

L even was surprised to find that she was to ride in the chariot with the queen's daughters. In fact, it seemed that not only was she to ride with them, she was to smile and wave to the crowds.

'There, look,' said the woman who had introduced herself as Princess Epona, 'stand in between us at the front of the chariot, that's it, my sister will take the reins.' Her accent was strange to Leven's ear, yet oddly musical despite the bossy tone. Princess Epona was a short, slender woman with sleek dark hair cut in a straight line from one ear to another, her skin perhaps a shade browner than Leven's own. She wore a loose silk tunic the colour of a robin's egg with a heavy woven belt of gold at her waist, and her face was painted with delicate blue streaks that put Leven in mind of the stripy alley cats she had seen around Stratum. Epona's sister, who had nodded once and told Leven her name was Bronvica, was taller and sturdier-looking, legs planted firmly apart as she took up the leather reins. She wore a torc made of golden wires around her neck, and her long dark hair was tied back from her head in a net of more golden wires dotted with tiny white seed pearls. She also had blue paint on her face, but it was thicker, applied in a slash across her eyes and across her lips. Her arms were firmly muscled, and also daubed with blue paint.

Bronvica touched the reins and the two horses leapt into a lively trot. The chariot gave a lurch, and they ploughed forward into the crowd, who gladly leapt back, apparently well used to the chariots of their princesses. Ahead of them, the harbourside gave way to a number of winding streets, all of them thronged with people. Leven saw men and women hanging out of black-timbered windows, children chasing along the sides of the chariot. The crowd seemed lively and cheerful, calling out questions and comments, although Leven wouldn't have described it as entirely friendly. More, *interested*.

'Stop looking around like a frightened rabbit,' said Princess Epona. 'You're a warrior, aren't you? Wave at them, smile. Look happy to be here.'

'I wasn't expecting such a welcome.' Reluctantly Leven raised her arm and waved at a knot of people outside a tavern, who all cheered and raised flagons at her.

'This is a great honour,' said Princess Bronvica. Her voice was lower than her sister's. 'For you,' she added. 'Just in case that wasn't clear.'

'Where are you taking me?' Leven cast a glance over her shoulder, and saw another, less regal chariot was following on behind, this one bristling with guards and their halberds.

'To see our mother,' said Princess Epona. 'You are to be welcomed at the palace, and probably paraded around a bit more there, too. She has hardly talked of anything else since we heard you were coming.'

'It has been quite tiresome,' added Bronvica.

Leven nodded. It seemed like a lot of trouble to go to, to simply fetch her up and throw her in a dungeon, so perhaps she was truly to meet the queen and be treated like an honoured guest. Even so, the smile on her face felt awkward and false, and she wondered what would happen if she summoned her Titan wings here, in this small chariot. Bloodshed in all directions, probably. And what would happen if she had one of her strange visions here, with hundreds of people watching? She gritted her teeth and forced herself to look at the buildings and people that were passing by; all sights that no Herald had ever seen.

They turned another corner, quite sharply, causing Leven to knock into Princess Epona slightly. The streets were irregular, she noticed, and so were the buildings; each one appeared to bear no resemblance to the one next to it – in one short row she saw buildings of wood, brick, stone; buildings with straw roofs, delicate clay tiles, tall windows glazed with black lead and windows that were merely holes with shutters. She spotted several ornate carvings of bears, often with a stripe of silver paint across their brows, and even one or two griffins, carved over the lintels of the grander buildings. *This is Titan country.* She thought of what Captain Elisa had said about Londus-on-Sea, about how the queen had burned it to the ground and then rebuilt it. She wondered if the queen was naturally given to chaos, or if chaos was simply in the nature of Londus-on-Sea itself.

Queen Broudicca's home stood on top of a hill overlooking the city, and to Leven's eye it looked not dissimilar to a number of solidly built castle forts she had seen whilst travelling through the Unblessed lands. It was built of dark grey stone the colour of rain, and everywhere she looked there were black birds – perched on battlements, hopping across the lawns, scattered through the sky like dead leaves. From the parapets there were several tall poles, with tattered blue flags flying, and on the top of each of those poles, a human skull, painted blue. Leven found her eyes returning to the skulls over and over as the small chariot rattled its way over the drawbridge, and then they were under the walls and through them, out into a courtyard. A team of young women in well-worn, practical-looking clothes came running out of an arched doorway to deal with the ponies and the chariot. The princesses jumped down themselves. Princess Bronvica paused to have a word with one of the young women.

'Herald, you will come with me,' said Princess Epona. 'We're to go straight to court.'

'I'm not really a Herald anymore, you know. My service to the Imperium is finished.' Leven looked around the courtyard with interest. There were more of the black birds here, and now that she got a better look, she could see that there were two types: a hefty bird with a beak like a dagger, oily black from top to bottom, and a smaller, slighter bird with a grey head and eerie pale eyes. All of them made a racket. The stones of the courtyard walls were a different colour at their base. Leven wondered if this castle had been built on top of something else too, just like the city. 'My proper title, to you, would be Blessed Eleven.'

'Really? How interesting. Come on, this way.' Epona was already heading off to the other side of the courtyard, where another arched entrance awaited them. She walked quickly, her head held up as if she owned the place – which Leven supposed was correct. 'My mother will be waiting, and she's not a patient woman. Especially not if she's excited about something.'

'We're to see the queen now? Can I not get changed?' Leven hurried behind the smaller woman, glancing back at the chariot. Her bag had been tossed in the back, and someone had already carried it off, it seemed. *Not that I have any clothes appropriate for a royal court*, thought Leven. 'At least have a wash?'

'I never thought a Herald would be so fixated on cleanliness. Are you not an unstoppable, brutal warrior?' Epona stopped and turned to her. They were in a wide stone corridor, lit with squat oil lamps. From somewhere nearby Leven could hear a lot of people shouting. 'Let's have a look at you.'

Epona looked her up and down, frowning slightly. She peered closely at Leven's face. After a moment, she licked the pad of her thumb and, reaching up, rubbed at a mark on Leven's forehead. Leven stood very still, caught somewhere between confusion and outrage. 'There, I say you'll do.'

'What—'

'Hurry up, come on, this way. My other sisters will have heard the commotion in the courtyard and will be trying to find us, but I am determined to be the one to present you to the court.'

'What about Princess Bronvica?'

'Oh Bronny doesn't care about this stuff, she only likes horses.'

Eventually, after Epona had scampered down several corridors and stomped up at least one flight of steps, they arrived at a vast set of double doors. Each had a bear on its hind legs carved into the grey wood, and there was a pair of guards standing outside. At the sight of Princess Epona they both nodded and stood to one side.

'Here we go,' said Epona. She took hold of Leven's hand, grinning, and then threw open one of the doors.

Leven's first thought was that it was surprisingly light. The court was housed in a great hall, built of the same dark stone as the rest of the castle, with warm wooden beams crossing the vaulted roof, and up above their heads there were several wide windows, thick panes of slightly warped glass held in place with strips of black lead. There was a pair of long wooden tables in the room, but no one was sitting at them. Instead, around a hundred people were gathered, standing and talking at the tops of their voices, brandishing cups foaming with ale. At the far end of the room there was a great wooden throne, carved out of a living oak tree which grew straight up through the flagstones. There were more black birds perched in its branches and across the back of the throne.

There had been a ripple of extra noise at their entrance and then the smaller woman was pulling her down the centre of the room. The crowd of people grew quieter, their shouted conversations dying down to excited whispers.

'My queen, I present to you the Herald Eleven, from the mighty Imperium.'

Leven focused on the figure sitting perched in the tree-throne, who was leaning forward avidly to watch their approach. She had expected the warrior Queen Broudicca to look more like her other daughter, the sturdy Princess Bronvica, but instead she saw a woman who looked strikingly like Epona, although quite a bit older, in her late fifties perhaps. She was short, with delicate features, and her skin was a warm brown save for a pair of lighter coloured scars on the top of her left cheek – a strike from a bladed weapon was Leven's guess, made many years ago. Her hair was dark like her daughter's too, but much more unruly. It fell around her face and down her back in tangled waves, and there were feathers and beads woven into it. She wore a silk tunic dyed sky blue, and her eyes – which were also blue – were narrow and watchful. There were three younger children clustered at the bottom of the throne – like Epona and Bronvica they had blue paint on their faces – but the woman on the throne muttered something to them and they scattered, disappearing into the crowd.

'Welcome,' she said. Her voice was low and warm, and every other voice in the hall fell quiet at the sound of it. Leven cleared her throat, aware that everyone in the room was looking at her. All at once it was very clear she had made a mistake. What was she thinking, to come to this savage island, alone, with no one to advise her on how to speak to queens? What would happen when news of this meeting got back to the empress? She cleared her throat again, louder, and nearly choked.

'This is an unexpected honour,' she managed.

The queen smiled, apparently delighted with this response. Epona, who still hadn't let go of her hand, squeezed it.

'Herald Eleven,' continued the queen, still speaking for the entire room, 'we could hardly let such a distinguished guest arrive at our shores without due ceremony. Epona, put her down, please.'

Epona let go of her hand, and Leven felt an odd pang of regret. There had been something almost comforting about her fierce grip,

and now she stood alone in front of this woman with the sharp
blue eyes.

'You do realise, Herald Eleven,' Queen Broudicca leaned forward
on the throne, 'that the Imperium is not a friend to Brittletain.'

Leven glanced to the edges of the room, waiting for the guards
with halberds to come surging out of the corners to decapitate
her, but no one was moving. Instead, she caught the eye of a young
man standing slightly apart from the rest of the crowd, his arms
folded across his chest. To her astonishment, he had a pair of
curling horns sprouting from his temples. The gaze he returned to
her was not a friendly one. With some difficulty, she turned back
to the queen.

'Not friends, no.' Leven desperately tried to think of something
clever to say. What would an Envoy be doing in her place? Building
bridges, threatening reprisals? 'But perhaps we could be. We, that is,
the Imperium, is always keen to bestow its blessings on anyone who
might want them.'

There was a low murmur of laughter from the court, and despite
herself Leven looked round at the crowd. There were other men and
women there with horns, she saw, and many of them wore crimson
sashes over their shoulders. When Leven turned back, the queen had
tipped her head to one side.

'That's an interesting way to put it.'

A stout woman with horns tipped with green paint stepped
forward from the crowd. She shot a look at Leven, and then addressed
the queen.

'Broudicca, what are you thinking? Bringing one of the Imperium's
murderers into the heart of Londus? Letting them stand shoulder to
shoulder with your daughters?'

Leven blinked. She couldn't imagine anyone being allowed to speak
to the empress in such a tone, but Broudicca looked unfazed.

'Would you rather she were let loose to wander Brittletain as she
wished?' the queen replied. 'Allowed to wander the Paths alone?'

'If she did,' called another horned man, older and bearded, 'it might solve the problem quickly enough.' There was a rumble of laughter at that. Another man stepped forward, this one hornless but richly dressed; he wore a gold torc around his neck as Princess Bronvica had done.

'We must know why she is here,' he said. Unlike the others, he looked at Leven while he spoke, his brown eyes speculative. 'Attempted invasions by the Imperium we have grown used to. But messengers?' His tone, previously neutral, grew darker. 'A messenger who wears the pulverised bones of Titans on her skin. Can this be anything other than an insult to the Druidahnon?'

The crowd grew quiet again, waiting to see how Broudicca would react. Leven felt as though each of her ore-lines were burning with light. *They know nothing about me, or the Imperium.*

The queen stood up and left the tree-throne. Her feet were bare. 'Alright, that's enough of everyone gawping at our guest. Epona, Master Cillian, you will join us in the rookery.' She stepped down from the dais and made her way to a door in the corner of the hall. Princess Epona gave Leven a gentle shove.

'Come on, my brutish warrior, it's time for the real talk now.'

The next room was much smaller and more comfortable than the hall. The stone walls were covered in thick tapestries, and there was a long, low fireplace, a banked fire giving out a fragrant heat. There was a circular table in the centre, and on it was a big clay pot with a spout, and several earthenware cups. The queen had already seated herself at it, and began pouring something hot. The room had a single guard, a tall woman with broad shoulders and ginger hair cut so close to her scalp it was barely more than a fuzz; she stood at attention by the wall, a notched short sword hanging at her hip. The horned man Leven had spotted earlier had followed them in too, although he seemed reluctant to get close to the others.

'Sit down,' said Epona, shoving her towards a chair. Leven sat. Would this woman ever stop shoving her about? 'Never mind Cillian, we'll get to his part in all this soon. He's got the arse about it, of course, although it's difficult to tell. The Druin are never very friendly to us hornless ones, even when we're royalty.'

'Sister, you forget yourself,' said the guard. 'Can you stop showing off for long enough for anyone else to speak?'

'Now then, girls.' The queen was concentrating on the clay pot. She had taken the lid off and was poking the insides with a thin metal stick. 'Do you want our friend here to report that the royal women of Londus spend all day sniping at each other and drinking tea? Here, drink this.' She passed a cup to Leven. It was steaming gently. 'It's just nettle tea, one of my own blends. It would be an enormous insult to us if you did not drink it.'

Leven looked down at the cup, her mind racing, but when she glanced up she saw that the queen was smirking, and the guard – who was apparently another princess – was rolling her eyes. Leven blew gently on the tea and took a sip.

'Your majesty.' She put the cup down. Epona had seated herself at the table and was pouring her own cup. The horned man she had called Cillian still stood by the door, as if he were trying to sink into it and vanish. 'I'm really not here in any official capacity for the Imperium. In case you think that I... that is to say...'

'In case I think you are a spy?' Broudicca raised her eyebrows. 'Or a one-woman invasion?'

'Yes. I'm not these things. I am just a soldier – a retired soldier, actually.'

'That can't be,' put in Epona. 'How old are you? Twenty-five? Twenty-six?'

'And you expect us to believe that you are no longer a Herald?' added the woman with the sword. 'The markings are there, plain on your face and arms.'

'Herald Eleven, I should have introduced my other daughter. This is Princess Togi.' The queen waved her hand at the woman, who nodded shortly. 'The problem, you see, with having seven daughters is that they are all as highly strung as cats, and see conspiracies everywhere. Their day is not complete if they are not engaged in some underhanded intrigue.'

Epona laughed. 'Where do you think we learned it from, Mother?'

'Heralds only serve for eight years,' Leven said carefully. She could see the main thread of the conversation slipping away again and she was determined to snatch it back. 'Then we are free to do as we like. The markings themselves are with us for life. I wanted to see the great nation of Brittletain. There are so many stories about the forests, about the Druidahnon, the many great queens.' An image came to her then of the cold place from her visions, the vast, unreal winged shape passing over her. 'And the griffins. I wanted to see Enonah's last great Titans.'

'The world's last Titans, and our forests, are not entertainments for the Imperium.'

This was the man, Cillian. Leven turned to look at him. He was, at her guess, around the same age as her, perhaps a few years older. He had untidy brown hair, some of which was pulled back into a simple braid, and he had eyes the colour of good green jade. He wore ranger's clothes: soft leather, warm knitted tunic, tall sturdy boots. There was a slim loop of crimson leather across one shoulder, and at his belt, all manner of bags and pockets and baubles. And there were the horns, sprouting from his temples and curling back into his hair. They were ridged, and the colour of aged bone.

'You might well stare at me, butcher of the Imperium,' he said quietly. '*I* am not an entertainment for you, either.'

Epona laughed. 'They certainly sent us the right Druin for the job, Mother. Did you ask for an extra tactful one?'

'You are here by invitation, Druin,' added Princess Togi. 'The Herald here isn't the only one being granted an honour beyond their station.'

'Magog take us all...' muttered Broudicca. 'Why are you here, Herald Eleven? The Nost captain sent me what you told her, but I want to hear it from your own lips.'

'I'm here to see the island, as I said. That's all.' Leven made herself look directly into the queen's eyes as she said it, trying to fill her every word with certainty. 'I want to go north and see the griffins.'

There was a long moment of silence, broken by a low squawk. The women all turned to look at the horned man.

'Is there a bird in your bag?' asked Epona.

'Right.' Queen Broudicca put her cup down. 'Epona, go and see that our guest's room for the night has everything she might need.'

Leven expected the young woman to protest that clearly this was the work of a servant, but instead the princess raised her eyebrows.

'You are dismissing me?'

'I am dismissing all of you. Except the Herald. Master Cillian, go and do whatever it is the Druin do before a long journey through the Paths. Togi, get back to your duties at the guard house.'

Togi looked less than pleased at this. Her fair freckled skin turned scarlet, in that quick way of blushing redheads often had. 'Mother, what if this Herald really is an assassin from the Imperium? You would speak to her alone?'

'Child, if what we have heard about the Heralds is true, this young woman could have killed us several times over already, but instead she is sitting here like a stunned rabbit, so I think somehow I am safe for now. Go, all of you.'

Her tone gave no room for further argument. When they were alone again, Queen Broudicca let out a long, low sigh.

'You might not think it,' she said eventually, 'but it is entirely possible to have too many daughters.'

'Your daughters are very impressive,' said Leven, carefully.

Broudicca laughed. 'Are you sure you are not a diplomat, Herald? That is one way of putting it. In Brittletain, royal sons and daughters are encouraged to make themselves useful – the rule of kingdoms is not always passed to the eldest, but usually the most capable. It's why we have so many queens, and not so many kings.' The queen smiled to let her know this was a joke. 'So, is there anything else you would like to tell me about why you are here, Herald Eleven?'

For a strange moment, Leven thought of telling her: about the disappearance of Foro, her visions of a cold place where griffins flew. It would be a relief to share the burden with someone. But then she remembered what the Nost captain had told her – Queen Broudicca was an ambitious and clever woman. Any piece of information could become a weapon in her hands.

'I wish only to see this wild place,' she said. 'Is that possible? For someone like me?'

'A living weapon, dropping out of the sky onto my shores.' For a long moment the queen was quiet, looking at Leven closely. She rubbed her thumb and forefinger together, as if she were testing the silkiness of a piece of fabric. 'Tell me. Did you see much of my city on your way here, Herald? I imagine my daughters swept you through it all fairly quickly.'

'I saw a little. It's lively.'

'How does it compare to your Stratum?'

'Stratum is more orderly, I suppose,' said Leven. She thought of the many concentric rings that made up the city. 'If you're in the First Ring, or the Second, or the Fifth, you know where you are by looking at the buildings, and the people around you.'

Queen Broudicca nodded, apparently pleased by this. 'And Londus-on-Sea is everything at once – every *place* at once, isn't it? It's one of Brittletain's busiest ports, second only to Kornwullis in the west. We have traders from all of Enonah calling here. And we have travellers from all over Enonah calling the city their home. Go out into my streets, and you will find spices from Caucasore, marble from Taroknor, even pink salt from the Sea of the New Moon.'

'I'll take your word for it. But the Imperium is not welcome. Why do you turn us away?'

'What sort of island would not welcome those who came open-handed, those who came to trade, to live and to work? An island with its head up its arse, of course. No, the Imperium are turned away because they come only to *bless* us with conquest.'

Leven opened her mouth to protest, but the queen waved her down. 'You asked me if it is possible, Herald, for you alone to travel through Brittletain, and I have decided that yes, it will be, more or less. One woman is not the Imperium, unless she is the empress, and I do not think you are her in disguise – she is a lot shorter, I have heard. Here is what will happen. You will travel through each of our kingdoms, and you will visit each of my fellow queens and kings – it will put their minds at ease, to see you as you are, rather than as the nightmarish conqueror they will imagine. As a favour to me, you will take with you several... items, that I wish sent to them. You will be acting, for a little while, as an agent of mine. A messenger. I am sure you will not find this a problem. After all, I imagine you are very grateful for my generosity, and very eager to make it up to me.'

'Your generosity?'

The queen gestured around the small, cosy room. 'You are in my rookery drinking my tea, rather than in my dungeons, having the Titan ore stripped from your flesh.'

Leven sat back in her seat. 'I see what you mean. And what are these things I'll be taking with me?'

'Just small things, nothing to be concerned about. I will not send you out into the Wild Wood alone, of course. Cillian, the Druin you met a moment ago, will be your guide.'

'The horned man?' Before she could stop herself, Leven grimaced. 'Is that really necessary?'

'What do you know of the Druin, Herald Eleven?'

'I thought they were a story, to be quite honest with you. So much of Brittletain feels like a story.'

'Not a story, but a very real and vital part of Brittletain. Without the Druin to keep the old Paths safe, no one would survive a journey through the Wild Wood. Believe me, to give you the service of one of our Druin is a high honour.'

I am being given so many honours, thought Leven, *so why do I feel like I am being packaged up for the butchers?*

'Thank you,' she said, trying to sound like she meant it. 'You are generous.'

'Good. And thank you, Herald Eleven, for providing such an entertaining afternoon. I am sure this arrangement will only benefit us both.'

16

The question of Titans and language is a mildly interesting one. It has long been accepted wisdom across Enonah that it was the Titans who raised humans up out of the mud of earliest creation, setting them on their feet to walk upright, and giving them words to speak. As fanciful as it might sound, every piece of historical research only seems to confirm the fact, and the most compelling piece of evidence can be witnessed around us every day: across Enonah's three great continents and their surrounding islands, there is one single root language. A thousand flavours, shades and dialects, of course, but at their heart, there are the words the Titans gave us. For me, the more interesting question is: why? Why take these creatures – and we must have seemed so vulnerable and weak to them – why take us and make us something more? What did the Titans themselves gain from our advancement? Now that they are largely extinct, that is something we may never discover. The people of Unblessed Lamabet have a saying – 'The book of the griffin is written on the mountain', which is, I believe, a phrase used when something is especially impossible to understand or even entirely incomprehensible. It's interesting because it's also a literal fact. The griffins of Brittletain have a long tradition of oral history and storytelling, often detailing the exploits of their trickster god, T'vyn, but they also carve their stories into the sides of the mountains where they live. There was a riddle when I was a child – 'how hard is a griffin's beak?' – well, harder than a bloody mountain, it turns out.

From Gynid Tyleigh's notes

When the sun rose, the griffins took Ynis and T'rook to another glacier across the lake. There was a hole bored into the side of it, large enough even for Brocken to enter. The big griffin led the sisters down the tunnel until they entered a nesting-chamber. The walls of the space were covered with dark wool, while the glassy ceiling let in a diffuse, blue light. There was a griffin lying on the floor on her side. Her chest was rising and falling rapidly.

'I've brought some help,' said Brocken. 'Are you still with us, Witch-seer Frost?'

'You've come to take me to the Fall, then?' The voice was weak. 'That's the only help for me now, Brocken. I wish you would just have done with it.'

Brocken put her head behind Ynis and gave her a push towards the prone griffin. 'The wound, human clan, is on her shoulder. You will see it clearly enough.'

Ynis approached the griffin called Frost cautiously. She was claw clan, her paws displaying sets of scarred pads; her feathers were yellow-brown, although the feathers and fur on her neck and head were black. Her wings were not tucked neatly away on her back, but sprawled out across the floor, as though she had been flying when this icy room somehow reached up and caught her. In the corner of the chamber there was a pile of old griffin bones, blue and black – a headdress like those the other griffins wore.

'What is this? Food?' The griffin snapped her beak, a small parody of hunger. 'The fever fills my belly, Brocken, I've no appetite.'

'I'm not food,' said Ynis, with one eye on the griffin's powerful paws. 'I am help. I mean, I am someone who can help.'

The griffin called Frost half lifted her head in surprise. 'It speaks to us! It smells of griffin too. What is this thing, Brocken? You bring me another mystery even as I lie here dying? Just kill me as I asked you days ago. I want to go to the Bone Fall.'

Ynis decided to ignore what the griffin was saying. She moved to the creature's shoulder, and there, sure enough, she could see a small wound, running with blood and yellow pus. On the icy floor by her feet there was a narrow wooden shaft, one end broken, the other fletched with bird feathers. She bent and picked it up, turning it over in her hands.

'An arrow?'

'A human weapon,' said Brocken. There was an undertone to her voice that Ynis couldn't interpret. 'Look at the wound. Do you see? It will not close up.'

'A human shot a griffin?' asked T'rook. The outrage in her voice was clear, and Ynis felt her own stomach clench at it. The idea was unthinkable. Humans were food, not a threat. She put the broken arrow shaft down, and, standing by the griffin's furred belly, she placed her hands to either side of the wound. It was hard to see anything clearly. The pus had turned the fur around it slick and sticky, and the flesh itself was swollen. There were splinters deeply embedded there, where the arrow had struck.

'You pulled this out?' She turned her head to address Brocken. 'The arrow did not pass through?'

'It struck her there, in the shoulder,' said Brocken. 'And stuck. I yanked it out, but it broke.'

'Then the head of the arrow is in there somewhere.'

'Yes,' Brocken agreed.

Ynis turned back to the wound. She was thinking of how Brocken had looked at her when she had said she must heal the griffin, or die. There had been no question in the Edge Walker's expression, no doubt in her stance, and why should there be? Ynis was very far from the home of her fathers, and here, she was just another prey animal, no matter how she smelled. They would eat her, pick her bones clean, and think nothing more of it. She reached into her satchel and pulled out her claw-knife, which was still covered in dried blood.

'I will need this cleaned in water, and then fire. You can do this?'

Brocken came forward and took the knife carefully in her beak. The blade needed sharpening but it would have to do. The thought of trying to pick away at the half-formed scabs with her hands made her feel shaky and strange.

'I'm going to have to cut the wound again,' said Ynis. 'So that I can reach inside it. Witch-seer Frost, you will have to be very still for me. As still as you can, although it will hurt. Do you understand?'

'Hmph,' said Frost. 'Still it speaks.' There was a pause, and then, 'There is nothing a human can do that I cannot endure.'

Ynis pursed her lips. *A human has hurt you well enough already*, she thought. When Brocken brought the knife back, still warm from the fire, Ynis took it and placed her hand on the griffin's neck, seeking to calm herself. She noticed that the black on the feathers there had rubbed off on her fingers; they were dyed black. All of these griffins had dyed their heads and necks black. Blinking away her confusion at that, she brought the knife down across the wound, and fresh blood, red as poppies in the spring, ran down the griffin's filthy fur. Ynis realised she was sweating; the chamber inside the glacier was warm, despite the ice, and her fingers on the knife were slick.

'Hold still,' she said again. 'I'll be as quick as I can.'

She pushed her hand inside the hole she had made, her fingers questing for anything that shouldn't be there. Hot blood pulsed over her wrist, smearing her arm, her face. Frost grunted, once, twice, and Ynis felt the griffin's muscles contracting as she struggled to keep still.

'Almost... it must be here somewhere.'

The tips of her fingers brushed against something hard, and she pressed harder, trying to get a purchase on it. Slick stone moved under her hand, slippery and warmed with the griffin's body heat. Her fingernails caught on an edge, and she pulled back, spattering more blood.

'Fionovar save us,' muttered Brocken.

'There.' Ynis gave another yank and the arrowhead came free, suddenly enough that she fell backwards, hitting the icy floor with her rump. Frost grunted, moving her legs as though she was trying to get up. 'No, stay there, stay down. It's out but it's not all done yet. I need more water. I need to clean the wound as much as I can.'

They brought her what she asked for in a steel bucket that must once have been stolen from a human camp, and Ynis stripped off her own scavenged outer tunic to use as a rag. She wiped the blood and pus away until she could see the edges of the wound clearly – rawer now than they had been – and from her pack she pulled out her own precious bone needles and the lengths of twine she used to patch her own clothing. She stitched the wound shut with large, clumsy stitches, but she made sure there were many of them, holding the pieces of flesh in place. When it was all done, she leaned back on the griffin's belly, barely able to stand up. Every inch of her felt covered in sweat, blood or pus.

'My sister has done as you asked,' said T'rook. The feathers on the back of her neck were standing on end, a clear sign she was in distress. 'Now what? Will you leave us be?'

Brocken ignored her, addressing herself to Frost, who was still breathing rapidly.

'How do you feel, Grandmother?'

'Pained. But lighter. We shall see, I suppose.'

⁓

Ynis and T'rook were taken to another part of that place, a nesting hole deep in another glacier, where the ceiling was so close to the top that daylight shone through in a peaceful, eerie blue glow. Ynis was brought another bucket of melted ice water and allowed to wash, and although she shivered violently as she peeled the sodden clothes from her skin, afterwards she found that with the thick woollen layer on the walls and the warmth of her sister, she was quite comfortable in the ice den. They were kept there for some days, eating scraps of raw meat

Brocken brought them, until eventually, Frost herself appeared. She still looked small and thin, especially next to Brocken, and she walked with a significant limp, but her eyes were sharp and intelligent. She stood in the entrance to the nesting hole for a few moments, her beak open as she took in their scent.

'What do you know of the Edge Walkers, yenlin?'

Ynis and T'rook looked at each other.

'Not much,' Ynis said eventually. 'I had never even heard the name. T'rook, my sister, said that Edge Walkers are the griffins who tend the Bone Fall.'

'Hmm. It is more than that, but I can hardly expect her to know better – she is barely out of the egg.' Next to her, Ynis felt T'rook bristle with annoyance, so she placed a soothing hand on her sister's wing. 'We tend the Bone Fall, yes,' continued Frost. 'We tend the griffins who have come to the end of their lives, and exist in the space between life and death. We give up the names given to us at hatching, as we give up lives in Yelvynia, and we choose names for ourselves. We also live in the space between life and death, watching and waiting, tending the bones. It is a strange place – an uncertain place. For some of us it is possible to see and hear things, on the Edge, that others cannot. Do you understand?'

'You are killers,' said T'rook, hotly. 'I know *that*. When griffins come here, because they are old or cannot fly, you kill them, and strip them down to their bones.'

Ynis felt a cold hand walk down her spine. Witch- seer Frost gave them a long look, but she did not seem especially offended.

'Tell me now,' she said. 'Tell me what brought a human child here, with a griffin calling it her sister. Leave nothing out.'

T'rook had snapped her beak shut, clearly intending to say nothing more, so haltingly Ynis began to tell their story: how sixteen winters ago their fathers had found her on the borders of Brittletain, a screaming egg at the end of a trail of blood, and how Flayn had believed her to be fate-tied to them, and to all griffins. She told Frost how Queen

Fellvyn had agreed to tolerate her presence until, one day, she could not anymore; until the day they had been exiled from Yelvynia. When she finished, Witch-seer Frost cocked her head to one side, peering at them both, and was quiet for a while.

'When you came to us, yenlin, I was in the place between life and death, more fully than I had ever been,' the griffin said eventually. 'And when I looked at you, at first I saw a hatchling and her food. But then, as the pain moved me closer to the Edge, I saw something else. A red line that spread out from you and seemed to encompass everything.'

'What do you mean?' asked Ynis. 'What red line?'

'A fate-tie, although with you, it is like a spider's web,' she said. 'The more you tell me, the more I see that you were brought to us for a reason. Your fathers saw it too, all those years ago, and everything about you, human child, speaks of the Edge. The border between the human world and ours. How you stood in the place between life and death and pulled me back from that other land.'

'I just did what Brocken told me,' said Ynis. Her cheeks felt hot. 'She said she would kill me otherwise.'

Frost chuckled. 'Yes, that sounds like Brocken. She doesn't see as clearly as I – very few can – but even she sensed it. You are both welcome here. You will have a place with the Edge Walkers, if you take it – and I suspect you will. This place between worlds is where you are meant to be.'

17

*We reached the borders of Unblessed Houraki with little trouble
and have found lodgings in the trade city of Nawatabor – here, at
least, outsiders are not so uncommon. Finding our destination is
proving to be more complicated. Although the locals clearly know
of the place, they will not talk about it, and in fact bringing the
subject up appears to be a kind of extreme social faux pas; several
people simply walked away when I indicated I wanted to know more
about the Black City. With this in mind, Belise and I have begun
making enquiries in the seedier parts of Nawatabor, where large
amounts of coin can more easily loosen tongues. It seems that there
are men and women who make their living guiding people through
the various jungle territories of Houraki, and there are some that
are willing to venture into forbidden areas, although it was made
clear to me that only a desperate few will travel anywhere near
the Black City. All of these dramatics were quite wearying, but it
appears we have a lead with regards to a guide – a man known as
Riz will take us. We have arranged to meet at a public location in
the city to discuss terms.*

*Our alchemist has made it very clear several times that she
doesn't appreciate the delay, and will be writing lengthy complaints
to you about my incompetence. I thought it fair to warn you.*

A decoded communication from Envoy
Kaeto to the Imperator Justinia

T he tavern didn't look like any Kaeto had ever known, and he had travelled widely on the Imperium's business. For a start, instead of a roof there was a series of wide silk panels stretched between poles, so that the humid air passed quite freely through the place. The tables were built from sand-coloured stone with rich seams of quartz running through it, and all the tables were sat within a lattice of low stone walls. Kaeto had not been able to puzzle out the point of the walls, which could easily be stepped over by anyone of adult height, until he had spotted the first of the fire beetles skittering smoothly along the top of the one nearest to him. It had been fitted with a neat wooden box on top of its shining carapace, and within carefully cut holes tall glasses of some honey-coloured liquor were slotted. He watched it carefully as it went, fascinated, and noted that it didn't spill a drop.

Belise, who was seated on the opposite side of the tavern, dropped one hand to her side in apparent boredom, and he saw her fingers flicker through a few of their private signs.

Strange place.

He reached up to rub his beard, subtly signing back:

Keep your eyes open.

The strangeness of the beetle couriers notwithstanding, the tavern – called Mother's Third Eye, according to the banner at the entrance – was a pleasant enough place to pass the afternoon. There were lush plants and flowers spilling over the natural borders created by the beetle roads, and the black dirt smelled good; like soil after the rain. The place was busy too, filled with men, women and children all pausing for a midday meal – glad, no doubt, to get out from underneath the punishing sun. And everywhere you looked, the skittering jewel-coloured beetles carried drinks and orders back and forth.

They had been in Unblessed Houraki for less than two days, and Kaeto was beginning to adjust; to the air that felt as thick and as damp as wet wool; to the lush, teeming greenness of the jungle; and the scuttling, ever-present insect life. Gynid Tyleigh had declared it a 'hot bucket of shit' the moment she stepped off the boat, and had immediately retired to their tents, instructing Kaeto to find a guide and get them moving. Belise was reserving judgement on the place, but she was certainly keen, Kaeto had noticed, to try every bit of food and drink available. He glanced at her again, and she was licking some powdered sugar off her fingers in an overly elaborate fashion.

Where is he? she signed. *He's late.*

Kaeto looked away from her, casually looking for a man of their guide's description in the tavern-tent, but there was still nothing.

Be ready to move if we have to.

On the boat they had presented themselves as simple travellers from the west, a husband and wife and their adopted daughter, on their way further east – going to visit family, a long-awaited reunion. Luckily no one had questioned it; with his darker colouring Kaeto looked as though he could be from anywhere further east of Stratum, and Tyleigh had kept to their room studying the papers and books she had brought with her. He was certain that any prolonged attempt at pretence would quickly expose them for what they really were: an arrogant alchemist and a spy who could barely stand to be in the same room as her.

The precariousness of their situation was balanced on two difficult facts: Unblessed Houraki had no love for the Imperium, so declaring their official business would likely get them rounded up and executed; and the region they wished to travel to was strictly forbidden, even to the members of Houraki's scattered aristocracy. On their first night in sweltering Nawatabor, Kaeto had slid out into the humid evening and made some extremely careful enquiries. He had been told to look out for a tall, heavyset man with a web of tattoos on the right side of his face – easy enough to spot, he had thought. And yet...

From the corner of his eye Kaeto caught a quick signal from Belise, and he looked up to see a man approaching their table. He was slim and wiry, a little shorter than Kaeto, with smooth unlined skin and quick, bright eyes. He was wearing a loose silk vest tucked into grey trews; the silk had a thin band of what looked like coloured glass threaded through it, until Kaeto realised it wasn't glass at all, but tiny pieces of beetle casings. There was a belt at his waist, hanging from which was a short sword. Judging by the wear on the grip it had seen a lot of use. The man grinned crookedly as he approached the table. Kaeto leaned forward in a friendly manner while his hidden left hand eased a knife from his own belt.

'You look hot, sire.' The Houraki language was no more than a step removed from Imperial Common, and easy enough for Kaeto to understand, who had spent much of his life as an Envoy studying the unique dialects of Enonah. 'Can I buy you a drink?'

'I'm waiting to meet a friend,' said Kaeto. He could feel Belise watching them closely from the other side of the tavern. The man did not seem concerned. He sat down at the table across from Kaeto and leaned back, one arm hooked over the back of the chair.

'You know how it works here, sire? You grab a passing beetle, write your order on the scrap of paper, and it'll tottle off to the bar for you. I'm guessing you're not from Houraki?'

'I'm here with my wife and daughter,' said Kaeto. 'And today I'm meeting an old friend. We're from the west, just travelling through.'

'Is that so?' The man leaned forward and spoke in a low voice. 'A knife, really? Is that what you take to the taverns where you're from, sire?' He winked.

Kaeto moved very slowly backwards. With his free hand he signed a quick message to Belise. He smiled warmly.

'Do I know you?'

'That doesn't seem possible, does it, sire? I've never been outside of Houraki.'

Belise appeared like a tiny shadow at the man's shoulder and Kaeto watched with satisfaction as the man went rigid in his chair. The relaxed smile remained, but his eyes narrowed slightly.

'Another knife. You're fond of your blades, aren't you, sire?'

'They are some of my *daughter's* favourite toys. Do not move, friend.'

Around them the hubbub of the midday rush continued.

The man raised his hands.

'You're here looking for a guide, sire. And that guide is me. I'm sorry, please forgive my teasing. It's just that you looked so serious I couldn't resist it.'

'You are the guide? You do not resemble the description I was given.'

The man shrugged. 'I wanted to get a good look at you first. You'd be amazed, sire, how many people will ask for a guide and then rob them the moment you get out of Nawatabor. We all have to be careful in this game, don't we? I am Riz. I'd be very happy to take you… where you need to go.'

Kaeto waited a moment longer, watching the man – Riz – closely. He looked back steadily enough, his posture remarkably relaxed for someone with a short deadly blade positioned somewhere around the kidneys. His skin was the warm coppery gold typical of most of the people of Unblessed Houraki, and his hair was a deep, shining black, jaw-length and hanging loose. He wore a simple gold ring on the smallest finger on his left hand.

'*Father*,' Belise asked quietly. 'Shall I stick him?'

Kaeto shook his head slightly, and Belise's posture loosened. Riz leaned forward and looked down at the girl's feet.

'And you can stand down too, ReRe.'

Belise looked where he was looking and took a sudden hop and skip backwards, her eyebrows lost under her mop of hair. It wasn't often that Kaeto saw the girl truly surprised.

Riz patted his lap, and a fat beetle around the size of a small cat flew up and settled there. The thing was covered in a dark red-black carapace that shone as though it were regularly polished, and long antennae quivered as it turned in circles on the man's lap.

'ReRe is a fire beetle with an especially nasty nip, aren't you, my sweet?' Riz patted the beetle's shell fondly. 'A kind of sudden, agonising paralysis. No fun at all, if I'm truthful with you.' Riz grinned at Belise. 'ReRe doesn't take kindly to me being threatened by children. Not at all.'

Kaeto could see that Belise was itching to get her knife out again.

'Enough of this. If you are the guide, fine. When do we leave?'

Riz drummed his fingers on the table top.

'Come with me.'

———

Out on the street, Riz led them away from the tavern of tents and down a narrow dirt path that split off from the main road into the dense forest that seemed to creep in at every corner. Immediately, Kaeto felt himself on edge – if there were ever a place for an ambush, this was it – but Riz walked ahead, following the muddy path as it weaved its way through the towering jungle trees, until they came to a small building of reddish-brown clay. It looked old, the uneven bricks crumbling at the corners; a thick species of vine with glossy green leaves appeared to be the only thing holding it up. There was a high-pitched whine and the deeper, thrumming buzz of insects all around, and Kaeto could see a large number of the colourful fire beetles, most much smaller than ReRe, crawling in and out of the twisting vines and crumbling brick. Partially hidden by the plants was a small open hatch in the centre, and standing on it were three simple figurines made of clay, painted in vivid colours. Riz picked a fat pink flower from one of the vines and laid it before the figurines. There was no one else around that Kaeto could see.

'We can talk here,' said Riz. Some of the arch amusement had faded from his voice, and when he turned back to them the smug grin was gone too. 'It's quite a dangerous thing you've asked for, my friend. Dangerous for you and your girl, and dangerous for me.'

'We're quite aware,' said Kaeto.

'Do you know what these are?' Riz nodded to the figures.

'Household gods,' said Kaeto. 'Houraki has a great many of them.'

Riz nodded. 'So you've done some reading. That's good. They say we have as many ways to die as there are gods, and there are five or six gods on every street corner.' The smile came back, muted now but to Kaeto, much more appealing. 'Fire beetles, wild cats, poisonous snakes, hungry spiders, river lizards, sudden floods, mudslides, earthquakes. There are tiny flying creatures, so small you can barely see them, and they can give you a disease that will have you shitting your guts into a bucket until you die. With all these dangers, you want to go to the most dangerous region of them all?'

'We do,' said Kaeto. His patience was wearing thin. 'We are aware of what we'll be facing.'

Riz shook his head. 'Are you? I wonder. Still. You are paying a good heap of coin for the opportunity to die in the most lavishly exotic way possible, so who am I to argue?' He looked then at Belise, as if taking her in for the first time. 'Not a good place for a kid to go, though. Is there somewhere you can leave her, perhaps?'

Belise was instantly furious. 'Who are you calling a kid?'

Riz raised his eyebrows as though pleased with the response. Kaeto sighed.

'We are willing to pay you handsomely, as you know. And I'm assuming you've done this before. So what is the problem, exactly?'

Riz had turned back to the figurines on the altar.

'You know what these are. Do you know *who* they are?'

'It's not important.'

'Maybe not to you.' Riz picked up one of the clay figures. The endless humidity of the jungle had worked on its features, turning its face soft and somehow unnerving. 'A year ago, a woman died in an accident just up this road. A cart, a delivery of logs that hadn't been secured properly.' Riz shrugged. 'This is Essensan, a god that watches over the souls of young women who die before their twentieth birthday. This one,' he put the first clay figure down and picked up another, 'is Eroc, who watches over all the journeys we make in a single lifetime.' The figure had a definite insectoid cast to it; too many limbs, a bulbous head. 'And here, last of all, we have Rissen, a god of bravery, chance and taking dangerous risks.'

Riz and Rissen. Kaeto wondered if their guide had been named after the god, and if he had, whether that was a good omen or a bad omen.

'Yeah, you've got a lot of gods,' said Belise. 'What do you want? A prize?'

'You're a charmer, aren't you, kid?' Riz put the figurines back in their original places. 'My point is – if you have no interest in the gods and superstitions of Houraki, then why do you want to travel to the Black City? The darkest gods of all are buried there. It's forbidden because they are sleeping, and the possibility of waking them up is too dangerous to contemplate.'

The Othanim, thought Kaeto.

'And what are they exactly?' he asked. Even Tyleigh with her papers and her books knew very little about the Black City and its supposed occupants, and he was keen to get every scrap of information that they could. 'Do the people here truly believe them to be gods?'

Riz looked away, shaking his head. He looked uncomfortable.

'I've no idea what they are, and I don't want to know.'

'How can the place be forbidden when you don't know what the danger is?' put in Belise.

'Sometimes the only thing you need to know about a snake is that it will kill you.' Riz ran his hands through his dark hair, pushing it behind his ears. 'My point is, you are not Houraki citizens, intent on pilgrimage to some obscure gods because you need a very specific prayer answered. Houraki specialises in specific prayers. So why?'

Kaeto looked at his feet for a moment, then removed a small bag of coins from one of the inner pockets of his jacket. He put it on the altar, and spoke without looking at Riz, who was watching him closely.

'An extra pound of gold for a lack of curiosity. How's that? You can leave it here in offering to your gods if you like, I don't care. It sounds like we might need their support. Do we have an agreement?'

Riz picked up the bag of coins and hefted it in his hand. His face was serious, and now that they stood so close Kaeto could see that the shorter man's eyes were not black, as he had originally assumed, but a very dark blue; almost the deep indigo of a night's sky.

'I didn't say they were *my* gods, did I? Alright, we have a deal. Bring yourself and your charming kid to the Broken Gate tomorrow afternoon, and we'll get ready to leave.'

'There will be one other to our party. A woman. Will that be a problem?'

Riz turned back to him, and for a second there was a new expression there – disappointment? But then as quickly as that it was gone, and the crooked smile was back in its place.

'Fine with me. Bring everything you need, but if you can, travel light. We'll be going fast, and through the thickest part of the jungle.'

Kaeto nodded agreement, and he and Belise left Riz to walk back up the road. When he looked back, he saw that the shorter man with the night-sky eyes was taking a single coin from the bag, and as he watched he placed it in front of Eroc, the god of journeys.

Perhaps he is wise after all, thought Kaeto. *We need all the help we can get.*

18

The empress has enquired after the possibility of bringing the Nost into the Imperium. This was a question back in Emperor Lumious's day, of course, and I'm afraid the conclusion is still the same. While it may be entirely possible to take the archipelago of islands in the north, the simple fact is that the vast majority of Nostia men and women live aboard their ships, and whatever military action we take against their homelands, we would always be faced with an armada once the word got out. It is the opinion of the Bureau of Envoys that the Nost must remain, sadly, Unblessed – at least until we have a navy of equal size and strength, which will be a long time coming, or Heralds who are able to stay in the sky for longer periods.

Note written from a fellow
Envoy to Envoy Kaeto

The room they had given Leven was the grandest she had ever seen, with a huge canopied bed and rushes on the floor heavy with perfume. There had been a bowl of fruit on a table, and as she sat on the bed eating an apple, she had begun to relax a little. They were treating her well, and with honour. Surely they did not intend to cut her throat the moment she went to sleep?

But the next morning, as she was hurried through the palace and back out onto the road again, she began to wonder. The horned man was waiting for her with a pair of horses, one black and one white, and there was a small bird seated on his shoulder, which Leven had learned was called a jackdaw. Princess Bronvica escorted her there, a tense expression on her face; Leven had the distinct impression the princess was glad to be rid of her. Cillian turned away as they approached, as though he'd rather look at anything else. The road they were on rose up behind Londus-on-Sea, so it was possible to see much of the bustling city port, and the strip of dark grey sea glittered on the other side, already looking too far away for Leven's liking. She thought of Sans Rosen, far on the other side of that strip, and looked in vain for any sign it was still there.

'Take the white horse,' said Princess Bronvica. 'He will take you as far as the edge of the Wild Wood, and from there you will carry the bags containing our mother's gifts to the queens and kings of Brittletain. Cillian is carrying supplies for you both.'

'Thank you,' said Leven, although she wasn't sure how grateful to be. So far no one had given her any hint of what exactly she was carrying to the other kingdoms. The road they were on was deserted, and that made her wonder too. Were the people of Londus-on-Sea so fickle they had lost interest in their Imperial visitor already, or was she being smuggled out in secret? 'I am glad to have met you and your sisters.'

Bronvica grunted at that. 'Just stick to the Druin, and you will make it through well enough.'

When she and Cillian were mounted on their respective horses, they left without any further ceremony. The princess stood in the road, watching them as they went. The morning was full of sunshine yet there was no heat to it, and Leven felt like she would never warm up. The chalky road was a high one, taking them over several green hills studded here and there with grey marker stones carved into different Titan shapes: bears, griffins, bristling boars and fierce unicorns. The horned man's jackdaw flew ahead periodically and circled back again, as if it were scouting and reporting to him. For all Leven knew, it could be doing exactly that.

Eventually, the movement of the horse and strengthening of the sun began to warm Leven's limbs, and she started to take more notice of the space around them. To the north, she noticed, there was a dark line on the horizon, getting closer all the time. The forest, she realised. The Wild Wood. That's where it truly started – the great forest of Brittletain, where to wander from your Path likely meant a slow death, far from human eyes. She cleared her throat.

'So. Are we to spend the entire journey in silence?'

The black horse was a few feet in front of her. The horned man turned his head slightly.

'You are welcome to talk if you want,' he said.

'To what? My horse? Your bird?'

'You can talk to the hills, for all I care.'

Leven nodded, and looked around. This was not going to be easy.

'You could tell me...' The wind picked up, snatching her words away, so she raised her voice. 'You could tell me about this forest of yours. And the Paths. And why it is I need someone to hold my hand through them.'

Cillian cast a quick look over his shoulder. The bird took off into the sky again.

'What do you want to know?'

Leven tapped her heels to the white horse's flank and he briefly cantered, catching up with the horned man until they rode side by side. She looked over at Cillian, trying to catch his eye, but he was keeping his gaze firmly on the road ahead.

'Won't this be easier if we're friendly with each other?' she said. This was the first time she had gotten a proper look at him up close, and she saw with some mild surprise that he was quite striking: dark stubble on a strong jawline; thick, expressive eyebrows and those green eyes. The hand that rested on the horse's neck had clever, long fingers, and he had a number of small scars, paler strikes against his tanned skin. 'I asked Princess Bronvica how long it takes, this journey we are about to make, and she said it can take up to two whole moons, from Londus to the northern edge of Brittletain. And that's without stopping to deliver whatever it is I have in these packs.' When the horned man didn't say anything to that, she raised her voice a little more. 'Will you really avoid speaking to me all that time?'

'I'm waiting for you to ask a question worth answering.'

Leven grinned. 'I have heard stories about the horned men and women of Brittletain. I had no idea they were so charming, though.'

This surprised him into glancing at her. Leven laughed.

'What sort of stories have you heard?'

'Oh, exactly the sort of stories the Imperium loves, of course. That you are born with those horns, and each one of you kills their mother at birth.'

'That's not true,' said Cillian. He sighed and went back to looking at the road ahead. 'We're gifted our horns by the forest when we are ready.'

'It is said that the horned priests of Brittletain know all sorts of dangerous magic.'

'That may be so.'

'It is also said that you eat and sleep and rut with animals.'

Cillian shook his head slightly, not deigning that with an answer, and fell back into silence. From somewhere overhead, his jackdaw was calling. Eventually, when he spoke again, his voice was light and considering.

'We hear stories about the Heralds too, here. Even on this little backwater island, we have heard about the butchery you bring to each country not willing to become blessed. That you have murdered your way across the continent, that men, women and children alike fall to your monstrous blades. Is that true, Herald Eleven?'

Leven thought of Blessed Lamabet, how they had chased the exhausted soldiers into the river, slicing them in half with glittering wings. And there had been villages too, small places with no great resistance; farmers with makeshift weapons who made the mistake of attacking first. Boss had had no qualms about designating them enemies who must be wiped out. Of course she hadn't – it was their duty.

'I am a soldier. *Was* a soldier. What do you expect?' But the words on her tongue tasted sour, and she found she no longer had any appetite for the conversation.

They fell into another silence, but sooner than she had expected, the thick band of darkness that was the forest was nearly upon them. Trees, taller than any she had seen in her years across the continent, reached up towards the clouds. At their level, the road narrowed, bottlenecking into a path that led into the woods, as though the trees would only take a thoroughfare so wide. Leven frowned at it. She was sure it should have taken most of the day to get here, but already the land around them had changed, the cobbles under their horses' hooves becoming scarce, the grass taller and thicker. The wind had died down to nothing. She wondered, a little uneasily, if she had somehow fallen asleep during the ride, slipping in and out of naps without realising. Could it be another symptom of whatever was currently afflicting her? Or was it the presence of the forest itself?

'This is the beginning of the Wild Wood,' said Cillian. 'We will leave the horses here.'

'You mean it's your job to maintain these roads and you still haven't cleared the paths enough for horses?'

To her surprise, rather than being angry, Cillian shook his head as though she had simply misunderstood. 'These Paths will not be like other paths you have known. Most horses will not willingly travel them. They have to be specially trained.' He turned to her. 'Listen. The Wild Wood is dangerous. These Paths are dangerous. Go only where I tell you to, and don't question my decisions. There are threats beyond these trees that even I barely understand, and I've lived with these trees for most of my life. Do you understand?'

Leven raised her eyebrows. 'If I say yes, will you give it a rest?'

'This is ludicrous.' From above them somewhere, the jackdaw appeared, alighting once more on the horned man's shoulder. Cillian sighed. 'At least try to get this through your thick Imperial skull – no one travels these Paths alone. Anyone who does, doesn't make it back out of the forest. This place is ever shifting, and only the Druin know the safe routes.'

'Alright. Fine.' Leven glanced up at the clouds gathering overhead. It looked like it was going to rain soon. 'I promise I will stick by your side at all times. You'll be sick of the sight of me, I promise. Now can we go?'

Cillian looked at her for a moment longer, and for a second Leven thought she saw another expression there – was he worried about something? Was there something he wasn't saying? But then he turned away from her, and together they dismounted and began the task of unpacking the horses. When they were done, he pressed his hands to either side of the black horse's long face and seemed to murmur something to her. The black horse pushed her face into his shoulder once, almost affectionately, and then both of the horses turned back to the road. Leven stood blinking with surprise as the two of them trotted away.

'Wait. Are you not going to tie them up? Won't someone come to collect them?'

'They will make their way back to the castle stables,' said Cillian. He was adjusting a strap on one of his many packs. 'Faster too, without a human to slow them down.'

'But won't...' Leven looked at the horned man in astonishment. 'Did you just *tell* that horse to go?'

'I just told her goodbye, and thank you. She wanted to go. Like I said, horses will not walk willingly into the Wild Wood. They've got more sense. Now. Shall we go?'

Together they stepped into the treeline. At once, they seemed to pass into a deeper shadow, and Leven shivered. The scent of the undergrowth was powerful and green in her nostrils, and the path – now little more than a dirt track – circled around the trees and dropped from sight. She was struck by the quiet, and the stillness; it felt a thousand miles away from the bustling city of Londus-on-Sea. This place felt *old*. She had to admit, it was impressive.

'Listen, Cillian.' She lowered her voice instinctively. For some reason, she felt like she needed this horned man to be on her side. 'I honestly—'

'Hey, you two, wait for me!'

The shout came from the trees off to the left. Leven, dumbfounded, saw Cillian reach for the knife at his belt, and then a slim shape crashed out of the foliage. It was Princess Epona, grinning widely.

'What—?'

'I thought you'd never get here. And then I had to stand there and listen to the Druin's speech about how dangerous this place is, and I thought I was going to burst with the need to surprise you.'

'Princess.' Cillian sounded as though he were talking past a throat full of brambles. 'What are you doing here? The Paths—'

'Yes I know, but I'd already decided I was going to accompany the warrior, and I just wanted to get out here and be ready. Besides, if I'd told you, you'd have told my mother, and then where would we be? Drinking tea and listening to lectures, that's where.'

'So you've just been waiting here, in the trees, by yourself?' Leven couldn't resist a glance at Cillian. He had closed his eyes and looked like he was counting in his head. 'I'd been led to believe that is very dangerous.'

'Oh, it is, it is.' Rather than the silk tunic she had been wearing to meet Leven off the docks, she had on a fine set of black travelling clothes – thick wool, shining leather. The cat-like blue stripes across her face had been freshly painted on, but she wore no obvious jewellery save for a narrow thread of tiny blue stones around her neck. 'When my mother came down the country from her old kingdom, she brought with her an entire company of Druin to make sure her army travelled the Paths safely. Cillian here will be a vital addition to our party. Do you still have that bird with you?'

'With respect, Princess...' Cillian had opened his eyes again and had lifted his hands up in front of him, as if he could force Epona back beyond the treeline. 'You can't come with us. That's not part of the plan, and I... I am not willing to be responsible for the wellbeing of one of Queen Broudicca's daughters.'

Epona grinned. 'You don't have to be. I've always been responsible for myself, ask anyone.' She caught Leven's eye. 'If there's one thing my mother has always impressed on us, it's that we have to be willing to look after ourselves. And I want to see what she's playing at, sending this Imperial brute to our friends and neighbours.'

'You make it sound as if I'm acting on her orders,' said Leven.

'Besides which, Druin,' Epona continued, 'what are you going to do? Force me to go back?'

In the end, they all moved on along the Path together, Cillian leading the way with Leven bringing up the rear.

'Have you travelled through the wood often, Princess?'

'Oh yes,' Epona replied. 'It's hard to get anywhere at all in Brittletain without going through the Wild Wood. But most of the time I have travelled with Mother's court, or my sisters.' She made a face. 'It'll make a nice change to have some *interesting* company for once.'

'And the griffins? Have you seen them?'

The princess gave her an odd look. 'I've never seen one up close, and believe me, you don't want to. If you're close enough to see their feathers, you're likely about to get eaten. My sister Ceni's kingdom lies along the border to Yelvynia, and when I've visited her there I have seen them, flying in the distance. There's no mistaking them for birds.'

Leven nodded. She was thinking of the ruins she had seen in her 'visions', the threatening shadow of a winged beast overhead. The place she was seeking had to be to the north – if indeed it existed at all.

After around an hour of travelling in silence, they came to a place where the muddy Path seemed to end. Ahead of them was a solid wall of trees; Leven could see no clear path through.

'Are we lost already? That was quick.'

'No, watch this,' said Epona. She took Leven's arm and squeezed it. 'I never get tired of seeing it, and I've seen it a hundred times. A thousand times, probably.'

Cillian, ignoring the pair of them, had stepped up to the closest tree, a huge old gnarled thing with thick green bark. He placed his hands on it, and lifted his head as if looking for something in its branches.

'What is he—?'

In that moment, the forest ahead of them seemed to shimmer and shift. Leven felt her whole body jerk with alarm as the tree that had been facing them vanished. Instead, there was a new, broader path ahead, the ground level and packed down as though from the passage of hundreds of people. The forest in front of them felt different too; lighter and airier, and full of bird song.

'What just happened?' Leven turned and looked behind her. There was the dark and imposing wood they had just been walking through. Yet ahead of them was clearly... someplace else.

'A Druin trick,' said Epona brightly.

Cillian cast her a dark look over his shoulder.

'Well, it's more than a trick,' Epona conceded. 'This is how they navigate the Wild Wood. They know all the secret ways and can open up new Paths where needed.'

'I don't understand.'

'Imagine a corridor lined with locked doors,' said Cillian. The three of them stepped out onto the new Path together, although Leven found herself sneaking looks at the old Path. 'I can unlock some, but not all, of the doors. Each doorway leads to another corridor, with more doors... It's through these mazes that we can move across the Wild Wood safely. Or mostly safely.'

'The more experienced the Druin, the more Paths they can unlock,' added Epona. 'And since the Druin conclave sent Cillian here to serve my mother, he must be fairly experienced.'

'The Druidahnon sent me,' said Cillian, a flicker of annoyance passing over his face. 'And I'm a ranger. Navigating these Paths is my life.'

'The last bear Titan?' asked Leven. 'You've spoken to him?'

'The old bear *trains* them,' said Epona. 'It's the Druidahnon who joins them to the Wild Wood.'

'What's he like?' asked Leven, looking at Cillian. But Cillian would say no more about it, and walked on ahead of them.

'Don't worry. He's not very chatty, even for a Druin.' Epona picked a leaf from a nearby sapling and twirled the stem between her fingers. 'But now you have me to talk to instead. Won't that be marvellous?'

Eventually, when the sun was directly overhead, the horned man suggested stopping for food, and Leven found she was enormously glad of the suggestion. She had walked for miles every day during their campaigns across the Unblessed lands, but there was something about walking through the Wild Wood that seemed to sap her strength. Perhaps it was the curiosity that had built up inside her since she had left the castle that morning; she found that she was constantly looking back and forth, watching birds flying overhead, or trying to keep track of the Paths that Cillian and Epona spoke of. Or perhaps it was simply the effects of the strange illness that had its claws in her.

Cillian instructed them to stay put in a narrow clearing while he found fresh water. Princess Epona stood with her hands pressed to the small of her back, stretching.

'Waiting around in the cold to surprise you has made me all stiff. It was worth it though. The look on your faces.'

Leven smiled, despite herself. 'What will your mother say about it, when she realises you're gone?'

'Oh, it'll take her no more than a handful of seconds to figure it all out. I borrowed one of Bronvica's ponies to get out here before you both, and she never was any good at keeping secrets. Have you looked in the bags then?' she asked. 'At what my mother has given you?'

'The boxes are sealed,' said Leven.

'*Tch*. And? Surely a fearless warrior like yourself can break a seal?'

'I am a guest here, your majesty.' Leven pulled one of the bags from her back and set it on the ground. 'It would hardly be wise of me to pry into the queen's business.'

'You can stop calling me that, for a start.' Epona crossed her arms over her chest, then shook her head. '*Your majesty*. Magog's balls, I thought people from the Imperium would be cleverer, really. Can you truly not see what my mother is up to?'

Leven shook her head. She felt cold again, and tired. It seemed to her that the trees were pressing in all around them, standing like sentinels; trunks covered in grey and green bark, punctuated with fleshy white pockets of fungi. It made her uneasy. If she were on campaign with Boss, her old leader would have led them out of this place quickly, she was sure of it.

'I don't suppose you feel like just telling this dim-witted warrior what you're talking about?'

Epona grinned and tucked a lock of black hair behind her ear. 'It's a demonstration of power. She has taken you, a symbol of the might of the Imperium, and got you delivering parcels for her. And it just so happens you are delivering parcels to those people she is keenest to impress and threaten.'

More games, then. 'That's not why I'm here,' said Leven, although she was no longer really paying attention. There was movement in the dark space beyond the grey trees, something shifting in the shadows. Epona was laughing.

'It doesn't matter why you're here,' she said. 'Haven't you figured it out yet? You've been in Brittletain less than a raven's blink and you're already one of my mother's tools.'

Leven nodded absently. In the shadows between the trees the wind was picking up and then, to her shock, she saw a gust of snowflakes in the dark; icy white flecks against a winter's sky.

'Wait, how is it...?'

There was a high and pitiful scream, like something very small lost in the night, and a slow clicking, clacking sound. As she listened it grew faster and faster, and the faster it got the more afraid she was. Leven wrapped her arms around herself. *Why did I come to this place? I knew it was dangerous.*

Click. Click. Click. Clickclickclick.

'Blessed Eleven, are you alright?' Epona's voice seemed to come from very far away. 'What's wrong?'

'I can't... I don't...'

Darkness shuttered Leven's eyes and the ground came up to meet her.

19

The Herald had been remarkably light in his arms.

Cillian wasn't sure what he'd been expecting. Did he think that the ore-lines etched into her body would weigh her down, somehow? Instead, he had scooped her up from where she had fallen – after Epona had hollered for him to come back – and brought her over to a softer patch of ground sheltered by an old oak tree. He pressed his fingers to the skin of her throat, and was relieved to feel a flutter there. Her heart was still beating, then.

'What happened?'

Epona was crouched next to them, frowning. 'I hardly know. I was talking to her about this nonsense task my mother has her on, and then she just wandered towards the trees, and stopped talking to me. It looked like she had seen something there, and then she dropped like a stone. Which reminds me,' the princess straightened up, 'I am going to see what is in these packages.'

'You can't do that,' said Cillian, although he wasn't paying her much attention. They had barely left sight of Londus-on-Sea and the person he was guarding had already had some sort of accident he didn't understand. Unconscious, with all the animation from her face fled, she looked younger, and oddly vulnerable. Her hair had fallen over her face a little, so he pushed it back, and then wished he hadn't. Everything about being this close to another human was making him uncomfortable. 'Wake up,' he said, trying to sound firm about it. 'We don't have time for this.'

'Huh. They're little boxes.' Epona was busying herself with going through the Herald's bags. 'Wooden boxes. There's a green wax seal on them.'

Cillian glanced up. 'You won't be able to open them. That is a Druin seal. It can only be opened by someone joined to the forest.'

'Well that's ridiculous.'

The Herald made a small moaning noise in the back of her throat. Cillian took a skin of water from his belt and poured a little into his hand. He tipped the water onto the woman's forehead, watching as it moved down the silvery ore-lines that were etched there. She shivered and her eyelids flickered, but then there was a cry from Epona. He looked round to see that she had dropped one of the wooden boxes. Cillian sighed.

'What did you do?'

'I wanted to see what would happen.'

He went over to the box where it lay in the mud. The whole thing was tightly wrapped in thick greenish-brown roots, with no sign of the lid of the box. He picked it up and pressed his finger to the green wax seal, and instantly the roots shivered back, revealing the warm brown cherry wood again.

'I picked at the wax and green shoots just shot out of it all over.' Epona no longer sounded startled. 'So that's what a Druin seal does, is it?'

'It is.' Cillian put the box back inside the bag. 'The other kings and queens of Brittletain will have Druin advisors who will be able to open the boxes for them. Or I can do it. It was very wise of your mother – this way our *guest* won't be able to plunder the boxes.'

'*You* could open it now,' said Epona.

Cillian opened his mouth to reply to that, but then the Herald woman was sitting up, one hand on her head.

'Stars' arses, what hit me?'

'Too much fresh air?' Epona stepped neatly away from the bags. 'Overcome with the beauty of our fair forest? The wonder of my company?'

'I... I don't know. Perhaps it was just the long journey by sea.' The Herald leaned her elbows on her knees, looking down at the ground, but there was something in the way she turned her head away from them. *She is lying*, thought Cillian. *But I can't see why.* He went over to her and offered a hand. The Herald looked at it, then took it, allowing herself to be pulled to her feet.

'Will you be able to continue?' Cillian cleared his throat, trying to keep some of the hope out of his voice. If she was too unwell to make the journey, he could simply lead her back to Londus and return to his actual responsibilities. But she shook her head, smiling ruefully.

'I'll be fine, I just need to walk it off.' The Herald rubbed her hands over her face. 'Perhaps some food would help.'

They ate a hurried lunch standing up, washing down some dried meat and hard cheese with the fresh water Cillian had found. While Epona and the Herald were stretching their legs and preparing to set off, Cillian made his way back to the big old oak tree, and pressed his hands against its ancient, rippled bark.

Father Oak, carry a message for me.

Talking to the trees was different to talking to creatures with blood in their veins. The thoughts of animals thundered with the sound of their heartbeats, living in the moment, *nownownow*, so that to speak to them was to be filled with their energy... Whereas the trees of the Wild Wood did not so much speak as listen in long, green silences. The birds at Dosraiche carried messages to and from the many kingdoms of Brittletain, but amongst themselves, the Druin used the trees.

We start the journey from here. The Princess Epona has joined us. It might be best to let Queen Broudicca know.

The tree would take the message inside itself and pass it down through its roots into the wider web of the Wild Wood, and eventually a Druin at Dosraiche would sift it out from all the other slow messages they received that day. Cillian had performed this duty himself a number of times, and knew that when the Druin withdrew his or her mind from the web after many hours' work, they would feel as slow and as calm as a tree themselves, a taste of sweet sap in the backs of their throats.

Inkwort, who had been preening herself in the branches, hopped down onto Cillian's shoulder.

'There you are.' Cillian reached out for her mind instinctively, but again felt only the anonymous warmth of a living thing.

'Are you coming then?' called Epona. 'We've still got a few hours of daylight left, I reckon.'

Cillian paused with his fingers still pressed to the tree, wondering whether to mention the Herald's fainting fit, then decided against it. They might assume he had been pushing their guest too hard, and it wasn't important. He broke his connection with the tree, and went to join the others.

For the rest of that day, as they walked the endless winding Paths through the forest, Leven found her eyes returning again and again to the darkness between the trees. She was surprised to find how much she missed the presence of their horses – the forest would seem less quiet and foreboding with the pleasing bellows of their lungs or the muffled clop of their shoes on the dirt path.

I am going insane, she thought, as for the hundredth time in the last hour she turned her head back to watching the slim shape of the Druin walking in front of her. *What do these visions mean? Even in this place, I'm not any closer to getting answers.*

Eventually the dappled light through the canopy turned orange and red, and Princess Epona began to complain about the weight of their packs. Cillian agreed that they would rest for the night, and he asked them to stand to one side while he found them a place to sleep. He went to the edge of the Path and stopped, one hand resting against the bark of a tree. Here, the forest appeared to be at its thickest; Leven could not see how they would find space enough for one of them to lie down, let alone the three of them with their packs. She glanced at Epona, who was grinning.

'Am I about to see more Druin magic?'

'Oh this is a pretty good trick, I have to give it to them.' The princess pointed over Cillian's shoulder. 'Watch the space between those trunks. You'll know it when you see it.'

Leven did as she was told, but could see nothing but more trees and bushes. The shadows were growing longer all the time, and the temperature was dropping. For the first time, Leven considered the fact that she would be sleeping out here, under this alien sky, and – she jumped. The light between the trees had flickered, as though a great mirror had appeared to reflect the last of the light, dazzling her, and now... the space beyond the tree trunks had changed. Cillian turned back to them, already lifting the bag straps from his shoulders.

'This will do,' he said shortly. 'We can build a fire here, if we keep it small.'

Where there had been trees crowded close together in the waning light, there was now a small clearing, the ground covered in short grass and soft green moss. The space above it was clear of branches too, and two thirds of the space was gently walled in with carefully placed stones. It was, in short, the perfect place to make a camp. There was even a pile of dry kindling stacked on the moss. Epona took her arm and pulled her off the Path and into the clearing. Cillian was gathering sticks and preparing a fire.

'Don't ask me how it works,' said the princess. 'But it's bloody clever, isn't it? This is why they are such good guides. Otherwise you'd be trying to sleep with sticks poking in your arse all night. Or you'd just get dismembered and eaten by something nasty. And not necessarily in that order.'

'How *does* it work?' Leven directed the question at Cillian, who seemed to be avoiding her eye even more than usual. Had been avoiding her eye all afternoon, in fact. 'Where are we, exactly?'

'In one of the wood's secret places,' said Cillian. He was pulling things from his belt and setting them on the ground next to the pile of kindling. 'There are little pockets like this all over Brittletain, small spaces given to us by the forest, by the Dunohi. If we stay here, we are safe.' He paused, then shrugged. 'Mostly safe.'

'What are the Dunohi?'

'The spirits of the Wild Wood. They are the souls that this place truly belongs to – they were here before us, and they will be here long after us. Part of the work of the Druin is to make sure that we don't upset them, or harm them in any way.'

Leven shook her head slightly. 'But what *are* they? Animals? Ghosts? People?'

'Yes,' said Cillian. For half a second something like a smile touched the corner of his mouth, and then it was gone. Leven thought briefly about picking him up and throwing him into the branches of one of his precious trees.

'Is it also your job to be bloody mysterious all the time?' Next to Leven, Epona laughed. 'Alright. So are they dangerous, your forest souls?'

'They can be.'

'And you just live alongside them?'

Cillian knelt by the kindling and began arranging the dry sticks into a five-sided shape on the ground. 'We co-exist. It's possible, you know, to live alongside people who are different to yourselves, without driving them from the land. A lesson the Imperium could do with taking to its heartwood.'

Leven bit her lip. Epona was brushing the dust from her clothes with short, sharp movements, but there was no mistaking the faintly amused expression on her face. *They think they know all about me*, she thought. *They think I am little more than a talking sword.*

'So rather than clearing the trees and building real roads, you live in thrall to spirits,' said Leven. 'Forgive me for not being more impressed.'

'I wouldn't expect you to understand,' said the horned man. His hands were working small pieces of wood, showering sparks over the kindling. A tiny curl of smoke wound its way into the air, followed by another, and a glimmer of amber light. 'It's Brittletain magic.'

Epona patted her arm. 'Druin business. Don't worry, hardly anyone understands it really. The best way to look at it is that the Druin carry the secrets of the forest, and sometimes they are useful.'

The fire was flickering into life. Leven moved towards it gratefully. Until she'd felt the faint push of its warmth against her shins, she hadn't realised just how chilled she was.

'We care for the Wild Wood, and the Dunohi, and in its way, the Wild Wood cares for us,' added Cillian. He glanced up at her, and she caught a flash of his green eyes. 'It's a compromise. Something else I wouldn't expect the Imperium to have much time for.'

The sun bled quickly out of the sky from there. The three of them crowded around the small fire, and ate a cold but tasty supper of ham and strong cheese, which Epona produced from one of her bags. There was a small bottle of a strange golden wine that Epona called mead, which was sweet and moreish on the tongue. After that, the princess announced that she was exhausted, spread out her bed roll and promptly went to sleep. When the princess's small snores began to break the silence, Leven smiled to herself.

'I had friends like that in the Heralds,' she said, gesturing to the sleeping woman. 'Wherever you were bedded for the night they could be asleep before their heads hit the floor. Useful skill when you're a soldier.'

For a long moment, the horned man didn't say anything at all. The small jackdaw that followed him around had perched on the top of his pack, its head tucked into its chest.

'You may as well sleep too, if you wish,' said Cillian eventually. 'I can watch over us, through the night.'

'What about you? Will you wake me for a watch?'

'Would you know what to watch for?' He shook his head before she could answer. 'I don't need your help.'

Despite herself, Leven bristled. 'You might think me useless—' she remembered how she had passed out, and the Druin had had to revive her, and carried on anyway, 'but I have spent more than one night out under the stars. I am also the best equipped to deal with trouble.' She moved her arm into the firelight, knowing that the ore-lines on her skin would glitter in the glow from it. 'Or have you forgotten what I am?'

'I could hardly forget that, it's written all over your face.'

Heat leapt to her cheeks, and her fingers itched to summon her blade. The Druin wouldn't be so full of himself with his guts sitting in his own lap. The jackdaw chose that moment to chirp, and they both looked at it, startled. Cillian cleared his throat.

'I mean that I do not need to sleep. At least, not in the way you would think of it. I can remain connected to the forest while I rest, and it will warn me of anything approaching. So. You may as well sleep.'

Leven looked at him for a long moment. He was gazing into the fire, a troubled expression on his face, and when he looked up again he appeared uncertain of himself somehow. She picked up a stick and poked the fire, wanting to look at something else.

'Is that another secret of the forest? How you can do that?'

Cillian nodded slightly. 'Everything here is connected.' He touched his fingers to the moss they sat on. 'Under here, in the black earth, there are thousands upon thousands of tiny roots. The roots of trees, shrubs, bushes, every kind of fungus you can think of – and they all link together, where we can't see them. It is a huge web, running under the forest floor.' As he spoke, his voice warmed up a little. 'Did you know that trees speak to each other this way, sending messages along the roots? That when a tree knows it is dying, it sends the last of its strength to its brothers and sisters? They care for one another.'

'The trees?'

'It's all joined in the web. The trees, the animals, everything that grows here. And the Druin are connected to that web too. It is who we are. And why we have these.' He touched one of the curling horns that sprouted at his temples. 'We give our lives to the forest, and in turn, it sends us strength, as though we were brother-trees.'

'You give your lives to the forest?'

'We don't marry, we don't have families, and we have no other loyalties. We live our lives in the service of the Wild Wood.'

'Don't you find that... lonely?'

Cillian's dark brows drew low over his eyes. 'Is it so different to being a Herald?'

'They're not the same at all!' Leven shook her head, smiling crookedly.

'Then you have a family? A partner?'

'Well...' Reluctantly, Leven thought of her time in Stratum after their discharge. She had always thought of her fellow Heralds as her family, yet they had all drifted away when they no longer had any orders holding them together. As for relationships... there were no rigid rules about fraternisation between Heralds while they were on campaign, and Leven knew of several couples who sought each other out when night fell over the camp – and she had hardly been chaste herself over those eight years. But where were they now? 'It's different for us,' she finished awkwardly. 'We were soldiers. Brothers-in-arms. And now I have my life back anyway.'

'And you've chosen to spend it here, in the lands of your enemy?'

Leven couldn't think what to say to that, and after a few moments' silence, Cillian looked as though he regretted speaking at all. He threw a handful of dry leaves onto the fire.

'Herald, you should sleep. Perhaps another night you can stand a watch, if it means so much to you.'

Leven nodded and lay down on her own bed roll. But with the unfamiliar noises of the forest and the wild man of Brittletain watching over her, it was a long time before sleep found her.

20

In the heart of the Imperium, in the lands directly around Stratum, even the most monstrous and impressive insects grow little bigger than a hand's breadth – the constellation moth, for example, has been recorded to reach a wingspan of six inches; or the much reviled earthworks spider, rarely seen, but widely reported to grow to the size of a pomegranate when it reaches adulthood. The 'hound bugs' of Unblessed Houraki then are perhaps difficult for the average Imperial citizen to imagine. The species is known rather prosaically as the 'fire beetle', and most grow only to be around ten inches long, or the size of an especially robust rat. Some, however, carefully bred and fed and cared for, can grow to the size of a dog, and can indeed be trained to do much of what a dog can: fetching, protection of property, or simple companionship. During my brief stay in Unblessed Houraki I was initially horrified, and, eventually, strangely charmed by these slippery beasts. I witnessed these huge, buzzing, many-legged nightmares delivering documents, carrying pots of wine and even, on one particularly memorable occasion, chasing off a would-be burglar. Awful to contemplate for the civilised person perhaps, but an ingenious solution for an Unblessed land with a lack of useful mammals.

Notes from the travel journal of Envoy Castius,
who travelled extensively in the Unblessed
lands during the reign of Emperor Lumious

The Broken Gate was a huge arch of sandstone, largely held together by thick ropes of red and green vine; here and there it was pocked with the straggling nests of colourful, raucous birds. If it once had a door it was long gone, and the wall that marched out from either side of it was in a similar state of disrepair. It faced the rising sun, so that as they approached Kaeto, Belise and Tyleigh were dazzled by a sea of pale golden light flooding the slightly sunken jungle plain on the far side. It occurred to Kaeto that, as early as it was and as blinded as they were, it would make another great place for an ambush. He gritted his teeth and looked around as best he could. There was no sign of Riz.

'Where is he?' Tyleigh was frowning, as she had been all morning. She held up one hand to shield her eyes. 'I've no interest in hanging around this bug-infested shit hole a moment longer than we need to.' She had dressed in loose, flowing pale fabrics, the better to deal with the heat, although she still wore the thick headband that crossed her forehead; Kaeto had never seen her without it. Belise was wearing a wide-brimmed straw hat she had bought at the market; it kept the sun off her face but every now and then she had to tip it back to get a proper look at something. *Not the most practical attire for a trainee assassin*, thought Kaeto, but then, he reminded himself, hopefully they wouldn't be murdering anyone today.

'Bug-infested shit hole? I'm so glad you're enjoying your visit.' Riz stepped out from beyond the ruined gate.

'This is it? The guide? Envoy, you could have found a less shady-looking bastard amongst the rats infesting the inn where we stayed last night.' Tyleigh shook her head. 'We'll be lucky if we're not murdered on the way there.'

Kaeto cleared his throat and spoke in a low voice. 'Did we not discuss the use of names and titles in front of strangers?'

'I wouldn't bother,' said Riz. He beckoned them over, and Kaeto saw that he had three sturdy-looking horses with him. 'I've no interest in who you really are, and I already know that you are from the Imperium

on some dark errand of your own. As long as you pay me, we're golden.'
He led one of the horses over to where Tyleigh and Belise were
standing. 'I thought your lady and the child could share a mount, no?
Don't worry about Bertino, he's a sturdy boy.'

'Absolutely not.' Tyleigh stepped away from Belise sharply. 'I don't
even know why the child is here.'

'Belise will ride with me,' Kaeto said, taking the larger horse's reins.

'As you wish.' Riz helped Tyleigh into the saddle, and then mounted
his own horse. Once they were all ready, they rode through the gate
and on down the wide, overgrown road that led away from it. For some
time they rode in silence. As the sun climbed higher and higher in
the sky, the day grew oppressively hot and still. The sound of chirping
insects was so constant it seemed to form one continuous hum,
until Kaeto was no longer sure he was hearing it at all. Remembering
the varied insect population, he looked at Riz's horse where he rode
in front and was not surprised to see his trained fire beetle, ReRe,
perched neatly on the man's pack. It was so still it could almost
have been dead.

'How long will this take?' Tyleigh was the first to speak. 'I assume
we're going the quickest way?'

'It's not so far,' said Riz. 'On horseback, a few days, perhaps.'

The jungle enclosed them on both sides, while the foliage that crept
in over the sandstones made it appear as though it were growing
closer all the time.

'We'll be making camp overnight in this place?' asked Tyleigh.
'I can hardly wait.'

Riz chuckled. 'The path to the Black City is not a pleasant one, but
what you do with your time and your coin is your business.'

'It's not *my* coin,' snapped Tyleigh.

Kaeto leaned forward to speak into Belise's ear, who was sitting in
front of him on Bertino.

'What are your observations, Belise?'

The girl sighed noisily. 'You want me to report now? In this heat?'

'If you can't report on an actual mission, then I have wasted my time in training you.'

'Fine.' Belise took her big straw hat off and used it to fan her face. 'Unblessed Houraki is too hot, that's my first observation. Heat, vegetation and humidity are the things you notice first. Then it's the giant bugs.'

'What do you think about those?'

'They're interesting. They treat them like pets here, or working animals. And much of their culture seems to be tied in around them.' Belise's voice had lost its usual sarcastic edge and had gained a more musing tone. Kaeto smiled. 'The little god statues we saw yesterday – most of them had too many legs, or wings, or those things that stick out their heads.'

'Antennae.'

'Yeah. And the people often wear pieces of beetle sewn into their clothes. The shiny shells and casings – they use them like the Imperium uses jewels. The other thing that makes me curious is this Black City. The place we're going.'

'Yes?'

'Every person we asked didn't want to talk about it. At all. In fact, they usually looked pretty angry we even brought it up. And the letters and maps and stuff Crafter Tyleigh has don't tell us much about it at all. It's almost as though the whole thing has been, I don't know, taken off the records and everyone has agreed not to talk about it. And from what I know about people they don't often agree on anything.'

'How wise of you. So what *do* we know?'

Belise shrugged. 'That it's haunted. By what? We don't know. We don't even know why that makes it dangerous. That it's cursed. But we don't know what the curse is. It's not much to go on, chief.'

'Correct.'

'Which leads me to the other thing I'm curious about.' Belise lowered her voice even further. 'If nobody even wants to talk about this place, then why is this scruffy thief happy to take us there? Either he doesn't understand the danger, or he doesn't care – which raises its own problems – or he's so desperate for money he'll do anything.'

'All valid points. And there's always the possibility that he has no intention of taking us anywhere near the Black City. Did you consider that?'

Belise turned round in the saddle and looked at him.

'There's three of us and one of him,' she said. 'And us two are pretty lethal.'

'He might not be working alone. Easy enough for a gang of cut-throats to hang out in these trees. Keep your eyes open, Belise. Watch our friend Riz closely. In particular, look out for anything that may be a signal to someone we cannot see. Make sure your throwing knives are close to hand.' He leaned back a little in the saddle. 'And keep that hat on your head, or you'll get sunstroke.'

Towards the end of the day, the fat orange sun sank into a bed of deep grey clouds, and the air around them became a little cooler. They made camp some distance from the overgrown road, seeking out the colder spots under the shade of the trees. Tyleigh ate a small amount of the food they had packed and then declared that she needed to stretch her legs.

'Don't go far,' said Kaeto. 'It will get dark quickly here.'

'You don't want to be lost in this jungle at night,' added Riz. 'It's not just beetles you have to worry about.' He tapped his fingers to ReRe's carapace, and the beetle waved its antennae.

Tyleigh curled her lip at them. 'Save your warnings for the kid,' she said, before tramping off through the bushes.

'With a bit of luck she'll get bitten by a snake,' said Belise. Riz laughed at that, then nodded to the space where Tyleigh had vanished into the heavy undergrowth.

'She's an odd one,' said Riz. He was using a small knife to peel a fruit he had picked from a nearby tree; to Kaeto it looked like some sort of red pear. 'It's like she absolutely doesn't want to be here and at the same time she's furious that she wasn't here yesterday.'

'I believe that is her attitude about everything,' said Kaeto.

'Who is she to you? Your boss? Your sister? Your wife?'

Belise gave a bark of laughter at that, and Kaeto gave her a sharp look. She hid her smile under her sleeve.

'I believe I am paying you extra for a lack of curiosity.'

'Just making conversation.' Riz cut the top of the pear off and threw it to ReRe, who fell on it with furious movements from her mandibles. 'She's not your blood sister, anyway – you couldn't look more different – and I seriously doubt she's your wife.' He grinned, and took a bite from the pear. 'So, your boss.' He chewed noisily. 'She's used to ordering people around, you can see that.'

'How much longer will we be on this road?' asked Kaeto, pointedly changing the subject.

'There's a little way to go yet,' said Riz. 'And then we turn off the road, and that's where the going gets harder.'

When Tyleigh returned from her walk, both she and Belise bedded down for the night; the alchemist curled up on her bed roll with her knees pulled up to her chest, Belise spread across hers as though she wanted to take up as much room as possible. As full dark fell around them, turning the air soupy with heat and insect calls, Riz began to pull small clay figures out of his pack. Kaeto watched him, a tin cup of weak tea in one hand.

'More gods?'

'In Houraki, there are always more gods,' said Riz, smiling. There were three of the figurines, and he set each of them in front of their small fire. He then took a tiny glass bottle from his pack, and placed a drop of what appeared to be oil on each of the figurines. A warm, woody scent briefly filled their makeshift camp, and Kaeto was reminded uncomfortably of his own home, before the Imperium took it. His father had burned incense on certain feast days, and they had eaten honey cakes with their hot tea.

'What do these gods signify?'

'Ah, you are curious?' Riz shot him a smile. 'This one is Layla, god of dark places.' The figure he touched looked to Kaeto a little like a moth, with a fat body and low-slung wings. 'Teefa is her sister, god of the night.' This one had many legs. 'And here is Teibo, the god of... I'm not sure how you would describe him. A god of bravery, perhaps? It'd be more accurate to say the god of, ah, walking willingly into danger.'

'Hmm.' Kaeto took a sip of his tea. 'Not an auspicious group.'

Riz raised one shoulder in a shrug. 'They will watch over us tonight, and tomorrow, as we get closer to our destination. Where we are going... it's certainly a dark place.'

'These gods will protect us in the Black City?' Kaeto said it half smiling, but Riz shook his head, his own easy smile gone.

'I'd rather you didn't name it here, my friend. Not when the sun is down, at least.'

A small silence grew between them. The jungle was alive with the trills and clicks of thousands of insects, as well as with the calls of various night birds. Every now and then Kaeto caught the faint whistle of Belise's snores.

'Sorry,' Riz said eventually. 'I am... superstitious, I think you would say, in the Imperium. I didn't mean to frighten us both into silence. I was enjoying talking to you.'

Kaeto glanced away, an unfamiliar warmth growing around the back of his neck. Riz was watching him very closely now, his dark eyes reflecting the smoulder of the fire.

'We don't see many people from the Imperium here, since we are *Unblessed*,' Riz continued, 'and even fewer men like you.'

'What's that supposed to mean?'

Riz shrugged one shoulder again, but he didn't take his eyes from Kaeto's face.

'I suppose I mean handsome Imperial spies.'

That surprised a laugh out of Kaeto. It occurred to him that theirs was a vulnerable position – the suffocating dark of the jungle, two of the party asleep, far from any civilisation – but then Riz did not look like a man waiting for the rest of his criminal gang to arrive. If anything, he looked nervous, as though he had put himself at risk somehow. Perhaps there were other, less obvious dangers here.

'I am almost sorry I am not as interesting as you believe me to be,' Kaeto said, keeping his shoulders relaxed. 'An Imperial spy sounds like an exciting life.'

'The woman isn't your wife, and the girl isn't your daughter,' said Riz. It wasn't quite a question.

'No,' agreed Kaeto. 'But that hardly makes me a spy. What exactly is it you want to ask me, Riz?'

'That's a good question.' Riz took a battered bronze bottle from his pack and unscrewed the top. The scent of strong, sweet alcohol drifted between them. 'I suppose I wondered if you might want to share a drink with me. And then perhaps... who knows?'

21

The nest-pit they had been given was in the side of a cliff overlooking the Bone Fall, but perhaps in concession to Ynis's lack of wings, there was a rough set of steps leading down from the entrance. When she had asked about it, Brocken had told her that the Edge Walkers often made such places, for those griffins who could no longer fly. There was no shame in it, she had said, in her abrupt way. It was simply a way to make their lives easier. Inside, the hollow was thickly padded with layered wool, so that it was quite cosy, and the sisters each had a small burrow to curl up in, although they still preferred to sleep next to each other – at night, when the temperature plummeted and the wind howled past the entrance of their nest, their new home seemed less dark when they were together.

Ynis sat on the steps as the sun went down and thought about this. The Bone Fall spread below the cliffs like a great bowl, the wall that surrounded it looking small and insignificant from her vantage point. Of the interior, Ynis couldn't see very much – shadows grew quickly in the griffins' graveyard, bleeding together around the bones – but here and there she could make out shapes; strange, half-familiar forms that caught her eye again and again. The last orange light of the sun turned the remains into golden relics, edged with fire. Onward, beyond the Bone Fall itself, was the unfamiliar mountain range at the very end of the world, half hidden in dark purple clouds. Above her, the first of the stars were shining in an indigo sky.

'This is it, then,' said T'rook from behind her. The young griffin stood in the entrance to their nest-pit, the feathers around her neck fluffed up. 'This is our life now.'

'It's not so bad,' said Ynis. The cynicism in her sister's voice made her feel guilty for enjoying the view. 'The Edge Walkers look after each other, so they look after us.'

'Look after?' T'rook snapped. 'This place has drained you of your yost. We are hunters, fighters. Not scavengers or parasites.'

Ynis sighed a little. 'It's just until we know this place well enough to hunt ourselves. There is no use in starving until then.' T'rook snorted, and Ynis felt a little flicker of annoyance with her sister. She had barely left the nest-pit since they had been given it, and refused to have anything to do with the Edge Walkers. When Brocken or Frost or another brought meat to their home, T'rook would retreat to her own burrow and avoid them entirely. All of which meant that they were little closer to learning about the Bone Fall, and therefore still unable to hunt themselves. 'Perhaps if you would explore with me...'

T'rook snorted again. 'There will be nothing to eat here but skinny rats.'

'That's not the point!' Ynis stood up and turned to face her sister. 'You are behaving like a stone-licker! You do not want meat brought to you, but you don't want to hunt for it, either. Why do you hate them so much?'

The feathers on T'rook's neck puffed up even further. 'Why are you so keen to become one of these eaters-of-the-dead? Does your human stomach long for the taste of griffin flesh?'

Ynis picked up a stone and threw it at T'rook, who batted it away easily with her wing.

'You don't understand,' continued T'rook. 'These griffins are... yost-torrosa. They feed upon the souls of the dying, like ticks. They have unnatural appetites. It is why they cannot live in Yelvynia.'

'You are talking out of your feather-hole!' Ynis stamped past T'rook into their nest-pit. She snatched up the thick coat she had made herself out of scraps of wool and pulled it on, before grabbing her pack and slinging it over her back.

'What are you doing?' demanded T'rook. 'Where are you going? It's nearly nightfall.'

'I am going to hunt,' said Ynis. She shoved past her sister again and went to the steps. During the short time of their argument, the sun had all but vanished from the sky, and the glinting golden lights from the Bone Fall had dimmed. It was a clear night, and cold, and not the best time for a creature with no wings to go hunting, but her frustration with her sister was like a hot stone in her chest. Her claw-knife was tucked into her belt, and she gripped its handle, trying to take solace from its small, lethal shape.

'That is madness,' scoffed T'rook. 'You will freeze out there, or be eaten by wolves.'

Ynis turned and stretched out one hand. 'Come with me then. We'll fly together and get to know this place. We'll kill some wolves.' T'rook's eyes flashed, and she flapped her wings in a showy manner – this was a gesture Ynis knew of old, and it meant 'go away'.

Ynis set off down the steps. Behind her, she heard the clatter of T'rook's talons as she made her way back into the nest.

Fine, she thought furiously. *We shall see who has more yost.*

But the steps were tall and not easy for a human to navigate, and by the time she reached the bottom of the cliff face her own anger had been cooled by the chill wind and eerie silence of the Bone Fall. And once at the bottom, it was easier to see how big the place was, and how long it would take her to get anywhere – when travelling on her useless human legs, at least. Still, the thought of clambering all the way up the steps again only to face her sister's quiet triumph was even less appealing, so she set off across the rocks and ice, her eyes fixed on one of the spindly towers that lined the wall. As she walked, she paid attention to each of her senses, just as her fathers had taught her to. This was the way of the hunter, the way of claw and talon.

Her weak human eyes told her very little, at first. The darkness was creeping up faster all the time, but when she made herself really look, she realised it wasn't quite as dark as she was expecting. The moon was half full, and the sky was thickly dotted with the first stars, and they lent their light to the ice and snow around her. The soft eerie whiteness of the snow; the deep blue heart of the glaciers; both meant that the Bone Fall seemed to have its own, secret light.

The longer she walked, the warmer she became, and the argument with T'rook seemed to drift away, replaced with a genuine curiosity about the landscape around her. Picking her way carefully over the scree at the bottom of the cliff, she saw that the land there wasn't as featureless as she had thought. Bushes of hardy thistle erupted from the ground, and big swathes of heather too gave part of the ground a soft mauve covering. The scent of heather and moss was everywhere underfoot, and there was the clean, mineral taste of snow on her tongue. The wind gusted fiercely, and then stopped, then gusted again, as though playing a game with itself, and interwoven around that sound were the cries of birds – owls, night eagles, snow hawks, too far away to be seen other than as a brief flicker of darkness against the stars.

The wall, when she reached it, was still tall and imposing, but she saw that the sides of it were covered in a tough kind of creeping plant with leathery purple leaves, and after a few experimental tugs, she found it sturdy enough to climb. Years of living in the valleys and nests of Yelvynia had given her strong arms, strong fingers, and a healthy respect for heights, and in an hour or so she was at the top, looking out across the rocky territory of the Bone Fall itself. She had come up next to one of the spindly towers, built of long, cold-hardened branches and griffin-spit, and she leaned against its side for a moment, getting her breath back.

The graveyard of the griffins. If the territory surrounding it was full of surprising light, then the inner part – the part where the griffins laid their bones down to rest – was an eerie place of shimmering blues and greys at night. Ynis could see piles and piles of bones in all directions, piles of skulls with their eye sockets gaping up at the stars, ribcages so huge she could have walked inside them, her arms outstretched. The bones themselves were a burnished blue, like human metal exposed to the elements; not at all like the yellow and white and brown of prey bones. Looking at them all, Ynis felt a strange shiver move through her body. She knew that the bones under her own flesh did not look like these. Her bones were white, easily broken, unmagical. For perhaps the first time, the true gulf of the distance between her and her sister opened up inside her, leaving her cold and oddly empty.

I'm the only human to have ever seen this place, she told herself, but it only made her feel worse.

And then, a movement on the bone-covered field caught her eye. A shifting caul of light, pale blue and then green, drifted across the rocky ground and was gone. Ynis frowned, wondering if her eyes were playing tricks on her, and then she saw it again, in a different place, but now there seemed to be more substance to it. She thought she could see feathers, the sharp curve of a beak. But then it faded from view again, flowing away like blood spilled in a river.

'What was that?'

There was a gust of wind then, and the soft thump of paws landing on stone. Witch-seer Frost was with her, and she was looking out towards the graveyard too. Ynis shrank back against the wall of the tower, uncertain whether she would be welcome so close to such a sacred place.

'You see them, don't you, yenlin?' The griffin spread her wings, then folded them neatly away. The place where Ynis had pulled the arrow from her was a white mark on her fur. 'I thought you might. How interesting.'

'See what?' asked Ynis, although her skin was already crawling with the knowledge of it.

'Our dead. Not the bones, but the other things they leave behind. Not all Edge Walkers can, you know. See them. Only those who walk the line between the living and the dead so closely they are half crossed over themselves.'

'Ghosts,' said Ynis. Her mouth had dried up. 'You're talking about ghosts.'

'Tell me, Ynis. Have you ever been close to death?'

'What? What do you mean?'

'Have you nearly died? Fallen from your sister's back, perhaps?'

Ynis opened her mouth to say that of course she had never fallen, and then closed it again. No, she had never been badly hurt in an accident, not truly, but she had been ill so much as a yenlin; always burning up with fevers, unable to eat anything given to her, wracked with chills and her head thumping like it would burst. And there was the place where her fathers had found her – left on the snow, exposed to the weather and anything that might come along and eat her. There had been blood that day. Violence on the wind. Perhaps she had almost died then, too, and would never know the details of it.

'It's possible,' she said eventually.

Frost nodded as though she agreed. 'How many did you see? Of our ghosts?'

Ynis looked again, and now she could see more ethereal shapes moving across the griffins' graveyard, as though talking about death had summoned them. She felt panic rising in her chest; some of them were turning to look at her. Empty eyes settling on her, no doubt wondering what a human was doing in such a place.

'One,' she said, before swallowing hard. 'I only saw one.'

'You should not fear them,' Frost said. 'Although...' The griffin shook her head, apparently changing her mind about what she was about to say. 'So, you have the sight as well as being fate-tied to us. Interesting. I would never have thought a human could live among us, let alone become an Edge Walker, yet in you we seem to have found the most naturally talented of our kind we have seen for generations.'

Ynis bit her lip, uncertain what to say. Across the graveyard, more spirits were seething into life, so that the bone-ridden place teemed with uncertain light. She didn't know why she had lied to Frost.

'My sister...' Ynis looked away from the gathering ghosts. 'T'rook doesn't want to stay here. She will not want to be an Edge Walker, and she won't like the idea of me being one either.'

'And what do you think, Ynis?'

The wind picked up, blowing a thin veil of tiny snow particles down over the graveyard. Ynis watched them pass through the ghosts there, scattering over the strange magical bones of the griffins.

'I don't know.' She took a deep breath. Was this a place where she could be accepted by the griffins as one of their own, even though she couldn't fly, had no feathers of her own, had not hatched from an egg? It seemed impossible, yet her eyes were drawn back to the ghosts. She *could* see them. What did that mean? '*I don't know,*' she said again.

'The best way to find out about anything is to do it,' said Frost. 'I will show you some of the duties of an Edge Walker. We will start tomorrow, at dawn. I will send someone for you.'

And with that, Frost spread her wings and was gone. Ynis noticed that she favoured one wing over the other, and she wondered if the injury was still causing the old griffin pain. The wind seemed to vanish with her. Ynis found that she was standing in an eerie silence again, a field of ghosts spread before her. Hunting would have to wait for another night.

'She could have given me a bloody lift.'

The skin on the back of her neck crawling, Ynis walked to the edge of the wall and began to make her way back down, as quickly as her cold hands and feet would take her.

22

A curious thing about the written records of Unblessed Houraki: Titans are barely mentioned in it. Taken in context with the other nations of Enonah, both Blessed and Unblessed, this is more than a little strange – across the world, the Titans have been worshipped as gods, revered as leaders, legends and even the creators of the human race. In every place that Titans once walked, they left behind stories and certainties about their importance to us; they gave us the words to speak when we were little more than apes scrambling in the mud; they elevated us from animal to personhood. Yet there is no such reverence to be found in Unblessed Houraki – instead their spiritual focus is on tens of thousands of 'small gods', household gods that seem almost to leap into being when needed.

Another observation that Crafter Tyleigh might want to take particular note of: the written record seems to come into existence quite abruptly around two thousand years ago. What happened before then in Houraki is anyone's guess – if there were any histories written of that period, they are gone.

Notes from an unnamed Envoy
for Crafter Tyleigh

'Wait.'

Kaeto put his hand to Riz's chest, trying not to notice the rapid thunder of the guide's heartbeat just under his skin. They were stood together in the trees, some distance from that afternoon's camp, and only partially dressed.

'What is it?'

'I thought I heard something. A cry.'

Riz smiled and shook his head slightly. 'You think everything is a danger. Just relax. Enjoy yourself. I certainly am.' He bent his head back to Kaeto's throat, where he had been carefully placing lingering kisses. 'You taste of salt.'

Kaeto let himself be kissed for a time, feeling the burgeoning heat inside him gently push away his concern at leaving Tyleigh and Belise alone together. When he could bear it no longer, he took hold of the younger man by the shoulders and turned him, so that he was the one leaning against the smooth grey bark of the tree. For a time he lost himself as they moved together, pressed tightly to each other, and then Riz's busy hands were at the laces to his trousers.

'It is soft here, on the ground,' Riz murmured into his ear. 'Come and lie down with me.'

'We should get back,' Kaeto murmured, although there was little force to it. He was finding it difficult to think clearly.

You have a duty to the Imperium, he told himself. And then he thought, *Fuck the Imperium.*

'You said the kid can handle herself,' said Riz. His bronzed skin looked almost golden in the dappled midday sun, and it glimmered with sweat. 'And Tyleigh barely takes any notice of you anyway. Just for a few moments, what harm can it do?'

Kaeto was about to give in to his honeyed words when there came another cry, unmistakable this time: it was Belise, shouting something, probably a swear word. And on the heels of that came Tyleigh's voice, and the alchemist sounded angry. Kaeto pushed Riz away sharply and set off at a run through the undergrowth towards their camp. When he got there he found Belise sitting on the ground clutching her arm, and Tyleigh standing over the girl. The older woman whirled on him as he crashed through the bushes.

'Where the bloody hell have you been? Your child has gotten herself bitten!'

'Bitten?' Kaeto dropped to his knees next to Belise. Behind him, he heard Riz enter the camp and wondered what Tyleigh would make of that, but a glance at Belise's face chased all such thoughts from his mind. Her cheeks were flushed, and her lips were pushed into a thin line as though she were trying not to cry – but her eyes were full of tears anyway. 'What happened?'

'There was a beetle...'

'His beetle?' Kaeto nodded at Riz. *If his beetle has hurt her I will kill them both.*

'No, a different one. It was blue, and sniffing around the camp, so I was looking at it.'

'She poked it,' Tyleigh put in. 'Although I told the brat not to.'

Gently, Kaeto took Belise's wrist. 'Show me your arm, please.'

The girl released the death grip on her forearm, and underneath there were two bloody puncture wounds, each the size of the smallest coin in his pocket. The skin around them was inflamed.

'There is a type of fire beetle that will bite like that,' said Riz. Kaeto glanced up; the man was standing over them. He had put his shirt back on at least. 'It can... it is poisonous, I'm afraid.'

Kaeto gave Belise's hand a squeeze and stood up to face Riz.

'And the antidote?'

'It's not as easy as that, my friend...'

Kaeto took another step forward. He was thinking of all the places his knives were hidden, calculating how much pain he would need to inflict, and how quickly.

'Speak swiftly, *my friend*,' he said, his voice low so that Belise would not hear him. 'Because more than one life depends on it, believe me.'

Riz held his hands up. 'You've made your point. There *is* an antidote, alright? We make it from the roots of the teefan plant, but it doesn't grow here. We'll need to get closer to... your destination.'

'And how long do we have?'

'A good few hours, I should think.' Riz glanced down at the girl. He looked a shade paler than he had out under the trees. 'Kid, you're going to feel like shit, but we'll have you well again soon, I promise.'

'Right.' Kaeto bent down and helped Belise to her feet. 'Gather everything together, Tyleigh, we're going now.'

For a long second it looked like Tyleigh might argue, just for the sake of it, but in the end she simply rolled her eyes and began kicking dirt over their cookfire. Riz grabbed his own pack off the ground and slung it over the back of his horse before turning back to Kaeto.

'We'll have to ride fast now, my friend, if we're to get there in time.' He cleared his throat. 'Much faster than we were travelling.'

It seemed to Kaeto that the guide had raised his voice slightly as he spoke, and had there also been a quick glance into the trees? Whatever it was, for now he would file it away for future contemplation. He lifted Belise up onto the horse – despite her protests that her legs were working fine, thank you very much – and in moments they had left the camp behind.

23

There are many legends of the Wild Wood, all about as ridiculous as the next, but one that interests me particularly just for the sheer strangeness of it is the so-called Green Man. This is a figure so sacred to the people of Brittletain that it is barely even spoken of – whereas we in the Imperium talk often of our ancestors the stars, in that backward country it is considered dangerous to speak too casually of the Green Man. He is a changing figure, sometimes human, sometimes animal, sometimes even plant; he is said to be linked to fertility, but also to death; to the harvest and to the wildest places. Questioned closely over many years, few of our captives from that island ever spoke of the Green Man, but there was one elderly prisoner who gave us a few scraps of information. He hinted that the Green Man was himself the forest – that if the forest had a mind, it was the Green Man. Gibberish mostly, I suspect, but it made me wonder if there was some link between this mythical figure and the Druin beast men and women that supposedly litter the Wild Wood. Could they be one and the same?

It's worth noting that when the elderly Briton finally succumbed to many years of punishment, he used his last words to ask if his body could be buried near some trees, so that the Green Man could find him easier. Such notions. His corpse was passed on to Gynid Tyleigh, who has a grisly interest in such things.

Extract from one of the research journals
gathered by the empress's Envoys

Over the next few days, Leven, Epona and Cillian moved steadily through the Wild Wood, following the horned man's lead down a bewildering variety of paths and hills. They might walk for hours on one path, and then Cillian would stop and twist the forest to his will, and the path ahead of them was something different again; a dirt track across a wide meadow peppered with yellow and blue wildflowers; a winding set of flat stones half hidden beneath huge bushes of dark brambles; a high, hilly place where the trees were dropping their leaves like copper and gold coins. It was here that Leven stopped to pick a leaf from her hair. It was dry and it broke to pieces under her fingers.

'Is it autumn here?' she asked. For a moment she felt dizzy, and she wondered if perhaps she had been walking in these woods forever. 'That can't be right, can it? It was summer in the Imperium.'

Epona dropped her bag on the ground and pressed her fingers into the small of her back. The princess, Leven had realised after only a few days in her company, would take any opportunity for a break. Cillian stopped too, turning back to look at them with some impatience.

'Time can be changeable in the Wild Wood,' he said. 'Sometimes we borrow a Path that doesn't quite belong to the here and now.'

Leven turned to Epona. 'That doesn't make any sense. Does it? Please tell me that doesn't make sense to you.'

Epona grinned. She was fishing a small bottle of mead from its place at the bottom of her pack.

'I told you, Herald, it doesn't do you any good to think about it too closely. These things were never meant to be understood by the Imperium's sword. Or by anyone without horns.'

'Yes yes, I know, I am merely an unthinking soldier with nothing but bloodlust in her head. Magic isn't completely unknown to me, you know.' Leven held up her arms and the Titan ore in her skin glittered darkly in the sunlight. 'You might even say I'm close to it.'

'The brutal, twisted magic of the Imperium,' said Cillian, 'is not the magic of the Druin.' On his shoulder, Inkwort gave one of her little honking squawks, and his voice softened. 'I'll do my best to explain. Sometimes, we might find a Path has become impassable – a tree has fallen, or the snows have blocked it off. Sometimes the Dunohi themselves won't let us pass, for reasons of their own. When that happens, we look for an older version of the path. One before the snow fell.'

A gust of chilly wind pelted them with more red and gold leaves.

'I still don't understand what the Dunohi are. They're spirits of some kind? Wood ghosts?'

Cillian put his own pack down on the ground. 'They are like… they are beings made from the wood. Branches, plants, roots, living trees, brought together to make a new thing. They are shy creatures, especially to outsiders. We probably won't see any.'

'Although,' added Epona, 'I'm pretty sure there are ghosts too. Just to be clear.'

'So what is this place?' Leven gestured at the trees around them, which were shedding their leaves in a light golden rain. 'Or should I say, *when* is this?'

'Another autumn,' Cillian said, as if that explained everything. 'But we shouldn't linger here, I'm afraid, Princess.' He gave Epona a meaningful look as she pulled a half loaf of bread from her pack.

'What? This looks like a great place to have lunch.'

And it was, reasoned Leven; they were high up, with the Wild Wood stretching away all around them. It would be possible to see any approaching threat from up here.

'When we take these older Paths, it opens us up to other dangers.' Cillian shouldered his pack again, and began walking back under the trees. 'The longer we stay here, the greater the risk is.'

'The risk of what, exactly?' asked Leven.

'Stay here long enough and you start to… forget. You come unstuck in time.'

'And what does that mean, exactly?'

The horned man didn't answer, and after a moment, Epona put away her bread and honey wine with a great deal of sighing, and she too began to walk down the Path. Leven lingered a little longer, looking out across the wood to a strip of hazy blue on the horizon. If this was last autumn, did that mean that somewhere across the wood and the sea, there was another version of herself, freshly arrived home from the campaign, drinking away her cares in the many taverns of Stratum? Or could it be another autumn entirely, years in the past, when Leven had been Blessed Eleven, a new Herald in the Unblessed lands, the ore-lines in her skin still painful from where they had been burned into her skin?

Or what if it was nine years ago? Or longer? Who was I then?

The question seemed to drop into her head from nowhere, and Leven was afraid. She thought of her visions of a wood in winter; the screaming in the distance, and the unnerving clacking sound she couldn't identify. She made herself look around boldly, to face whatever might be creeping in the spaces between the tree trunks, and then she began to follow the other two. She found that she believed Cillian after all; it wouldn't be wise to be left behind in such a place.

24

Darling Epona,

I will have to invest in a better lock for your apartments, or find some guards who aren't so easily swayed by your nonsense. Still, since you are there, we may as well make use of you. Keep a close eye on the Herald. I will want a full report on your return. Be sure to try and have a hot meal at least once a day, and change your clothes if they get wet.

Yours, in endless tolerance,

Mother

A message sent by bird to Princess Epona,
intercepted by the Atchorn

T wo days after the autumn Path, Cillian led them down out of the Wild Wood and into a stretch of land that felt eerie and old to Leven. The landscape was flat and littered with vast misshapen rocks and boulders, dark grey and covered with red and green lichen, and all around there were stretches of yellow gorse and lilac heather. The sky overhead was huge too, with tall grey clouds moving rapidly across the rich blue. Summer was back, present in the snatches of warmth Leven felt on her face when the wind died down.

'Where are we?'

'The kingdom of Kornwullis, to the west,' said Epona. 'The first place on Mother's little checklist for you.'

Leven frowned. This place did not look anything like the snow-bound forest of her visions. She also couldn't see anything indicating that anyone lived there at all, let alone a thriving kingdom. As if sensing her confusion, Cillian nodded to the rocky bluff they were approaching.

'From there we'll be able to see more clearly where we are going.'

Climbing between the thick mounds of gorse, they reached the top of the small hill, and beyond it there was a long, low stretch of land that dwindled to a jumbled archipelago. This was the furthest western reach of Brittletain, and Leven could see several port towns clustered on the very edge of the land, as well as swarms of busy ships moving in and out on a choppy sea. Far from being a desolate wasteland, Kornwullis was clearly a thriving kingdom of its own.

'I like this place,' said Epona. The wind had blown her black hair over her face and she pushed it out of the way with a grin. 'What is it they say about Kornwullis? *They call a boat a boat.* They *are* very keen on fish though, fair warning.'

'What else can you tell me about it?'

'Ah, figured out that you might need to be prepared?' Epona took Leven by the arm, and together they began to pick their way down the rugged path on the far side. 'I will, of course, be glad to – what would you call it, in the Heralds? Give you your orders? Your briefing?'

'Any information you'd be happy to share, your highness...'

'Alright, alright. Kornwullis is lately the kingdom of Queen Verla, who has three sons and one daughter, all of whom spend most of their time at sea. The royal family here say they are the oldest in Brittletain, claiming that their ancestors were favoured by the oldest Titans, and, well, they do not usually take kindly to diplomacy.'

'They don't?' Leven kept her eyes on the path ahead of her to hide her growing dismay.

'As far as Kornwullis is concerned, they don't need the rest of us, and we don't need them, and they'd be happiest pretending we don't exist. *Especially* Londus. My mother has made various attempts to befriend them over the years, and as yet all we've received are icily polite refusals.'

'And now she's sending me with a... *box*?'

Epona continued as if she hadn't spoken. 'Having said all that, they are a great tradespeople, and their ports are open to all ships.'

'It's said that if you can't find it in a Kornwullis market place, it probably doesn't exist,' added Cillian. His face was turned up to the sun as though he were enjoying its warmth.

Epona tapped her hand sharply. 'I know he's pretty, Herald, but please do pay attention.' To her horror, Leven felt her cheeks grow hot, but Cillian didn't appear to have heard her.

'I've spent the last few months in Stratum, one of the biggest cities in any land, Blessed or Unblessed,' said Leven, largely speaking to cover her embarrassment. 'I doubt there will be much in a Kornwullis port to surprise me.'

'The Imperium truly does believe itself to be the be all and end all, doesn't it?' said Epona, cheerfully enough. 'I still think there's a chance you might be impressed, oh worldly Herald. What else should you know? Oh, and they believe in *pixen* down here, don't they, Cillian? A kind of story for children.'

'The pixen aren't stories,' said Cillian.

'What are they?' asked Leven.

'The word means "little spirit", and it's thought amongst the Druin that they are possibly related to the Dunohi. Spirits of stone and heather, spirits of springs and even the sea.'

'Yes, well. They are very respectful of the pixen down here – the first apples of the harvest are left out for them, the first spoonful of cream from the day's milking, the best of that day's catch left on the rocks. It's really rather sweet.' Epona drummed her fingers across one of the huge boulders that sat by the path. 'We don't go in for that sort of thing in Londus.'

'Londus is too noisy for pixen in any case,' added Cillian. 'And the milk is never fresh enough.'

Leven shook her head. She had the sudden impression that they were mocking her in some subtle way, and she was tired of it. The wind blowing in across the wild, flat landscape was growing colder.

'Your mother would have sent a bird to tell them we were coming?'

Epona nodded.

'So they will send someone to meet us?'

'Oh no,' Epona looked genuinely surprised, 'Queen Verla has no time for any of that. We will get there when we get there, and likely have to knock on a few doors before we find anyone who cares.'

Not for the first time, Leven felt a wave of helplessness move through her. What was she doing here, in this strange kingdom, on a mysterious errand for a queen she didn't know and couldn't trust? Every day seemed to bring more questions, and all the while the biggest of them all – why was she having visions of this backwater country? – was very far from ever being answered.

The young jackdaw, which she had heard Cillian call by the name Inkwort, flew down from the darkening sky and landed on the rocks just to Leven's right, startling her.

'There's a place we can take shelter not far from here,' said Cillian. 'We won't have the light much longer.'

That night they camped between a set of tall standing stones, the bulk of the rocks becoming ever more black and solid as the sun sank beneath the horizon and the stars came out. When the fire was set, Cillian moved beyond the circle of light and into the dark, listening intently. He could hear the wind moving across the heather, and the cries of crows somewhere close by. Princess Epona and the Herald were talking quietly. Out in the dark, lost to shadows already, he could feel the presence of the Wild Wood; teeming and green and full of life, it was calling to him. To be even this far from it was gently painful, like a persistent tug in his chest, and he had considered telling the two women that he would wait for them on the edge of the wood –

let them go to Queen Verla without him, and he could stay where there were familiar roots under his feet. But he knew that Epona would argue, and the Herald wouldn't, which was worse somehow, and most of all, the Druidahnon would expect him to do as he was asked, and not to try and wheedle out of it as soon as he was out of sight of his elders.

And despite his desire to get back to the Wild Wood, there was something else – something that meant that for the first time in his life, he had felt relieved when he had passed out of that sacred place.

You're afraid.

Cillian jumped, casting about to see who had spoken, and then a flutter of soft wings in the dark passed close by his head.

'Inkwort.' He took a slow breath to calm himself and spoke in a murmur. 'So. You're not so silent after all.'

I speak when I wish, child.

And in fact far from being silent, her voice was unwaveringly precise in his head, as clear and as sharp as blackbird song in the morning. He couldn't believe that when he'd quested towards her before he had felt so little. Had she hidden from him? Cillian held himself very still, just in case a sudden movement might cause her to withdraw this confidence. And 'child'? It was unusual for any animal to take a specific tone with a human, let alone a parental one.

You're afraid, she said again. Now that his eyes had adjusted to the dark he could see that she had alighted in the grass and was stalking around in the prancing way that jackdaws had.

'Yes,' he said, reluctant. 'The Wild Wood... feels wrong. I told them that before, the other Druin, but they wouldn't listen. It's angry. About something happening... in the north? I can't make it out.'

Inkwort pecked at something unseen in the grass.

'And it's getting worse.' He paused, and then focused on the atmosphere he had felt in the woods over the last few days: the shadows that felt particularly cold, a darkness that seemed to seep in at the edges. And worse: a half-formed sense of anger, of threat. He felt the jackdaw there with him, feeling what he was feeling. 'What is it? Do you know?'

She ruffled her feathers, and he felt the bird withdrawing her consciousness from him. After another peck at something he couldn't see, she flew off and was lost to the night. Cillian took a step back, trying not to feel the wave of loneliness that threatened to wash over him. Home had never felt farther away.

Leven woke with the dawn, which came fast to that high place. The sky turned lilac, and around them the craggy landscape of Kornwullis crept out of the dark and into a strange, pale light that edged every leaf and stone with silver. Epona was still asleep, curled so deep under her blanket that only a tuft of her black hair was visible, but Cillian was awake. He came over to where Leven stood, leaning against one of the tall stones. As they watched, the lilac was chased from the sky by a pure golden light as the sun peeked out over the horizon, gilding the bottoms of the clouds and tracing the delicate veins of the rivers that lay beneath them. For the first time in a long while Leven forgot about her troubling visions and dangerous blackouts.

'It's certainly a beautiful place,' she said softly. 'I'll give you that. Where did these stones come from?'

Cillian smiled. 'We don't know. Some say that the great bear Titans made the circles, raising stones all across Brittletain, but why they did that has been lost to time. The Druidahnon doesn't talk about them. But we think they serve a similar purpose to the Paths, for those who are no longer living.'

'What?' Leven turned to look at him. 'Dead people? We've been sleeping in a dead-people place?'

'All places are dead-people places,' Cillian said in an infuriatingly reasonable tone.

'Just when I think we're in a quiet, peaceful spot...' Leven stopped. There was movement on the hill below them, a fast, darting shape that made the hair on the back of her neck stand up and her ore-lines prickle. 'There are wolves, down there – look.' She pointed. Now that she had seen the first one, the landscape seemed alive with them. Lithe grey shapes moving around the gorse and the rocks, all heading towards the circle of standing stones. Barely even needing to think, Leven summoned her shimmering blue wings. Behind them, alerted by the blue light of the Herald magic, Epona groaned and sat up.

'What's going on? Hey, your wings—'

Leven summoned her sword. 'Get behind me, both of you.'

'Wait.' Cillian's hand on her arm was warm. 'There's something strange going on here. The wolves are not—'

'There's nothing strange about getting torn to pieces by wolves, it happens all the time.' Leven stopped. The closest wolf, the one she had her eye on, had looked perfectly solid as it wound its way through the dense gorse, but as the first full rays of sunshine fell across it the animal seemed insubstantial, a shadow creature. As she watched, the others vanished and reappeared in a similar fashion.

'What *are* they?'

Epona had appeared at their side. She pointed down the slope, eyes squinted against the sun.

'And who's that?'

Leven would have sworn there had been no man there a moment ago, but now there was; a tall, lean man dressed in raggedly armour, his chain mail riddled with holes and an enormous sword slung across his back. He had a single horn curling from one side of his head, and he wore a thin circlet of bronze. It was clear that he was moving with the wolves, that they were flanking him, almost as though they were his escort.

'It's a spirit,' said Cillian, in a low voice. 'Herald, put away your weapons and stand aside. We have to let it pass.'

Leven hesitated. The wolf man was coming up the hill directly towards them, and she could not quite take her eyes from the vast sword.

'Herald,' Cillian spoke again, impatience in his voice. 'It's a ghost of the dawn. It likely will move straight past us without even noticing we're here.'

Leven took a step back as the wolf man crested the hill. The wolves came up alongside him, their yellow eyes bright even as their bodies faded and flickered like shadows. Now that he was closer, Leven could see that the man was old, ancient even, although he moved easily enough. His white beard was tied into a neat braid, and his eyes were sharp and blue. Epona and Cillian moved back, and Leven let her wings and sword vanish.

When the man and his wolves stepped inside the circle, the soft warmth of the early sun was replaced with a bitter cold, harsh enough that Leven could see her own breath in front of her – the man and wolves had no such vapour in front of their mouths. As Cillian had predicted, they did not look at the three of them as they passed, and didn't appear to be aware of them at all. As he came close enough to touch, Leven could see scars on the old man's leathery skin, and thick bands of silver on his fingers; one of his ears had once been cut away in some brutal fight and what was left was partly scar tissue, and the single horn that curled from his head had been carved with leaping, swirling shapes. Without knowing why, Leven felt a great wave of sadness move through her. *Who was this man? What did he witness during his long life, and what has he lost?*

Just as Leven had accepted that the wolf man and his charges would pass them peacefully, the old man stopped, and turned. He raised one hand uncertainly, and sunlight slanted through it like it was made of glass. He was staring, thunderstruck, at Cillian.

'Can it be?' The ghost's voice was like the rushing of a river. 'Can it be I've found you, after all this time?'

Epona raised her eyebrows. She spoke out of the corner of her mouth.

'He's talking to you, Cillian.'

The Druin looked lost for a moment, and then stepped forward. The little jackdaw on his shoulder gave a short *tchack* and fell silent.

'Spirit, I am not who you seek. Please, we don't wish to delay you. Keep on your journey.'

'But it *is* you, my lord. I've wandered for so long, from stone to stone, and never thought that I would actually...' Inkwort spread her wings and was gone, up into the early-morning sky, and the movement seemed to confuse the old ghost. He looked away from Cillian, his eyebrows drawing together, uncertain now. 'I'm sure... It's said he would come back... He swore it.'

Around him the wolves were moving on, across the middle of the stone circle and back down the far side of the hill, and like a grey shadowy tide they seemed to take the old ghost with them. He looked around once, as though he'd lost sight of something and could not quite remember what it was, and then his features cleared. He walked on with his wolves, and as Leven watched, all of them faded into the shadows and were lost.

For a long moment, no one spoke. The cold that had invaded the stone circle faded, and as the warmth returned so did the early-morning birdsong. Epona let out a noisy sigh.

'What was that all about, Cillian? Who did he think you were?'

The horned man shook his head, looking troubled. 'I don't know. The dead that travel the stones can be very old indeed, and the stones, like the Paths, have a strange relationship with time.' He stopped, although Leven had the distinct impression he had more to say. 'I don't know. We may as well clear up the camp and get moving, as early as it is.'

Epona yawned. 'Don't worry,' she said, 'after that little encounter I doubt I will ever sleep again.'

25

It was full dark by the time they reached the area Riz insisted contained the antidote plant, and the jungle itself was closer and wilder on all sides. The road was gone, the wide slabs of sandstone getting smaller and then breaking up into pieces, until the undergrowth had eaten it entirely. Tyleigh and Riz were both carrying lamps, while Kaeto kept one hand on Belise's shoulder, to stop her from toppling off the horse. Over the last few hours she had grown increasingly shivery, and was complaining of feeling dizzy.

'Here, look.' Riz slipped from the back of his horse and pushed his way through the thick green foliage. The light from his lantern sent dagger-like shadows skittering across the bushes. 'Here is the teefan flower. We'll need to dig up three or four of the roots, and make a tea. And your girl will feel better quickly.'

'Get on with it then,' snapped Tyleigh. 'The sooner this nonsense is sorted out the sooner we can get on with the real reason we are here.'

'For once, I agree with you,' said Kaeto, ignoring the poisonous look she shot him. 'Belise, you can sit with the lamps while we find your medicine.'

An hour or so later it was done. They made another small camp, and Riz cut up the roots of the teefan plant before stewing them over the fire with water from Kaeto's pack. The result was a thin yellowish liquid that looked, according to Belise, like 'hot piss'; Kaeto sampled it before passing it to her and had to agree she wasn't far off in her assessment. The soft fibrous remains of the teefan root were made into a bitter-smelling poultice that Kaeto fixed to the wounds with a bandage, but by that time Belise was already looking a lot brighter. She sat by the fire, the cup of tea held in her hands. To Kaeto, she looked very small, and younger than her years.

'We may as well camp here for the night,' he said. 'We won't get much further in the dark, and Belise should try and get a full night's sleep.'

Tyleigh shook her head, her lips quirking into a bitter smile.

'This is what the Imperium gives me,' she muttered. 'A nursemaid.'

When, eventually, Tyleigh and Belise were asleep – squeezed into the tiny area of flat ground they'd found amongst the trees – Kaeto found himself once again facing Riz across the fire. All their earlier intimacy had fled, leaving behind a husk of something else; a wall built of equal parts longing and mistrust.

'She's a strong kid,' said Riz, a little too brightly. His own beetle was keeping out of sight. Kaeto wondered if Riz had ordered it to do so. 'She'll be back to herself in the morning, you'll see.'

'You're very lucky that the tea worked,' said Kaeto quietly.

'And you're lucky I knew where to find the antidote,' said Riz, but there was no heat to his words. 'She's not your daughter. But that doesn't really matter, does it?'

'Belise is my responsibility,' said Kaeto. 'And that is all you need to know.'

'For what it's worth, I'm glad she's alright.' Riz smiled hesitantly. There was something very like hope in it. 'I did tell you that there are a thousand ways to die out here, didn't I? If anything we've been lucky.'

Kaeto looked at the younger man for a long moment. In another place, in another time, if he were a different man with other loyalties, this evening might have ended differently. But pleasure and affection were treasures for other people. His domain had always been the dark, and the careful application of pain.

'For your sake,' he said, 'I hope our luck holds.'

The next day was hot and oppressive, the air so thick that it seemed to turn into something wet and filthy the moment it touched Kaeto's lips. Belise was undoubtedly back to herself, peering from under her broad hat at every strange plant or colourful bird, asking Tyleigh questions and watching everything in her careful way. Most people, Kaeto knew, took Belise for what she appeared to be – a gutter-born child making the most of her new station in life. But such people were precisely as unobservant as Belise was cunning; he knew that everything she saw and learned was carefully parcelled away for future examination, ready for when he needed a fresh pair of eyes or a new angle on an old subject.

'We are close.' Riz's voice floated back from the head of the party. 'Not much further to your destination, my friends.'

'Close? The Black City is out here in the middle of this stinking jungle?' Tyleigh was riding just behind Riz, her blue headband dark with sweat.

'I'd rather you didn't name it, especially not here.' Kaeto could hear the wince in Riz's voice. 'But yes. Within the next few hours.'

They picked their way through the jungle until the sun began to sink behind them, finally summoning a cooler period of twilight. The noise from the insects all around increased, becoming a cacophony that drowned out even the birds. And then, just as it seemed they would be spending the night walking through the Houraki jungle in the pitch black, Riz stopped. He slid down from his horse's back and stood waiting for them.

'Well?' demanded Tyleigh. 'What are you doing? Are you saying we should make camp again?'

'We are here,' Riz said, simply enough.

'If you have led us out here into the middle of nowhere as a joke, I will have the Imperial backstabber here string you up from the nearest tree…'

'Mistress Tyleigh,' said Kaeto, and to his surprise she grew quiet. Feeling deeply uneasy, he climbed down from his own horse and went over to the guide. It was dark enough that he couldn't quite make out the expression on the man's face. Inside his pocket, his fingers closed over the handle of a small dagger.

'We are here? At the Black City?'

'ReRe,' said Riz. 'Show them, please.'

With a whirring of wings the beetle flew off the saddle bag and suddenly it was a flying lamp; the lower half of its abdomen glowed a fierce greenish-yellow. For a second Kaeto was sure this was it, this was the ambush – the light served both as a way to dazzle them and signal the bandits. His dagger was half out of his pocket before he saw the structure, now revealed in the light from ReRe, just beyond the trees. He heard Belise swear from her spot on the back of the horse.

'It's a wall,' he said.

Although it was difficult to tell in the harsh glare from the beetle's belly, it looked to be made of more of the sandstone, and it stretched up and up, out of sight. The trees themselves grew right up next to it, and there were vines tracing all over it, like veins across a body. It was the proximity of the trees that had made it so invisible in the near dark.

Kaeto walked forward, following Riz and ReRe. As he got closer, he saw that the wall wasn't entirely featureless. There were recesses in the stone, around every four or five feet, and at about head height. Each one housed a small clay figurine, much like the ones Riz had produced from his pack.

'More of your gods.' Light flowed into one of the recesses revealing a squat figure with many legs, its shadow climbing the wall behind it like a spider.

'A bloody wall?' snapped Tyleigh. 'What's the use in that?'

'The use of it,' said Riz, 'is that it keeps everyone out. The curious, the stupid, and the spies of the Imperium.' From around them, the lights of many beetles flickered into life amongst the trees, illuminating a number of men and women with a variety of weapons, all of which were aimed at their small group. 'Welcome to the Black City.'

26

S cree was furious; Ynis could see that immediately. His crest and neck feathers were bristling like the needles on a pine tree, and his dark eyes flashed dangerously. She planted her feet in the snow and forced herself to stand where she was and face him.

'I can think of no greater insult to our order, Frost,' he said. They were stood on one of the high snowy paths that led to a series of resting caves. Frost had been taking her to see one of the recent arrivals, to give her a better idea of an Edge Walker's duties. Until Scree had arrived. 'A human, learning witch-seer secrets? I've never heard the like.'

'We are hardly known for our adherence to tradition, Scree.' Witch-seer Frost did not sound concerned at his display of anger. She turned her head from him to preen at a shoulder feather, and Ynis felt a spike of alarm; to show your bared neck to an angered griffin with such indifference was a significant insult – it suggested you saw them as no kind of threat. 'We have always walked on the outer edges of griffin tradition. That's why it attracts... eccentrics. We are practical, though. The human girl has a gift, and I intend to use it. To not do so would be wasteful.'

'A gift?' sneered Scree. 'She claims to see the dead? Any child could claim such.'

'Like you do, Scree?'

The older griffin gave a harsh cry of outrage, and despite herself Ynis shrank back.

'You dare? I am your natural successor, Frost. We've known that for years.' He laughed then, and shook his head. The bones of his headdress rattled. 'You're making a fool of yourself.'

'If I am such a fool, Scree, then get out of my way and let me be. I haven't the energy to scrap with you today.'

The older griffin regarded them in silence for a moment, and then he took off, huge dark wings lifting him up into the sky. Frost shook her head wearily and began to clamber up the final part of the path.

'Scree has considered himself a witch-seer in training for much of his adult life, although Great T'vyn knows I've never bloody encouraged it,' Frost said, cheerfully enough. 'Convinced he is special, that one. Ynis, beware of those who are convinced of their own specialness – it usually means they can't see further than their own beaks.'

Ynis nodded, although she felt deeply uneasy. She turned and looked behind them. The Bone Fall stretched away like a great bowl of dark glass dusted with snow, and Scree himself had already vanished beyond it. Ahead of them were the bleak rocky hills that stood to the north of the graveyard, and now that they were closer, Ynis could see caves that pitted the face of them like honeycomb. The path they were on led past a series of them.

'Witch-seer Frost, why could we not fly here? Walking takes so much longer.'

Frost shot the girl an amused glance over her shoulder.

'Think yourself important enough to be carried around on my back, do you?'

Ynis grimaced. She felt almost woozy with embarrassment.

'Oh, no, not at all! I just meant... I am very used to travelling with my sister. She gets so annoyed with how long it takes for me to walk anywhere, and...'

Frost gave a harsh bark of laughter. 'I am teasing you, yenlin. We approach these caves cautiously and reverently, our wings carefully folded – not that you'd have any trouble with that – because the griffins who come here are in the very last moments of their lives, and we owe them our respect. That, and some great beefy fool dropping out of the sky might just shock a greatly aged griffin straight into their grave before they are ready. And it is our duty to make sure they are ready, girl.'

Ynis found that she was half smiling, so she carefully rearranged her features.

'How do we do that?'

'You will see very shortly.'

They had arrived at the entrance to a cave. Someone had left large sprigs of hare's blood, a mountain plant with bright red flowers, on the ground outside, the long stems weighted down with stones. The interior was full of shadows. Frost placed her great brown paw on the threshold.

'We mark the entrances of occupied caves with hare's blood.'

Ynis thought hard. 'The colour is significant? Because these griffins are losing their own life's blood? Is it to do with the colour of Fionovar's feathers?'

Frost cocked her head. 'Perhaps. But mainly it is easy to see in this cold, grey place. The last thing a dying griffin needs is another dying griffin blundering their way into their cave. It makes things very awkward.' The old griffin clicked her beak with amusement. 'You will find that much of the work of an Edge Walker is about practicalities and kindnesses, Ynis, something that Scree and his ilk find rather frustrating.'

Witch-seer Frost gave a low call in the back of her throat, and the sound echoed down the cave ahead of them, a haunting, uneasy noise that made all the hairs on the back of Ynis's neck stand up. Then she walked into the tunnel, and Ynis followed on behind. To her surprise, the place wasn't as dark as she had initially thought; on the ceiling were small pieces of stone that glowed with their own pale blue light. They were both beautiful and unsettling.

'What are these lights?'

Witch-seer Frost glanced upwards. 'Shards of griffin bone from the Bone Fall, their last pieces of soul-light held within them. A *lot* of our work is practical, yes, but a fair amount is full of that sort of uncanny malarky, too. Here, we are at the chamber now, so keep your ears and eyes open and your beak shut.'

The chamber was small and round, with just enough room for three griffins to stand close to one another. On the floor lay the oldest griffin Ynis had even seen. His feathers and fur were the colour of dust, and as he breathed – slowly, and with difficulty – it was possible to see the outline of his ribs moving against his skin. Standing over him was a much younger claw clan griffin, the fur on his body a warm tawny brown and his long flight feathers a deep, striking blue. The younger male looked up at their entrance.

'Witch-seer, my father is very close to the end now. Will you... is that a *human*?'

Ynis attempted to shrink back, but Frost only shouldered her further into the room.

'A student of mine. She is here to observe only.'

The younger griffin snapped his beak together, tasting the air. 'Very well. The ways of the Edge Walkers have always been strange.' He took a step back, and Ynis realised that he was not just wary of her; he was scared of Frost, too. She remembered T'rook's reaction to the Edge Walkers and the Bone Fall – how horrified she had been. Again, she was reminded that this was an aspect of griffin life – and death – that had been kept from her entirely. The thought made her feel strange inside.

'Your father's name?' asked Frost.

'He is called T'wesen, of the talon clan.'

Frost then asked the younger griffin all about T'wesen's life; about the breeding partners he'd had, the yenlin he had hatched and raised, the places he had hunted and flown all his life. T'wesen himself appeared to be in a thin kind of sleep, and watching him Ynis would sometimes see his eyelids flicker as certain names were mentioned.

He is listening, she thought. *Somewhere, he is listening.* And the reciting of the names seemed to calm his son too – soon the powerful muscles on his shoulders became slack, and some of the manic fright eased from his eyes.

It feels like a ritual, thought Ynis, *but it has a practical use, just like Frost said. It has put the frightened one at ease, and let T'wesen know he is no longer among strangers. We know all about him now – all the important parts of his long life.*

When that was done, Frost turned back to Ynis and beckoned her to come closer. By this time the young griffin had settled on the ground next to his father, one of his own paws resting, almost timidly, on T'wesen's outstretched leg. When Frost spoke to Ynis, the younger griffin paid no attention.

'Remember, Ynis, when we were at the Bone Fall and you saw one of the ghosts of our ancestors, moving in the dark? Do you remember how that felt?'

'I do,' said Ynis. *I felt bloody frightened,* she thought.

'I want you to sit here now, with T'wesen, and I want you to put yourself into that mindset again. Look for the things that are hidden.'

Ynis did as she was told, sitting cross-legged on the ground, which was covered in soft down and old, dry grass. She tried to relax in the quiet gloom of the cave, but her eyes kept being drawn back to the old griffin's son. She thought he might be the most beautiful griffin she had ever seen; the small feathers on his head shaded from warm brown to the blue of a summer sky, and his eyes were crystal green.

Frost nudged her.

'Concentrate. Watch T'wesen. He is very close to the end now. Pay no attention to what I do – I just want you to observe T'wesen.'

It was true, Ynis realised. T'wesen's breaths were more infrequent, the soft rise and fall of his chest slowing, slowing. She looked at him closely, taking in his old bones and his thin fur, and wondered what it must be like to know you were at the end of all things. Frost was standing over him, her head bowed, and she was murmuring something to him, words Ynis could not catch. Instead, she watched and watched for what felt like hours, until her eyes began to hurt and the image of the old griffin seemed to shiver and double. And then she realised that it wasn't her tired eyes after all. There was another image of T'wesen, a soft ghostly double that moved almost, but not quite, in tandem with him, and the longer she watched, the more out of sequence it was with the physical body. This double image was pale and watery, the same pale blue as the lights that had lit the tunnel. Surprised, and more than a little afraid, Ynis looked up to see if the young griffin with the handsome blue feathers had noticed. She was sure he must have, it was right there in front of him, his own paw crossing that of the ghostly griffin, but no... He sat, unmoving still, watching his father die with sadness, but no surprise. He could not see it.

Witch-seer Frost stopped her murmuring and turned slightly to Ynis.

'You see him, don't you, child?'

Ynis nodded.

'Good. I knew that you would. Now. Look at what surrounds T'wesen. Look for where his life leads.'

Frowning slightly, Ynis let her eyes move around the ghostly form, but she didn't know what Frost was talking about. The ghostly figure itself was starting to move independently of the body lying prone on the floor. She saw it lift its head and look around.

'Ah, he is leaving us now,' said Frost. The witch-seer dipped her head and tenderly touched her beak to the young griffin's bowed head. 'Prepare yourself, young one.'

'Wait...' Ynis squinted desperately. 'I can't...'

'Watch me now, Ynis.' Frost leaned forward, opening her beak over the head of T'wesen, and that was when Ynis saw it: a thin red thread with the consistency of smoke rising up from the ghost form of the dying griffin. The thread rose and twisted in strange shifting patterns, and led straight to the son. Frost bent her head and snapped her beak shut, cutting through the thread cleanly. Ynis watched as one end of the thread curled back, sinking into the ghostly form of T'wesen, making him appear somehow brighter, while the other end sank into the body of the younger griffin. It shone, bright as fresh blood on white snow, and then it was gone. All of it was gone: the thread, the ghost, and the life of T'wesen.

'There.' Witch-seer Frost smoothed an errant feather on T'wesen's bony head. 'It's done. You did well.'

Ynis didn't know which of them she was talking to. She rubbed at her cheeks and was amazed to find tears there – she scrubbed them away quickly with the backs of her hands.

'Come.' Frost was brusque again, shoving Ynis back towards the tunnel entrance. 'We'll leave our friend here for a moment, and more of our order will arrive shortly to help take T'wesen to the Bone Fall, where he can rest.'

Ynis cast one more look at the griffin with the bright blue feathers, but he was still looking mournfully at his father's body. Outside in the daylight once more, she shivered. Inside the cave she had not felt the cold at all. It was as though she had just woken from a dream.

'I feel... strange.'

'Yes. Witch-seer magic. That is what it is like.' Frost ruffled her feathers as if throwing off a creeping sense of strangeness herself. 'Tell me what you saw.'

'I saw him. I saw his... spirit. And I saw a thin red thread that led from him to his son.'

Frost eased her claws from their sheaths in pleasure. 'Yes, good. What you saw was a fate-tie. And you saw it very quickly too – it took me many such vigils before I could see them.'

'But what was it?'

'When we make close bonds to other griffins,' she paused, 'or, with other humans, I suppose, part of our soul is tied to them for life. Some will have many such ties. Some, like T'wesen, will have only the one. Sometimes there will be those sad souls who make no such bonds...' She shook her head. 'They are impossible to see, for most.

Not for you though, Ynis. It is like I told you when you arrived here. You have been close to death, you have lived already in the place that sits between this world and the next. You can see the structures and the substance of the Edge.'

Ynis swallowed hard. She wasn't sure how she felt about this. 'Then why... why did you cut it? With your beak?'

'Ah.' Far to the west, the sun was easing towards the horizon, a pale orange ball of cold fire. 'It is hard to lose someone you are so bonded with. Very hard. We cut that tie at the end so that the one left behind isn't half pulled into death with their loved one. You see it, sometimes. The husband who loses his wife and then cannot move on with his own life – he becomes ground-stuck, he does not groom his wings or hunt, he wastes away. The mother who loses the newly hatched and cannot bear to see each new morning without them. This way, a piece of the fate-tie remains with them, something that becomes a part of them and can never be taken, while the soul that moves on is able to do just that – to move on. Cleanly and with joy. Do you see?'

Ynis did not reply. She was thinking of the way the thread had curled and snapped back into the younger griffin, as if it belonged there. And of how the ghost had seemed brighter, just before it vanished.

Frost nodded, as though Ynis had somehow given the correct reply anyway.

'You will be able to see them easier now, yenlin – the fate-ties and the souls. It will mark you out as different to the others. To the other Edge Walkers, to your sister. It is not easy what we do, but it is an honour.'

'We?'

'Witch-seers.' Frost stretched one wing, briefly sheltering Ynis beneath it. 'That is what you are, child, make no mistake. Welcome home.'

27

The hierarchy of Brittletain is about as chaotic as you would expect. There is no overall ruler, no high-king or emperor. Instead, the island – which is small enough already, compared to the territories of the Blessed – is split up into several kingdoms, each ruled over by a king, or more usually, a queen. Even the term queen here has a slightly different meaning than a citizen of the Imperium might expect. Rather than a hereditary title passed down from royal parent to royal child, the queens of Brittletain are more rightly warlords, the privilege of queendom passed to whoever has caused the most carnage in recent years. Queen Broudicca, of the south-eastern kingdom of Londus, is perhaps the most prominent and, although I hesitate to use the term in connection to Brittletain at all, perhaps the most civilised. Her portion of the island contains one of its largest ports, and consequently, is one of the richest territories. She is said to be a pragmatic woman, with several equally formidable daughters.

Extract from *The Foundations of Conquest*,
a text originally commissioned
by Emperor Lumious

The land to the west of the standing stones was sparsely populated, but for the first time Leven began to spot signs that people were living in the wilds of Kornwullis. They passed tiny cottages built of dark grey stone, their roofs covered in gorse and lichen so that they looked more like barnacles on the landscape than human dwellings, and once they saw a figure on the top of a distant hill, driving great horned beasts across the grass and scree; to Leven they looked a little like the cows she would see in Stratum's markets, but much larger, and covered in shaggy brown and red hair. The figure was clearly watching them, but gave no reaction to Epona's enthusiastic waving. Over the course of that day the blue vault of the sky was filled with dense grey cloud that seemed so close Leven felt she could almost touch it, and a cold, wild wind started to blow. Not long after that, their path took them across another rocky hill, and here Cillian suggested they stop to eat and rest for a while before making the final push towards Zenore, the sprawling port town Leven had spotted when they'd left the Wild Wood.

Epona sat down on one of the rocks and began unlacing her boots.

'I dread to think what I am about to unleash on you, given we've been walking for days, but my feet need some air.'

Cillian, who had been in the middle of building a fire, took a few steps to one side to avoid standing down wind. Leven laughed.

'While you do that I'm going to have a look around.'

Cillian spared her a glance. 'Don't wander too far. I'm not chasing after you if you get lost.'

Despite herself, Leven felt a prickle of annoyance. 'I've travelled across Unblessed nations you've likely never heard of, Druin. I reckon I can cope with a stretch of open country.'

Without waiting to see what his reply would be, Leven left them in the rocky outcrop and began to make her way down the side of the rugged hill. In truth, the exposed landscape of Kornwullis was making her uneasy, and as they had started to see more people the closer they got to Zenore, she wanted to at least walk the perimeter of the camp to check that they were unobserved. Such behaviour was a throwback to her days on campaign with Boss and Foro and the others, and something about that offered a comfort of some kind.

The going was slower than she would have liked; the ground underfoot was sandy and unstable, pebbles and chunks of rock breaking away and skittering down the slope with every footstep. And then, just as she'd started to convince herself that they were indeed alone under the grey sky, she had the distinct feeling that she was being watched.

Leven looked back up the way she had come, in case Epona or Cillian had decided to follow, but there was no sign of them.

'Hello?' She kept her voice low. 'Is someone there?'

There was no reply, but the hairs on the back of her neck stood up.

'If someone is there, make yourself known. Or I will not be responsible for what happens to you.'

She lifted her hands, prepared to summon her wings and sword, but at that moment the cold wind turned freezing, and the edges of her vision went dark.

Stars' arses, not now.

The ground underneath her seemed to tip and roll, and she was back in the wintery wild wood. She was frightened, and somehow small, and someone had a firm grip on her shoulder. Leven tried to turn, to see who it was, but the fingers dug in, as cold and as hard as iron, keeping her facing forward.

'Who are you? What do you want?'

She stumbled in the roots and leaf litter, but the hand never left her shoulder. And then out of the dark came the sound she had come to dread.

Click click click. Clack clack clack. Clickclickclick.

'No! You can't—'

A sudden sharp pain at her elbow made the winter forest wobble and then vanish, and Leven found herself lying awkwardly amongst the rocks at the foot of the hill. The day seemed darker than it had, and as she sat up, the landscape itself seemed untrustworthy; parts of it scampered and moved away from her.

'Shit.' She sat up. She had clearly fallen or slipped, and struck her elbow on the rocks. Her shirt was torn and bloody. '*Shit.*'

As she lifted her arm to examine the damage, she spotted a small creature near the offending rock. The tiny thing was crouched over it, lapping at the smear of blood, and even as she took this in she realised she was surrounded by things just like it, tiny scampering creatures that were watching her with bright black eyes like beads of glass. To her eye they looked like a strange amalgamation of landscape, human and rodent – the thing that lapped at her blood had arms and legs, tiny, long-fingered hands, and a furry face with a twitchy nose. Long blades of grey-green grass sprouted from the back of its head and the bony curl of its spine, while yellow and orange lichen covered its torso like a crusty jacket.

'What... what are you?' Leven rubbed one hand across her eyes. 'Wait, are you the pixen Epona was talking about?'

At the sound of her voice some of the creatures took a few steps backwards; others glanced at each other, as though wary or amused. The one that had tasted her blood came closer and actually reached out to take hold of her shirt. It tugged at the fabric, pulling her arm down sharply with surprising strength. With a cold feeling Leven realised that it was trying to get to the wound on her elbow, no doubt to continue its feast.

'Get off!' Leven scrambled to her feet and the pixen scattered with a noise that sounded suspiciously like laughter. She had one last glimpse of tiny, darting shapes and then in less than an eyeblink they were all gone; vanished, she assumed, into the dark spaces between the rocks. Leven shivered, brushed herself down, and began to climb back up the hill. All desire to walk the perimeter of their camp had fled.

When she got back to the top, Cillian had the fire burning merrily and Epona was brewing tea in a small clay pot. The princess raised her eyebrows.

'You've missed the first pot so I'm making a fresh one,' she said. 'I was beginning to think you had made a run for it.'

'What would you do if I did?' Leven came and sat down next to the fire, glad of its merry heat after the cold slopes of the hill. 'Send your horned man after me?'

'You think you are untouchable, Herald, but you likely wouldn't survive long in the wilds of Brittletain alone,' Epona replied airily. 'Bears, wolves, the Dunohi. You certainly wouldn't get to see the griffins you're so keen on seeing.'

'And there are other things besides,' said Cillian. 'Even here, it's best not to travel alone.'

Leven thought of the pixen that had surrounded her, and the ancient ghost that had walked through the standing stones. She wondered if she should mention what she'd seen to the others, but it felt too much like admitting she had been in danger – and in danger from beings no bigger than her hand. Instead, she smiled sunnily at them both.

'Luckily I am much too charmed by your company to leave you both behind.'

'What's that?' Epona tugged at her sleeve, and the fabric of Leven's shirt clung stickily to the graze on her elbow.

'Just scraped myself on the rocks,' said Leven quickly, 'nothing to worry about.'

Epona nodded, apparently satisfied with that explanation, but Cillian gave her a long, considering look, as though he knew exactly how she'd injured herself.

'Drink your tea,' said Epona, passing Leven a warm clay cup. 'This is my own blend. Pink rose, cornflower, lavender, nettle, sorrel...'

'You drink a lot of this stuff,' said Leven. She took a sip, pursing her lips at the sharp floral taste. Much to her own annoyance, it was growing on her.

'Brittletain princesses are practically weaned on it.'

'Drink up,' said Cillian. 'If we get a few more hours' walking in before sundown we should reach Zenore tomorrow.'

28

I n a way, it was a relief.

Kaeto threw his knife towards one of the men waiting in the trees and he caught it in his throat, making a brief gurgling sound before he fell backwards and was lost in the undergrowth. He counted five more figures in the trees as well as a confusing number of beetles, their rear ends glowing, and when he glanced back towards the horses he saw that despite her sore arm Belise was already gone; he allowed himself a small smile as he charged forward and slammed Riz into the wall he had led them to. The shorter man gave a surprised grunt as all the air was crushed out of his lungs, and from behind them Kaeto heard a pair of shouts as two of the bandits found Belise's own lethal daggers buried in their kidneys.

And they thought the darkness was on their side.

Riz looked like he might be attempting to get up, so Kaeto punched him hard on the side of the head – something Kaeto didn't like to do often, because skilled hands were very important in this job – and the guide slumped back down again, his eyes unfocused. By this time the three bandits in the trees had surged forward, either to get away from Belise or to take him down. He slipped back behind a tree just as a crossbow bolt sprouted from the trunk on the other side. He pulled another, slightly longer dagger from his belt and stepped neatly out next to the man who had charged over to the trees after him. He had long dirty blonde hair, which Kaeto grabbed and yanked forcefully downwards, exposing the man's neck for a quick deep cut.

Somewhere back on the path, he could hear Tyleigh shouting about something.

Of course she would draw attention to herself, he thought as blood spattered down his good clean tunic. *Clever as the stars but with as much sense as a scalded cat.*

Two left, and one of them, a tall woman with a nasty-looking hand axe, was at Tyleigh's horse, trying to drag the woman out of the saddle. The second, another woman who could have been a sister to the first, was drawing back a short bow. Kaeto moved back out of her range but Belise was already there; the woman screamed in agony as the tendon in the back of her ankle was sliced neatly through, and then her scream grew choked and broken as Belise did something that Kaeto couldn't quite see. He ran instead to the woman with the axe, who was finding Tyleigh a more difficult prospect than she had expected. The Imperium's most celebrated alchemist and bone crafter had pulled her legs up in the air and was frantically kicking at her attacker, landing the odd strike across the woman's chin or throat. The horse was trying to walk sideways into the trees.

'That's enough,' said Kaeto. The woman whirled on him, and faster than he was expecting threw her axe directly at his head. Kaeto ducked, feeling the whoosh of air as the axe passed over, and then used his momentum to leap back up with the dagger in front of him. It caught the woman under the ribcage and he thrust upwards firmly. She closed her hands around his, a grimace of absolute fury on her face, and then the reality of the blade sticking out of her belly caught up with her. She slid slowly to the ground, her expression of fury fading to something between surprise and despair.

'All done, chief.' Belise was back at his side. The only sign of the activities of the last few minutes was a slight pink cast to her cheeks. 'No more in the trees that I can see.'

'Good. How is your arm?'

'It's fine.' Belise held it up. The poultice had fallen off. 'Just a bit itchy.'

'What in the stars' arses was that about?' Tyleigh, to her credit, did not look frightened, but she did look very angry. 'Did you just go out and find the most obvious bunch of criminals you could, Envoy? You do realise that I could have been killed? The lynchpin of the Imperium's success, murdered in the middle of bloody nowhere for the sake of a few coins. What would the empress have to say about that?'

'Well done, Belise,' Kaeto said, deciding to ignore Tyleigh for the time being. 'What happened to the other... bugs?'

'I skewered a couple, and the rest all scarpered once the fighting started,' said Belise. 'So much for them being good pets!'

'Hmm.' Kaeto went to each body on the ground and searched them, but there was nothing of particular interest. The coins and waterskins he found on them he gave to Belise to put with their own packs, and let her have the pick of the jewellery, although it wasn't an especially lavish selection. Lastly he went over to the wall where Riz was just beginning to come around. His beetle, ReRe, was scuttling over his chest, the long antennae whipping back and forth frantically.

'You will order your beetle to leave us, or I will kill it.'

Riz still looked faintly dazed, but when Kaeto held up his dagger the guide pulled himself up into a sitting position.

'ReRe, go,' he croaked. 'Go *home*, ReRe. I will be there later. Home.'

The beetle scampered off, did a frantic circle in the dirt, and then vanished into the undergrowth.

'Well, that didn't really go according to plan.' Riz coughed weakly. 'Who *are* you people?'

'I've a number of questions for you,' said Kaeto. 'I'm going to ask a few of them now, and a few more later. For each question that you don't answer, or if I feel you have lied to me, Belise here will remove a finger.'

Belise appeared at his side with one of her daggers. It was still bloody.

'She doesn't have her bone saw with her, but she can make do with the dagger. It'll just take longer.'

'Did you... did you kill all of them?' Riz sat up a little straighter. Now he had fully regained consciousness he was clearly starting to realise the trouble he was in. 'Gods strike me, I told them this would be an easy job...'

'Listen.' Kaeto gave him a little shake. 'They are all dead but you don't have to join them. Here are your questions. Is it safe here? Are there others? Will they come here?'

Riz licked his lips. 'N-no. No, that's it, that's the whole band. Gods. The whole lot of them, dead.' Somewhere behind them, the woman with the dagger in her belly was gasping her last.

'Alright. Your next question. Pay attention, please. Do you actually know the way into this place? Into the Black City? Or was that a lie?'

Riz blinked rapidly. His face had taken on a grey cast. This was something that Kaeto recognised; he was going into shock. He took a slim silver bottle from within his shirt and held it out to the guide.

'Drink that. Quickly.'

Riz looked up, then took the bottle. When it was uncorked he sniffed it, then took a big slug. He passed it back.

'Better? So, do you know the way into this place, or was that a ruse?'

Riz shook his head. 'I know a way, yeah. It's not far.'

'Good. You will tell me where it is.'

'If I do that, you'll just kill me.'

'Belise...'

The girl stepped forward, a big smile on her face. She never got tired of the wet work.

'No, honestly, I'll take you there,' said Riz. 'I'll take you to the entrance, I promise.'

'Oh you're coming in with us regardless,' said Kaeto. 'After all you've cost me, I'm quite determined to get my money's worth, you see.'

'Inside the Black City?' Riz spluttered. 'No way. Nope. You will in fact have to kill me, because there's no way...' He scrambled to one side, trying to wriggle away from them, but Kaeto grabbed him by the shoulders, and as quick as a whip Belise was there, her dagger poised over his hand.

'The place?' asked Kaeto again.

'There are no gates into the Black City, but down the wall to the east there is a way in,' said Riz. 'There's a broken section there where it's possible to climb through. Alright? That's all you need, surely. Let me go. Please? I am not going in that place. I thought that, when we were together, in the trees—'

'You thought wrong. Belise, the ropes.' Kaeto took his own knife and held it to the other man's throat. 'Our guide needs to be secured for his own safety.'

29

'This is truly where the queen of Kornwullis spends her time?'

They were stood on the docks of Zenore, the busy port town that clustered on the very tip of the westernmost landmass of Brittletain. In front of them was a ship with a complicated array of black and red sails and a thick crust of barnacles on the hull. There were huge nets bunched on either side, and the crew were moving briskly back and forth, unloading enormous barrels that smelled strongly of fish.

'Oh yes. Isn't it marvellous? I'd kill for a ship like this.' Epona was gazing at the vessel as though it were a jewel-encrusted crown.

'You sail?'

'Oh no, I know nothing about boats or the sea. But it must be wonderful to be able to disappear off over the horizon whenever you feel like it.'

Leven turned to Cillian for help, but the Druin wasn't looking at them or the boat. Instead he was watching the crowds moving around the harbour, his gaze shifting every few seconds or so. He looked even more uncomfortable than Leven felt.

'So how do we go about—'

There was a flurry of shouts, and a second later a dark shadow fell over the three of them. Leven looked up just in time to see a fishing net, tangled here and there with clumps of seaweed, falling down on them from above. It landed with more weight than she would have believed possible, almost pushing her to the ground. Epona, even shorter and slighter than Leven, did fall, and Cillian crouched low. Immediately the stink of salt and fish was everywhere.

'Halt, interloper!'

Leven couldn't tell where the shout was coming from. She stood up straight and took hold of the net, meaning to throw it off, but it seemed to pull in all directions.

'Magog's balls,' Epona muttered from somewhere near the ground.

'Let us go!' Leven yanked at the net again, but it did no good. Cold sea water trickled down through her hair and soaked her shirt. A piece of slimy seaweed flapped unpleasantly next to her ear. 'Right now!'

'Weapon of the Imperium, silence! Foreign Druin! Daughter of a false queen! All of you will be silent!'

'For the love of the gods,' Epona sighed. Next to her, Cillian was trying to untangle his horns from the net. Somehow, the sight of this made Leven even angrier. Very quickly, the Titan strength was tingling at her fingers in a way it hadn't in days. Her ore-lines seemed to crackle with it.

'I warned you!' she called through the net. Between the sturdy cord and her own bedraggled hair she thought she could make out a powerfully built woman coming towards them, but she was too furious to care. She let the Titan magic surge through the ore-lines and her great blue blade of magical glass leapt to her hand. She turned and neatly cut through the net that surrounded Cillian, leaving him with a ragged hood made of netting, and then she released her wings...

'Stop it!' Epona cried, trying to get to her feet. 'You can't do that here! You have to stay calm.'

Leven wasn't listening. Her wings outstretched, she leapt into the air, bringing the net with her and yanking it away from the ground. She heard a chorus of shouts as the men and women holding it down were unceremoniously pulled up after her. Two of them – the only two with any sense – let go almost immediately, dropping down onto the wooden panels of the dock. The other two held on longer, rising up almost to the level of the ship's sails, and then she spun herself in a quick circle. There was a shriek, and then a splash, and a moment later, a thud and a scream. Leven heard Epona shout, and she wondered, just for a moment, if she might not have made a mistake, but then her anger swept back over her just as strong: she was a soldier of the Imperium – not just that, but a Herald. And they had thrown a net over her! They sought to trap her like some sort of rodent.

Flying above the dock she flung her magical blade through the remains of the net and it parted as easily as wet paper, pieces of it scattering down to the people below. There was more shouting, sounds of panic. She looked down and saw Epona on her feet, her hands outstretched as if to reassure the bulky woman who was standing on the dock, staring furiously up at Leven. On the ship itself there was a man lying on the deck with his leg at an awkward angle. He was surrounded by people trying to help him up.

'Herald! Blessed Eleven!' Epona had cupped her hands around her mouth and was shouting in an exasperated tone. 'Come down! You're here representing my mother, remember?'

Leven clenched her fists and the blue glass blade vanished.

'This isn't much of a welcome, is it?' she shouted back.

The stout woman seemed to scowl at that, but Epona just shook her head.

'A misunderstanding, Herald. I'm sure you've heard of those?'

Leven hung in space a moment longer, the magic of the ore-lines coursing across her body. More than anything she wanted to show them what the Heralds really were – to smash their small and pointless port into timber and sink all their boats. The feeling of the net closing over her head had made her frightened in a way that... well, in a way that she hadn't felt before. Except, she realised, that wasn't entirely true – the moment the net had closed over her head, she had felt like she was back there, in the snowy forest, in the midst of whatever memory it was that she had lost, so long ago. *I was tied up, once*, she thought. *Held somewhere I didn't wish to be.* She didn't know how she knew that, but it felt true. She shivered.

Slowly, she realised that everyone on the ground was staring at her in horror; that the man on the deck with the broken leg was sobbing; and perhaps worst of all, Cillian was looking at her warily, every dark opinion he'd ever had about the Imperium confirmed. With an odd feeling in the pit of her stomach that she barely recognised, Leven let herself sink back towards the wooden boards of the port and folded her wings away.

Epona pushed her wet hair out of her eyes, and bowed neatly in the direction of the stocky woman who now stood frowning at them all with her arms crossed over her chest.

'Herald Eleven of the Imperium, *it is your honour* to meet Queen Verla, ruler of Kornwullis.'

Leven picked a piece of seaweed off her shirt and dropped it onto the boards. The woman glaring at her had skin the colour of cream, with strong cheekbones and short, pale blonde hair. She looked to be in her late fifties to Leven, although her skin was almost entirely unlined save for a clutch of crow's feet at the corners of her eyes. Her lips were narrow and pink, and her cheeks had a rosy flush. There was a solidity to her bearing that made Leven think that even with her Titan strength, she could not have pushed her way past that woman in a crowded market.

Leven cleared her throat. 'A pleasure.'

'Interesting.' Queen Verla tipped her head to one side, rather like a seagull considering its lunch. 'The fancy blue wings are impressive, girl, I'll give you that. A little overdramatic, maybe.'

'Do you greet all guests of Kornwullis with a big stinky net?'

Next to her, Epona sighed heavily.

'Only those we think might chop all our heads off.' The queen turned away and gestured to the crew still standing around her. 'That's quite enough excitement for one day. Get the fish to market, and yourselves to whatever taverns you'll be pickling yourselves in. And get that silly sod to a healer.'

The man who had broken his leg in the fall from the net was being carried gingerly down the gangplank by four other crew members. Verla squeezed the man's shoulder as he passed, and Leven felt that unfamiliar clenching in her stomach again. Guilt.

'Will he be alright?'

'We're no stranger to injuries here, girl. He'll get patched up.'

A small group of armed men came forward to stand at the queen's back. They wore salt-crusted leather and coarse woven tunics, their beards threaded with seashells and twine. There were brutal short swords at their belts, which almost made Leven laugh – until she remembered the man with the broken leg. Queen Verla sniffed and gestured to one of the streets leading away from the harbour.

'Now, Princess Epona, if you could bring your Imperial pet with you, it's time for her to receive judgement.'

30

Oh where are you going?
I hear the bones on the coast calling,
All the live long day,
I hear the bones on the coast calling, mother,
And I can no longer stay.

Oh where are you going?
I hear the trees in the forest singing,
All the live long day,
I hear the trees in the forest singing, mother,
And they must have their way.

Oh where are you going, child, your face so bare and bloody?
I hear the griffins in the north crying,
All day and into the night,
I hear the griffins in the north crying, mother,
And none can deny their might.

Traditional song of the northern
tribes of Brittletain

'Judgement?' Leven whispered to Epona. 'What does that mean?'
'I don't rightly know.' When Leven shot her a sharp look, the princess shrugged. 'You have to understand, Herald, we don't

get to visit Kornwullis all that often. A great number of their rites and rituals remain secret.'

Queen Verla and her guards led them away from Zenore's port and up a winding, narrow street. The buildings on either side seemed to lean towards each other, and in contrast to the raucously interested crowds of Londus, the people of Zenore seemed keen to avoid them altogether – as they climbed the cobbled road, Leven saw people drawing back, some even heading indoors or closing their windows as they passed. One man leading a shaggy-haired pony turned the animal's head away as they approached, as though looking at them was bad luck.

'What about you?' Leven glanced at Cillian. 'Do you know what this is about?'

'I only know what the trees tell me, and they are few and far between in Zenore.'

'Thanks. Very helpful. Am I to be tried for the fool who broke his leg? Only the queen didn't seem all that concerned about it.'

'It won't be that,' Epona replied, her voice low. Ahead of them, Queen Verla kept pace with her guard, moving with an easy grace. To Leven she didn't look out of place in that group of fighting men. 'They might be wary of strangers, but the people of Kornwullis are deeply pragmatic. The man was attempting to restrain a Herald of the Imperium, one of the most infamous soldiers in all of Enonah. They would have expected someone to get hurt.'

'Right.' Leven did not feel reassured. When they reached the top of the hill they came to a wall at least twenty feet high, built from wood with a deep reddish tint. The wall curved away to either side, and here and there Leven could see that people had tied things to wooden pegs that protruded from the rough surface – a posy of flowers, a bushel of corn that had clearly been there a while. There were even tiny hessian bags hung on the pegs, although what they contained Leven could only guess at. There was a simple door in the wall, which the queen unlocked with a large brass key that hung from her belt. Beyond the threshold Leven could see a verdant green space: lush grass, peppered with wildflowers.

'You'll see the Queen Consort now, girl,' Queen Verla said gravely. 'And we'll see what she makes of you.'

The armed men stood guard either side of the door. Leven, Epona and Cillian followed Queen Verla through, and it was like stepping outside again. Leven stopped, wondering briefly if this was some new kind of Druin magic; inside the circular wooden wall there was a steep hill, covered in grass and marked with a spiralling path, which led to the top. There was a woman seated at the summit, a pale, shifting shape. Without another word Queen Verla made for the rugged stone path and began to climb it.

'Queen Consort? How many queens are there in this place? How many could one island possibly need?'

'The Queen Consort Verbena.' Epona raised her eyebrows. 'Even I've never met her! You shall have to come with me on all future trips to Kornwullis, Herald.'

'This counts as a *good* experience, does it?'

'Only one injury so far? This is practically a party.'

Walking slightly behind the queen, the three of them climbed the hill. It was quiet, the only sound their breathing and the lazy hum of the bees visiting the wildflowers, almost as though the hill wasn't in the middle of the busy port city. As they neared the top, Leven spotted the sea beyond the wall, a glittering band of blue dotted with ships. It would make, she reasoned, an excellent lookout point to ward against approaching invaders, yet clearly this was not a place that was used by many people – the grass was long, and the stones under their feet were clean and unworn.

When they reached the top Queen Verla stopped and knelt before the woman who was seated in the grass.

'My love,' Verla took one of the woman's pale hands and kissed its knuckles, 'I've brought you our guests.'

The Queen Consort looked up, her eyes glazed, and blinked slowly, as though focusing on them took a great deal of effort. She was tall and willowy, with masses of thick blonde hair that was so pale it was almost white, and she wore an odd patchwork garment, hundreds of pieces of mismatched fabric sewn into a loose, shapeless outfit; to Leven it looked like she had taken the scraps of an entire village to make a single robe. Her feet were bare and dirty, and her eyes seemed to bulge slightly from their sockets.

'Who is it who comes?' The Queen Consort wore a silver thread around her neck, and from it hung a single acorn cup, its interior painted gold. She held it with her long white fingers as she spoke.

'The Herald, remember, Verbena? I told you she was coming. Will you tell me what our lords and ladies think?'

Leven looked around, expecting perhaps some more people to appear, but instead the grass was rustling as though caught in a stiff breeze. As she watched, the tiny forms she had glimpsed after she had fallen on the hill began to scurry out of the undergrowth, all rushing towards the Queen Consort. Leven took a hasty step back, but neither queen appeared to be alarmed by the sudden invasion. In fact, Verbena laid her hands on the ground, palms up, and the tiny creatures clambered up her arms and across her shoulders, disappearing into the thick terrain of her hair.

'Those things...' Leven took another step back, which made her collide with Cillian. 'What *are* they?'

'The pixen,' he said, his voice little more than a murmur. He steadied her with one hand, then quickly let go. 'I'd keep quiet if I were you. They are easily offended.'

'What?'

One of the rodenty little creatures had settled on the Queen Consort's hand. On its head it wore a small blue cap, and its tiny hands were folded neatly in its lap. Verbena lifted the creature up to her chest, where it snatched up the acorn cup that hung around her neck. Belatedly Leven realised that the blue cap was in fact a mushroom.

'What is happening?'

This time, it was Epona who shushed her.

The pixen lifted the acorn cup up to its hairy face, and its little snout disappeared inside it; there was the tiniest sound, like a bird singing in the dark. Then Verbena took the cup from the pixen and pressed the tip of her tongue to the golden interior. She looked perplexed for a moment, then nodded. During all of this Queen Verla remained kneeling, watching the pixen scamper over her consort with a solemn expression.

'My lords and ladies, they say that this one is full of secrets,' said Verbena in a scratchy voice. 'She has a dark purpose, or her purpose leads to darkness, but it doesn't concern us.'

'Hey.' Leven took a step forward. 'What's that supposed to mean?'

Verbena continued as though she hadn't spoken. 'Her future is a red thread that binds us all. She will spill blood, for love and for ruin – but it will not fall on these rocks. My lords and ladies say that she has given them a great gift already, that which they prize the highest.' Verbena stopped and for the first time looked directly at Leven. When she spoke again it was in an entirely normal tone. 'You gave them some of your blood?'

'Oh.' Leven could feel Cillian and Epona looking at her. 'I suppose I did. Or they took it, anyway.'

The laughter of the pixen sounded like tiny silver bells.

'Then you are welcome.' The Queen Consort stood up, and as quick as a bird taking flight the pixen scattered, vanishing back into the long grass. 'My love, the pixen say they like this soldier, and we should invite her to feast. Go on and take her up to the Sea House.'

Queen Verla nodded and stood. 'If you say so, my dear.' Verla turned and began ushering them back down the spiral path. 'I wasn't in the mood for a fight today anyway, truth be told.'

'That's it? The pixen like me?' Leven glanced over her shoulder, but Verbena was already turning away. 'What would've happened if they didn't?'

'A right bloody mess, is what,' said Verla. She seemed completely at ease now that the ritual was over with, and even clapped Leven on the shoulder in a companionable way as they made their way down the path. 'Come on then. Since I can't cut your head off I suppose I should probably feed you.'

31

From the pixen hill they were taken to a tavern called Clever Jack's and told to amuse themselves until they were called for. It was clear to Cillian that Leven was instantly at home in such a place, eagerly ordering tankards of ale and bringing them over to their rickety table. The place wasn't crowded, but every man and woman in the place watched the Herald as she sat down, as she sipped at her drink. Epona's face paint marked her out as Londus royalty, and there were no other Druin in the place. Altogether they made, he supposed, the sort of group that every patron would be telling stories about when they got home. The thought made him deeply uncomfortable. Inkwort had refused to enter the place.

'Are you going to tell us, then?' asked Epona, after she had tasted her ale and wrinkled her nose slightly.

'About what?'

'The pixen,' said Cillian. He was curious about it too. The pixen were notoriously shy, and even the Druin had very little to do with them.

'*Of course* the pixen,' said Epona. 'When exactly did you gain their favour? And by feeding them blood, of all things!'

'Oh.' The Herald looked down into her ale. 'When I slipped and scraped my elbow, they were there. It was such a small thing, I didn't think it worth mentioning.'

'A small thing.' Epona grinned. 'You owe the pixen now, Herald Eleven. Without them I suspect you'd be trussed up in some dungeon now, waiting for good Queen Verla to have you burned on a pyre.'

'I'd like to see them try,' said Leven, scowling. 'I've not done anything to Kornwullis, yet I get dragged up a hill and judged by hairy little rat things, not to mention having a stinking net thrown over me.'

'The net was thrown over all of us,' Cillian added quietly. 'But Princess Epona is right, Herald. The Queen Consort's deep connection to the pixen makes her one of the most respected people in Kornwullis, if not all of Brittletain. That you have her favour is quite a feat.'

'A mad woman on top of a hill?'

Epona's smile became a grimace. 'Keep your voice down, Herald – we are still guests here. Queen Consort Verbena spends much of her time in seclusion, gleaning secrets and prophecies from the fair folk. It's said that she arrived on the shores of Kornwullis from the west, from an island in the Broken Sea where the pixen are lauded as kings.' She lowered her voice. 'And more to the point, if Queen Verla hears you talking about her wife like that it'll be all-out war before we finish these pints.'

'Fine.' Leven lifted her hands, palms facing outwards. 'I'll keep my gob shut.'

They passed the time, mainly listening to Princess Epona's stories of her older sister Ceni, who was now a queen in the north; how when she was younger than Epona she had been a respected warlord in her own right; how she had won chariot races at the age of twelve, and found a silver chalice inside a wych elm tree. After a couple of hours the queen's guard returned for them, ready to take them up to the Sea House. Just as they were leaving, Leven paused and poured the last of her ale into a shallow saucer. Curious despite himself, Cillian asked what she was doing.

'Like you both said, I owe the pixen now.' To his surprise, the Herald was blushing slightly; her flushed skin contrasted prettily with the silvery-blue ore-lines that crossed her face, a fact he did his best to immediately forget. 'So I'll leave this here for them. I imagine they like a drink as much as anyone.'

32

I can't tell you how it hurts my heart to write these words, Elder Celynnon, but you will hear it from someone else sooner or later – young Cladd has gone thrawn, only three years after receiving his horns. There's no way of knowing how or why, and I'm as surprised as anyone: he was always so conscientious with his studies, so (apparently) dedicated to his connection to the Wild Wood. The small piece of good news I can give you is that he hasn't turned to violence yet. He is merely confused and angry with himself, so my recommendation is that he is banished, sent perhaps to live on the coast, far from the Wild Wood. The blue discolouration on his horns is growing by the day, however, so a decision will have to be made soon.

Private letter to the Druin
elder Celynnon

The Sea House was Queen Verla's idea of a palace: a vast old ship, turned upside down and crafted into a sprawling mead hall. The sun was inching towards the horizon as they made their way up the path, and the worn wooden structure was bathed in an orange, fiery light that promised storms. The queen's guard were keeping a close eye on the Herald, but one of them, spotting the confusion on her face, turned to speak to them.

'It was the queen's first ship, back when her father held the throne.

When it was too old to face sea water any longer, she ordered it brought ashore and turned on its head.' There was no mistaking the pride in the guard's voice. 'We don't waste things here. Especially not a Titan's worth of good cedar wood.'

There were lanterns burning in narrow windows, and across its wide belly, now facing the sky, a walkway had been built. There were more guards there, keeping watch.

'What a life those trees have had,' Cillian murmured, more to himself than the others. 'Grown tall and wise in the forest, and then cut and formed into a new shape, one that sailed the sea and saw so much other trees have never seen. And now, they've a new life, as a place of shelter.'

The Herald glanced at him. 'You talk as though the trees are aware of what happens to them. With their roots in the ground, maybe. But chopped up? Surely they can't be alive then?'

'They are aware of more than *you* could ever guess.' Cillian looked down at his feet. He was too used to being alone, being able to speak his thoughts out loud with no one but the trees to hear them.

The doors to the mead hall were thrown open, and from inside came a wall of noise and heat. Queen Verla was there shouting orders, and as they entered men and women immediately scattered to fetch food and more ale. Cillian hung back as much as he was able – the place was just so *loud*. Inkwort abandoned his shoulder and made for the rafters. The Herald was looking all around, her face tense, as though she still expected to be attacked at any moment.

'I hope your stomachs are ready to be filled,' Queen Verla barked. 'That's what we should do with visiting royalty, isn't it? Feast them? Visiting royalty and whatever you are, Herald. The bird she sent told me you were bringing a *present* from Queen Broudicca.' Verla chuckled, then seemed to remember that Epona was there. 'How is your mother, Princess?'

'Anxious that I convey her admiration and wishes for a stronger partnership between our two kingdoms.'

'Yeah, that sounds about right.' Verla heaved herself into a huge driftwood throne that sat behind a long table. The table itself, Cillian noticed, was decorated with carvings of the Titans that had long since vanished from Enonah: the wyverns, the kraken, the great boar and the firebirds, all cavorting above a tumultuous sea. 'Your mother never gives up, does she?'

'Not when it comes to the possibility of friendship with your good self,' Epona replied sweetly.

'Londus's eyes are bigger than its belly,' replied Verla. 'Queen Broudicca's appetite will never consume Kornwullis.'

'Your majesty...' Epona started, but Verla waved a hand at her dismissively.

'Your mother was hungry enough to travel south and devour a new kingdom when she should have been satisfied with Galabroc – but we're not here to dredge up that old argument.'

At that moment a door opened on the far side of the hall and Queen Consort Verbena entered. She looked very different to how they had seen her earlier; her skin was clear and shining, and her long white-gold hair was neatly plaited into an elegant bun, held in place with silver pins. Instead of her gown of pixen-scrounged fabric she wore an elegant robe of pink silk, with wide sleeves and a thick belt embroidered with daisies. The golden acorn was still on a silver thread around her neck. Verla rose from her throne and let Verbena sit in her place, pausing to kiss her cheek fondly. Around them, the other men and women in the hall grew quiet. Fierce human minds burned all around Cillian, all of them curious, a good few of them angry, and they were all focused on the young woman who waited next to him. The Herald stood very straight, her chin lifted as though she were ready to take any of them on.

'No, today we have something much more interesting to discuss.' Verla's words dropped into the quiet like stones dropped into a forest pool. 'A visitor from the Imperium. And not just any visitor, but a Herald, one of the empress's twisted magical creatures.'

There was a muttering from around the hall.

'Why are you here, Imperium?'

The Herald cleared her throat. 'I'm here to deliver a gift to you, your majesty. From Queen Broudicca. As you know.'

'I asked what you were doing here, girl, not what madness Broudicca has put you up to.'

Blessed Eleven seemed taken aback by that.

'Perhaps I'm here to get nets dropped on me from a great height?' Epona laughed quietly.

'I am here, your majesty, because I am a free woman and I wanted to see Brittletain. That's it. I have no secret plans, no underhanded orders.' The Herald held her arms out. 'I can tell you no more than that. Now, do you want this bloody present, or not?'

The muttering from the hall grew louder, and Cillian heard a couple of men by the door draw their swords. But the queen was grinning.

'Insolence. But why would we expect better manners from the sword of the Imperium? And Verbena tells me I should trust you. So. Present your gift, Herald, and we'll see what we make of it.'

For a long second the Herald didn't move. Eventually Epona leaned over to her and Cillian heard the princess whisper: 'It has to be you, Blessed Eleven. Coming from me it means nothing.'

The Herald shook her head slightly, and then bent to her bags, which she'd placed on the ground in front of her. From inside one she withdrew the box with its green Druin seal, and Cillian tensed, wondering if he would be summoned to open it, but instead Queen Verla gestured to a tall figure in the shadows beyond the table.

'Loveday, you will open it for us. And be quick about it, aye? Dinner is on its way.'

A woman in long scarlet robes stepped neatly around the table. She was willowy and beautiful, with long horns that spiralled from her temples almost directly towards the ceiling. She glanced up and caught Cillian's eye, and she gave him a quick, cool smile as she took the box from the Herald.

Again, the tension in the room seemed to soar, and from up in the rafters Cillian could feel the fluttering bird heart of Inkwort, beating so fast it was almost a hum.

He caught a couple of her thoughts. *Danger, danger, interloper...* And then the connection was gone again.

Cillian looked at the box, now being turned over and over in the hands of the beautiful Druin woman. It seemed like madness that he *hadn't* opened it, that he hadn't checked for himself what was inside it. They knew nothing really of what the Heralds were capable of; their magic was a complete mystery. What if she had tampered with the box somehow, and changed what was inside? Was that what Inkwort was sensing? Could the little jackdaw even have seen the Herald do it, one night on the Paths when Epona was asleep and he had been busy keeping watch in his trance state? A low bubble of panic pushed its way up his throat and he took half a step forward, ready to dash the box from the Druin's hands.

And then the seal fell away, and the wooden lid popped open. Nothing happened. Cillian heard several people breathe out, and he knew he wasn't the only one to wonder if the box itself was a trap.

'Oh. Is that it?' Epona was standing on her toes, trying to see inside the box. 'Just some sort of trinket?'

'A fine one,' said the Druin called Loveday. She had a warm voice, full of quiet power. She reached into the box and brought out a short blade, the handle of which was a bear standing on his hind legs, a crown of twigs on his head: the Druidahnon. The whole thing had been carved from Titan bone, and it gleamed a dark blue under the flickering lamplight. The Druin placed the bone dagger on the table in front of Queen Verla, who picked it up and turned it to catch the light. Even from where he stood, Cillian could see how the lamplight shone through the thin blade as though it were coloured glass; how it lit up like the bluest seas on a summer's day. Queen Verla smiled.

'It's a beautiful gift. You will tell your mother thank you, Epona. For all our differences she knows me well enough. And here, at last, comes the pig.' She stood up and gestured to the places next to her at the table. 'Let's eat – it's been a long day fishing for Heralds and I am famished.'

Cillian found himself seated next to the tall Druin called Loveday. As the feasting went on, he ate only small portions and drank only sips of the powerful, salt-tinged mead that was being poured into every flagon with great abandon. He still felt deeply uneasy. The gift from Queen Broudicca had turned out to be harmless, but being this close to so many people made him very uncomfortable. There were too many warm bodies, too many busy minds, all pushing in around him. It was hard to hear himself think. Further up the table, Epona was remonstrating with one of the queen's advisers about something – she was using a pair of long silver forks and half a loaf of bread to act it out – while the Herald was having some sort of shouted conversation with Queen Verla, which was making them both laugh.

Even she fits in better than me, he thought.

'Here.' Loveday had been quiet during the meal too. She laid her hand on his forearm. 'Would you like to go outside and get some air, Druin Cillian?'

It was a cool night, and the sound of waves crashing at the bottom of the nearby cliffs was clear and somehow calming. Cillian took a deep breath; he felt instantly better.

'Thank you,' he said, and meant it. 'Will the queen not need you?'

'Need me?' Loveday smiled crookedly. 'They have very little need of me at any time. Take a look around… Or I suppose you will have noticed already, being from the Wild Wood. What are we missing around here?'

'Trees.' Cillian had felt the distance from the Wild Wood with every step, and it was true; Kornwullis was a wild and rugged place, but it was mostly open country, crowded with stones and boulders, gorse and briars. The only trees in sight were a few lonesome mulberrys, twisted and stubbornly isolated. 'How do you cope?'

She shrugged. They had walked some distance from the Sea House, and the sound of the feasting had faded to a vague rumble. It was dark, but the moon was fat, and Cillian could see the woman's face quite clearly. Her hair was the colour of polished conkers in this light.

'Once, the Wild Wood came all the way down to the edge of the sea here. It used to stretch from coast to coast. Did you know that? And then humans came, and we started to parcel the land up into little pieces, and then whoever had the biggest sword got to call themselves king or queen. And now the kings and queens get to order us around, even though we hold the true power of Brittletain.'

Cillian frowned slightly. 'I'm not interested in power,' he said. 'I just want to be left to walk the Paths by myself.' He thought of his current mission; that it had been given to him by the Druidahnon couldn't erase the fact that he was doing Queen Broudicca's will. 'But even that seems to be too much to ask.'

She smiled at him and shrugged. 'I do my best here. You can't have a royal court without a Druin, can you? Unless you are Mersia, of course. But Queen Verla barely needs me – they are a seafaring folk, and they will take their ships wherever they need to go and barely use the Paths at all. It has been, oh, nearly a year since I walked the Paths. Tell me – what are they like? What have I missed?'

She turned to him and grabbed one of his hands in both of her own. Cillian stopped, looking down at them. Her fingers were very white against his tanned skin.

'It has been... strange lately,' he said eventually. 'The Wild Wood is unhappy. Angry even. It's hard to describe.'

'Ha! I am not surprised. Not when that Imperial creature is walking our Paths and tainting them.'

'The Herald? No, she hasn't done anything wrong.' And then he stopped, because he wasn't sure why he was defending Blessed

Eleven. 'I've felt this before. Something has unsettled the Dunohi. That's all I know for certain.'

'I miss them.' Loveday stepped closer to him, close enough that he could feel her breath on his neck. 'Would you share a little of what you've felt with me?' She squeezed his hands and pressed them to her stomach. She felt warm through the thin material of her dress. 'I wouldn't ask, but it's been so long, Cillian.'

'I don't...' Cillian laughed and glanced around. They were quite alone. 'That's a little forward of you.'

'Aren't you lonely, so far from the Wild Wood?' Loveday pressed her cheek to his. 'Just share a little with me.'

He sighed and closed his eyes. Her warmth was shot through with the green of the wood, and it was easy enough to connect to, mind to mind. He gave her a sense of his memories from the last few days: the sound of birds in the trees; the chattering of magpies; the eerie purple smell of foxgloves and the tart taste of wild garlic. Craving more, she pressed herself even closer, and he could feel her hands in his hair.

'Come back with me to my bed, Druin Cillian,' she said in her low, lovely voice. 'I want to taste more of this, and of you.'

Cillian's eyes flickered open, and he swallowed hard. After a moment, he took a step back and broke contact with her. She drew her breath in quickly over her teeth, as if he had pinched her.

'What's wrong?'

'I gave you what you wanted,' he said. He smiled to lessen the chill of his words. The wind dropped and the noise from the mead hall sounded closer.

'Not *everything* I wanted,' she said, a smile in her voice. 'What if you could have what you want, Cillian? Freedom, the ability to walk wherever you wanted without question, and an end to the false divisions in this land. An end to queens.'

'I didn't say anything about that.' Cillian took half a step back. 'The Druidahnon...'

The smile on Loveday's face quickly became something cold and bitter. 'What is wrong with you? The Druin that come out of the Wild Wood are usually much more receptive. Too busy with your *queen's* work. Or are you tainted by the Herald, is that it?'

'Tainted? I don't know what you're talking about.'

'Oh please. I could taste her all over your memories. You've been watching her. And she's been watching you.' Loveday smoothed the creases from her robe, her horns gleaming in the moonlight. 'More fool you. That monster will eat you alive.'

She turned away and walked off down the cobbled path. Cillian watched her go until she was out of sight, uncertain whether he was disappointed or keen to see the back of her. Inkwort's words – *danger, danger, interloper* – kept occurring to him.

'Hey! What are you doing, standing out here in the dark by yourself?'

The Herald was crunching across the stones towards him, silhouetted by the open doors of the mead hall.

'I needed some air.' *It's too dark for her to see my face clearly,* he told himself, although he wasn't sure why that was important. 'It's too loud for me in there.'

'I'm afraid it's only going to get louder. Epona has challenged the queen to a drinking contest.' The Herald smiled at him, and there was something in her manner – a kind of shyness, almost – that made him panic even more than Loveday's sudden intimacy had. 'I was worried that perhaps you had left us.'

Cillian cleared his throat. 'This is only the first of our stops, Herald. I've a long way to go yet before my job is over. More's the pity.'

'Then you'll come back?' She nodded to the open doorway. 'I don't know much about these things, but I reckon if there isn't at least one sensible head in the room there's going to be a diplomatic incident.'

Cillian glanced back at the cobbled road, down which Loveday had vanished. *There's still time,* he thought. *I could catch up with her. She's the only one of my kind for miles around.*

But in the end he turned back and followed the Herald into the Sea House.

33

Ynis woke before sun-up, her eyes snapping open in the gloom of their shared nest-pit. Something had woken her – a noise or a shout, something that had lurched out of her dream to shock her to consciousness. Sure that it must be important, she closed her eyes again and tried to remember the dream, but all that would come was the odd sensation of being held in arms that were like her own – smooth, featherless – and some breathless sense of danger. Annoyed, she wriggled her way out of the warm wool and feather blankets and crept closer to the cave entrance. The first light of the day was painting grubby marks on the heavy clouds hanging over the Bone Fall, and in this faint glow she could see her sister sleeping soundly, her head and beak tucked snugly under one wing.

Looking at her sister made her think of the old griffin and his son, and the bond they had shared between them. Did their own fathers still think of them, at home in Yelvynia? What would they think if they knew that their wingless human daughter was learning to be a witch-seer? Would they be proud? Or disgusted? It was hard to imagine T'vor being anything other than proud, or Flayn ever being less than understanding, yet T'rook had reacted so violently to the Edge Walkers and their duties. Perhaps they would be the same.

And she still had yet to accept it. The lessons with Frost had continued all week, much to T'rook's annoyance, and Ynis had weathered endless cutting remarks at every meal they shared. But she sensed a growing curiosity too, even a kind of jealousy. For better or for worse, Ynis had found her place at the Bone Fall, whereas T'rook was still a stranger on the outskirts, looking in.

'What are you doing?'

Too late Ynis realised her sister was awake, watching her with one eye from under her wing.

'Nothing. Do you want food? There's some meat left over from last night here.' Ynis picked up the dried meat and brought it back over to the nesting spot. The down and straw was still warm and it felt good to be close to her sister again. They divided up the meat between them and ate in silence for a while.

'You are off with the seer again today?' asked T'rook. Ynis chewed and swallowed, feeling the tension flow back into the cave again.

'I am. She's taught me so much these last few days.'

'About the dead? About how we die?'

Ynis shifted, folding her legs underneath her. T'rook was still being very brusque, but there was perhaps an inquisitiveness that hadn't been there before. Or was she imagining it?

'I suppose so. She has shown me how to see things that are normally hidden.'

T'rook held a piece of meat with one talon and pulled it into two parts with her beak. 'The old stone-licker is filling your head with lies.'

'No! That's not it at all.' Ynis shook her head. Why was it always the same with her? 'It's just a different way of looking at things. She says that because I nearly died when I was yenlin, I am closer to this... other world. So I can see things easier, like she can.' T'rook opened her beak to object, so Ynis rushed in to speak before she could. 'I can see fate-ties, T'rook. The things that Flayn was always talking about, they're real! They really do connect griffins to other griffins.'

'Can you see one between us then?' asked T'rook.

'I...' Ynis stopped. 'I haven't looked.'

'Look now then. Show me this tie, and where it is.'

'It doesn't work like that.' Ynis stood up and stepped out of the nesting space. She felt afraid. 'I have to be thinking the right way. It's complicated.'

'Or, it is made up. And you pretend to see things to impress these corpse eaters.' T'rook rose from the nest-pit, stretching out her front legs and letting her talons score the stone. She pecked at an errant flight feather, then stalked her way past her sister to the entrance of the cave. 'I am going to go and do something useful, and not made up. Like hunting.'

Ynis watched her sister leap from the cave entrance up into the sky, which was already much brighter than it had been. Quickly T'rook was a small shape in that vast expanse, lost in the early-morning light. It was good that her sister had found her love of hunting again, but Ynis was still afraid, and she had a terrible feeling she knew why.

'I'm afraid that there may not be a fate-tie between us,' she said quietly, her voice parcelled up by the wind and carried off over the glacier. 'I'm afraid that there can't be one, whatever Frost says, because of what I am and what you are, sister.'

Later in the day, Frost came and took Ynis back to the caves where they had watched T'wesen die. The body of the old griffin himself had been taken to the Bone Fall, but his son, with his fine blue feathers and green eyes, was still in the cave. When they arrived, he stood up to meet them, the crest on his head displayed, yet he still looked bedraggled somehow, his wings held low and his eyes downcast.

'How are you, Festus?' asked Frost.

'I survive,' the young griffin said brusquely. His green eyes flashed, as if daring them to say any different.

'These are the hardest days, Festus,' Frost said in a matter-of-fact tone. 'Sadness and pain are nothing to be ashamed of. They are important parts of our lives, the darker twin to love and joy. Without them, without all these things, we are incomplete. But it is hard to lose those we are fate-tied to – you might think that everything you shared with your father has been lost also. But this is not the case.'

Ynis stood to one side of Frost, feeling like an interloper, but Festus barely seemed to notice she was there.

'Your memories, Festus, are an essential part of who you are,' Frost continued, 'and that is why nothing is ever truly lost. If you like, we can help you to experience some of your memories again, to ease some of your pain. Would you like that?'

Ynis found herself marvelling at the softness in Frost's voice. Growing up in Yelvynia, she had been taught that it was the griffin way to shrug off pain, to keep going regardless. And here Frost, in her role as witch-seer, was offering to ease it. To share it.

Festus looked as though he was confused by the idea too, but after a moment he turned his head away from them.

'I would like that, yes,' he said quietly. 'I would like to hear his voice again.'

Frost nodded, then turned to Ynis.

'The paste I gave you earlier, Ynis. Please give it to Festus.'

Ynis opened her bag and pulled out a broad hairy leaf, folded in half. Inside it, Frost had told her, there was a paste made from finely ground griffin bones, various dried plants and rabbit's blood. It smelled strange; it smelled dangerous. Holding it carefully by the edge, she went to Festus and held it out to him, but he peered past her to Frost.

'What am I supposed to do with this?'

'Eat it, my dear,' Frost said. 'It will make you sleep for a time, and Ynis and I will guide you through your dreams to the memories beneath.'

'The human?' Festus looked directly at Ynis for the first time. 'You will take the prey animal inside my head too?'

Frost tipped her head to one side. The younger griffin was larger and more vital than her, but when she spoke her voice had become stern, almost admonishing.

'Ynis is an apprentice witch-seer, and you will show her respect, regardless of the weight and colour of her bones. Do you understand?'

Festus looked as though he might disagree further, but in the end he simply took the leaf from Ynis's hands with his beak and with one sharp flick, swallowed it. He then settled down on the floor of the nest-pit, the blue crest of feathers on his head drooping. Frost brought her head down to speak quietly in Ynis's ear.

'Sit down, and watch carefully. Witch-seer initiates are guided by their seniors during their first experience of the Death's Remembrance ritual, but in truth I do not know if it will work with a human.' Ynis nodded, and made herself comfortable on the floor of the cave. 'Just remember, yenlin, how you saw the spirit at the Bone Fall. That is the presence of mind that you will need.'

By then, Festus's head was curled on top of his paws, his breathing slow and steady. He was already asleep. Ynis let herself relax, remembering everything Frost had taught her, letting her natural awareness of unseen things move through her. Gradually, as she did so, she became aware of a crown of blue light across Festus's broad forehead. A soft glow at first, becoming brighter, and sharper. She could see points of light seeping out from the crown, like the dazzle of sunlight on new ice.

'You can see it,' said Frost. 'Good. Now then, keep close to me...'

Frost opened her wing and curled it over Ynis's head, as though sheltering her from the rain, and then after that moment of brief shadow they were elsewhere. Ynis rubbed a hand roughly over her face, dizzy and disorientated.

'Remember what I said, yenlin,' Frost said quietly. 'Stay close to me. I don't want you getting lost in this young griffin's dream.'

A griffin dream. Ynis swallowed hard, caught between fright and wonder.

In front of them was a mountain unlike any she had ever seen. It burst forth from the ice like the tooth of a wolf, long and sheer and white, and all around it there were griffins flying. Each one of them was bigger even than Brocken, and they had feathers of all colours. Their eyes winked like crystals in the bitter winter sun, and they called to each other with thunderous voices; voices like the mountain itself. Some of them, Ynis noted, wore armour of silver and gold.

'What is this place?'

Frost chuckled. 'Festus dreams of our past. We don't talk of it to yenlin now, but those of us who are left are shadows of what we once were. Little good it does us to try and hide the truth – the young are still granted these fate-dreams, every now and then. Who we are lives in our bones, after all.'

Ynis shook her head. 'I don't understand. Why don't...' Her words trailed off as she noticed another figure on the mountain. It was a vast bear, stood on his hind legs. He wore a crown of leaves and branches about his head, and he appeared to be talking to the griffins.

'Oh *him.*' Frost made a disparaging clicking sound with her beak. 'Never mind all this, Ynis. We are in a dream, and we need to find Festus. And a door to memory. Ah, there, look, he is ahead of us.'

Near the foot of the strange tooth-shaped mountain there was a cave, and waiting outside it was the young griffin. Next to the huge griffins of the mountain, even Festus with his colourful plumage looked drab. In the way of dreams, Ynis found that she was standing next to him, with Frost standing next to her, without them having to move at all. She looked down at her feet, at the snow under her boots. It all looked real enough.

'Witch-seer, there you are,' said Festus. 'What am I doing here?'

'We're to take you into your memories now, Festus, memories of your father.' Frost's tone was kindly and faintly impatient. 'Here we go now, down into this cave, this is the way. Ynis, grab a handful of my feathers. I don't want to lose you as we pass through.'

Ynis did as she was told – the idea of being lost in a griffin dream was both marvellous and terrifying – and the three of them stepped into the shadowy cave. Almost straight away, Ynis could see light on the other side. Within moments they were stepping out onto the lush grass of a valley in summer; this place, with its purple gorse and milky grey stone was recognisably Yelvynia.

'Home,' Festus said. He no longer sounded confused. He sounded happy. 'This is where I was hatched. Father taught me to fly from that crag over there.'

'And who do you see there now, Festus?' asked Frost.

Ahead of them there was a rocky outcrop, and there were two griffins on the top of it, the youngest of whom looked strikingly like Festus, with blue feathers and green eyes. A second later and Ynis realised it *was* him. *This is his memory*, she reminded herself, *of a time when he was still yenlin*. The second griffin was larger and somehow more robust; his taloned legs were the colour of cream, and the feathers on his chest were buttercup yellow. He was talking to the younger griffin, and occasionally sifting his beak through his hatchling's feathers.

Festus laughed. 'He would groom me before each attempt,' he said fondly. 'He was convinced that having neat and clean feathers would make it easier for me to fly.'

'Your father,' said Frost.

'Yes,' said Festus. 'He took such care over it.' His voice grew quiet. 'It was weeks before I could fly without crashing into the ground or the trees, but he was always patient.'

'And do you still groom yourself, before you fly? Perhaps before long journeys?' asked Frost.

Festus looked at her in surprise, his green eyes widening. 'I do! Always, just a little. It makes me fly better. I do believe that.'

'Your father is with you, you see, always.' And then she added, 'And I think he was proud of your fine blue feathers, Festus. You are a link to our colourful past.'

The young griffin fluffed up the feathers on his chest and looked back to the two figures on the rocky crag. Ynis thought of the silvery feathers she had cut from the head of the griffin who had mocked and attacked her and T'rook, and felt a coil of something like guilt tighten in her stomach.

When they had watched Festus jump from the crag a few times, wings flapping with enthusiasm but no experience, Frost took them to other memories, moving from place to place with the ease of dreams. They saw T'wesen and a female griffin Ynis took to be Festus's mother, building a larger nest-pit while hatchling Festus provided newly scavenged sticks; they watched the family fly through a storm, calling reassurances to each other; they saw T'wesen teaching his son how to make griffin-spit, and how to use it to form great spiralling sculptures from branches.

'He was obsessed with them,' Festus said fondly. 'We made a whole series of them on the side of the hill, and when the wind blew they made a kind of music. It was his great project.'

Finally, Frost led the two of them out of the memories and Ynis was surprised to find herself back in the small cave near the Bone Fall. The last of the daylight was seeping in through the mouth of the dwelling, and Festus himself looked groggy. Frost touched her beak to his quickly, a kind of farewell, and then herded Ynis back towards the entrance.

'We'll leave him be for a while now,' she said once they were back on their way down the long rocky path. 'It is our calling as Edge Walkers to help the bereaved accept what has happened, but ultimately they have to make most of this journey alone.'

Ynis nodded, although her mind was still on what she had seen in Festus's memories. When the silence between them lasted to the bottom of the path, Frost gave her a friendly nudge.

'What is on your mind, apprentice?'

Ynis looked up shyly. Beyond Frost, she could see the blue and green wisps of spirits moving across the Bone Fall. It was much easier to see them now.

'How can I be a witch-seer when I have never been taught to fly? When I have no feathers to groom, and my spit doesn't stick branches together.' For a moment it was hard to speak, as though there were a clod of mud in her throat, but she made herself continue. 'I have never dreamed of our ancestors, Frost. Maybe I am... just too different.'

Frost tutted. 'There is more to being a griffin than feathers and spit, yenlin. You also have memories of your fathers, do you not? Of your life in the nest-pit with your sister? If a griffin was born without any feathers, would she be any less a griffin?'

'I...' Ynis blinked. 'No. She would not.'

'Your *yost* is what counts, Ynis. And you are as full of that as a rabbit is full of blood. Come on now, enough talk and magic. I want food.'

Ynis turned her head away and smiled a little, as fragile as ice in spring.

34

'So why drop a net on me in the first place?'

They were walking back along the high lonely headland towards the Wild Wood. Queen Verla had seen them off herself, along with several tightly packed bags of food and supplies – mainly, from the smell of it, dried fish. Cillian had been quiet all morning, hanging back and saying very little, but Leven found that she was – hangover aside – in a remarkably good mood.

'It's complicated.' Epona seemed full of energy too, and they matched each other stride for stride as they made their way along the rocky path. The princess had carefully reapplied the blue stripes of paint to her face and they seemed especially bright and cheerful under the brittle morning sun. 'They couldn't have you just turn up without remark, could they? But equally they did not want to lose their reputation of having little interest in the outside world. So, no big official welcome with parades and what have you. Instead, a little demonstration that they could still cause you trouble if they wanted, and trial by pixen. If you'd failed that, they would have had every excuse to run you out of Kornwullis, or worse.'

'But I liked Queen Verla,' said Leven. 'And she seemed to like me. None of this makes sense.'

Epona shrugged. 'It's because you see yourself as this lone traveller, a woman quite separate to your job.'

'A job I don't even have anymore.'

'But to Kornwullis, and the rest of Brittletain, you are a symbol. A symbol of an ancient enemy. Of course you will be treated differently because of it.'

'And you know, that net was hardly a problem. I was out of it in seconds.' Leven laughed and shook her head. 'Does Brittletain really think something like that would worry the Imperium?'

Epona gave her an odd look.

'Whatever else you might think, you see yourself as the Imperium still. It's not so easy to shrug off an old identity.'

They had reached a narrow gully between two high walls of rock, punctuated here and there with a twisted mulberry tree, roots intwined with the stone. Perhaps if Leven hadn't been quite so hungover she would have recognised it as a great place for a trap. Instead, she found herself looking at the brightly coloured lichen and moss that grew all over the grey boulders; yellows and reds, deep, fleshy-looking greens. She had just turned to ask Cillian if he knew what these tiny plants were called, when a rattle of falling pebbles made her glance up to the ridge of rocks above them. There was a figure there, outlined against the sky, and he was drawing back a bow.

'Get down!'

She pushed Epona into the shelter of the rocks, causing the princess to squawk in indignation, and a second later an arrow clattered against the stones where they'd been walking. A man's voice, made thin by distance, floated down towards them.

'Leave the Imperial monster where she is and you won't get hurt! We're not here for you.'

Cillian caught up with them, his face tense.

'Outlaws,' he said in a low voice. 'Rebels.'

Epona leaned out of the shelter and shouted up towards the man with the bow.

'This Imperial monster is a guest of Queen Broudicca!'

'Thanks for that,' muttered Leven.

'Furthermore, she is in the middle of carrying out my mother's orders,' continued Epona. 'So would you kindly sod off?'

Leven, who had pressed herself against the rocks beneath the archer, could feel a faint tremble in the stone.

'There are more coming,' she said quietly. 'They are on the path as well as above us.'

'Magog take us all,' muttered Epona.

'You get one more chance!' the man on the top of the rocks shouted. 'Leave the Herald behind and let us deal with her. Or we'll assume you are an Imperial loyalist and you'll get the same treatment.'

'This is ridiculous. I will fly up there and knock him off his perch.' Leven made to leave the cover of the rocks but Epona grabbed her arm and yanked her back.

'Do you want to start a war? You can't go about murdering the people of Brittletain. You have my mother's trust! People will blame her for letting you run riot.'

'Murdering? They started it!'

'What do you want with her?' shouted Cillian.

'She will pay for the Imperium's crimes.' The answer came not from above them, but further down the rocky path ahead. 'And for her own. She has killed *thousands*.'

The voice was female. Leven leaned out from behind the boulders and peered down the path. There were two men and one woman coming towards them; all three of them had horns like Cillian, and the woman she recognised – the Druin who had opened the seal on Broudicca's gift.

'Loveday?' Cillian stepped out onto the path. 'What are you doing?'

'What you should have done, you fool.' The female Druin raised her hands. As far as Leven could tell, she wasn't armed. 'Her presence here is an insult to the Dunohi. You told me yourself the Wild Wood was angry.'

'This has nothing to do with that,' said Cillian, although to Leven he sounded less than sure. 'The Druidahnon himself told me to take this woman where she needed to go. Are you telling me you know better than our lord?'

The Druin called Loveday shook her head. Her russet hair had been tied back into a braid, and the two men behind her came forward, also with their hands raised.

'This is your last warning, brother Cillian,' said Loveday. 'Join the Atchorn or die with your Imperial pet.'

'Hey,' called Epona. 'Have you forgotten I'm here? Are you really willing to kill a royal daughter of Londus?'

'Queen Broudicca has many daughters,' said Loveday. 'She will not miss one.'

'She bloody well will,' muttered Epona.

'Alright, that's enough,' said Leven. She shrugged off Epona's grip and stepped out onto the path so that the Druin could see her. 'I'm not going to kill anyone, I'm just going to give out a few bruises. And for what it's worth, I feel they are thoroughly deserved.'

Leven summoned the Titan strength to her fingertips, and her great glass wings unfolded, taking up most of the room in the narrow gully. At the same moment, the three Druin ahead of them lifted their hands as one, and the earth all around them began to jump and shake so violently that Leven was almost thrown off her feet.

'What—?'

There was a shout from above, and Leven looked up in time to see that several of the larger boulders lining the top of the gully had come loose and were bouncing their way down towards them, followed by a large amount of loosened earth and scattered pebbles. They were directly in their path. She spread her wings and held them over the three of them like a shield just in time for the first boulder to hit; it struck the magical glass of her wing and bounced off with the sound of a great bell being struck.

'What are they doing?'

'Moving the earth,' Cillian said, as though that explained everything.

'Burying us alive is what they are doing!' cried Epona.

More boulders fell, all at once, half pushing Leven to the ground. Ahead of them, Loveday and the other Druin were retreating. Now that the rocks were falling, it seemed they needed no more help to crush them flat.

'Hold on,' Leven said to the other two. 'I just need to throw these off...'

'There's no time, the whole thing is coming down.' Cillian jumped out from the safety of Leven's wing shield and scrambled up the debris ahead of them.

'Where's he going?' cried Leven. 'Is he actually leaving us here?'

But Cillian had stopped and turned, and he lifted his hands in much the same way as Loveday had done. He grimaced and gritted his teeth, and the cascade from the cliffs slowed, and then stopped. There was a last rattle of pebbles bouncing off Leven's wings, and he dropped his hands.

'There,' he said. He was panting with the effort. 'It's stopped, you just need to—'

He jerked to one side, an arrow sprouting from the top of his left shoulder.

'Right, that's it.' Leven slung one arm around Epona's waist and took off. With the gully so narrow and full of dust it wasn't the most graceful flight, but in seconds she was at the top of the cliff, dropping Epona onto the scrubby grass there before turning to find the Druin. The man with the bow was moving back rapidly from the drop, and some feet away, the other Druin were running to join him. Leven summoned her glass sword, and to her satisfaction all four of them scattered.

'This is more like it.'

She felt as though she were back in the Unblessed lands, watching the enemy as they fled below her, as tiny and as insignificant as ants.

With all their strange Druin magic, they could not get to her up here, whereas she was a lethal thing, a hawk on the wing ready to pounce. One swoop, and they would spill their guts onto the dry grass...

'Leven! Leven! You have to help him!'

Reluctantly Leven turned back to the gully. Epona was stood on the edge again and was pointing down to where they had left the injured Cillian. He was on his feet, but barely, and the rocks had started to fall again. His small jackdaw was circling him frantically, squawking over and over.

'Shit.' She gave one last look at the retreating enemy, then flew back down into the gully. She grabbed Cillian under the armpits and swept him up and out of the narrow path. Epona reached up for him as she flew back over and once the two of them were safely away from the falling rocks, Leven turned back to see what had happened to the Druin. They had vanished, all save for the woman, who was standing with the bow, her back straight and the bowstring pulled taut. Leven had perhaps half a second to realise that she was the target, and that she wasn't wearing any armour, and then a force that felt like being kicked by a mule smacked into her right arm. The blue glass sword flickered and vanished, and she fell back towards the ground.

35

Father and I have drawn the lot this year – it will be our job, from spring to winter, to circle the wall and make sure it is not breached, and if it is, to repair it. We are to be given the supplies to do it, and we will be paid handsomely, so that is something, but when we were back home behind our own walls, he fell into despair. He cried in a way I have never seen before. I know it is bad, but I am determined that we will be careful. People do return from this duty. Perhaps I will go and speak to some of those who have returned, in case they have any advice.

Nizran agreed to speak to me about the wall, but he was so nervous that I'm not sure I understood all of what he told me. He said not to sleep near it at night – it will take more time, he said, but it's worth making camp each night out of sight of the wall. That goes double for any repairs you have to make, he said. Once the sun is close to the horizon, get out of there. Don't be there after dark. And keep your gods close.

Today we set off, and I got my first glimpse of the wall. It is not what I thought at all. There is nothing scary about it, but I can't ignore how it has changed my father's mood. While we walk the perimeter he barely speaks at all, and my every attempt to lighten our work with chatter or songs is met with disinterest or even fury. He says we shouldn't make light of it. The ghosts won't appreciate it.

Series of notes found in a journal
abandoned near the Black City

The hole in the wall was a significant one. At the base it was easily wide enough for a man to walk through, and the line of broken masonry carried on above, as if the wall had split open at some point, or someone had struck it with an enormous axe. The place was accessible enough, which immediately put Kaeto on his guard. Surely the place would not be abandoned in that case? In all his years working for the Imperium, Kaeto had never seen a building or a village completely abandoned. There were always people who needed shelter, always people who were desperate enough for any kind of roof over their heads. He held Riz next to the gap in the wall and lifted him up until he was at eye level with the thief.

'Who else is in there? Are we about to walk into another ambush?'

The man actually laughed. 'You are out of your mind. There is no one in there. No one is crazy enough!'

Kaeto looked at him steadily. 'I will kill you if you're lying to me. Do you understand that?'

The brief merriment faded from Riz's face. He turned his head away. 'Yeah, I understand that alright. You've got my friends' blood all over your knives.'

'Good.' Kaeto dropped him and began pushing him towards the gap. Immediately, Riz fought back; his hands were bound behind him but he dug in with his heels, tried to throw himself to one side.

'You can't make me go in there!' He lurched back again. 'You don't need me, I promise, you can just leave me out here, can't you? Wait!'

'He really doesn't want to go in there,' Belise said, her hands on her hips. 'I'll go, chief! I can have a quick look around and report back.'

'No,' said Kaeto shortly. 'He goes first. If any more of his friends are waiting, I want him to be first in line for the arrows.'

'All this shouting.' Tyleigh had dismounted from her own horse and was picking at the crumbling bricks of the wall. 'Get this over with, Envoy. I'm losing my patience.'

With one hand gripping the collar of Riz's shirt and the other clamped around the man's bound wrists, Kaeto shoved the smaller man through the gap in the wall. Riz was trembling all over, and when they got inside he seemed to deflate, as though all the strength had gone out of him.

'Gods help me,' he whispered. 'I'm inside the Black City. I'll die here.'

'Stop gibbering,' snapped Kaeto, although to himself he admitted that he was unnerved. He had expected the Black City to be little more than a pile of ancient ruins. Instead, it seemed to be an entire abandoned city, bricked up behind an enormous wall with no gates. From where they stood he could see several grand buildings, with tall windows and crow-stepped gables, all carved from black stone. In the moonlight it was difficult to tell the condition of everything, but aside from a thick covering of vines and other crawling plants, what he could see looked largely intact. Yet the place was eerily silent.

Belise came through the hole behind them, one hand on her injured arm. She turned in a slow circle taking it all in.

'Stars and arses,' she whispered. 'Is this the place we were after? I thought it was going to be some big pile of broken stone. This can't be that old, can it?'

'This does complicate things.' Tyleigh climbed through last, leaving the horses tethered to the trees. She stood up straight and glared around at the buildings as though they were a huge inconvenience, which Kaeto supposed they were, in a way. 'Finding anything Titan-related in all this is going to be a challenge.'

'You're all mad,' Riz cried. He had fallen to his knees on the broken paving. 'There's only death here. If you had any sense you'd leave now.' He turned to Kaeto. 'Let me go, alright? Do I...' He lowered his voice, and he kept his dark eyes on Kaeto. 'Do I really mean so little to you, my friend?'

Kaeto frowned, but Tyleigh was busy glaring at the buildings and didn't appear to notice the man's tone.

'This evening your friends attempted to rob us and leave us for dead,' Kaeto replied evenly. 'I'll leave you to work out how much you currently mean to me, *friend*.'

Riz smiled sadly and shook his head. 'I suppose I should have expected that, but it's always been in my nature to look for pleasure in the darkest places. Listen. You don't need me for anything more. I've shown you to this cursed place, so let me go. You don't even have to untie me, just let me run.'

'Up you get.' Kaeto took hold of the man's arm and yanked him up. The dark and the stillness of the abandoned city was catching at his nerves. He wanted to get undercover quickly. 'Belise, check the doorway of that house. We need to find shelter for the night.'

Glad to be given something to do, Belise trotted across the broken paving stones, her dagger held lightly in one hand. Kaeto watched as she disappeared through the open doorway. Tyleigh was peering around at the buildings and sighing. A few moments later Belise reappeared in the doorway and waved them over.

'It's a bit musty,' she said, 'but there's a fireplace, or at least what I think is one, and the floor is dry. There were loads of beetles in there. I heard them all scuttling off when I went inside.' She pulled a face and unconsciously her free hand touched her arm again. 'But I reckon all of these buildings will have beetles.'

'A good point. Go and fetch our supplies from the horses, Belise, and we'll make up a fire.'

Inside it was much as she said. There was a rectangular hole in one of the walls that did appear to lead to a flue, but an iron contraption that had fallen to one side in pieces made Kaeto wonder if it was some sort of cooking apparatus rather than a fireplace. Either way, it would do. He made Riz sit in the corner, and when Belise returned he built a fire quickly, lighting it with the tinder box he kept in one of his pockets. When it was burning merrily, he took some time to look at the room more closely.

'I had expected to camp out in the rough, but I suppose this is better. There's a roof, at least,' said Tyleigh, although she didn't sound convinced.

Kaeto nodded. Aside from the metal contraption and the hole in the wall, there was barely anything inside. In the firelight the walls revealed more crawling vines, and a few tattered remains of what might have been silk-paper, painted with shapes and figures he could barely make out. Beyond the room there was a hallway that led to a steep set of steps. Something about the place was wrong, but he couldn't put his finger on it.

'Belise,' he said. 'What is wrong with this room?'

The girl stood up from where she was warming her hands by the fire and looked around. As he had taught her, she spent some minutes carefully taking in each part of it, looking at things from different angles.

'Hmm,' she said.

'Are you serious?' said Riz. 'Everything is wrong with it. This is the Black City. No human should... We shouldn't be in here.'

'It's the proportions,' Belise said, as if he hadn't spoken. 'Look at this doorway.' She went and stood in the entrance to the room and held her arms out to either side of her. She spun around slowly. 'Look at the size of it! It's too big. The ceilings are really high. And those steps,' she nodded to the stairway, 'not made for human feet.'

'Ah.' Kaeto smiled, pleased. The girl was like an extra pair of eyes. 'That is it. How very strange.'

'Very curious indeed.' Tyleigh went and looked at the steps herself. 'Very interesting. I'm going to look upstairs.'

'Be careful,' said Kaeto. 'We don't know how sturdy this place is.'

'I will take the girl with me,' said Tyleigh. 'If there's anything dangerous, she'll find it first.'

'Fine. Belise, you be careful.'

The woman and the girl headed up the stone staircase. Kaeto waited until he heard their footsteps disappear, and then went and sat opposite Riz.

'I take it you wish to leave.'

Riz boggled at him.

'Are you out of your mind? *Yes* I wish to leave. This place is more dangerous than you can know.'

Kaeto nodded once, firmly. 'I will allow you to leave, Riz, even though you have threatened my life, the life of my employer, and most significantly of all, the life of my assistant. I will allow you to leave even though you tried to rob us and leave us for dead.'

'Are you trying to make out you're some poor confused tourist?' Riz shook his head. Much of his fine black hair was stuck to his cheeks and forehead with sweat. 'I saw you kill five people in less time than it takes me to put my trousers on in the morning.'

'Your issues with your trousers are of no interest to me,' said Kaeto evenly. 'What I want is for you to tell me everything you know about this place – this Black City – and I will then allow you to leave.'

The young thief shook his head rapidly. 'You don't understand. We don't even talk about it. It's bad luck. It's like asking the curse to come and get you.'

'You think this curse will kill you?'

'Yes!'

'Riz. I will definitely kill you if you do not tell me what I want to know. The curse is not quite as certain as that, is it?'

The young man went quiet. In the light from the fire Kaeto could see that his eyes were growing wet. He sighed.

'The woman who went upstairs just now? She is a terrible person, what the Imperium calls an *alchemist*. A bone crafter. She has done terrible things to people to get information – not, you understand, torture, exactly, but what she calls experiments. Over the years she has gotten very used to it – doing things to people, and learning from it. I could ask her to come down here and experiment on you.'

Riz shifted on the floor. He looked vulnerable, and the memory of his kisses seemed to burn on Kaeto's throat... but then Kaeto remembered how the gang of cut-throats had emerged from the trees with their weapons ready.

'I don't know much, not really,' Riz said eventually. His voice was very quiet. 'Like I said, it's not something we talk about. When I was a kid, we used to swap stories of the Black City, but then we got caught, and nothing puts you off talking about something than seeing your grumpy old bastard of a father afraid because of some words you said.' He sighed deeply, as if committing himself to something. 'A people built this place. They were old, very old, and they weren't like us. The city... it's said to be taller than it is wide.'

'What does that mean?'

'I mean, supposedly there's not much of the city above ground. Most of it, they built below, because... because they were devils.'

Kaeto cocked his head to one side. 'Devils.'

'Yes! I know what that sounds like, but that is what was always said. Devils. Demons.'

Above their heads it was just possible to hear Belise and Tyleigh speaking. Kaeto hoped Belise wasn't antagonising the older woman, even inadvertently.

'When was all this?'

Riz shook his head. 'How would I know? When there were Titans all over Enonah. Hundreds of years ago, thousands. Who knows things like that?'

'Normally, it would have been written down somewhere,' said Kaeto. 'We have many libraries in the Imperium.'

'With books stolen from all over the world, I suppose.'

Kaeto nodded. This was perfectly true.

'But our research suggests that the Houraki historical record was purged at some point. Go back two thousand years, and there is nothing. The odd mention in the histories of your neighbouring nations, but contemporary accounts of Houraki from your own people? They don't appear to exist. And from everything written since then, yours is apparently the only nation on Enonah that had little to do with the Titans. But sometimes a hole isn't just a hole – sometimes a hole is proof that something was once there.'

Riz laughed, shook his head. 'I'm just a thief. Go and ask your alchemist about this stuff, I'm sure she knows more than me.'

'Fine.' Kaeto leaned forward. 'What *can* you tell me? In my experience, the history that is passed down through hearsay is much more difficult to kill.'

'The story I was always told was about a priestess of the devils. She rose up among them, became more powerful than the rest. She told them it was their destiny to destroy the other Titans, and rule over us. Enough of them believed it that they talked of war, and they built something, but...'

'What?'

Riz shook his head. 'There were many different versions. I've heard that it was a great machine, some terrible thing that tore the bones out of other Titans. And I've heard that it was no machine, but a Titan god, a creature beyond any of them...' He fell silent again and shook his head. 'It's forbidden to talk about it – about that especially. I don't think anyone really knows, and no one with any sense wants to find out, either.'

'There was a war?'

'Yes. The other Titans stood together against them, and they were driven back, to this place, and it's said they were forced underground and sealed up there by some terrible magic.'

'What became of the machine that might not be a machine?'

Riz shrugged. 'I don't know. The devils can't leave the walls of the Black City, but can come up out of their tunnels – or at least, that's what we used to say when we were kids. We used to dare each other to come up to the wall and touch it, knowing a devil could be on the other side.'

'Interesting. But nonsense.'

Riz laughed weakly. 'Believe what you like. But every now and then you'll get someone foolish enough to break into this place, and they never come back. Something in here is hungry, I believe that.'

There was a clatter of footsteps on stone as Tyleigh and Belise made their way down again.

'The third floor had a beetle nest in it,' said Belise. 'Like a weird warren of mushed-up leaves.'

'It was fascinating,' added Tyleigh. 'I don't know any species of beetle that builds in that way, like a bird does. I've left poison up there, should have a lot of beetle carcasses in a few days.'

'Why would you do that?' asked Riz. He sounded sickened. 'They don't do any harm to anyone!'

'Apart from *biting* people who are only going about their own business,' Belise muttered.

Tyleigh gave Riz a hard considering look, as if wondering if she had some poison for him too.

'I'd like to cut one up,' she said bluntly. 'See how they work.'

Kaeto stood and pulled the knife from his belt. Riz cringed back against the wall, but Kaeto knelt and cut the bonds from his wrists.

'You can go,' he said. 'But please do keep in mind that if I see you again, or if Belise sees you again, we will kill you immediately. Especially if you should think to return with any more of your friends.'

'Don't worry.' Riz was on his feet already, rubbing his wrists where the ropes had left pinkish marks. 'There's no way I'm coming back to this accursed shit hole.' He glanced around at all three of them. 'If you've got any sense, you'll follow me out.'

And with that he left. They stood and listened to his footsteps outside, growing faster as he broke into a run, and then fading to nothing.

'What an odd little man,' said Tyleigh. 'Did he tell you anything useful, Envoy?'

They sat and heated up a small meal over the fire, and Kaeto recounted everything that Riz had told him, about the 'devils' and their war with the other Titans, and the strange machine that might not be a machine.

'The Othanim,' said Tyleigh. 'I knew I was right. They lived here, two thousand years ago, and their remains must be around here somewhere, Envoy. We are on the cusp of the greatest discovery in the Imperium's history.'

'What about this machine thing?' asked Belise. 'Could that be here too?'

'It's interesting, but it's not important,' said Tyleigh. 'Othanim bones are our priority.'

Before she bedded down for the night the alchemist made a series of notes in a leather-covered notebook she had in her pack. When she had taken herself off to the other side of the room and was snoring steadily, Kaeto and Belise prepared their own routines for the rest of the night and early morning.

'Do you believe it, chief? What Riz said about this place?'

'It's likely that parts of it are true, and others are not – when a story has been around for a very long time, it grows strange and warped in the telling.' He had heated them up some tea, and as he watched Belise downed the last of hers. 'We should be careful, but don't go jumping at shadows.'

'What if it is cursed?'

'Curses are for children's tales, Belise. Remember, we are here to dig up Titan remains, and it seems very likely that the last of them died thousands of years ago. If there was any Titan magic here once, it's long gone. I will take the first watch. Get some sleep.'

When the child was settled, Kaeto made his own brief search of the building, and went back down to the wide doorway and looked out. The street remained dark and silent, save for the faint skittering of thousands of beetles, out of sight. He watched and waited for a time, unsettled by Riz's stories despite what he had said to Belise, but the night remained quiet, and no ghosts loomed out of the dark. He returned to the fireplace and settled in for his watch.

In the morning he left Belise to prepare some bread and dried meat for Tyleigh's breakfast and went outside – he was eager to see what the place was like in the daylight. The first thing he saw when he stepped beyond the entrance was Riz's broken body, lying no more than twenty feet away. The man had been torn open from sternum to groin, and the long sticky ropes of his guts had been yanked out so far that they tangled around his feet. There was blood in great quantities everywhere but only around the body – no tracks or drips led to it, and there were no flies around the corpse. It was as though Riz had changed his mind and come back towards the building, only to simply explode where he stood.

36

L even was walking in the winter woods again, alone. She knew this place well; she had spent hours playing in the ruins, tracing the broken walls and picturing the splendour of a long-lost castle. She had spent whole days picking through the tangled undergrowth, seeking out exactly the right flowers and plants for her mother, and she had hunted here with her father, learning patience as they tracked a lone deer for hours or how to make traps to catch rabbits. They had to be careful where they went. Mother had lectured them on this subject over and over again – anywhere beyond the Paths was not truly safe, especially if she wasn't with them – but Father had never really been one for obeying rules.

Today though, she was alone. The woods were alive and wet, the dripping of half-melted snow creating its own kind of music between the trunks and branches. The ground was wet and squelched satisfyingly under her boots, and she could hear ravens calling, harsh lonely cries that seemed spooky to her, as though they were announcing bad news in a language she couldn't understand. She sang under her breath to drown it out.

'A thousand birds will carry you,

Carry you far away,

A thousand birds must carry you,

Because only the dead can stay.'

Ahead of her she spotted something moving in the undergrowth. Dropping into the crouch her father had taught her, Leven crept forward, her hand holding an imaginary spear. At first she thought it must have been a trick of the light, that there was nothing there at all, but then the creature turned its head and she saw what it was, so cleverly camouflaged in the winter ground-muck. It was a jackdaw, a very young one.

'What are you doing on the ground, little one?' Leven straightened up and moved forward slowly, so as not to frighten it. 'If I had wings, I'd never come down.'

The chick gave an outraged little squawk and left its beak open, tasting the air. Leven looked around, trying to spot the nest it might have fallen from.

'I will move you at least,' she said. 'Somewhere with a bit more cover, otherwise anything could come along and step on you. Or eat you.'

She leaned down to pick up the chick and caught sight of her own hand, pale and unmarked, and for some reason that struck her as strange.

'Where have the lines gone?' She held her hand up in front of her face. '*Where are my ore-lines?*'

As if her voice had called it into being, the ominous clicking and clacking started up again – almost a gentle noise, the satisfying sound of a key turning in a lock. There was nothing terrible about the sound really. So why did it fill her with such a crawling sense of dread?

Click click click. Clack clack clack. CLACKCLACKCLACK.

And then the world seemed to turn sideways. She wasn't crouching in the mud, she was lying on the ground, and it wasn't cold and wet, either; there was a fierce warmth on her face, although it wasn't quite strong enough to distract her from the pain in her arm.

'Fucking *ow*.'

'She's waking up.' Epona's voice was close, then far away. 'I thought Heralds were supposed to be tougher than this, you know.'

Leven forced her eyes open. 'We do heal faster than normal. The ore-lines won't tolerate being broken.' And then, 'What happened?'

'They caught you with one of their arrows. Hold still.' Cillian was seated next to her and was busily bandaging her arm. They were in a small, summery clearing, filled with thick green grass and fringed with tall, shaggy old trees. 'The arrowhead grazed you but the thing is poisoned, which is probably why it knocked you out of the sky.'

'Oh.' Leven tried to sit up, and the small summery glade spun crazily. 'How bad is it?'

'It's lethal,' said Cillian mildly, 'but luckily you had me here to treat it. Let me finish this.' He pulled the last piece of bandage tight, and somehow the pain eased slightly. Gingerly Leven lifted her arm and turned it back and forth. The dream still felt very close, and she found herself looking around for Inkwort.

'Hold on,' she said, pushing her hair out of her eyes. 'You took an arrow too. I saw it hit your shoulder.' She also remembered the pulse of panic and anger that had overtaken her at the sight of it. 'But you look fine. Why aren't you poisoned?'

'No poison made in these woods can harm me,' he said, and then, 'the arrow caught my flesh but not deeply. Most of the damage was to my tunic, truthfully. And Princess Epona is remarkably good at dressing wounds herself.'

'My mother believes in practical skills,' said Epona. She was standing over the pair of them with her arms crossed over her chest. She looked pensive, the blue lines on her brow drawn together in a frown. 'I don't like this. Who were those Druin, Cillian? Did you know them?'

'No,' he said, although he did not look up. 'They were not known to me.'

'You *did* know them,' said Epona. 'You called one of them by name.'

Cillian sighed and shook his head. 'Why do you ask if you know the answer?' He stood up. 'Loveday was the Druin who opened the gift from your mother, Princess. That is all I know.'

'So these Druin are the Druin of the Kornwullis court?'

He shook his head. He looked tired, his long brown hair especially untidy. 'No, I don't think so. I don't know. I don't think they were acting on Queen Verla's orders, if that is what you're asking.'

'Well I'm glad to hear that – one queen ordering the murder of another queen's daughter would be a storm of shit I would not like to have to dance through.' Epona put her hands on her hips and pushed her shoulders back until her bones popped. 'Ugh. I slept in a real bed last night and already I feel like I've been hit with a bag of sticks. So what are they? Rogue Druin?'

'They called themselves the Atchorn,' said Cillian. 'There have been rumours...'

'Whatever they are, you should have let me kill them all.' Leven scrambled to her feet and very nearly pitched back into the mud. Cillian caught her elbow and for a brief second she clung to his arm, grateful. 'Alright, I'm fine, you can let me go.'

'You should rest more,' he said. 'Even with the healing I've done, the poison should have weakened you considerably.'

'I'm tough. It's fine.' She caught sight of Inkwort, seated on Cillian's discarded pack. The little bird was watching her closely with its eerie blue eyes. *Do you know I dreamt about you, bird?* 'What happened out there? They moved the earth somehow. And you stopped it?'

Cillian went over to his pack. Inkwort hopped easily onto the Druin's shoulder. 'Druin magic, an especially rare type. We're only supposed to use it when all else has failed,' he said. He opened the pack and pulled out one of the packages of dried fish, which he passed to Leven. 'Eat something. It'll chase the poison out of your system faster. These other Druin, they knew the earth of Kornwullis, so it was easier for them to move it. But I know that land, and I'm not without power there either.'

'Which is a relief, because without that we'd all be painting the bottom of that gully right now,' said Epona. 'I wish I could speak to my mother about this. She might have heard of them.'

'We could send her a message through the trees,' said Cillian, 'but it is slow. And since the Atchorn are also Druin they might be able to intercept it.'

'Does it matter?' asked Leven. 'We got away from them. And if I ever see any of them again, I'll drop each of them from a great height.'

'Of course it matters!' Epona threw her hands up. 'A group of rogue Druin, going against the orders of my mother, and Queen Verla? If we had been killed today, there would have been a real war between Kornwullis and Londus, and despite what Verla may pretend about her dislike for outsiders, no one wants that.'

Cillian took a long drink from a waterskin and wiped his hand across his mouth. 'There may be someone we can ask,' he said. 'About the Atchorn. But you will not like it.'

'What is this place?'

Cillian had led them from the secluded clearing down another Path, and then he had made the woods change again. Now they walked under a sky heavy with twilight, while around them the bright green wood had become a much darker place; the ground underfoot was marshy and wet, and the trees were sparse. Those that did grow were sad, stunted things. The insect life here was loud and enthusiastic, and there was an earthy, overpowering scent of rot.

'If it's the place I think it is,' said Epona, 'then we definitely shouldn't be here, and frankly I am shocked that Cillian, respectable Druin that he is, would bring a princess to this bog.'

Cillian was walking ahead of them, using a long stick to probe the ground. Inkwort flew in distracted circles around the three of them.

'We call it the Lich-Way. Technically it is simply another pocket hidden within the Wild Wood that we are able to access. But in truth the Lich-Way is... different. We shouldn't linger here. We'll ask our questions and get out again.' He glanced at the darkening sky. 'Definitely before it gets fully dark.'

'I can't help noticing that neither of you are actually answering my question.' Leven shifted her pack again. Her wounded arm was aching.

'There. The place we need is just ahead.'

About two hundred feet away the marshy ground gave up its pretence at solidity and relaxed into a meandering stretch of greenish pond. Hanging over it were several diffuse points of light, floating and moving gently around each other. In another place Leven thought the lights might have been beautiful – there was something about the pale golden glow that was hypnotic – but here, in this stinking place, they felt more like a warning or a deception.

'The Lich-Way,' Epona said, picking her way carefully along in Cillian's footsteps, 'is a place where lost souls gather. They group together, you see – misery loves company, I suppose. And a lot of people lose their lives in the Wild Wood. Give them long enough, and they will seek each other out. This is the place where they end up.'

Leven waved a group of tiny flying insects away from her face.

'Of all the places to come after a near-death experience... And why have we come here, exactly?'

'Because sometimes the dead know things.' Cillian had led them to the edge of the pond. It was thick with bright green algae and covered with broad lily pads that sprouted fleshy yellow flowers. The wispy points of light rose and fell slowly, as though moving with the breath of the forest. Leven found she could hardly take her eyes off of them.

'Are those the lost souls?'

'No.' Cillian threw his stick into the pond, disturbing the algae and revealing, very briefly, the whirling black mud beneath the surface. 'We'd have words with you, sisters.'

The water churned violently and three large objects bobbed to the surface. Leven initially took them to be big bundles of waterlogged wood; they were knobbled and twisted and water gushed from several holes. It was only when one of them opened its jaws that she realised that they were three skeletons, turned rigid and black by the brackish water. It was difficult to see where one ended and the other began.

'Speak then, green-boy.' The one in the middle spoke first. The skull still had most of its hair, which clung like seaweed to its peeling scalp.

'Bog bodies, we've come—'

'What is that *thing*?' The middle corpse turned its attention to Leven, its blank sockets still pouring with pond water.

'What has the green-boy brought here? Surely not that? Surely not that which is forbidden?'

Leven gritted her teeth, trying to ignore the way her skin was crawling. The other two skeletons were watching her closely too, although she couldn't have said what they were watching her with, given their lack of eyeballs.

'Bog bodies,' said Cillian, raising his voice slightly. He took a step forward, and as one they all turned back to him. 'I'm here because you wise ladies know more about the days and nights of the Wild Wood than anyone. Your wisdom is unmatched. Nothing moves in the wood without your seeing it. They say that—'

'Yes, alright,' said the central skeleton. 'You needn't lay it on so thick. What do you want?'

Cillian cleared his throat. 'We have encountered Druin that seem to act against the code of the Druidahnon. They attacked us, against the wishes of our queens. They called themselves the Atchorn. Who are they?'

'Oh those. Yes we know about *those*.' To Leven's surprise, the rotten skeletal creatures, with their black bones and fibrous remnants of flesh, sounded oddly familiar. How many times had she stood with the gossipy landlady of a tavern and listened to her drag her customers through the mud? 'Druin who have been away from the Wild Wood so long the sap in their veins has turned hard, lost all its vital greenery. There is more salt in their blood now – the sea has them. The Atchorn feel themselves drifting from the Wild Wood, and it makes them murderous.'

Cillian frowned. 'What do they want?'

'What they think is for the best,' said the skeleton on the right. 'They want an end to the time of queens, particularly those they believe to be especially... *modern*. Like your mother, little cat.'

Epona jumped like she had been pinched. 'What do you mean? Do they intend to do her harm?'

'Oh in the long run yes, I'm sure of it. In the long run they would string up her guts for streamers and drink from her skull, little cat.' This was from the skeleton on the left, who poked her long, blackened fingers into her own empty eye sockets as she spoke. 'The Atchorn want to turn all things over to the Wild again, as it all was when the Druidahnon himself was a cub and the Titans shook their way across these isles.'

'Who are they? Can you give us names?' asked Epona 'Tell us where the cowards are hiding.'

As one the bog bodies laughed wetly.

'The dead don't care for the names of the living, little cat. They don't mean anything on this side of the forest.'

'Thank you,' said Cillian. He turned to Leven and Epona. 'That's all we'll get from them. We should leave now, before it gets darker.'

'Wait!' One of the bog bodies lurched forward, sending a little ripple of foul-smelling water across the marshy grass towards them. 'What about the other one? What about this bone thief? Won't you tell us of her?'

'What are you talking about?' demanded Leven.

'A great disgrace, a defiler, a grave robber – the most forbidden, yet green-boy brings her into the Lich-Way as though she were his sweetheart and in need of hiding. Does your lord know what you do?'

The sky darkened, and the humming of the insects died away. The floating lights over the pond sank backwards into the gloom, and a strange skittering noise grew in the distance. Cillian turned away from the bog bodies.

'We've outstayed our welcome here,' he said.

'Tell us about her, tell us,' the three skeletons demanded. 'The bone thief has mysteries inside her, can't you feel it? Tell usssss.'

'What do you know about me?' Leven demanded, but the bog bodies shrank back from her, black water slapping at their knobbly chests.

'Come on.' Epona grabbed her arm and pulled her after Cillian. 'I think the green-boy is right. I don't like this place. The sooner we get to Mersia the better.'

Cillian was already opening up the new Path ahead of them. Bright daylight broke through, clean and beautiful after the stinking darkness of the bog, and the three of them ran headlong into it, leaving the clamouring voices of the dead behind.

PART TWO

THE BONE FALL
TO GALABROC

37

The horror and the violence of the Imperium grows with each sunrise, with each season, each turning of Enonah. They take our neighbours one by one, calling the bloodshed 'blessed' while we hear stories of their butchery in our ports. We have held them back from our shores for generations, but the threat cannot be ignored. Their desecration of the Titans has reached new heights; they have taken the precious bones from beneath the cesspit of Stratum, and the empress has ordered that her soldiers have the souls of Titans sown into their skin, creating monsters that the forest can barely imagine.

The Druin must resist them, as one. The Heralds are a dark shadow of what we are, and an insult to the Druidahnon himself. The forest speaks.

Notes from the Druin conclave
on the Imperial threat

I t was dusk, and the last of the Atchorn were fading back into the summer mists. Loveday watched them go from the threshold of one of their hideouts; it was little more than a hole dug in the earth with flat stones bracing its walls, but the strong earthy scents of the dirt under her feet were a comfort. They had failed today, and the failure nipped at her heart with sharp teeth. The Herald and a princess had been in their grasp, and what a feather in their cap that would have been, yet the Herald had shown herself to be stronger than expected, and the Druin had thrown his lot in with the Imperial monster. *I should have tried harder,* she thought, narrowing her eyes at the growing dark. *Pushed him to come with me. Once I'd had him in my bed, he wouldn't have looked twice at the Herald creature.*

She was just turning to extinguish their small peat fire when a flicker of something unexpected moved across her senses. There was no Wild Wood in this part of Kornwullis, but she still had her connection to the earth, as stony as it was, and it was telling her that some large warm-blooded animal was approaching. It was too late to get rid of the fire as whatever it was would have seen the light already, so she stepped away from the barrow, hoping to hide herself in the growing shadows. There was a figure approaching through the gorse, someone tall, and without a horse. For a brief second she hoped it was the other Druin, Cillian, that perhaps he had changed his mind and returned to her, but as it drew closer she saw that this could not be; the Druin was slender, with hair that fell to his neck. This person was powerfully built, and they wore a hooded cloak that couldn't disguise their broad shoulders.

'There's no use in hiding.' A woman's voice, low and terse. 'Stay where you are.'

Loveday scowled. She brought her hands up in front of her, ready to use the earth magic again. She'd drown this person in soil and rocks before they drew that sword at their hip.

'Who are you? What do you want?'

The figure stopped when she was still some ten feet away. Between the growing dark and the shadow of her hood, it was difficult to make out her face. Loveday thought she could see pale skin, a scattering of freckles.

'The Druin Loveday. One of the leaders of the Atchorn.'

It wasn't a question, but Loveday shook her head.

'I don't know what you're talking about.'

'Oh please.' The woman flashed a grin. Loveday felt cold. There had been no humour in it. 'Don't waste my time. I know who you are and I know the Atchorn – a group of rebel Druin dedicated to giving the rule of Brittletain to the Wild Wood.'

'Returning it,' Loveday said sharply. 'When the Titans walked this island, they didn't tolerate human queens. But if you've come to kill me, or drag me in irons back to Verla, you've made a mistake. I may be alone but I can summon the earth to crush you in seconds.'

The figure tilted her head to one side. 'I thought the Druin had forsworn the more… violent of your magics?'

'The Druin have forsworn a number of things that should never have been set aside,' said Loveday. 'But that will all change when the queens of Brittletain are toppled from their thrones.'

'What would Queen Verla say, to hear you speak like that?' The figure shook her head, and in doing so the hood fell back a little. Loveday saw a pair of striking blue eyes, and the curve of a ginger brow. A pulse of recognition made her draw in her breath sharply.

'I know you,' she said, although she wasn't entirely certain, not truly. 'Are you not—'

'It doesn't matter who I am,' the woman said, raising her voice slightly. 'You need to listen.'

'Doesn't matter?' Loveday laughed. She wondered if any of the other Atchorn were close enough to hear if she called out. Probably not. 'Are you making a poor joke?'

'I did you the honour of coming here myself because I believed it was the best way to make you listen. Did I make a mistake?'

Loveday held herself very still. When she didn't reply, the other woman began to speak slowly.

'I came here with the offer of an alliance. A way that we can work together, for a time. The Atchorn are angry, and have many grand ambitions, but they lack knowledge and resources, lashing out randomly when what they really need is a plan.' The woman took a slow breath, in and out. 'We both want the same things.'

'I doubt that very much,' cut in Loveday.

'Perhaps, ultimately, our highest goals would not align.' The woman flashed her cold grin again. Loveday thought it looked very much like the moonlight glinting off the pommel of her short sword. 'But that isn't to say we couldn't help each other in the short term. A summer of grace before a winter of hardship. Who knows what you could harvest to help you in the lean times?'

'What is it you want from us?'

'We need someone who does not hold loyalty to any particular queen. Someone who can move through the Paths of the Wild Wood and is willing to go against the wishes of the Druidahnon. I think that is the Atchorn.'

Loveday looked back at her peat fire. Somewhere, an owl was calling to its mate, and there were bats over the barrow. Little flashes of life; nothing in comparison to the thriving glory of the Wild Wood.

'Then we would hear your plan,' she said eventually.

The figure took a step forward, apparently no longer concerned about hiding her face. There was a line of royal blue paint circling her forehead.

'Go to Mersia. You will learn more when you get there.'

38

Some distance to the north of the Bone Fall there was a stretch of land known as the Barrens. The name was misleading; although it was certainly bleak, even by the standards of Yelvynia, the tundra was dotted with dense patches of gorse and short black mulberry trees, and it was home to a sizeable population of snow-white rabbits. Ynis leaned forward over T'rook's shoulder, her eyes watering with the effort of trying to spot the creatures before her sister.

'There, there's one! It's stopped just beyond that pile of rocks.'

T'rook darted through the air and dove, moving so fast that Ynis felt like her stomach had exited through her throat. There was a thump and a squeak, and they were soaring off again, something limp and spattered with red clutched in T'rook's talons.

'That'll be a good lunch.'

Ynis grinned into her sister's neck. It was good to be out flying together again. As much as she had come to enjoy Witch-seer Frost's lessons, there was no denying that they were full of strange, unsettling knowledge, and even a fair amount of hard physical work. Out here there was just the simple joy of watching for prey animals and chasing them, and then the satisfaction of the kill. It was the first time they had hunted together in weeks, and she thought her sister was beginning to warm to life amongst the Edge Walkers – and she also thought she might know why.

'Let's stop and eat this,' she called against the wind. 'I'm half starved.'

T'rook banked and turned into a spiral, bringing them in to land neatly on top of a raised section of rock. Ynis hopped down and kicked some of the ice crystals off the stone until there was a relatively dry place for them to sit. T'rook dropped the body of the rabbit.

'You can open it,' she said. 'It's too small for my beak to bother with.'

Ynis took her claw-knife from her pack and quickly slit the animal along its belly. She yanked out the organs and sorted them, pausing to pop a nugget of kidney into her mouth, still hot with blood.

'You seem happier lately,' she said, not quite looking up at her sister.

'Do I?'

'I thought you were in a permanent sulk here. But perhaps I was wrong?'

T'rook snapped up the other kidney. 'You have made a place for yourself with these death-lickers. So we are stuck here. I will make the best of it.'

'Yesterday,' Ynis continued, 'I saw you preening your feathers very carefully. And then later I saw you flying with T'wesen's son.'

Ynis kept her head down, concentrating on separating the rabbit's skin from its flesh, but she felt quite keenly the look that her sister was now directing at the back of her head.

'What is your point?'

'Nothing,' she said. She bit her lip to keep from grinning. 'He has very fine blue feathers, doesn't he?'

T'rook flapped her wings dismissively. 'I can't say I noticed. Festus is staying here until the next dark moon, at least. I was keeping him company to be polite.'

'Oh *Festus*, is it?'

T'rook's beak opened dangerously wide at that, but before she could answer the quiet of the tundra was interrupted by a piercing scream. It came from beyond a ridge of small hills to the north of them and was followed by a flurry of shouts. Ynis felt her stomach turn over: the shouts were not griffin shouts. They sounded small and flat, like her own.

Without exchanging a word, Ynis climbed onto T'rook's back and they were up in the air again, heading towards the hills. Very quickly they saw a griffin in distress, flying in a confused circle some distance above the ground.

'Is that Brocken?' Ynis leaned around T'rook's neck, trying to get a closer look. 'She has arrows in her!'

The big griffin was obviously in trouble, and although her huge wings had kept her aloft so far, with each beat she was lurching closer to the ground. Beneath her, standing in the scrubby grass, were five humans, three of them holding bows. Seeing them, Ynis felt her heart almost stop – she had never seen any of her own kind so close before. They seemed ugly to her, their bare faces raw and somehow obscene, their bodies stringy and unappealing. In her fist, she gripped her claw-knife a little tighter.

'Get away!' cried T'rook as they came over the top of the hill. The humans on the ground below scattered and then re-formed, clearly reluctant to leave their prize, but at that moment Brocken turned and roared at them. Ynis and T'rook added their voices to hers, and that seemed to be enough for the small band of humans. They picked up a net they had cast on the ground and then they ran, moving surprisingly quickly across the flat ground.

'I will catch them,' said T'rook. 'Catch them and we'll eat their guts still steaming.' But at that moment Brocken fell from the air and crashed into the ground awkwardly, half landing on one of her own wings. There was a sickening crunch. Ynis tugged on the feathers on the back of T'rook's neck, but she had already gotten the message. Ignoring the fleeing attackers, she circled down and landed by the injured griffin.

'Brocken!' Ynis jumped down and ran to her side, but she could see almost immediately that it was very bad. There were a couple of arrows piercing Brocken's wings, and there was blood spattered all over her tawny fur and feathers, but the real problem was an arrow so deeply stuck in her broad chest that there was only three inches or so of the shaft protruding; the rest of it, including the arrowhead, was deep inside her. Blood pumped steadily from the wound so that the scrubby hillside was quickly soaked and steaming.

'Ynis?' Brocken rolled an eye towards them. 'Humans. So brazen. They... tracked me. Attacked from all sides.'

'Be quiet,' snapped T'rook. 'You'll wear yourself out.'

But Brocken wasn't listening. 'You have to tell Frost. About the humans. I knew that they...' She paused to pant heavily. With a horror that turned her cold all over, Ynis saw that blood was oozing from the corners of her beak. 'They have never come so far before.'

'We'll tell her.' Ynis was still examining the wound. She curled her fingers around the shaft that was visible and gave it the barest tug, and Brocken bellowed with pain. 'I don't know how to get this out. It's too far in.' She glanced at T'rook for help, but her sister looked as terrified as she felt. 'Can you fly, Brocken? Perhaps if my sister helped you...'

'No, it is done.' Brocken shuddered on the grass, her huge chest rising and falling with obvious effort. 'Ynis, you must perform the rites for me.'

'What? No. I can't, I've barely... We'll get Frost, just wait here.'

'No time. Please, Ynis. I know that this... is what you were brought to us for. It's who you are.'

Ynis looked at T'rook again. Her sister pressed her head against her shoulder briefly.

'You can do it,' she said, very quietly.

'I...' Ynis slumped to her knees in the grass. Her hands were still deeply buried in Brocken's bloody fur. 'I'm not ready.'

'You ask me about my life,' croaked Brocken. 'That is the first part.'

The wind picked up across the Barrens, howling down from the mountains.

'Brocken of the Edge Walkers.' Ynis took a deep breath. 'Tell us of your life.'

'My mother and father were kind. They understood little of me, so I... left.' It was obviously costing Brocken a great deal to keep talking, and Ynis felt transfixed by the surge of her blood as it left her body. 'It was here, in the Bone Fall, that I found my real life. My real... family. Is here. I was given my true name. And I walked the Edge until it was my time. The time is now. I am not afraid. I step beyond the Edge.'

She hadn't been looking for it or even concentrating, but Ynis realised she could see Brocken's spirit, rising a little above her body, blue and shimmering and beautiful. The thin red cord of her fate-ties streamed up into the air and seemed to move slightly with the wind. Ynis could not see its end; instead it seemed to split, high up in the blue sky, into more threads than she could count, all streaming off into the distance.

So many ties, she thought. *All the griffins she was closest to in life.*

Ynis reached up with the claw-knife and held it close to the thin red thread.

'Brocken, thank you,' she said. Tears were running down her face, so hot they felt like blood. 'Thank you for bringing us here to find our real lives.'

Brocken chuckled. 'You are welcome, yenlin.' Her voice was fading to nothing, a whisper in the wind. 'I will go now. Tell Frost...'

Ynis waited a heartbeat longer, but Brocken had no more words left in her. She slipped her knife across the cord and watched as one end curled away into the sky. A moment later the spirit that was Brocken stood up from her old body and was lost in a bright splash of sunlight. Ynis dropped the knife.

'They *killed* her.' T'rook's throat feathers were puffed up, and her flight feathers were trembling. 'Humans killed a griffin!'

Ynis stood. She felt very shaky herself. Once again she had the blood of a griffin on her hands. She looked down the hill where the humans had run. They had left their tiny footprints in the thin layer of snow. She wondered if they had seen her at all, and if they had, what they had thought.

'Come on,' she said. 'We have to tell Frost.'

39

The girl is talented and dedicated, no question. She will become a Druin with no trouble at all – she's already half wild, spending more time outside than in. And it's given her a structure she needed, alone as she was. But the girl is too fascinated with the Dunohi – she seeks them out on the Paths, and if you're not watching her closely, she will leave the Paths behind altogether and go looking for them in the Wildest Wood. Three times now we've caught her and brought her back, and I still don't believe she understands the danger. I don't think there's anything else she can be but Druin, and yet I fear it's also how she will meet her end. She has no fear of them, no fear at all.

A personal note from a Druin
elder to the Druidahnon

Leven watched, fascinated, as a huge blue butterfly opened and closed its wings slowly in front of her. She had been picking berries off a bush by the side of the Path when the insect had landed on a cluster of blossoms. She stood very still, not wanting to scare it off.

'What are you doing?' Cillian appeared next to her. He and Leven had decided to scout ahead for some fresh water while Epona stayed back at the camp, ostensibly trying to cook a fat wild bird they had managed to trap. 'There's a small creek back here, we can fill our skins from that.'

Leven didn't take her eyes from the butterfly. 'Look at this thing! I've never seen anything quite this colour. Have you?'

'I've seen butterflies just like that before, many times.' But when she glanced at Cillian she saw that he had a curious expression on his face, like he'd seen something funny where he wasn't expecting it. Leven straightened up, feeling her face grow warm.

'Where was this creek?'

She followed him over to the narrow channel of water, but not without a backward glance at the butterfly. It was, she realised, something of a novelty simply to have the time to stop and look. When she had been travelling with the Heralds there had been no opportunities to admire the local wildlife. If anything, showing undue interest in the Unblessed lands was considered, at best, embarrassing, and at worst a kind of treason. Here though, finally, she was out from under the unrelenting gaze of Boss. She could stop and look at anything she wanted to. Or just enjoy the quiet.

'Are you alright?'

Leven realised she had been staring at nothing again. Cillian was stood over the creek, carefully filling up his waterskin. She took the second one from him and crouched down by the water.

'I'm fine. Great, actually.'

'Your arm isn't hurting you?'

Leven held her arm out and flexed it back and forth. 'It's more or less as good as new. One of the perks of being a Herald – we heal quickly. I just...' She grinned and shook her head. 'It's so quiet here. I don't think I've ever been anywhere this quiet.'

'Your campaigns for the Starlight Imperium never took you through forests?'

'Oh they did, but there was always something to do – setting up camp, breaking up camp, foraging supplies, drills.'

'Killing the natives.'

Leven stood up and wiped her wet hands on the backs of her trousers. 'There are no second chances with you, are there, Cillian?'

He put the waterskins away. 'I'm not sure it's my place to give you a second chance. I can only tell you that the Imperium is not loved. Not here.'

'I'm not the Imperium. I'm just… never mind. If you hate me so much, Cillian, then why did you bother healing my arm? You could have just told Epona that you didn't know the antidote for that poison and let me die.'

She made herself look him in the eye. In the dappled green light, with the ridged horns curling over his forehead and his hair falling about his face, he looked more than ever like a creature of the forest.

Why do I care what he thinks? A savage of Brittletain could never understand the might and the glory of the Imperium. The voice in her head sounded like Boss.

'I suppose because I don't want to see any life thrown away,' he said eventually. 'Even yours.'

Leven scowled and rolled her hands into fists. 'Right. Don't trouble yourself next time. Heralds are tougher than you think, and…'

Her words dried up as a black shadow cast Cillian into darkness. Behind him, a huge shambling shape with an elk's skull for a face had lurched out from the trees. Leven could see tiny points of green light deep within the shadowed sockets, and there was movement in the bulk of its body, as if it were made up of thousands of teeming creatures. Cillian, reading the expression on her face, touched a finger to his lips.

'Don't move,' he whispered.

'If that thing goes for me, I'll bloody move alright,' she whispered back. Already the ore-lines that ran the length of her body were thrumming. Her fingers itched with the need to summon her glass sword.

Slowly, Cillian turned round to face the forest soul. The thing hadn't moved beyond tipping its head slightly to one side, as though listening to their whispered conversation.

'Lord Dunohi, master of the forest,' Cillian said in a low, pleasant voice. 'Forgive our presence. We are following the Paths as agreed, and we won't be here much longer.'

The jaws of the skull fell open with a *clack*, and something seethed where its tongue should be. Leven could hear a fierce buzzing noise, growing in volume.

YOU MUST LEAVE. Leven heard the voice as a shout in her head, so powerful it was like a blow. YOU MUST LEAVE. GET OUT!

The last was so loud that Leven cried out, clapping her hands over her ears. Cillian turned back to her, startled.

'You must be quiet!'

'Tell it to stop shouting at me then!'

Cillian looked like she had struck him. 'It's speaking to you?'

The forest spirit lunged forward, bodily knocking Cillian into the creek and thundering towards Leven. Without a conscious thought her ore-lines blazed to life and a second before the creature struck her, Leven opened her wings as wide as they would go. Together, she and the forest soul crashed backwards through the foliage and off the Path, the sound of branches falling and splintering trees a cacophony in her ears. She was caught just below the creature's skull, pressed into the strange matted, fibrous material that made up its body. Small branches whipped at her face as she tried to bring her sword around.

'Get. Off. Me.'

WINGED MURDERERS. YOU MUST LEAVE. NEVER RETURN.

There was a crunch as they collided with a huge old tree. The Titan strength inside her seemed to well up in response, and Leven pushed, using the tree as leverage. The forest soul fell back, its bleached skull agape – the tiny points of green light, she noticed, had turned red.

That doesn't seem like a good sign.

She brought her blazing blue sword around in a two-handed grip above her head, ready to strike.

'Stop! Don't you dare!'

Cillian appeared at the edge of her vision, although he looked so different that for a moment she thought the forest soul had shaken all the sense out of her head. He rose up next to them on a moving tide of roots and branches, and his skin was tinged green along his jaw and across his eyes. There were tiny plants twined through his hair and along his horns, and his green eyes were a bright tawny yellow. He lifted his arm and stretched out his fingers, and a stream of living tendrils shot out from the wave beneath him and pushed the forest spirit back. The thing hissed and buzzed angrily.

'Let us pass, lord!' Cillian shouted. 'The Druidahnon commands it!'

The forest soul drew back a few more paces, shaking its skull back and forth. Leven dropped down to the ground, wincing at the places where she had been grazed on her abrupt journey through the forest. To her surprise, Leven spotted Cillian's jackdaw flying in circles between them, chattering in its own strange tongue.

INTERLOPER, thundered the forest soul again. NEVER TO RETURN.

But it sounded less certain now. Cillian, on his wave of vegetation, pushed forward, moving the forest soul back into the trees, but gently now.

'Go, lord,' he said again. 'There's nothing here to concern you. Go back to the secret places of the Wild Wood.'

As Leven watched, the forest soul seemed to step into shadows that weren't there, its solidity fading, and then it was gone entirely, vanished back into the darker wood. Cillian hung there for a moment, his hands up, and then the wave of squirming roots he stood on sank back into the ground, and he fell with them, unmoving, into the mud.

'I'm telling you, the thing was angry. It was shouting at me.'

When Cillian woke up, he was lying on his back at the camp. Princess Epona and Leven were both sitting by the fire. Leven looked tattered and covered in scratches, while Epona was poking at some sort of stew she had cooking over the fire.

'So you say,' said Epona, 'but the Dunohi would hardly talk to a stranger. They barely even talk to us! Why would it speak to you and not me, a princess of Brittletain?'

'Well it wasn't Cillian it was trying to squash into a tree. Believe me, you're welcome to all future conversations with the bastard things.'

'And yet poor Cillian seems the worst off.' Epona clattered a spoon against one of their tin cups. 'This stew will sort him out. Or at least, I'm certain it can't make him feel worse.'

Cillian sat up, groaning. It had been a full year since he had tapped into such a direct link with the Wild Wood, and he had forgotten quite how exhausting the process was, and how disorientating. He could still hear the creaking and hissing noise the trees made as they grew, and he could taste on his tongue the sweet and bitter flavours of the lively soil.

'He's awake.' Leven stood up but came no further. The look she settled on him was suspicious.

'Did you carry me here?' Cillian immediately regretted asking. The thought of being slung over Leven's shoulder was unnerving. As if she guessed his discomfort, the shadow of a smile passed over the Herald's lips.

'I've carried heavier men than you, believe me.'

'Here.' Epona came over with the cup of stew, which he took gladly. 'The bird was taking too long to cook so I chopped it up into bits for the stew. What happened? Did our Herald pick a fight with the Dunohi?'

'I did no such thing!'

Cillian shook his head. 'I don't know what's happening. This has... been going on for a while. The forest souls are angry about something.

They're becoming violent, unpredictable. I told the conclave but they didn't believe me.'

Epona sat back on her heels, her lips pursed. 'Magog's balls, that's worrying. And Blessed Eleven claims the forest soul spoke to her. That can't be true, can it?'

'I'm not making it up,' said Leven, her arms crossed over her chest.

'I heard it too,' Cillian said, reluctantly. 'Not at first, but then it was almost like an echo. As if I were hearing it from a great distance.'

'What did it say?' asked Epona.

'It said something about "winged murderers",' Leven answered. 'And it said "never return".'

'How curious,' said Epona. She stood up and turned back to the fire. 'How would the Dunohi know about your life in the Imperium? You haven't been doing any sneaky murders while our backs are turned, have you?'

'Of course I haven't,' said Leven, although Cillian noticed that she turned her face away from them as she said it. He remembered how the bog bodies had told them that Leven had mysteries inside her.

'The Dunohi are known to be dangerous,' said Epona in a musing tone. 'That's the whole reason we're supposed to keep to the Paths. And why the Druin exist in the first place really. Perhaps we've just been unlucky.'

Cillian shook his head. His sense of himself was returning, and with it came all the aches and pains of the bruises he'd gained from being knocked into the creek. He could feel Inkwort in the tree above his head, chirping in a slightly garrulous tone.

'No,' he said. He reached up and pulled a leaf from his hair. 'I've lived in the Wild Wood all my life, and I've never felt anything like it. The Dunohi are unpredictable and dangerous, like any wild creature, but like most animals they won't hurt you unless you attack them, or trespass in their territory. It's like... it's like there's an infection somewhere, and it's making the entire Wild Wood feverish.'

'We'll have to keep out of their way then,' said Epona. 'That's easily done. We'll be extra careful from now on, no wandering from the Path at all, and when we're fetching water or food, we'll all go together so we can watch each other's backs.'

Cillian nodded, and Leven muttered her agreement from the fire, but when they set up camp for the night in one of the hidden pockets of the woods Cillian found himself staring out at the darkness between the trees, straining to hear anything out of the ordinary. He hadn't told the others, partly because it seemed ludicrous and partly because it was frightening, but the sense that the forest souls didn't want them there was only half of it. More and more, with every day that passed, it felt as though the trees and the great connected network of roots beneath their feet were actively angry with human beings themselves. Angry enough to hurt them, or worse.

Cillian kept his watch that night with one hand on the dagger at his belt; as little help that would be if the Wild Wood itself wanted them dead.

40

There is no doubt that this experiment of Tyleigh's has been wildly successful. I don't dispute that, your Luminance. The Heralds, as she calls them, have taken Unblessed lands we thought were forever beyond our reach and brought them into the Blessed light of the Imperium. I am happy to throw all the accolades and honours at them we can muster. But I must make it clear to you that I find – and have always found – the Heralds to be an enormous risk: a weapon that could harm us as easily as it harms our enemies. I do not need to remind you what these people were before Tyleigh burned her weird magic into them. They must be contained, for the good of the Imperium.

Personal note from Imperator
Justinia to Empress Celestinia

'Where do we even start?'

Kaeto, Belise and Tyleigh had packed up their supplies and were walking the streets of the Black City. Belise's question, Kaeto had to admit, was a pertinent one. The tall buildings clustered in close to one another, looming over the streets and blocking out the sun; they walked in shadows, half the time. There was no map to this place, no signs that he could see, and certainly no citizens to show them around, or at least, he hoped not. After he and Belise had examined it, they had moved Riz's body back through the hole in the wall and left it in the jungle foliage. He was no closer to knowing what had happened to the guide, and it made him uneasy. He looked closely at every dark corner and watched for movement in the windows.

'We need to look for a place where we can get underground,' said Tyleigh in a matter-of-fact tone, as if exploring cursed cities was something she did every day. 'That idiot guide claimed that the *devils* had built things under the surface, which seems to be in line with my own reading on the subject. If there are any viable remains still around, that's a good place to start looking for them. There must be stairways, passages, tunnels of some sort. We just have to systematically search for them.'

'A good chance for you to put your map-making skills to the test, Belise.' When the girl groaned, he raised an eyebrow at her. 'If this place corresponds to the maps I have on Unblessed Houraki, it cannot be very big. Certainly not a city in the way the Imperium uses the word, anyway.'

It wasn't like any city he had ever seen. In the harsh light of the Houraki sun, it was clear that every building and structure had been built from a kind of shining black stone which looked a lot like fire-glass, a kind of hard crystal that was often used to make Imperial arrowheads. Yet if that was the case, then the builders of the Black City must have had access to a truly extraordinary amount of the stuff. The effect of it was oddly unsettling; whereas houses, taverns and warehouses in Stratum were built using all manner of materials, this place was uniform, even when the design of each new building was wildly different to the next. Despite the vines and plant life creeping in at the edges, the black stone remained unblemished and intact; it made it look as though the inhabitants might be back again at any moment. And the walls themselves seemed to absorb sound; the flat slap of their footsteps was muffled, and when they spoke it felt like they were throwing words into a yawning silence. He had to admit, whatever this place was, it was no human city.

'We'll explore today and see where it takes us. Tomorrow, we can arrange a more methodical way of finding what we need. We have enough supplies with us to last a few weeks, if we're careful. We have plenty of time.'

But even as he said it, Kaeto wondered if that was true. He could not quite dispel the feeling that every moment they spent in the Black City was putting their lives in danger. As if she sensed it too, Tyleigh wrinkled her nose.

'With luck, it should not take that long, Envoy.'

They walked along a wide thoroughfare, the street lined with huge black paving slabs carved with interlocking geometric shapes. The sun above their heads was hot and the sky was clear, but in the shadowed streets of the Black City it was chilly, as though the place had fallen from the sun's graces thousands of years ago and had never earned it back. Tyleigh moved ahead, too eager to see what lay around each corner.

'What happened to Riz was... bad.'

Kaeto looked down at Belise. He had thought the girl had accepted the guide's death with her usual pragmatism, but there was an uncertain tone to her voice and her wide-brimmed hat hid her face from him.

'Yes. For all that he was a thief and a liar, he did not deserve that.' Kaeto remembered the weight of the smaller man's body against his when they stole time in the trees together, the heat of his mouth against his. 'Perhaps no one does.'

'What could have done it?' She glanced up at him, one hand curling around her recently injured arm. 'A giant beetle?'

'I don't think so, Belise. If there were beetles so large, I'm sure we'd have heard of them. But there are other dangerous animals in places like this, so it's best to be alert.'

'Hmm.' Ahead of them, Tyleigh had paused to examine some detail in the black rock that surrounded them. Belise lowered her voice. 'Anyway. I'm sorry, chief. I know you liked him a little.'

Kaeto looked down at the girl, a strange tightness around his heart. It was never wise to underestimate Belise, and what her sharp eyes picked up on. They didn't speak again until they caught up with Tyleigh.

'This place is spooky,' said Belise, brightly enough.

'Spooky.' Tyleigh shook her head in disgust. 'It's a long-dead ruin. No more to it than that. Save for the extremely valuable remains I intend to excavate from it.'

'There is certainly a strained atmosphere to the place,' said Kaeto. 'Look, the street drops a little in front. A step?'

When they reached it they all stood on its edge for a moment. The drop was around two feet in height, and it was clearly a deliberate part of the road; there were no cracks or broken pieces of stone to indicate that some cataclysm had sunk it. They jumped down, and then in around a hundred feet there was another one. And then another, after that.

'The street is gradually taking us downward.'

It was curious. The longer they followed the street, the further down they went, and the taller the buildings on either side became, until the sky was an ever-narrowing blue strip above them. Kaeto also noticed that they were seeing more beetles – large ones, as big as cats, with iridescent carapaces. They fled when they got too close, either scuttling away into the dark or unfolding stiff transparent wings and flying up and through windows. Periodically Kaeto would check the compass sewn into the inside of his sleeve. He was fairly sure that the street was heading into the centre of the city.

'Do you think what Riz told us was true?' asked Belise after a while. 'That there were devils living here.'

She had not been addressing Tyleigh, but the alchemist gave her a dark look nonetheless.

'*Devils*,' she said, her voice dripping with derision. 'They were Titans, Titans of a unique shape and species. The Othanim. That is all. Stars save us from ignorant children.'

Belise narrowed her eyes. 'If you believe the stars are our ancestors, it's not so much of a leap to believe in devils, is it?'

Kaeto had to hide a smile behind his sleeve.

'It's a turn of phrase, whelp. And keep that tone out of your voice when you speak to your betters.'

Belise didn't reply, but Kaeto caught the eye-roll when Tyleigh had turned her attention back to the street.

The idea that they were deep within the city was irresistible now. The buildings on all sides rose up into the sky, and they were walking in the near dark, shadows thick all around them – a kind of false twilight. The beetles gave off a soft luminescence from their rear ends; combined with the dark, the shining black rock of the buildings and the silence, it felt as though they were walking through an enchanted grotto – although, Kaeto suspected, the magic here was anything but benign.

And then the way ahead of them was clear of buildings. Instead, the street they had been following barrelled into the ground, becoming a tunnel. And all around them were other streets, all becoming tunnels at the place where they almost met. Above this great confluence of roads, at the very centre of the city, was an enormous statue wrought in the now familiar black rock. The three of them stopped in their tracks, looking up as one.

'Fuckin' stars,' said Belise.

The statue depicted a thickly muscled woman, one hand reaching up as if to pluck the sun from the sky. A pair of vast wings sprouted from her back, each feather carefully carved from the faintly translucent black stone, and she wore an elaborate war helm of gold; two twisted prongs, almost like horns, burst from the temples, displaying more feathers all wrought in the shiny metal, and the front was a mask, with slim bars over the eye holes and hinged jaw-pieces framing the chin. There were also, Kaeto noted, deep scratches marring the stone in places, as though something had once tried to tear it down.

'Extraordinary.' Despite himself, Kaeto was impressed. 'She could almost be one of our own Heralds.'

'She's magnificent!' For the first time that Kaeto could remember, Tyleigh was grinning broadly. 'Proof, if any were needed, that my hypothesis is correct. A new breed of Titan, hidden away in the stinking jungles of Houraki.'

'But they're not here now, are they?' asked Belise. Her voice was uncharacteristically quiet. 'They're all dead, right?'

'Of course they're all dead,' snapped Tyleigh. 'Idiot child. The Othanim would hardly be secret if they still lived, would they? Now, fetch my sketch book from out your pack. I want to make some notes of my first impressions.'

Belise said nothing in reply to that, but Kaeto saw the hand by her side make several deft movements that only he could see.

Kiss my bum, you old bat.

As Belise and Tyleigh set about the note-taking, Kaeto walked on down the street, under the unnerving gaze of the winged Titan statue. He came to the very edge of the tunnel and paused there – beyond the lip it was difficult to see anything, but he thought he saw carvings in the walls, and an oddly clean floor. *Even this far from the jungle, there should be some debris in there*, he thought. *Old leaves, dead beetles, dust.* But there was nothing. He turned back to make this observation to Tyleigh and caught a flicker of movement out of the corner of his eye – for the barest second he thought he had seen a figure moving, back near the buildings they had passed on the way down. He stood very still, watching closely, making himself aware of every noise and gust of wind.

'It was just a beetle,' he murmured to himself. 'Or a shadow of one.'

And yet, the sensation of being watched had increased. He went back to Tyleigh and Belise. The former had sat herself on the floor and was quickly sketching the looming statue. She was fast, and accurate.

'Envoy,' she snapped, not taking her eyes from the statue. 'Today I wish to take notes and sketches of this entire outer tunnel system.

Tomorrow, we will return and explore the tunnels. You have brought the torches?'

'Yes,' he said. 'There are plenty.'

Again he felt that pressure on the back of his head, and he turned to look at one of the far buildings. The windows there were just holes in the rock, but he had the distinct feeling that a moment ago they had not been empty. He settled in for a long afternoon of jumping at shadows.

They were not alone.

41

'**B**rocken is dead?'

Ynis hung her head. They had stopped on the flight back so that she could wash some of the dried blood from her hands, but still it felt as if every griffin there could see it. *Is this how it will always be for me?* she thought wildly. *Griffin blood on my hands and a circle of accusing eyes?* They had found Witch-seer Frost at the heart of the Edge Walkers' home, the glacier that sat in the pale blue lake, and she was apparently in the middle of a tense discussion with several griffins there, including Scree, who scowled at them openly as they landed. Ynis had told the whole story, stammering through it painfully as she remembered how Brocken had fallen, and bled. When she came to the ceremonies of the witch-seer, to her surprise T'rook spoke up, telling them all how her sister had done what Brocken had asked and made certain that she didn't leave this world without the proper rituals. There were a few gasps and angry beak snaps at that, but Witch-seer Frost did not react.

'I am sorry,' said Ynis again, 'I tried to help her, but it was… there was just too much blood.'

'You did what you could,' said Frost softly.

'Aye, she did far too much!' Scree pranced forward, his dark eyes flashing. He glared at Frost. 'This is exactly what I was talking about. You have let this human live among us – unconventional, perhaps, but our ways are not those of Yelvynia. But to let her think she can be a witch-seer? To tutor her and encourage her? This is what it has led to, Frost. One of our bravest and kindest Edge Walkers dead, and without the proper rituals in place. Her soul will be trapped in her mouldering corpse!'

'No.' Ynis stood up very straight. 'That's not true. I did it right. I saw her fate-tie and I cut it. Her spirit was freed.'

'Nonsense,' spat Scree. 'Lies and nonsense. As if a ground-stuck human could free the spirit of a griffin!'

There were twenty or so griffins on the glacier with them. Ynis saw many of them looking at each other uneasily. She could hear muttering, and one or two puffed out their crests in anger.

'Brocken was my friend,' she said, but a lot of the certainty had gone out of her voice. 'I wouldn't lie about this.'

'If my sister says she did it, she did it,' said T'rook. 'And all you stone-lickers are missing the point! Brocken is dead!'

'Yes,' said Witch-seer Frost. She turned to a pair of griffins that stood off to one side. 'You will go and retrieve our friend's body. She must be brought back to the Bone Fall so she can rest here with her ancestors.'

'Idiots!' squawked T'rook. Ynis glanced at her sister, alarmed at the anger in her voice. 'Brocken didn't fall out of the sky on her own. She was killed. Don't you want to know who did it? Don't you want to pull out their guts and eat their livers?'

Scree shook his head dismissively, while the other griffins seemed to grow quieter. To Ynis's surprise, Witch-seer Frost sighed.

'It's not our purpose to stop death, or deal justice for a death unjust,' she said. 'This will be very hard for you to hear, both of you so young as you are, but that is not an Edge Walker's task. We are here for the dying and the dead, and the living must do what they will.'

'What?' Ynis shook her head. 'You mean you don't care that Brocken is dead?'

'Watch your words, yenlin,' Frost said mildly. 'Brocken was a dear friend of mine long before either of you were hatched, and my heart is broken today. My duty now is to see that her remains are cared for and allowed to rest.'

'This is how they are,' said Scree, pitching his voice loud enough that all the griffins on the glacier could hear him. 'Now they are here, and being taught our ways, they want to change them. This is what comes of your human witch-seer, Frost.'

'Toross!' T'rook shook her head angrily, digging her talons into the ice. 'Your friend was murdered and you don't care.'

'Frost,' Ynis stepped in front of her sister, worried she might actually lash out, 'something is wrong here. You were shot too, remember? And now Brocken. There are humans in the north, and they're here to kill griffins. Shouldn't we find out who they are and stop them?'

'Ynis, it's just not our way.' Frost's voice was kind, but Ynis felt a cold hand close around her heart at the sound of it. 'Griffins die every day. We do not ask why.'

The bitter wind that had been blowing all day rose up then, and for a few seconds all was silent as it ruffled feathers and fur. Ynis pulled her hood up over her head.

'I will not stand for this,' Scree said. He spread his wings wide and brought them down heavily as if to challenge the wind itself. 'I am the next witch-seer, Frost. You have known that for a very long time. This creature,' he jabbed his beak in Ynis's direction, 'is no better than food. And I know that I am not the only one who thinks so.'

He leapt up into the air, and for a terrible second Ynis thought that was it; he would land on her and tear her throat out and be done with it. But instead he flew off, followed by ten or so other griffins who had been watching. Again, Ynis was reminded of their banishment from Yelvynia. *Will it always be like this?*

'Ynis.' Frost spoke softly now that Scree had gone. 'You did well today. And I think it is time you were given your Edge Walker name.' She turned her head to one side and yanked at a piece of twine around her neck. It fell to the icy ground. Tied to it was a long, black arrowhead that Ynis recognised. It was the one that she had pulled from Frost's shoulder on the day they had first arrived at the Bone Fall.

'Take this,' Frost said. 'Our names are given to us in lots of different ways – sometimes it is a word associated with the day we arrived at the Bone Fall, sometimes a significant moment or task will suggest the name. For you, Ynis, I think your life changed when you saved mine. Welcome, Witch-seer Arrow.'

Ynis bent down and picked up the arrowhead. It was made of a shiny black rock she wasn't familiar with, and when she held it up to the light she saw that the thinnest portion of it was translucent and filled with grey shadow. The point of it was still sharp. *A beautiful and lethal thing*, she thought. Next to her, T'rook squawked with amusement.

'Arrow is a word for a human tool,' she said. 'But it is a better name than *screaming egg*, sister.'

Ynis smiled crookedly. 'Maybe. I don't know...'

'You'll get used to it. I did,' said Frost. 'Rest yourselves, then come and see me. You might have been given your name, Witch-seer, but there's still more you must learn.'

'Wait.' Ynis put the arrowhead into her pack. 'Please listen, Frost. T'rook is right. We need to find out who these humans are that are using their weapons against griffins, and what they're doing here.'

Frost shook her head sadly. 'No good will come of it, Arrow. Will you not take my advice on this?'

'I'm sorry.' And Ynis did feel sorry. She could sense what a great honour Frost had done her by sticking up for her against Scree, and for giving her this Edge Walker name. To leave now would be like throwing that honour back in her face. But the image of Brocken's fate-tie kept coming back to her, that red thread cut short, so much sooner than it should have been. 'We need to find out what's going on. What if they keep coming? What if they come all the way up to the Bone Fall, and find those griffins who are already weak? It's not right.' She took a deep breath. 'Me and T'rook will go back to that place, and see what we can find. And then... then I will finish my witch-seer training.'

T'rook nodded brusquely.

'As you wish.' All at once, Frost sounded very old, and very tired. 'You must find your own way, I suppose.'

The old griffin left them there, and Ynis turned back to her sister.

'When do we go?' T'rook asked. Then, cheekily, '*Grand Witch-seer Arrow.*'

'As soon as we can.' Ynis put her hand in her pack and closed her fingers around the arrowhead. 'We'll need to rest, get some food together. But humans can't move as quickly as we can, and especially not over the mountains. We'll find them.'

'We'll *hunt* them,' T'rook said. 'Hunt them and tear out their guts.'

42

The civil war was a terrible time for our people. The Druin are not war makers; the whole idea of destruction and fury stands against everything we are, in fact, and to take up arms – using the gifts given to us by the Druidahnon and the Wild Wood – against the people of Mersia was a wrenching experience, like a tearing deep inside. It's possible to use our gifts for violence, of course it is; just like any rock of sufficient size can be used to bash a man's head in. And Druin must be vigilant against the temptations of thrawn magic at all times. Using Druin magic for violence hurts us; it is a wound that will not heal. An inner rupture. And in a very real way the injuries and the slaughter of the war with Mersia live on today. The earth and the roots soaked up the blood and the pain and the death and kept it all, and in our connection to the Wild Wood we feel it still. So if you wonder why the Druin, usually so diplomatic and so neutral, are reluctant to assist Mersia that is your answer. To us, the civil war was yesterday.

Personal journal of Kirka,
an elder Druin

They emerged from the Wild Wood into the soft rolling hills of Mersia. Leven stood for a moment to take it in. It was a bright hot day, with only a few scattered white clouds in the sky, and the landscape that spread before her was deliciously green and remarkably ordered. Long meandering lines of dark green hedges divided the land into neat squares, and it was possible to see tidy little settlements tucked into the bottoms of the hills, threads of wood smoke rising against the lush grass behind them. In the distance she could see what looked like a much bigger city, a place of tall towers of grey and white stone. It looked very different to the wildness of Kornwullis, or the gritty sprawl of Londus.

'This is very orderly,' she said brightly. 'Is that where we're headed? That big city to the north?'

'Yes,' said Cillian, although he immediately led them to the west.

'There's no straight route? You people need to get more roads. We're very fond of straight roads in the Imperium.'

'This *is* the straight route,' said Epona, who then laughed at Leven's confusion. 'See that copse over there? That is where we get back on the Wild Wood path.'

'Oh.' There was a small group of trees in the corner of the field they walked through. Looking closely Leven noticed that they did look somewhat out of place – they were wild and unruly and clearly very ancient, whereas the part of the landscape they were in looked as though someone tended to it every day. 'This is one of those Druin things I don't understand, isn't it?'

'There is a story to this,' said Epona, putting her arm through Leven's. 'Do you want to tell it, Cillian?'

'Not particularly,' said Cillian.

'Don't mind him,' Epona said, patting Leven's arm. 'The Druin are still very cross about it. You see, hundreds of years ago, the ruling family of Mersia ordered that a large section of the Wild Wood be cleared for farmland.'

'Without asking any of those who lived in it,' put in Cillian.

'Yes, well... They started chopping down trees and digging out the roots, clearing away the plants and the wildlife and making it level. When the Druidahnon realised what was happening there were quite a few cross words.'

'We went to war,' said Cillian.

'It was infamous,' Epona said cheerfully. 'All the old kingdoms were constantly fighting, but for the Druin to take up arms? It was unheard of. It was like... a civil war with the land itself. Even the Druidahnon fought, and he was very old, even then. But in the end the Wild Wood lost.'

Cillian cast Epona a dark look over his shoulder. 'We didn't lose, Princess Epona. We compromised. The land you see around you now is the result of that compromise. Tamed, flattened, all but lifeless.'

'Not worthless though,' continued Epona, giving Leven's arm another squeeze. Leven smiled. She had grown used to the princess's tendency to grab her arm when making a point or how she punched her lightly on the arm when she wanted something. 'Mersia took the lands and turned them into crops, which in turn made them one of the richest kingdoms in Brittletain. Not richer than Londus, you understand. The soil here is the best in the country for growing crops.'

'Because the soil is full of our dead.' Seeing Leven's raised eyebrows, Cillian shook his head. 'I don't mean that in a morbid sense. But thousands of years of trees, plants, mushrooms, insects and the animals of the Wild Wood living and dying on that soil... and Druin, too. Of course the soil was rich. It's almost magical.'

'So, part of the compromise,' Epona continued as if he hadn't spoken, 'was that Mersia would maintain these copses throughout the kingdom, so that the Druin and the Dunohi could continue to move along their Paths.'

'They broke so many Paths doing what they did,' said Cillian bitterly, 'that the system will be broken forever. Which is why we must traipse across this field to the next copse.'

'You sound angry about it,' said Leven.

'That's because I am.'

'But it was hundreds of years ago.'

They had reached the copse of trees, and Cillian paused. In the brightness of the summer's day and out of the shadows of the wood, his eyes were very green indeed. Inkwort, the little jackdaw, flew down and perched on Epona's shoulder, making her laugh. 'I don't expect you to understand. But it's a wound my people have felt for generations, and I know it still grieves the Druidahnon, although he won't talk about it anymore. We lost a big part of ourselves.'

'You lost a part of yourselves when you went to war in the first place,' said Epona quietly. She sighed and shook her head, and Inkwort flew off into the trees ahead of them. 'The Druin really have never forgiven Mersia, which is why the Mersian royal family have no official Druin guard. There are instead a group of Druin from the Wild Wood who serve as their Path Keepers when they have need of them.'

'It's usually troublemakers who spend time in that group,' said Cillian. 'Druin who have annoyed the elders in some way.'

'And how often have you served in it?' asked Leven. Epona laughed again, delighted, and for the barest second the hint of a smile played across Cillian's lips.

'Often enough,' he said. 'Come on, let's not spend any more time in these stupid fields than we have to.'

Once inside the copse, Cillian performed his strange magic again, and they were walking once more in the Wild Wood. Leven had experienced it often enough that most of the disorientation she felt each time he opened a new Path had faded, but there was still something very unsettling about walking into a small group of trees and emerging into an enormous forest. An hour or so later, he led them out again and they were back in the carefully maintained fields, but the busy city that Leven had seen earlier was much closer. Beautiful soaring towers built of a shining white stone and tipped with gold were almost too bright to look at in the sunlight, while other shorter buildings clustered around them like children around a mother's skirts. There was a sturdy-looking wall that stood between them and the city, and just in front of that, at the end of the road that led to the gates, there was an armed guard.

As they made their way down the road, Leven felt the ore-lines crossing her hands and arms begin to sting and prickle. The men and women by the gate wore what were obviously guard uniforms, and they were armed to the teeth with spears, pikes and brutal notched short swords. *Still*, she thought, *nothing that could stand against me. As long as I'm not visited with visions of the winter wood.*

'Princess Epona.' A tall man at the front detached himself from the guard and approached. He was dressed differently to the rest, with a long white silk jacket lined with gold and his hair, which was black, was tied into a long braid. He wore a sword at his belt too, and the look he gave them was not friendly. 'I am glad to see you here. I can't imagine what would have happened if your mother had sent an agent of the Imperium here with a lone Druin.'

'It's good to see you too, Prince Gallan.' Princess Epona bowed in a way that felt deeply sarcastic to Leven. 'Are you going to let us into your precious city, or will I have to tell my mother that Mersia was too scared to open the gates?'

Prince Gallan gave a short bark of laughter. 'You haven't changed.' He turned his attention to Leven. She noticed that he didn't look at Cillian at all. 'We have been told of your arrival, Blessed Eleven. Welcome to the city of Wodencaester, the jewel of Brittletain.'

Epona gave a snort at that, which he ignored.

'I should tell you, Blessed Eleven, that any insult, injury or damage to this city, or to any persons in it, from you, will be considered an act of war by our Queen Ismere.'

'He means his mummy,' Epona said helpfully.

'I'm not here to cause injury to anyone,' Leven said, as levelly as she could, although in reality she had taken a sharp dislike to Prince Gallan and could have happily picked him up and dropped him from one of their fancy towers. 'I am here to deliver a gift from Queen

Broudicca, along with her greetings and good tidings to the kingdom of Mersia.'

Prince Gallan looked at her for a long moment. He had sharp cheekbones and cold blue eyes, and on the lapel of his jacket he wore a silver brooch in the shape of the towers of Wodencaester. It occurred to Leven that she hadn't seen the jackdaw Inkwort in a little while. Evidently the bird didn't think much of Mersia's greatest city either.

'Good,' he said eventually, although Leven wasn't sure what was good about any of this. 'You're to come with me. You and the Princess Epona are to be housed in the palace in our finest rooms, and tomorrow there will be a banquet where you can present your gift to our queen.'

He began to walk towards the gates in the wall, his guard moving neatly to one side to let him pass.

'And Cillian?' Leven found herself trotting to keep up with the skinny little git. 'Where is he staying?'

Prince Gallan cast one look over his shoulder, the only time he had acknowledged the Druin's presence at all.

'Your wood witch can find a place at the stables.'

'Hold on!' Leven stopped and held up her hands. 'Druin Cillian is my guide in this... in Brittletain. He stays with us and is given the same honour you would give me.'

As soon as she said it she felt stupid – she could almost picture Queen Broudicca rolling her eyes – but Prince Gallan stopped and turned to face her, a curious expression on his face that looked very close to amusement.

'Very well. He can share your rooms, Blessed Eleven.' And he began walking again, shouting orders to the men on the gate to open the doors ahead.

'Interesting,' Epona muttered, elbowing Leven. 'That was quite a power move, Herald. Been here for all of an eyeblink and you're already issuing orders.'

'I wasn't...'

'I would have been perfectly fine in the stables,' said Cillian. He was scowling and wouldn't meet her eyes. 'All Druin have come to expect this sort of treatment at Wodencaester.'

'It's insulting,' said Leven firmly as the three of them followed Prince Gallan through the gate. 'By which I mean it is insulting to *me*.'

Beyond the gate, they walked along a raised road made of the same white stone as the towers, although it was significantly dirtier. Below them was a sprawl of busy buildings built of a more prosaic grey brick: houses, taverns, warehouses, shops, inns and workshops. There was a narrow fast-flowing river too, carefully contained with high walls and neat bridges; it made Leven think of the little streams of perfumed water in the Imperator's building. On the raised road itself were various exits sloping off down into the city proper, and here and there portable cabins selling food, drink and tiny models of the towers. There were people around, mostly well-dressed and prosperous-looking, and all of them turned to watch the guards and their prince as they passed. Leven saw people pointing at the three of them.

The raised road eventually led to the towers themselves. They stood at the centre of the city, and beneath them was a series of interlinking courtyards of grey and white stone. Here were many men and women of business, merchants identifiable by their rich clothes and thick rolls of parchment held tightly under arms or stuffed into packs. They gave the group a wide berth. The guards led them up to the central tower, which had to be one of biggest buildings Leven had ever seen. It was very wide at its lowest point, sprawling so far across its courtyard that it was easy to forget it was a tower at all, yet above them it soared elegantly into the sky. Here there were more guards, and hundreds of long silk flags emblazoned with the same tower sigil that was on Prince Gallan's badge. Reluctantly, Leven was impressed. It was, she realised, very far from the vision of Brittletain that the Imperium liked to preach – grubbing barbarians, living off acorns and painting themselves blue. It looked like something from a star-story.

Most of the guards stopped at the courtyard. Prince Gallan led them forward himself. Inside the tower – which Leven was coming to realise was the palace they had spoken of – it almost felt like another small city. Men and women dressed in brightly coloured and richly decorated clothes raced back and forth on important business, visiting various alcoves and disappearing down a multitude of corridors that led away from the main foyer. The prince led them to the far side of the room, where an enormous flight of stairs swept up to the next level before splitting off to spiral up into the unseen rooms above. In front of them was a huge set of wooden double doors, painted blue and silver and intricately carved with trees and vines. Leven stole a glance at Cillian, and saw that he was glaring at the door as if it had done him a personal insult. He caught her eye and muttered, 'Built with the blood of the Druin.'

Prince Gallan turned, and for a second Leven thought he'd heard Cillian's comment. Instantly her ore-lines thrummed with Titan strength, but instead he shook his head slightly.

'Queen Ismere insists on seeing you before you are shown to your rooms. I suggested that it would be more proper to have the formal greeting tomorrow, during the banquet, when there's been a chance to make you more presentable, but... she does you a great honour today.' His eyes flickered between the three of them, and Leven fought down another urge to summon her sword. 'This is our throne room. Try not to get the rug dirty, it is very old indeed.'

He opened the doors and they followed him in. The room beyond was large and chilly. The wall directly facing them was given over to a spectacular set of hexagonal glass windows, fitted together like an intricate honeycomb. Through the windows it was possible to see, just below them, the bustle of the city, while the light they let in cast the throne itself into shadow. The floor was indeed covered in a long rug that led from the doors to the throne, and it was intricately woven with a pattern that continued on from the door: leaves and trees, flowers and birds and vines. All the bounty of the Wild Wood, laid in tribute to the throne of Mersia, ready for its people to walk all over. *Even I can see what an insult that is,* thought Leven. It was possible to see a figure sitting on the throne, although they had to walk some distance down the rug before the light from the windows lifted enough to make out any details.

'Queen Ismere, I present to you Blessed Eleven, the Herald of the Imperium, and Princess Epona of Londus-on-Sea.' The prince's voice filled the whole room, and Leven wondered if that was what the impressive chamber was for: shouting names and introducing people.

'And a hedge witch, I see.' The figure on the throne leaned forward to get a better look at them. The queen of Mersia was, at Leven's guess, in her late sixties, and she wore a thick fur-lined coat. She was bone-thin to Leven's eyes, with high cheekbones that pressed at the thin skin of her face. Her hair, which lay flat against her head, was an incongruous shiny brown, like a chestnut; Leven wondered if she dyed it. There was a thin circlet of gold around her forehead, and a small brown cat on her lap. As she spoke to them her fingers tugged on its fur relentlessly. 'Gallan, why do you bring a Druin into the palace?'

Prince Gallan bowed low in apology.

'The Herald insisted, Mother.'

Queen Ismere sniffed. 'There were always rumours about Imperial appetites.' And then, before Leven could figure out what that could possibly mean, she continued, 'Princess Epona. Has your mother sent you to woo Gallan? I have told her many times that he is promised to another.'

Epona grinned. 'My mother and I disagree on many things, your majesty, and her plans for my marriage is the biggest of them all.'

Ismere's mouth twisted as though she'd bitten into a rotten apple, and Leven was struck by the difference between this queen and the queens of Kornwullis. And Queen Broudicca, for that matter. Ismere plucked her robe, pulling it closer around her shoulders.

'As rude as you are, Princess Epona, we will feast you anyway. In honour of your Imperial *friend*. Gallan, take them away.'

Back out in the hallway, Gallan turned to them one last time, a sour expression on his face that made him resemble his mother.

'The gift,' he said. 'You will give it to me and I will see that it is kept safe until tomorrow's ceremony.'

Leven hesitated. Her instinct was to do the opposite of everything this pompous man requested, but she was a guest there and uncertain of how to proceed. She caught the slightest shrug from Princess Epona from the corner of her eye.

'Fine with me.' Leven dug around in her pack and brought out the box intended for Mersia, its green Druin seal still intact. 'Just don't peek at it or you'll spoil the surprise.'

Gallan took it with a faint frown, as though he were touching something dirty.

'The servants will show you to your rooms.'

Once Gallan had scuttled off, they were led up several long flights of stairs, passing more rich tapestries and beautiful sculptures of wood housed in narrow alcoves; Leven found herself wondering if they were carved from Wild Wood trees. Epona disappeared behind her own door with a wink, and the servant showed Leven and Cillian to the room across the hall. Leven hung in the doorway and caught at the servant's elbow.

'There really isn't a separate room for Cillian?'

The servant looked pointedly at her hand until she removed it. He was a small pallid man with a long, sad face.

'The Druin aren't generally guests at the palace. We have no suitable rooms for a Druin. No room with mud, or twigs, or animals for him to sport with.' A touch of a smirk appeared at the corner of his mouth. 'They're usually happier in the stables with the other beasts.'

Leven took hold of his lapels with one hand and lifted him an inch or so off the floor.

'I say...!'

'This is how you treat guests, is it?'

Behind her, she could hear Cillian speaking softly. 'We're not here to cause trouble. Remember, Herald?'

Leven dropped the servant, who gave her a poisonous look and scuttled off.

'I didn't like the look of him,' she said, and shrugged. 'Face like a weasel. Will you look at this room...'

It was a very impressive chamber. One wall was given over to the hexagonal windows, like the throne room, and as they were higher up, the view was even more spectacular. Tall white towers framed the city, while in the distance she could see hazy golden-green hills; purple-blue rainclouds hung on the horizon, like a smudge of ink. The floor was covered in another intricately woven rug, this one embroidered with hundreds of running horses of all colours, and there was a long wooden table, upon which had been placed a large bowl of fruit, a wide wash basin of white stone and a tall jug of water. In the centre there was the largest bed Leven had ever seen, with wooden posts at each corner and an elegant curtain of yellow silk surrounding it. Looking at this last, Leven felt a stab of discomfort.

'I'll get them to bring up a cot. The servants can't all be as rude as that arse they sent up with us.' For some reason she found she couldn't bring herself to look at Cillian. 'Or there might be something in Epona's room we could use. We can go and ask her.'

'You needn't worry.' Cillian walked over to the stretch of wall behind the long table. He tapped on it with his knuckles and a partially hidden door opened; it had been painted the same colour as the rest of the room so Leven hadn't spotted it. 'Servants' quarters.'

'Another room?'

Leven poked her head around the door. Inside there was a dark, narrow space with a bed in it and a jug of water on the floor. At the foot of the bed there was a simple wooden chest. The difference between it and the main room was stark. It didn't even have a window.

'The Mersian royals don't like to be far from the person who washes and dresses them,' said Cillian, and then a strange expression passed over his face. 'Not that I will be washing or dressing you...'

'No, I should think not!' Leven moved swiftly away from the door, not looking at him. She laughed and cleared her throat. 'Do you want some fruit? Help yourself. I'm going to... I'm going to see what Epona's room is like.'

At that moment her ore-lines lit up with a burning sensation, and a wave of weakness swept up from her feet to the top of her head like a tide. She felt herself falling towards the floor and put out one arm to stop herself – her hand brushed the edge of the table – and then she was kneeling in the snow again. All around her was the forest, the Wild Wood, the trees here so tall and old their trunks rose out of sight into the canopy, where birds called to each other day and night. The smell of the wood, peaty and gloriously green, was overwhelming. She had been running, she remembered, and she had fallen. Someone was coming for her.

Leven scrambled to her feet, scratching herself and catching her clothes on thorns. It was cold. She could see her breath.

'Who – who is it?' She turned a slow circle, peering in between the trees. How was it she knew she was being chased, but not by whom? 'Why am I here?'

CLICK. CLICK. CLICK.

The sound thundered out of the Wild Wood from every direction. Leven plastered her hands over her ears and squeezed her eyes shut, and then warm hands had hold of her own, pulling them away from her face. When she opened her eyes again she was on the vast bed with the yellow silk curtains, and Cillian was leaning over her with a worried expression. When he saw that she was awake, he dropped her hands.

'Ugh.' Leven tried to sit up, but pain sang down her ore-lines with each movement. 'What happened?'

'You passed out,' he said. He had drawn back slightly and was watching her closely. 'What is happening to you?'

For a long moment, Leven said nothing. She looked up at the buttery yellow silk. The cold forest had seemed so real.

'I don't know,' she said eventually. 'Listen, Cillian, can I tell you something?'

She tried to sit up on one elbow, wincing with every shift of her body.

'You shouldn't move,' he said. 'We don't have to be anywhere. Rest.'

'Will you listen for a moment?'

He stood up, and Leven felt an odd dropping sensation in her chest. All at once she remembered that she was not with the other Heralds; that she was a stranger here, and worse, an enemy. Cillian was here because he had been ordered to be here, not because he was her friend. He moved back to the door without looking her in the eyes.

'I will see if they have any wine in the kitchen,' he said. 'It will help.'

Leven watched him go.

43

The substance termed 'griffin-spit' is a minor mystery in and of itself. From what I can tell from a variety of somewhat dubious historical records and pure folklore, it seems that the Titans consume the fibrous wood of a particular tree native to Brittletain, and this mulch in combination with griffin saliva seems to create a kind of natural adhesive, which they use in the building of their more sophisticated structures. It is by all reports an extremely hardy substance, capable of creating buildings, statues, bridges and even works of art that stand for many years. I would love to get my hands on a sample of griffin saliva, or even a piece of the hardened 'griffin-spit' itself, but as with all things related to the Titan races, it's easier said than done.

Handwritten section in
Gynid Tyleigh's journals

Ynis and T'rook arrived at the place where Brocken had died in the late evening, just as the sun had sunk beyond the horizon. The sky was full of the fire of sunset when they landed, but by the time Ynis had constructed a small fire it was dark, with only a few clouds far to the west still dusted with pink and orange light. Of Brocken there was, thankfully, no sign; it seemed the Edge Walkers had already been and collected her body. She would be resting at the Bone Fall, waiting for the natural processes of decay and scavenging animals to strip her of her remaining useless flesh. There was still blood on the snow where she had fallen though, and Ynis found that she was glad that the darkness hid the stains.

When they had settled by the fire, Ynis pulled out a rabbit carcass from her pack and began to butcher it for their dinner.

'Can you smell them?' she said after a while. Her sister had been uncharacteristically quiet on their journey north, and she sat staring pensively at the fire, her eyes like molten gold.

'Yes. A little.' T'rook shifted her bulk and plucked briefly at a feather on her chest. 'It is hidden though, the scent. There's been a little snow since we were here last. And other animals passing through. The thread of it is mixed up with these.'

'Do you think they've been back?'

'I don't know,' said T'rook. 'All we know for sure is that they are not here now.'

The belly slit, Ynis yanked the skin off the rabbit. 'Do you think you can track them?'

T'rook clicked her beak dismissively. 'I have no doubt. But we will do better in the morning, rested.'

Propping the rabbit over the fire with the two sticks she kept in her pack for exactly that purpose, Ynis found herself frowning. It was strange to think that humans – other than herself – had been this far into griffin territory.

'We should keep a watch, though,' she said. 'In case they come back. We can take turns.'

When the rabbit was eaten and the full dark of night had fallen all around them, T'rook settled down to sleep and Ynis took first watch. She sat apart from her sister, as close to the fire as she dared, with her rabbit-skin cloak pulled closely around her. Normally, when they stayed out all night on a hunt, she and T'rook would sleep curled up next to each other. In the territories of Yelvynia, they had no fear of predators – *they* were the deadliest things in the skies. In this place there was a new threat, one that was more than willing to spill the blood of the world's last Titans.

After an hour or so of cold silence, the skies to the north began to glow with a flickering luminescence, green lights like ripples in a pond shimmering over the tops of the distant mountains. *Spirit lights.* Ynis had seen them many times growing up, but perhaps never so close or so clear. It occurred to her that the shifting green and blue light was very much like the forms of the spirits she had seen in the Bone Fall.

T'rook was sleeping soundly, her head half-tucked beneath her wing, and the spirit light played over her lightly, turning her brown and black feathers the oily magical colour of a magpie's wing. Around them, the wind picked up, and the sound it made across the hills made Ynis shiver; it was too easy to imagine the spirit of Brocken calling to them in that noise. And too easy to imagine a group of humans, making their way stealthily towards the light, their claws sharpened and their bows ready.

Ynis stood up and made herself look out into the dark. She walked a slow circuit around their campfire, her leather boots crunching over hard snow and stones.

There is nothing, she told herself. *Don't get caught up in the atmosphere of the place. Just because Brocken died here doesn't mean we will too.*

She thought instead of fate-ties, of the thin red cord that she had seen curling away from Brocken's body. Brocken had had so many ties to so many griffins; they would all be feeling her loss in the Bone Fall tonight. Reluctantly she turned back to look at her sister, who was still asleep.

'I could just look for it,' she said to herself, very quietly. 'I will look, and if there is no fate-tie between us, well, it doesn't matter. We are still sisters. Nothing can change that.'

But it would mean you are totally alone, came the treacherous voice within her head. *T'rook's ties will be to our fathers, and they with hers, and whatever Frost said, I will have... none.*

'It would still be better to know,' she said to herself firmly. Swallowing hard, Ynis let herself fall into the mild trance state that was becoming more and more familiar. Her eyes felt heavy, and her body felt light. She focused on T'rook, the gentle rise and fall of her chest, and the spirit light seemed to spill over them both, growing brighter and brighter.

'No, wait...'

The light coalesced between her and T'rook, taking on the form of a griffin. Brocken's spirit was there with them, shimmering between T'rook and the fire. Even in death she was huge, and when she turned her head towards her, Ynis felt her chest grow tight with fear.

'Brocken, what are you doing here?' For all her fright, Ynis spoke quietly so as not to wake her sister. 'The Bone Fall...' She realised she had no idea if the spirits could hear her or not.

'My brethren were too late.' The voice of Brocken seemed to come from all around, and yet it was so quiet it was possible to mistake it for the wind across the gorse. 'They came back for my body, not long after you left me.'

'Who did? Do you mean the humans?'

'My spirit was already free, thanks to you, yenlin. But they came and desecrated my body. You must be careful, yenlin. These humans are dangerous, and they have no fear of us.'

Ynis looked around, just in case the human threat should appear, and when she looked back the spirit of Brocken was already fading.

'No, wait! We need your help, Brocken.'

But she was already gone. Ynis saw the big griffin turn, as if she could hear something in the distance that Ynis could not, and then the light dissipated. The spirit of Brocken became a tattered thing, then nothing at all. Beyond the fire, T'rook stirred, pulling her beak out from under her wing and scenting the air.

'Are you tired?' she asked. 'Is it my turn?'

Ynis looked once more at the space where the spirit of Brocken had been. If she had woken T'rook up, would she have been able to see it? Would what Brocken had told her help them find the people who had done it? She forced herself to face her sister and give her a smile.

'I could do with a rest. Thank you, sister.'

The next morning, both of them tired and cold, they took some time to look at the area in the brittle early sunshine. Ynis looked with the knowledge Brocken's spirit had given her at the forefront of her mind, and she saw several things that supported what the ghost had said. The blood that had soaked into the snowy ground was smeared here and there with faint human tracks, and there was a long furrow in the deeper snow as though something large had been dragged through it. Ynis pointed out these things, and T'rook nodded.

'Their scent is weak, overpowered by griffin blood. But they could have been here. So...'

'So they came back for Brocken's body.' Ynis did not mention that she knew this for sure because Brocken herself had told her. 'What do they want with it?'

'It is an outrage.' T'rook shook her head back and forth. 'Why would humans dare such a thing?'

'I don't know. I know that humans use animal furs to keep themselves warm, and they use bones and claws for other things too, but to trap and kill a griffin, in our own territory... it is very dangerous. They would be killed on sight by any griffin who caught them. Have the humans become so poor and hungry that they would risk eating griffin meat?'

'To *eat* us? Like we are rabbits? Like we are snivelling prey creatures? They will be torn apart for this.'

Ynis nodded, but humans hunting them for food or supplies did not sound right. And why were they so far north? Human settlements were all to the south, far beyond the centre of Yelvynia. The border was easy to find, as it was famously scattered with human skulls.

'Let's find them then,' she said.

It was not difficult to follow the humans' trail. As weak as the scent was, it was distinctive, and once they had followed the trail away from the place where Brocken had fallen and Ynis had performed the rites of a witch-seer, there were even more signs that they had passed by. Footprints in the snow, old campfires, and discarded bones from their meals (none of which had the distinctive blue-black shine of Titan bone, thankfully). Ynis found the footprints especially compelling; more than once she put her own booted foot on top of the unknown human's print, frightened and somehow amazed at how closely they matched.

They wound their way through the foothills, travelling at a walking pace, much to T'rook's annoyance – if they flew, Ynis pointed out, it would be too easy to lose the trail from the air. Quickly the trail curled around the outskirts of one of the big northern mountains, and came alongside a quick-flowing river. Big pieces of white ice sped by, caught by the rapid current, and the water was startlingly blue.

'We are so far north now,' Ynis said. She had strung the arrowhead Frost had given her on a piece of twine around her neck, and she ran her thumb over its sharp edge as she spoke.

'Far north, and very far from our fathers,' agreed T'rook.

'Do you think they ever flew this far?'

'No,' said T'rook flatly. 'They have always had more sense.'

The trail led them upstream, and eventually they came to a deserted campsite. Ynis stood by the cold ashes of their extinguished fire, looking at their boot prints, the discarded pieces of food, the tracks that led to and from the river. They were getting water, possibly to cook with, in the same way that she sometimes boiled water to cook eggs or soften up dried and salted meat. It was something that Ynis did alone – griffins did not understand it – and the way that this activity tied her directly to these unseen humans caused a tight knot of horror in her chest.

T'rook dragged the point of her hooked beak through the ashes, tasting them. She ruffled up her feathers in disgust.

'We must be close now,' she said. 'Let's hurry.'

Ynis climbed up onto T'rook's back and they got on the trail again, T'rook almost running, her wings folded tightly behind her shoulders. Ynis kept her eyes on the ground, watching out for the boot prints and other marks, her eyes watering with the effort of it. After an hour or so, she felt the rhythm of T'rook's run change, and she sat up.

'What is it?'

'Something ahead,' said T'rook. 'More blood, perhaps.'

When they reached it, for a long time neither of them said anything. Eventually Ynis slid down from her sister's back, and approached the stain on the bank of the river. It was wide and bloody, stinking of death strongly enough that even Ynis's pathetic human nose could pick it up. There were feathers too, big handfuls of them discarded in the scrubby grass.

'They butchered her here,' said Ynis, feeling faint. 'They cut up her body.'

T'rook snapped her beak shut several times, and clawed the ground with her talons. When she didn't say anything, Ynis went and put her arms around her sister's neck and they stood that way for a while, listening to the river churning past them oblivious, just as though a good friend of theirs hadn't been murdered.

'Alright,' said Ynis, when she felt a little better. She pushed her hair out of her eyes and forced herself to look at what was in front of them. 'The trail ends here, too. They didn't go further on foot.'

'Well they can't fly, idiot,' said T'rook, and Ynis was relieved to hear some of the usual temper back in her voice.

'No, they had a boat. A human thing that floats on water.'

T'rook snapped her beak at her sister. 'I know what a boat is. So how do we follow them now?'

'We follow the river,' said Ynis. The river ran ahead through the foothills between two mountains, and then... 'They won't have been going back down the way we came, so we follow the river north. That's the way they went. Perhaps it leads to the sea.'

'Then we have to hurry,' said T'rook. 'If they get to the sea before we find them, we will lose them. And I have promised myself a breakfast of their guts.'

44

Report concerning the Imperium's last attempt to invade Brittletain:
'We sailed north of the Titan's Eye and crossed the final length of
the Channel of Giants with only fifty of our ships remaining – I'd
never seen storms like it; at the time it seemed like the sea itself
came to life and snatched our soldiers from the decks. It was the
middle of a black and howling night, cold and lashed with rain, but
we could see them on the shoreline well enough: hordes of Druin
wizards and other warriors, lit by eerie green witch-lights. Some
of them stood like giants, twelve or fifteen feet tall, and I heard the
murmur of discontent that moved through our troop. And they were
right to be unhappy about our prospects – I certainly was. We had
lost half of our force, and those remaining were half-drowned and
freezing. We had the job of launching the boats and then dragging
them up the beach, all while under enemy fire. As it turned out, it
was much worse than that... I scrambled out of the boat with the
others, and I remember the hot flash of a flaming arrow striking the
sea an inch from my leg. After that, shouts from our commander
to get into formation, but the men and women who had come in
ahead of us were already screaming. I looked up then, my mouth
full of salt spray, and I swear on the ancestor stars, it was as though
the sand and rocks had risen against us. I saw things, huge moving
shapes that could not have been men, snatching up our soldiers
and then our soldiers falling to the ground again, in pieces. What
could we have done, against that? ... Only a handful made it back

to the boats, and that was that, Emperor Lumious's great civilising
force sent back in tatters, shit in their trews and covered in their
fellow soldiers' blood. What could we do but get back in our ships
and leave? The survivors on our ship were silent. None of them
would speak of it, and I don't mind telling you that it fills me with
dread to speak of it now. Brittletain is a cursed and haunted place,
and the Imperium would be wise to leave well enough alone.'

Transcript of a report from an unnamed
member of the Thirteenth Legion

C illian made his way down the great spiral staircase swiftly, glad to be out of the ostentatious chambers. He wasn't familiar with the palace of Mersia; when he had served as Path guide for Mersian merchants, he had barely seen the inside of the city, let alone the complex that made up the royal towers. He had half a mind to go to the stables anyway and see if there was a place he could bed down for the night, but less than a minute out of the room he realised he had little chance of finding the stables without asking one of the servants, and since each one of them gave him a look normally reserved for bird shit on a fine robe, he was not in the mood to do so. He longed to be back in the Wild Wood, with the trees all around him and the gentle hum of the green under his feet. Here, in the tamed and trimmed Mersia, he was as far from the Wild Wood as he had ever been, and it made him feel panicky, lost. He was encased in the tower, trapped inside it like a rat in a tomb. Why had the Druidahnon sent him on this journey? What had he done to deserve this?

'Can I help you, *sir*?' A young man in a guard's uniform was smirking openly and looking at his horns. 'Are you lost?'

Here was his chance to ask about the stables, but Cillian couldn't bring himself to do it. *Don't let them see that it riles you.*

'I need some air,' he said. He made himself smile. 'It's too stuffy in our room.'

The guard raised his eyebrows. Clearly the story about the Herald and her pet Druin had already made its way around the palace.

'There's always the Round, sir,' the guard said. He nodded to a door across the way. 'It's the balcony that runs around the outside of the tower. It's open to everyone. Even you.'

Cillian decided to ignore the insult. He nodded his thanks and went to the far door. Beyond it was a long curving room that hugged the circumference of the tower, and here the hexagonal windows had given out to long simple planes of glass; beyond them was a balcony open to the air. The sight of the sun setting and all the open world before it was like a draught of cool water. He walked stiffly out to the balcony and leaned against its outer wall. A few seconds later, Inkwort landed on the stones next to his elbow.

'I wondered where you'd got to,' he said. The bird pranced and pecked in that way that jackdaws had until Cillian pulled some seed from his pocket and spread it across the stones. 'When I get back, I'm going to ask the Druidahnon exactly what he was thinking. They say you can't get a straight answer from him, but I think I deserve one.'

'He talks to you people, then?'

Cillian turned to see a figure walking towards him around the bend of the balcony. He had thought he was alone.

'Because I must admit I always thought he was a myth. A legend the Druin perpetuate to make the rest of us feel inferior. How could one bear Titan survive this long, alone?'

Cillian initially took the young man to be Prince Gallan, but as he drew closer he saw that this man was older, with a more open face. His shirt was unbuttoned at the collar, and he had several silver rings piercing his right ear. The resemblance, still, was uncanny.

'I am Prince Eafen, and you are the Druin given to look after the Herald,' he said. 'You're here to deliver a gift, am I right?'

'That's correct, your majesty.' Cillian looked away and brushed the last of the seeds from his palms, causing Inkwort to hop about madly. 'If you'll excuse me...'

'Oh, don't go yet. Cillian, isn't it?' The prince smiled warmly and pointed at the bird. 'That's remarkable. Do they all come to you like that? What a power that must be.' When Cillian gave him a sharp look, he raised both his hands and shrugged. 'I am not mocking you, Druin. I've always been interested in the Wild Wood and her caretakers. It seems to me that the power and prosperity of Mersia came at a terrible cost.'

Cillian said nothing. Prince Eafen came and leaned on the wall next to him, looking out across Wodencaester and the sprawling world beyond.

'I'm the oldest son,' said Eafen. 'Did you know that?'

'I'm afraid I don't know much about the Mersian royal family. My lord.'

Eafen chuckled. 'And don't care to either, by the sounds of it. I can hardly blame you. And you're not likely to have heard much about me – Mother has her favourite, and he's practically attached to her apron strings. Not that Mother has ever worn an apron.'

'Prince Gallan. We met him earlier. He brought us into the palace and introduced us to your... to Queen Ismere.'

'Wherever she is, he won't be far behind.' Prince Eafen grinned, quick and sharp, and Cillian felt his own unease deepen. Why was this prince talking to him, when all of Mersia preferred to pretend the Druin didn't exist? As if he had heard his thoughts, Eafen continued. 'You see, I know what it's like to be ignored, my friend. I think it's why I have so much sympathy for the Wild Wood and its keepers. I'm the *spare* son. Gallan has been lined up for the throne since the moment our mother's belly kindled with him. My youngest sister Sionne is the one given over to trade duties, or, as far as I can tell it, the one who spends all her time gathering gossip for Mother. I have heard that in other lands, the eldest child automatically becomes the heir, rather than the quaint little system that we have over here, where we pretend favouritism is something called *merit*. You don't talk much, do you?'

'I was just thinking that you talk an awful lot.'

'*That* has been said before.' Eafen grinned again. 'But I meant what I said, Druin. The civil war might have been hundreds of years ago, but it weighs on us still, doesn't it? That's why we will need you tomorrow to open Queen Broudicca's gift.' When Cillian didn't reply, he continued, a new weight to his words. 'Because the Druin order continues to shun Mersia.'

'With good reason.'

Prince Eafen shrugged. 'Perhaps you are right. But I think it has gone on long enough. Mersia needs the Druin on its side to reach its full potential. And it can't rest well with the Druidahnon that a great part of Brittletain is at odds with the Wild Wood.' He leaned in closer and lowered his voice. 'It is my intention, Druin, to change all that.'

Cillian looked at the man. Inkwort, having demolished the seeds, hopped away.

'You want to undo the civil war?'

'No. Well, yes, in a way, I suppose I do,' said Eafen. 'My idea is that we should cede some of the land we took back to the Wild Wood. Not all of it, obviously – most of that land is farmland now, settled by good people who have been working on it, growing crops and raising farm animals for generations. We could hardly kick them out. But there is still a good margin of land that remains open. Unused. Funnily enough, it turns out that most farmers don't want to live that close to the Wild Wood, and the wild things that live in it. That portion of land… we could give back. As a goodwill gesture.'

'Why are you telling me this?'

Eafen shrugged again. 'I suppose I wanted to sound it out with someone. With someone who has a good idea what the Druin might want from us. What do you think?'

'I think you are talking about it with the wrong person. I am a Druin of no real standing. Why do you think I am here, babysitting a soldier of the Imperium?' Cillian shook his head. He had wanted to get away from all this. Every time he looked at Blessed Eleven he was reminded how he had apparently fallen so low in the Druidahnon's graces he could be ordered to accompany an enemy of the realm. And here he was, back to talking the politics of Brittletain. His place was in the Wild Wood, tracking the Dunohi, not talking to a prince in a prison made of dead stone. 'I also think that I'm not the only one being given ideas above his station. Didn't you just tell me that Prince Gallan is set to inherit the throne, while you are just a spare son?'

For a brief second, the friendly expression on Prince Eafen's face flickered and Cillian caught a glimpse of something sharper underneath. 'Yes, well, just because I am a spare doesn't make me useless. I am sure you of all people can understand.' The easy smile returned. 'I have my ways. I just want you to think about it. And to know that in all of Mersia, you do have a friend.' He patted Cillian on the shoulder and turned to leave. 'Remember that, when you return to the Wild Wood. I won't see you again.'

Inkwort chirped and hopped onto Cillian's hand, her cold little talons a shock against his skin.

'You won't be at the feast tomorrow?' Cillian asked the prince's retreating back.

'Duties have called me away,' said Prince Eafen. 'Like I said, I'm not entirely useless.'

45

I t had been three days since they had arrived in the Black City. Already they had settled into a kind of routine; in the morning they would get up, stretch, eat some of the food they had brought with them, along with some fruits and roots foraged from the jungle beyond the wall, and one of them would check on the horses, which they had brought through the wall and stabled in one of the abandoned buildings close to their own camp. Then Tyleigh and Belise would go to the centre of the city and spend the day sketching and making notes. Kaeto would check in on them periodically, in between making his own careful explorations of the surrounding streets. The layout of the place, from what he had seen so far, was remarkably simple: a city like a wheel, with each main street a spoke radiating out from the centre; where the streets became tunnels, diving into the earth. It reminded him of Stratum, which was similarly circular – the idea had occurred to him that the Black City was the dark mirror of the Imperium's capital city, and the thought wouldn't leave him.

Frequently on these excursions he would feel that he was being watched, but despite his constant vigilance never managed to catch more than a flicker of movement on the edge of his vision.

And then, on the afternoon of the third day, he became convinced that a moment ago a figure had been standing in the empty window of a tower, and determined to know one way or the other, he made his way to the bottom of the building. The doorway, like all the others, stood wide and tall and empty; the doorstep, which was slightly too high to be comfortable for a human, was free of dust. It was another hot and still day, and the sunlight that crept in was flat and yellow, revealing an empty central chamber with a doorway leading to a set of wide stone steps that dipped slightly in the middle. Whatever was here now, Kaeto mused, people had once used these steps all the time, over the course of years and years – long enough to wear away the solid black stone under their feet. He paused at the bottom of the stairs, one hand curled over the slick banister that had been carved directly into the wall. He felt foolish.

You were imagining it, he told himself. *It's too hot here, too strange. You're seeing things because you're tired.*

Even so, he called out to the upper floors, his voice much too loud in the silence.

'I'm coming up! I don't mean you any harm!'

Despite his words, Kaeto took a dagger from his belt and held it loosely in his left hand. He walked up the stairs slowly, noting as he did so how much more effort it took than a normal set of stairs, because each step was ever so slightly too high. He came to another bare empty room, which he glanced at briefly before he carried on. There were windows at regular intervals, through which he could see the unnerving expanse of the Black City, and just beyond it, the ring of vibrant green which was the sprawling jungle of Houraki. Quickly he came to a second room, and then a third. This was where he believed he'd seen the figure, so he walked out into the room to check it over more closely, but there was still very little to see. There was a distinct lack of dust, and a few papery beetle corpses clustered in the corners. The walls, he noticed, had some sort of decoration on them, although it was difficult to make it out in the deep shadows. He had just taken a step forward, to get a closer look at them, when a powerful force struck him and he was thrown across the room. He was back on his feet in a second, the dagger that had been knocked from his hand already replaced with another, and he caught sight of the figure that now stood in front of the doorway, blocking his way out. His blood seemed to turn to ice water in his veins.

It looked to be a man, but unlike any man he'd seen before. The figure was at least a head taller than him, perhaps more, and slender through his waist and shoulders. He had long white hair, the colour of moonlight, and it hung down over his shoulders in bedraggled lengths, yet from his face he did not look to be much older than Kaeto. His limbs were smooth and well-muscled, and he wore an odd hodge-podge of clothes, heavily darned and patched, with a few pieces of armour that looked both very old and very expensive – there was a silver pauldron strapped to his left shoulder, and he wore a thin mail shirt made of silver hoops so fine it moved just like a heavy piece of silk. The eyes that glared back at Kaeto were the colour of amber, and he appeared to be carrying something on his back.

'Wait.' Kaeto held up his free hand. Too late, he had seen that the man's hands and feet were dark with what had to be dried blood. 'I'm not here to—'

Faster than Kaeto would have believed possible, the man shot across the room and threw him against the wall. One long hand circled his throat while the other batted away the dagger as easily as a child batting away a fly. The man brought his face very close to Kaeto's, and began to squeeze his throat.

'Wait!' Kaeto gasped. 'Who are you?' The face that glowered inches from his had high prominent cheekbones, and his eyes were narrowed to killing-slits – it was a look Kaeto had seen many times before, on any number of dark missions for the Imperium. 'Are you a Titan? Othanim?'

That word stopped him in his tracks. The tall man with bloody hands loosened his grip on Kaeto's neck and sensing his moment the Envoy threw himself free. He stumbled against the wall, his hands reaching for new weapons.

'That word...' The man's voice was low and musical, and his stance was wary, as though Kaeto had struck him with an unexpected weapon. 'I've not heard it for the longest time. Devils, and monsters, and ghosts, but not Othanim.'

'Who are you?' said Kaeto again. 'What are you doing in the Black City?'

'My name is Felldir,' he said. 'And the Black City is my home.'

'No one lives here,' said Kaeto. He was edging himself closer to the doorway. 'The place is abandoned.'

'It's dangerous,' said Felldir, as though he agreed, and then his face contorted. 'You shouldn't be here!'

'Tell me why, then.' Very slowly, Kaeto held up the dagger in his hand so that Felldir could see it, and then, just as carefully, he put it back in his belt. That done, he held his empty hands up in front of him. 'I am in your care now, friend.' He did not mention the poison-tipped blade that lay within a hidden pocket on his belt. 'Tell me why the city is dangerous. And tell me... what you are.'

The tall man stood very still. A faint breeze from the window stirred the papery casings of the dead beetles littering the floor.

'I've seen you down by the Undertomb, you and the other two,' said Felldir. 'You should not be there.'

'The Undertomb? Is that what you call the tunnels, Titan?'

Felldir stood very still.

'What is it that you know of Titans?'

'I know that they're all dead – or at least, almost all of them. Are there more like you in the city? What is dangerous about the Undertomb? Why are you here, alone?'

Felldir took a step backwards, towards the wide window behind him. He seemed even more uncertain, and Kaeto was put in mind of a spooked cat, staring at shadows.

'You killed the others, didn't you?' Kaeto took a careful step forward. Now that he was in the room with the creature that had been haunting him for days, he didn't want him to leave. 'Riz, the man who brought us through the wall. The others that have passed into the Black City. When you said it was dangerous, what did you mean? Surely you are the only danger here?'

'You ask a lot of questions,' said Felldir. He turned his head to one side slightly, his long white hair hanging down, framing his angular face.

'And more to the point, why haven't you killed us?' Kaeto knew he was pushing his luck, but the strength in Felldir's hands had been no illusion. He had the sudden idea that Felldir could have snapped his neck easily enough. 'Surely you've had plenty of opportunities to wipe out all of our little party.'

'Stay away from the Undertomb,' Felldir said. 'You should not disturb what sleeps there. Not if you value your little world, human.'

He stepped up to the window, and the wide bundle on his back that Kaeto had taken to be a pack of some kind unfurled into a pair of huge, feathered wings the colour of ash. Felldir stood there for a moment longer, framed by the bright sunshine outside, and then he was gone, stepping out into the sky. Kaeto ran to the window in time to see a dark shape disappearing beyond the buildings, and then the Titan was lost to sight.

46

Keep to the Paths, and the Paths will keep you.

A popular saying in Brittletain

'And then he said he was going to find some wine. And that was an hour ago.'

Epona laughed into her own glass of mead. The princess's room was, Leven couldn't help noticing, considerably fancier than her own. The walls were covered in rich tapestries, and there were elaborate glass oil lamps in each corner. There was also a fire recessed in the wall, which despite the warm day was roaring away – it was, Leven had noticed, cold inside the palace itself. The white stone did a good job of keeping the warmth out.

'There's no predicting the Druin,' said Epona. 'I mean, you probably could, if you were another Druin, spending all your time in the woods listening to the trees and so on, but to the rest of us? They live by different rhythms. That's what my mother says about them, anyway.'

'I thought I was doing him a favour,' said Leven, still aggrieved. 'They were treating him like… well, they were treating him like an animal.'

They were sat on the rug in front of the fire, a bottle of mead between them. Epona pulled her knees up to her chin and looked into the flames.

'That's Mersia for you. To think, my mother was trying to marry me off to that git. Can you imagine?'

'Prince Gallan.' Leven laughed. 'Like getting into bed with a patch of slippery ice.'

Epona hooted. 'That's practically what I said!'

'Then why? My impression was that your mother thought very highly of you.'

Epona grinned. 'Oh, that's exactly why. She wanted me here, getting my sticky fingers all over Mersian business. It would have brought our two nations together, you see, although what my mother really meant by that is "brought Mersia under the control of Londus, where they belong".'

'So, aside from the fact he's about as personable as a stab wound, what happened?'

Epona shook her head. 'I don't really know. Mother doesn't tell us everything. I think she has other plans for me. Someone has to succeed her when she goes, after all, and it would hardly do for me to have a Mersian husband if that were the case. Sometimes I wish I had ended up with my sister Ceni's fate – given a kingdom in the north to rule and left to get on with it. So far she's managed to avoid getting married to anyone.'

'Stars' arses.' Leven shook her head. 'This is all so complicated! Don't you ever just… marry whoever you fancy?'

Epona grinned lopsidedly. 'That's not how it works for royalty, Blessed Eleven. What about you? How does it work in the Imperium? Are soldiers allowed to have husbands and wives?' She stopped and sat up. '*Do* you have a husband? Or a wife? I never asked.'

Leven chuckled. 'Normal soldiers of the Imperium are allowed to marry. But the Heralds were different. We served for eight years only, and we were always on the move, marching through Unblessed countries and bringing the blessings of the Imperium.' Now, when she said it out loud, it sounded faintly sordid. Her smile faded. 'And before those eight years, I don't know… We have no memory of it.'

'I always thought that was a myth,' said Epona. She topped up their glasses. 'You really don't remember anything?'

Leven shook her head, although she was thinking of her visions of Brittletain. The frozen wood, the ruins, and the griffins high above her.

'So you actually could be married,' said Epona in a tone of wonder. 'You could have, I don't know, three husbands and twelve children.'

'I hope I don't look like I've had three husbands and twelve children.' They both laughed together then, raucously. When their giggles had died away, Leven sighed and took a sip of her mead. 'I don't know. I think, if I had a husband or a wife before I was made a Herald, it obviously wasn't going very well. It's one way to run away from a marriage, I suppose.'

What was I running away from?

'Still has to be easier than dealing with the politics of this place,' said Epona. 'And tomorrow you'll get more of it. Keep your wits about you, Herald. Prince Gallan and his mother are a slippery pair.'

Leven grimaced. 'Anything I should know?'

'Only that they don't like us much,' said Epona. 'And by that I mean me – Londus is their biggest rival, and they don't appreciate how my mother behaves like she's the one and only queen of all Brittletain. As for the Imperium... they wouldn't piss on you if you were on fire.'

'Right.' Leven took another swig of mead. 'I think I'm starting to get used to that.'

———

Later, when the moon had risen outside the hexagonal windows, Leven went back to her own room, mildly giddy on honey wine. It was dark in the chamber, with only a single candle burning on the table, but she could see a faint light spilling out from under the servant's door. She stood for a moment, holding her breath and listening, but if Cillian was in there he was asleep, or perhaps furiously sulking. Too weary to care much, she stripped off to her under clothes, pulled on an old shirt worn soft with too much washing, and crawled into the bed.

She awoke in the very dead of night with that disorientated feeling that comes from sleeping in a strange bed, and the sense that she wasn't alone. The candle had burned down to the nub, but there was enough light to see Cillian standing by the hexagonal windows. He wasn't facing her, but somehow he knew she was awake, because he spoke into the dark.

'I'm sorry,' he said. 'I couldn't sleep in there. It's too... closed in.'

Leven felt a spike of annoyance. 'I could have found you a bed from somewhere, if you'd have let me.'

'I know,' he said quietly. 'I don't like being in this place, and it makes me even more stubborn than usual.'

Leven sat up, surprised by his tone. She slipped out of bed, pushing the yellow silk to one side. She walked slowly over to the window, keeping her eyes on Cillian but not going too close.

'I'm sorry we had to come here, in that case,' she said. 'I think I preferred Kornwullis. Even with the nets and the pixen and the dried fish. Kornwullis was homely compared to this place. It was certainly friendlier.'

He smiled at that. In the moonlight he looked both older and stranger, the horns that curled out of his temples making him look like a statue of an ancient forgotten god. *I've gotten used to them*, she thought, surprised at herself.

'It feels strange to be so far from the Wild Wood,' he said. 'Cold, somehow. The Druidahnon wanted me to get some distance from it, I think, but he can't have meant this.' He gestured at the window. 'Even the animal minds here are quiet. I can hear their horses, their birds and their dogs and cats, but they all feel more human than wild. They've been tamed, restricted, brought up by human hand. The mind of a fox, out in the wood, doesn't give a fig about us. The dogs in the palace though, they think about humans constantly – where the master of the hounds is, when is he coming back, and will he bring them dinner. I went to the stables thinking it would feel more like home, but it only reminded me how far away home is.'

'We'll be back in the Wild Wood tomorrow night.' Leven crossed her arms over her chest; despite the rug on the floor, the room was chilly in bare legs. 'If not tomorrow, then the day after, surely. They can't keep us here for that long, can they?'

Cillian gave a short laugh, and for the first time he turned to look at her. He seemed surprised to see her so close, and Leven saw his glance flicker to her bare feet. All at once she felt painfully conscious of the ore-lines that tracked their way across her knees and down her shins and calves. *I must look so strange to him*, she thought, her cheeks growing hot. *I am a sword engraved with the words of his enemy.*

'Listen,' she said, hopping from one foot to the other. 'You take the big bed, okay? At least you can see the sky from there.' When he started to protest, she spoke over him rapidly. 'The truth is I'm not used to a bed that soft, or big, and I think I'd sleep better in the smaller room too. No one needs to know, do they?'

He looked at her for a long moment, an expression on his face she couldn't read. Eventually he nodded.

The narrow bed in the servants' quarters was still slightly warm. Leven lay without moving, uncertain how she felt about that. It was pleasant to be warm, and the blankets smelled a little of Cillian, which was also, she had to admit, quite pleasant, but there was that sense of being close to him that was slightly unnerving. She lay there in the dark for a long time, too aware of his presence to rest, until eventually the tiredness that had haunted her all evening overtook her, and she fell into a dreamless sleep.

47

The banquet was held at the very top of the royal tower. It had to be, Leven thought, the tallest building she had ever been in – and certainly the tallest building she had ever had dinner in. The roof itself was a remarkable structure: the hexagonal crystal windows she had seen in her room and Epona's were laced into a delicate shell that arched over them, catching the watery sunshine of Brittletain and holding it in place, so that it was quite warm; for the first time since leaving Stratum Leven felt hot enough to sweat. There were three long tables forming a triangle in the centre of a colourful roof garden, with scented straw thrown across smooth wooden boards underfoot. The tables faced a simple dais of dark wood, and on it rested the gift box that Queen Broudicca had entrusted to Leven. It was, she had been told, to be opened when they had finished their feasting.

'Have you seen the view?' Epona elbowed Leven in the ribs. They had been seated at the high table, given the honour of a seat near Prince Gallan and Queen Ismere. 'It's incredible. I shall have to tell Mother that we need some towers like this in Londus. Taller ones, if possible.'

'It's impressive.'

'You don't *sound* impressed.'

Leven looked out through the dome of glass panels. The cultured green lands of Mersia spread out below them in all directions, like a quilt made of green squares. The lands of the Unblessed had rarely looked so organised. 'I can fly, remember? I've seen countries from this height before, and there wasn't any glass in the way. Or any buildings to stand on. That's the best way to see any place.'

Epona grimaced. 'I'm not sure I can agree with that. Having something solid beneath your feet feels much safer.'

'Where is Cillian?'

There were three women strolling in front of the three tables, each of them playing a stringed instrument Leven didn't recognise whilst singing softly of rivers and wolves and long-lost loves. Men and women in servant livery were streaming up the spiralled stairs with large copper plates covered in food.

'He's over there, on the table I must assume is for the people Queen Ismere doesn't like particularly but feels she has to invite anyway. Do you know, the kitchens in this place are on the ground floor, yet these pastries are still piping hot! They must have some special system for transporting them up here. We will have to find out what it is. For our Londus towers.'

Leven looked for Cillian and spotted him at the far end of the third table. He looked very still and quiet, keeping his head down and stealing occasional glances out the hexagonal windows. Leven wondered if he was looking for the Wild Wood, somewhere in the distance. She had woken that morning in his bed, the blankets twined around her and the smell of him on her body. She had slept better than she had in weeks, which was something she did not want to look at too closely.

'Are you going to eat your pastry? They're very good.' Epona nudged her again. 'If you don't want it, I'll have it. After walking through the Wild Wood for weeks it feels like I've melted all the flesh off my bones.'

'Hands off, I'm eating it.'

Prince Gallan, who was sitting next to Princess Epona, leaned forward to address them both.

'May I introduce Queen Gwenith, of Dwffd?'

The woman on his other side leaned forward. She was, to Leven's eyes, young for a queen, perhaps only a year or so older than Epona. She had dark hair that fell in energetic waves across her shoulders, and her skin was pale and creamy, contrasting sharply with the dark slash of her eyebrows and the thick black smudge of her eyelashes. Queen Gwenith was dressed quite differently to the other men and women at the tables; she wore a red velvet jacket pulled tightly in at the waist, and loose trousers tucked into knee-high brown leather boots. The jacket was thickly embroidered with golden thread; serpents and moons wrestled across her sleeves. The new queen narrowed her eyes at Leven.

'You are the Imperium's great weapon? That brought so many nations to their knees?'

'Not me alone, your majesty.'

Queen Gwenith took a cloth from the table and dabbed at a corner of her mouth, although Leven could see no food there.

'Gwenith was a close friend of my sister Ceni, when Mother still ruled Galabroc,' said Epona. 'When they were both girls, she would come to the castle in the north and stay for the summer. Amazingly, Dwffd has even worse weather than Galabroc. Have you seen my sister recently, Gwenith? I'm sure she looks forward to your visits – it can get very quiet up north, with the Wild Wood on one side and the griffins on the other.'

Queen Gwenith continued as if Epona hadn't spoken.

'I came all the way from Dwffd when I heard that you would be visiting Mersia before us. You'll forgive me my caution, Herald, but I wanted to get a good look at you before you were let anywhere near the borders of my lands. We're not as at home to murderers as Londus.'

'I'm sorry,' said Epona, in a syrupy tone Leven was already learning meant trouble. 'What did you just say?'

'It's fine.' Leven held both hands up in a conciliatory gesture. She was in a good mood. The food – which had moved on to another course of sugared fruits – was very fine, and the wine was even better. No one had tried to kill her in days, and under the sunny crystal windows the strange visions of snow and forest felt very distant. Even the prickly nature of Brittletain's tribes seemed like a minor problem. 'I am not here representing the Imperium, your highness. I'm here to see an island that has been a mystery to my people for hundreds of years, and to do a simple favour for Queen Broudicca.'

'You know, Queen Gwenith,' Epona continued, 'we have all of the gift boxes my mother had made here in our rooms. If you do not want us to travel through Dwffd, we can fetch yours for you now and you can shove—'

'Ah, here is the next course,' said Prince Gallan rapidly. 'Perhaps we could divert our attention to the pig?'

On the far table, Cillian found himself looking around the banquet rather than at his food. The tower was high enough to be dizzying, and around the glass dome he could faintly hear the moaning of the wind. It was disconcerting, but better than being inside the tower; at least here he had all the sky he could ever want. He had not slept well; sleeping in the huge, soft bed with the yellow silk had felt ridiculous, and he'd woken up frequently from dreams where he'd been following Inkwort through the Wild Wood, a huge sense of anticipation in the green around him, as though they were waiting for him to do something. It hadn't helped that each time he awoke he became aware of Blessed Eleven's scent on the silk covers.

The diners next to him, as far as he could tell, were minor nobles and puffed-up merchants, and all of them were quietly furious to be seated with the Druin. The conversations going on around him had the solid feeling of ancient castle walls: he was not to be let in.

He found his eyes drawn to where Leven was sitting at the far table. She had dressed that morning in what she described as her best shirt, a simple garment of creamy white silk that contrasted well with her tanned, ore-marked skin, and a pair of simple dun-coloured trousers tucked into tall leather boots. Epona had tried to talk her out of these clothes, had attempted to lend her some dramatic silk dress that she had apparently squashed into her travelling pack, but Leven had turned the offer down. Seeing her now, seated amongst queens, princesses and princes, she clearly did not fit in, yet she seemed unfazed by it all. He realised that he admired her for that.

'Beast-witch.' A man lurched forward, blocking Cillian's view of the Herald. From the smell of his breath he had been making the most of the wine, and he had the bright silver buttons of a merchant. 'Shall I put some scraps under the table for you? Shall I find a dog to eat it with you?'

There were a few restrained titters from around the table. Cillian looked steadily back at the man.

'I'm fine as I am, thank you.'

The man sneered. 'Not rising to the bait? How boring. Why did they seat you with us, Druin, if you're not the entertainment?'

'Kanut.' One of the other diners leaned in close, her voice soft. 'The Druin is the guest of the Imperium's butcher. Even you don't want to make an enemy of that pretty little monster.'

'A guest?' Kanut spluttered. 'Do they dine with animals in the Imperium?'

'I wouldn't be surprised.' The woman smirked. 'And they think *Brittletain* is the backward little island.'

'I bet that he is *her* entertainment.' Kanut laughed. His voice grew louder as he warmed to his joke. 'Of course a bloodthirsty bitch like that ruts with beasts. How is she, wood witch? I imagine she's quite the handful.'

Cillian lifted his head. 'My lord, can I give you some advice?' The table grew quiet. 'The next time you travel through the Wild Wood, be very wary. It's a dangerous place. Who knows what terrible creature might take a fancy to your insides?'

The man took a step back, his mouth turning down at the corners. He wrinkled his nose at Cillian and wandered back to his own seat.

They were bringing out three spit-roasted pigs, their mouths choked up with apples and their skins brown and crispy and running with juicy fat. There was a murmur of excitement as servants stepped forward to carve the pork. Cillian looked back to the wooden dais where the gift box waited for him to open it at the end of the banquet.

Roots strangle me, when will this ever end?

When the final course of the banquet was cleared away – some kind of sweet milk pudding with a tart crimson jam – Queen Ismere leaned across the table and tapped her finger firmly on the wood.

'Have you ever eaten so well in the Imperium, Herald? I am sure the foods of Brittletain easily match anything your overlords have to offer.'

Leven smiled politely. She felt very full, very tired, and had no energy for any more political dancing. She wanted a nap. 'Truthfully, your highness, I have never had such a good meal in my life. We had decent supplies when we were travelling across the Unblessed lands, but even the best supplies boil down to stale bread and salted meat so many months into any campaign.'

Queen Ismere pulled back her scrawny neck, looking pleased. She then spoke to the prince at Epona's right.

'Where is Eafen? I told him to attend.'

Prince Gallan looked uncomfortable. 'I don't know. It is not my duty to know where my brother is at all times.'

'He shall miss the presentation of whatever this nonsense is Broudicca sees fit to send me. Perhaps he has more sense than I credit him with.' Queen Ismere smoothed her hair back from her brow in a preening fashion, and Leven realised something odd: that the queen, despite all her caution and her veiled insults, was thrilled to have such a reason to throw a banquet – was thrilled, in fact, to receive such attention from her rival Broudicca. *Epona's mother is a clever woman*, she thought to herself. *Clever and patient. Who has the time for these bloodless battles?*

'It's time,' Epona said, tapping her on the elbow. 'We'll give the gift now, and then hopefully there will be more drinking and carousing.'

She and Leven went to the dais with Queen Ismere and Prince Gallan. Cillian was already there, waiting quietly by the box with its green seal. The men and women at the tables grew quiet. Huge white and grey clouds as tall as sailing ships moved serenely through a blameless blue sky above them, and all at once Leven felt nervous. She wished she hadn't eaten so much. She wished she had thought a bit more about what to say. A lot of eyes were watching her.

'Your royal highness.' She paused and cleared her throat. 'It is my pleasure... I mean, it is my honour, to bring to you a gift from Queen Broudicca of Londus. Thank you for treating this stranger like a friend.'

Leven saw Epona nod slightly at that, and she knew she had done a good job. She caught Cillian's eye, and the Druin stepped up to the dais and picked up the box. He passed his hand over the green seal, and with a tiny snapping noise, the lid clicked open. Turning stiffly, he stepped away from the dais. The people at the tables were sitting up straighter, straining to see what the gift could be. Leven noticed Queen Gwenith watching especially closely, perhaps eager to find out if any present could be worth inviting an Imperium butcher into her lands. Standing close to his mother, Prince Gallan was smoothing down the white silk of his jacket.

The queen opened the box. Leven was only half watching, relieved that her part of the presentation was over, and then she caught a baffled expression passing over the older woman's face.

'What *is* that?'

She put her hand to the box as if to take something out of it, and a split second later a long shard of something dark and shining sprouted from the inside of the box, slicing neatly into and through the queen's throat; the far end of the object protruded a good eight or nine inches from the back of her neck, although on that side it was now glistening red with her blood. Leven's first shocked thought was that somehow a sword had grown from the impossibly small box, but then, as screams flew up all around the roof garden, she saw that the thing seemed to be made of a highly polished dark wood.

'Treachery!' someone screamed from nearby.

The queen's hands went to her throat, her expression of bafflement now one of amazement, and she sagged, held up only by the wooden stake. The fine silk robes she had been wearing were quickly turning a deep, ominous scarlet. Prince Gallan, who had appeared to be frozen in place for several long seconds, rushed to support her, his face a rigid mask of shock, all colour drained from it. Leven moved towards them – to do what, she wasn't exactly sure – and then the lethal wooden shard grew several more offshoots, striking the prince and running him through on the spot. A shard through his chest, a shard through the meaty portion of his bicep... a shard through his eye.

Epona, who had been struck by a lot of the blood, had her hands over her mouth.

'What *the fuck* is happening?'

'Treachery!' The cry came again over the general chaos of the banquet, and Leven realised it was the foreign queen, Queen Gwenith, who was shouting. She was already ordering guards to close in on them. 'Londus and the Imperium have murdered Mersia's queen and her heir! Take them! Take them now!'

48

A full two days of scouting through unfamiliar foothills and Ynis felt frozen to her core. The river they were following grew icy enough in places that they could walk across it, and a wind with teeth blew down off the mountains that towered over them.

'I can't believe I thought the Bone Fall was cold,' she said through gritted teeth on the second day. The days themselves seemed shorter here, gloom rushing in at the corners once the sun had made its blind progress to the centre of the sky, and already shadows were growing deeper all around them.

T'rook normally took such an opportunity to tease her sister about her lack of feathers or fur, but on that darkening day she simply agreed.

'Colder than stone, this place.'

They had been walking to give T'rook's wings a rest, but as they came out of the shelter of the last foothill, the landscape opened up and they stopped where they were. Ahead of them was a bay of dark green sea water, sliced here and there with frills of white foam. There was a beach of black sand, littered with larger black rocks, and in the distance they could see a wooden contraption up on the shore: the boat, the thing that Ynis knew was made to float on and move through water. Humans clustered around it, busily moving wooden crates onto it. Further out in the water there was another of the human contraptions, larger and with black sails that stood stiff in the freezing cold. Up on the rocks were clusters of black and white seabirds standing upright with slick, shining bodies, their wings too small to fly. They gave long mournful cries, as if they understood better than anyone what was happening here.

'That's them,' said T'rook. 'Get on my back. We'll make short work of it.'

But now that they were there, Ynis felt uncertain. There were around ten humans that she could see, and she knew that they would have weapons; the same weapons that had wounded Witch-seer Frost and killed Brocken. She touched the arrowhead that hung around her neck.

'Perhaps we should go back to the Bone Fall and get the others.'

T'rook tossed her head. 'What for? They already told us they were cowards. And we have chased humans before, haven't we? What's the difference?'

This was true. When they lived with their fathers in Yelvynia they had often protected the borders from human interlopers. If the humans were fast, and lucky, they simply ran back into the forests of Brittletain. If they weren't quite fast enough, they were dinner.

'Those humans were just straying out of their territory,' she said. 'These ones... *they've come to kill us.* I don't know why, but that's why they're here. I don't think they will be so easily scared off.'

T'rook snapped her beak several times and puffed out the feathers on her neck. 'I don't want it to be easy!' she said. 'I want it to be fun.' And in a lower tone, she said, 'I want them to pay for Brocken, who was kind to us.'

Ynis remembered her friend, dying on the cold ground, her hot blood running over Ynis's hands. She remembered the fate-ties scattering to the wind as she cut the cord.

'Yes,' she said eventually. 'You're right. But let's get a closer look at them first.'

She climbed onto her sister's back, and in moments they were in the air again. T'rook followed the line of the shore, approaching the boat cautiously. Ynis leaned out over her shoulder and narrowed her eyes at the group of humans.

They were dressed in heavy furs and leather. The crates they were loading onto the boat were made of a pale wood, and heavily stained with blood. *Griffin blood.* One of the figures appeared to be giving the orders, shouting at the others over the bitter wind. She had loose hair the colour of gold, and over her furs she wore a piece of shiny armour that winked and flashed in the last shreds of daylight. She also had strange lines drawn over her face and hands, lines of dark blue that perplexed Ynis. The other humans did not have such facial markings. Ynis couldn't see any bows, as all hands were occupied with the lifting and storing of the crates. And then she saw the woman with golden hair lift her face to the sky, and she saw the woman's posture change as she spotted them.

'They've seen us,' remarked T'rook. 'What shall we do?'

Ynis looked again at the blood staining the crates. *Brocken brought us to the Bone Fall and gave us a new life when no one else wanted us.* 'They are ground-stuck prey animals.' She pulled her claw-knife from her belt and held it ready. 'It's late in the day, so you can have their guts for dinner rather than breakfast.'

T'rook gave a harsh cry of joy, and they swept down from their vantage point towards the marauders. Ynis saw the men and women at the boat scatter, a few of them splashing backwards into the sea in surprise. T'rook was faster, though, and she crashed into one of the men and tore through his furs and leathers with her talons, lifting him up into the sky for a few seconds and then dropping him to the ground. Blood leapt through the air like red jewels.

'It's only an adolescent!' Ynis turned to see the woman with golden hair shouting to the others. She was their leader, then. Her accent was strange, quite unlike that of the humans who lived near the border of Yelvynia. 'The thing is barely grown. Load up your crossbows and we'll take this one to Tyleigh too.'

T'rook flew up and turned around, preparing for another attack.

Ynis leaned out further over her sister's shoulders, preparing to strike herself. She was no longer afraid or uncertain: she felt alive, and ready for the hunt.

'Wait! Is that a child on its back?' someone called. Ynis looked down to see human faces all looking up, expressions she couldn't read on their faces.

'It is!' someone else shouted. 'Boss, there's a kid riding the bloody thing's back!'

The woman with the golden hair peered up at them.

'Stars' arses,' she said. 'A filthy creature, but you're right. A child, of all things.' She waved down the men and women who were preparing their weapons. 'Hold off, I'll take it down.'

'But, Boss—'

'I've seen you fail to hit a barn door with that thing. Do you want to accidentally shoot the child?' The woman called Boss pushed her hair out of her face. 'The griffin is small. It's manageable.'

T'rook had made her circle, and was swooping down for another attack, her talons outstretched, when the woman below threw her arms wide as if to welcome them. A bare second later the lines on her face and hands gave a single pulse of blue light and a pair of huge wings burst from her back. They were blue and glittered in the daylight as though they were made from ice. Ynis felt T'rook's muscles jerk with surprise and then the woman was rushing up to meet them, a great glass sword clutched in one hand.

'What—?'

T'rook, thinking faster than Ynis, folded her wings and let herself drop, avoiding the first swing of Boss's sword, and then flew up underneath the woman, striking her from below with the top of her head. The human spun away, swearing, and spread her wings wider to bring herself back under control. Ynis watched with her mouth open, her own claw-knife held loosely in her hand. A human with wings.

A human who can fly.

'Sister!' squawked T'rook. 'You have to hold on or you will fall off!'

The woman was coming for them again, her blue sword slicing through the air so close to them that Ynis felt the hum of it as it passed. T'rook turned desperately, losing a few feathers in her desperation. From below, there was a chorus of shouts from the men and women by the boat.

'Let us shoot it, Boss! We won't miss!'

T'rook flew straight up, like an arrow herself, and the flying woman came after her. Ynis looked back over her shoulder and found herself eye to eye with Boss, who had snatched hold of her sister's tail. The woman had bright blue eyes and her cheeks were flushed pink – she was grinning too, as though this were the best feeling in the world.

And it is, thought Ynis, in wonder. *Because she is flying!*

Outraged by the weight on her tail, T'rook turned and struck at the woman with talons outstretched. Caught unawares and in the wrong position to use her sword, Boss let go of T'rook's tail and struck the griffin on her flank with her fist. To Ynis's surprise, T'rook bellowed with pain and lurched through the sky as though the very mountain had risen up to strike her. Before she knew what was happening Ynis was unseated and tumbling through the sky herself, and even as she fell she was thinking of those wings, those blue ice wings – where did they come from? How was it possible?

And then her arm was caught, nearly yanking it out of her shoulder socket. She looked up to see the woman with golden hair gripping her arm, her blue wings spread out to either side. The last of the sunlight winked across her golden breast plate, dazzling Ynis.

'Who are you, kid?' the woman asked. She looked fierce and bright and alive. 'What are you doing here?'

Ynis reached up with her hand still holding the claw-knife and struck the woman in the arm with the blade. It barely made a scratch, but Boss dropped her in surprise and Ynis fell again, tumbling towards the black beach. She had a last glimpse of T'rook, her yellow eyes wide with fright as she barrelled through the air to catch her sister, and then she was lost to darkness.

49

Like many Unblessed nations, Houraki persists in the primitive belief in a huge variety of small gods – so many, in fact, that it is apparently impossible to catalogue them, a fact of which the Houraki themselves seem perversely proud. If anything, gods seem to be summoned into existence at every whim, by any weaver who needs a dye to take, or any mother who wishes their child to survive a fever. Small clay figures of these gods litter the very landscape, although it does seem that there are other, older, more established gods who have their own dedicated cults. These are particularly prevalent in the south-eastern region – around the area where the Black City is rumoured to be situated. Whether that is coincidental or not is something you will likely find out for yourselves.

Preliminary research notes on Unblessed
Houraki gathered for Envoy Kaeto

'I have found the person who killed Riz. Or, I should say, the *Titan* that killed Riz.'

Tyleigh and Belise were both kneeling on the wide stone slabs outside the tunnel entrances – they were taking rubbings of the patterns inscribed there with charcoal and thin paper – but they both turned to look at Kaeto as he approached. Tyleigh's eyebrows had nearly disappeared beneath her ever-present headband.

'What?' she snapped.

Kaeto paused. As alarming as it had been to meet Felldir, the fact that Tyleigh would be furious that he had found something so significant before her gave him a certain satisfaction, and he intended to enjoy it.

'A Titan. He could hardly have been anything else. You were right, Tyleigh – the Titans of the Black City were human in shape. And they had wings.'

'Of course I am right.' She stood up, briskly wiping sooty marks onto her trousers. Behind her, Belise crouched, a stick of charcoal held loosely in one hand. 'Well? Spit it out, man. You are to report to me, remember?'

Kaeto cleared his throat. 'I had been catching movement out of the corner of my eye for days now, and I finally tracked it down to one of the towers.'

'Which tower, where?' Tyleigh shook her head at her own question. 'Never mind. Continue!'

'He attacked me, and told me we were to leave the Black City immediately. He called this place,' Kaeto nodded towards the nest of tunnels, 'the Undertomb, and he responded to the term *Othanim*. He was tall, with very pale skin and white hair.' Handsome and terrifying, he did not add. 'He had large wings, like an eagle, with grey feathers. He said his name was Felldir.'

'And he was human in aspect?' asked Tyleigh. Some of the anger had gone out of her voice. She sounded almost in awe. One sooty hand touched her own cheek lightly. 'A human face?'

'Strange enough,' said Kaeto. 'But certainly human, yes. He was also inhumanly strong.'

'Why didn't he kill you?' piped up Belise.

'That is a good question,' he said. 'I don't know. My impression, both from his behaviour and the local folklore, is that he has been here for hundreds of years, murdering anyone foolish enough to pass through the walls, so why he should leave me alive, I cannot guess.

Or why indeed he hasn't killed all three of us already. As lethal as you and I are, Belise, we would struggle to stand against him.'

'Hundreds of years,' said Belise. 'So it's not just the Druidahnon who is long lived?'

'Obviously, idiot,' snapped Tyleigh. 'Please keep your mouth shut if you have nothing useful to add. So, what then? He just left you in the tower? Where did he go?'

'He left, and I lost sight of him across the roofs of the city.' Kaeto shook his head slightly. 'It may well be impossible to find him again. He will know this city better than any of us.'

Tyleigh nodded, but she barely seemed to be listening. Instead she was looking fixedly up at the sky, which was filled with dense white cloud.

'I can hardly believe it,' she said, her voice soft. 'A living example of a lost Titan race. A race no one believed existed in the first place.' She scowled. 'And the discovery will be mine. Whatever it is he is protecting in this Undertomb, we must have it. There is no question about it now.'

'We just need to get those doors open,' said Belise cheerfully.

It was Kaeto's turn to frown. 'What doors?'

Tyleigh led him down the nearest tunnel, where small oil lamps were casting a soft buttery light against smooth walls. At the far end, they came to a large, circular door, also apparently carved from stone. Here, there were several of the small lamps burning brightly, and more sheets of the thin paper they had been making rubbings with. The stone itself was intricately carved with several different forms – Kaeto saw griffins, bears, wyverns, krakens, boar and firebirds, all interlinked with what looked like vines. In the centre there were odd curling interconnected shapes that looked almost familiar. There were also what he initially took to be blue-green spheres of glass sunk into the stone; six of them in all, with an empty space for a seventh. He reached out to touch one and was surprised to find it was faintly warm to the touch.

'Ingots of Titan ore,' said Tyleigh. 'Which might well prove that the Titans were smelting their own bones and using the ore to power magic hundreds of years before I came up with the idea. The pieces in this door are much purer than anything I've ever been able to produce from the ancient remains we've sourced.'

'Why would they do that?' Kaeto drew his hand away sharply. For some reason the thought unnerved him.

'I expect because it was a powerful magic that only they had access to.' Tyleigh grinned, and Kaeto looked away. Lit from beneath by the yellow light of the oil lamps, her face looked ghoulish. 'That empty space there? I think that is the key to opening this door. I've examined the colour and density of the other ingots and they appear to be made of a mixture of Titan ores – so much from the griffins, so much from the god-boar, and so on. I need to examine exactly what each is comprised of, and then... I think if we can create one to replace what is missing, we may well be able to open this door. Luckily, I have samples of all of these with me. It will just take time.'

'They locked the door with...' Kaeto cleared his throat, unsure how to put it. 'They used their own magical bones to craft the lock?'

'Certainly they did. Back then, who would have had access to their bones? The Titans were all-powerful, and now they are nothing. Now, I am the only one able to use their magic. Would you be able to kill this new Titan if we had to, Envoy?'

'What?'

'It could be that we need some of his remains to create the final ingot.' She paused and pushed a strand of greasy hair back behind her ear. 'Why are you looking at me like that? Killing is the one thing you are truly required to be good at, isn't it? It's what you are *for*.'

'I don't know,' said Kaeto. 'He is strong, and has survived here for hundreds of years.' He frowned, eager to leave the subject be. 'And the writing? I assume that's what it is?'

'Yes. A very ancient and apparently unique dialect of Hourakian.' Tyleigh narrowed her eyes and slowly drew one finger across the fluid shapes. *'This is not a place of honour. What is buried here is destruction, doom and shame. Leave here and forever forget this place.'*

'That bodes well, doesn't it, master?' said Belise brightly. 'Can't wait to get the door open now.'

Kaeto looked back to the far end of the tunnel, where daylight hung in a white circle, like an overcast sun. Having all three of them down here together made his back itch. How easy would it be for Felldir to collapse the entrance to the tunnel, leaving them in here to be crushed, or die of thirst? He wouldn't even have to get his hands dirty.

'We'll make sure one of us is outside at all times now, I think. We shall need to keep half an eye on the sky, in case our new Titan friend decides to pay us another visit.' He thought again of the strong hands that had closed around his throat. 'Work as quickly as you can, Tyleigh.'

50

Pixen: more superstitious nonsense from a barbarian island. According to the kingdom of Kornwullis every inch of their Unblessed land is teeming with mischievous spirits. A useful way to explain away spoilt milk, a miscarried calf or the drunkard husband who gets lost on his way home, I suppose. The pixen at least seem less lethal than their Dunohi cousins in the Wild Wood, which is an interesting distinction.

Excerpt from *The Lore of the Deep Forest: An Examination of the Myths and Facts of Brittletain*

'Wait, stop!'

Epona stepped in front of Leven, her hands held up, palms out. Guards with swords had surrounded them quickly, and the other dinner guests had melted back away from the tables – many of them had vanished down to lower levels. Queen Gwenith stood just beyond the guards, her pale face flushed.

'This wasn't us,' continued Epona. 'You have to see that! I had no idea what was in that box, or what it is that just… that has wounded the queen and her son.'

Wounded. Leven glanced at the bodies on the floor. They were very clearly very dead. Prince Gallan appeared to have died at the moment the spear of wood skewered his head, and although Queen Ismere had gurgled for a time as her life's blood rushed from the gaping wound in her neck, she was now still, her skin the colour of snow. Leven caught Cillian's eye, and he mouthed something to her: *this was Druin magic.*

Queen Gwenith wasn't listening. 'Take these three to the cells, and fetch Prince Eafen. He will want to see justice done himself, and swiftly.'

The guards advanced. Leven's ore-lines thrummed with life. She could feel the Titan strength waiting at her fingertips.

'Don't.' She addressed the guards directly. 'You don't want to do this. And I don't want to hurt you.'

She saw a range of expressions pass over their faces: anger, confusion, fear. But they didn't back down. Swords held at the ready, they advanced.

'Queen Gwenith!' Desperately, Leven called to the woman standing beyond the guards. 'Stand them down, or I will have to defend us. Please.'

'We can't fight them,' said Epona. 'It'll only make things worse.'

'Silence, Herald,' called Gwenith. 'Your kind should never have been allowed to touch the shores of Brittletain.'

'Leven, don't!' Epona grabbed her arm and attempted to pull her back from the guards. 'If you kill them now, they'll say it was our plan all along.'

'I think they're going to say that anyway.'

Three of the guards came forward, their swords ahead of them, and it was so like their years of travelling through the Unblessed lands it almost made Leven smile. People were always running at her with swords, and it never ended well. She stepped away from Epona and summoned her sword and her wings. There were cries of surprise and horror from the few dinner guests who had decided to stay and watch the confrontation, and the guards spread out, full of caution. Leven held up her sword, its sapphire light playing across wary faces.

'This is your last chance,' she shouted. 'Let us leave peacefully, and no one else has to die here today.'

They weren't having it. When the guards rushed her she brought her own blade round and up in a simple arc, knocking their weapons away easily, almost lazily. Another came around from the side and grabbed Epona's arm, yanking her forcefully away from the relative safety of Leven's side, while another lowered a pike at Cillian, preparing to strike.

'Alright,' Leven shouted, 'you asked for it.'

She leapt into the air, her magical wings holding her in place and putting her out of the reach of the guard. She swept down and grabbed the guard who was yanking Epona towards the doors and pulled him easily off his feet. She had a second to see his startled expression, eyes wide in a face framed by a ginger beard, and then she threw him, with considerable force, to the far side of the roof garden. He bounced off the hexagonal windows and landed with a crash on one of the long tables. Meanwhile, Cillian had been forced back himself, the lethal point of the pike inches away from his chest. Leven thought of how the Druin were disliked here, how it would be so easy for them to kill Cillian in the confusion of everything, justice be damned. She turned in the air and dropped down onto the long wooden staff of the pike, snapping it like a toothpick. Cillian moved to Epona's side.

'Get behind me, both of you!' Leven called.

'This won't work,' Epona shouted back. 'There are reinforcements coming up the stairs already – I can hear them.'

Leven looked towards the door and saw that she was right. More guards were filing into the room all the time. The place was filling up, and their chances of getting to the doors were dwindling.

'Fuck.' Leven glanced above her at the lattice of hexagonal windows that formed the roof over the garden. It wouldn't be pleasant, but it was hardly impossible. More guards were edging forward, and she gave them a warning slash with her sword.

'Get back then, as far as you can,' she shouted to Epona and Cillian. 'Cover your heads.'

'What are you doing?'

Leven summoned every bit of Titan strength she had, and with one great downward flap of her wings she propelled herself directly upwards. Her fist met the glass and there was a huge crash, and dark lights flashed in front of her eyes.

Hold on, she told herself. *Hold on.*

A large section of the glass roof fell, crashing down onto the guards with a musical explosion. They fell back, afraid of the falling glass and the maniac who had smashed the roof to bits. Leven blinked. There was blood running into her eyes, but there was no time to worry about that. She landed next to Epona and Cillian with a little more force than she was expecting. Cillian had picked up a discarded sword.

'We have a way out, come on.'

'A way out how?' said Epona. 'You aren't expecting us to climb up there, are you?'

'Not exactly.' Leven took a deep breath. The guards were approaching again, their boots crunching over the broken glass. She had only moments to gather the rest of her strength. She relinquished her sword and it vanished, back into the place where it waited for her. 'Take my arms, both of you. Quickly!'

Epona took hold of her left arm, while Cillian took her right. She grasped them back; it was her grip that really mattered, after all. She couldn't let them fall.

'Hold on. This is going to be hairy.'

She saw Epona open her mouth, whether to protest or whether to ask what she meant by hairy, she didn't know, and then she leapt up again, throwing her wings as wide as they would go. Keeping her head up and her eyes on the blue sky above them, Leven flew directly up, with Epona and Cillian hanging from each arm. She heard them shout, and Epona give a wild shriek, and then they were out of the glass roof and above the tower. Mersia lay all around them, gently rolling hills and fields full of crops. Below them, she could just about hear Queen Gwenith shouting more orders to the guards.

'Magog's balls,' cried Epona. 'I'm going to be sick.'

'Just hold on.' Leven flew slowly away from the tower. The city directly below was clearly no place to land; there would be guards there in minutes, if they weren't there already. She cast around beyond the city walls.

'Cillian, if I get us to a wooded place, can you get us to the Wild Wood?'

'Yes,' he shouted over the wind. 'There's a copse to the north, do you see it?'

Leven dragged her eyes up, blinking against the stinging blood that was still running from her forehead. Despite the Titan strength running through her ore-lines her arms were already burning. *I'm not what I once was*, she thought faintly.

'I see it,' she said. 'Hold on tight.'

With everything she had left Leven flew across the city, Epona and Cillian hanging from her arms. The tension across her shoulders and back was agonising. Below them, it was just possible to hear the citizens of Wodencaester shouting in wonder. They had been spotted.

'I don't want to sound like I'm being critical,' said Epona in a slightly manic tone of voice. 'But you're losing height really fast. Maybe too fast.'

Leven looked down. The princess was right.

'Just hold on,' she said through gritted teeth. 'I can make it.'

Leven pushed forward, forcing her wings to work harder than they ever had before. They passed over the city walls and were flying over the fields and grasslands of Mersia, while the wound in her arm, that had healed so well, woke up and began throbbing with pain. The copse of trees she had spotted from the air was growing closer and closer, and then, quite abruptly, the ground was very close indeed.

'I think...' Her head swam dangerously, and her vision dimmed. 'I think it's going to be a crash landing.'

She tried one last grasping attempt to gain height. Epona and Cillian were both shouting something, but she couldn't make out the words, and she could see the trees, coming up closer.

'Nearly there, nearly there...'

The next thing she knew it was like the ground leapt up and hit her, filling her nose with the smell of wet grass and dirt. Exhaustion rushed over her like a dark cloud, and it seemed like even lifting her head was beyond her. She felt hands patting her down, strong arms lifting her up.

'Leven?' Epona's voice, close to her ear. 'Leven, we can carry you the rest of the way. Don't move, okay? I think you hurt yourself when you smashed the roof. Leven?'

With the very last of her energy Leven opened her eyes a crack and was relieved to see the canopy of the forest closing over them. They were home. She closed her eyes.

51

Ynis could not remember opening her eyes, but she was there, standing on the Bone Fall. Not on the edge of it, as she had with Witch-seer Frost, but down on the plain, amongst the bones. The sky overhead was a strange, bruised violet, and pale wisps of green light moved across it, like lightning smeared and frozen in place.

'What am I doing here?'

As she spoke, spirits rose from the bones around her, hundreds of blueish-green lights swarming into being. Startled, she looked down at her own hands and realised she was made of the same stuff; her hands were there, but she could see through them to the gritty ground below.

'Wait. Am I dead?'

The thought didn't panic her in the way she expected. Instead she felt a rising tightness in her chest, like the feeling was too big for her to grasp.

'You're walking the Edge again.'

Ynis turned at the sound of the familiar voice and saw the ghostly shape of Brocken moving towards her. It was difficult to tell the griffin spirits apart – they moved constantly, a soft rush of light and form – but she realised she would know Brocken anywhere. She was glad to see her.

'What do you mean?'

The form that was Brocken shifted and flowed around her. 'You fell from your sister's back, didn't you? Onto the hard sand.'

'I didn't fall,' said Ynis immediately, offended. 'I... There was a human woman with wings!' It all came back to her: the boat on the black beach, the crowd of humans with their bloody crates... and the woman with golden hair who leapt up into the sky and *flew*. She had been graceful, powerful, unstoppable. Whereas Ynis had fallen. Twice.

'How is that possible, Brocken? Humans don't fly.'

Her friend shimmered and re-formed, like a reflection on a busy pond. 'There was a bad scent to them. I did not see them fly,' said Brocken. 'They came up on me slowly, creeping, hiding behind rocks. Cowards. And when I did see them, I was confused, because one of them smelt wrong. Not human at all. Something else. Something bad.'

'What was the scent?'

'Like death. Like this place.' Brocken shook her head. 'But wrong. This place is death that offers peace, and rest. The death I smelt on them was... corrupted. This is a thing for witch-seers, not me. I do not know how to describe to you what it was.'

Ynis shivered. Her head was beginning to throb.

'Is it some magic they have outside of Yelvynia? That gives them wings? I could... With wings like that, I could really be one of you!'

Brocken gave her a hard look. 'You *are* one of us, Witch-seer Arrow.'

'But I'm not, am I? I am weak, ground-stuck, a prey animal.' Ynis gasped. It seemed harder to keep her feelings in check in this place, and her head was hurting more and more by the second. 'If I had wings, I could fly with you, hunt with you, go where I wished without needing to be carried. I...' She hiccupped, dangerously close to crying – another human weakness.

'You are one of us, yenlin,' said Brocken again, her voice softer. 'I can't say it clearer than that. But you can't stay here much longer. The other side is calling you back.'

'What did you say?' Ynis clutched at her head. It was pounding so hard it felt like something was trying to hatch from it. 'I can't... Brocken?'

This time she felt her eyes open. Brittle yellow daylight, so much more alive than the strange twilight sky over the Bone Fall. It dazzled her and sent hot pins through her head. She cried out, and heard voices coming closer.

'She's awake. Arrow? Can you hear me?'

Witch-seer Frost's great beak reared into view, and then T'rook was there, impatiently barging her elder out the way.

'Ynis? Are you alright? We're back at the Bone Fall. Sister?'

Ynis groaned. She was tightly swaddled in furs of some kind. She recognised the walls of their cave, and the smell of it too was familiar. Her head felt heavy, and when she reached up to touch it, she realised they had done their best to bandage it.

'What happened?'

'You fell on your head,' snapped T'rook. 'Smack, crack, like an egg. I snatched you up and flew you back here.'

Ynis blinked rapidly. She knew what an extraordinary effort that would have been for her sister, yet she could only think of one thing.

'What happened to the flying woman?'

T'rook clacked her beak shut several times. 'That stone-licker didn't follow us. They were too busy with their stolen things.'

'T'rook, you have to let your sister rest. Head injuries in humans are quite serious.' Frost sounded weary herself.

'She is tough, my sister,' said T'rook. 'When we were yenlin she was often ill, but she was always too strong for it.' She sounded proud.

'Yes, I'm sure, T'rook,' said Frost. 'Arrow, you must keep still for a while. Let things knit back together. Arrow?' Ynis reached out and placed her hand against Frost's chest. She could feel the old griffin's heartbeat.

'The other griffins didn't get there in time, so the humans took her body. They butchered Brocken,' Ynis said. Her voice felt like it was coming from far away. 'Took her body on the boat. But she's happy enough. She said... she said I am one of you.'

She tried to say more, but the words slipped away into darkness, and Ynis fell backwards into dreams of blue glass wings, and freedom amongst the clouds.

52

Mother, this will be my last letter to you. I have gone thrawn, they tell me, and tomorrow I will be riven from the Wild Wood, cast out to some treeless place. I don't know, perhaps there I will finally know peace. I am sorry; sorry for me, for you, and for those people who met me on the Paths that day. I am sorry. Think of me when you sow seeds next spring.

Extract from a private letter to
the mother of a Druin novice

'Sit forward.'

'I'm trying.'

'You have to sit still, Leven, or it will be wonky. I thought Heralds were supposed to be impervious to practically everything, anyway?'

'Yeah, well,' Leven looked down at her boots sourly, 'I'm not quite the soldier I once was.'

Epona paused to push more of Leven's hair out of the way. When she had crashed through the roof of glass, Leven had managed to cut her head – a shallow cut, but it had bled a lot, so that when Epona and Cillian had dragged her into the Wild Wood she had looked like something out of a nightmare, drowned in blood. Cillian had taken them to a clear running stream, icy cold, and there Leven had washed the wound as best she could, and now Epona was sewing it up.

'When I was little,' said Epona, 'I took the role of princess very seriously.'

'Oh, I'm glad there was a time when you did.'

Epona laughed. 'I badgered my mother for any books with princesses in, and I read them all. You know what princesses mainly seemed to do in these stories?'

'Cause trouble?'

'Sewing. They used to sew.' Epona held up the needle to the light. 'So I thought, oh, sewing must be very important. I went to the people who made our clothes, to the family who made Mother's robes and shirts and everything, and I got them to teach me it. Spent hours on it, I did. My mother said I was making a nuisance of myself, and I have to admit, I haven't done a lot of sewing since. But,' she bent back to her work, pushing the needle through a raw piece of skin, 'it's finally come in handy.'

'You carry a sewing kit everywhere with you then?'

'Oh no. These supplies are Cillian's. I imagine he has all sorts in that belt of his.'

Leven sucked in air over her teeth as Epona's needle wriggled its way through her scalp.

'*Ow.* Where is Cillian?'

'He went to see what is happening in Mersia.' Epona's voice grew quieter, a lot of her usual good cheer leaking away.

'He's left us here by ourselves?' Leven, unable to move her head, moved her eyes back and forth. They were sitting under some trees near the stream, and a light summery rain was falling, turning the air around them fresh and lively. It was hard to imagine they could be in danger here, but she had learned not to underestimate the Wild Wood.

'He can move faster along the Paths without us. I told him to go. There.' Epona tied off the thread. 'That'll have to do.'

Leven reached up and touched her head gingerly. The skin there felt tight, and her hair still felt stiff with blood, but the pain had already started to ease.

'What do you think he'll find?'

Epona shook her head and sat on the roots of the tree. Her normally animated face looked very troubled.

'I hardly know. Mersia preparing for war with Londus, probably. They will be looking for us, I've no doubt. I still don't understand what came out of that box.'

'I've never seen anything like it. And it was so sudden. But they must see it had nothing to do with us...'

'Must they? We were the ones who brought the box, we were the ones who handed it to Prince Gallan at the gates. It was our Druin who opened the thing.' Epona bit her lip. 'And we've made such a song and dance about you being a Herald from the Imperium, doing a favour for Londus, for my mother. And then the gift we brought kills the queen and the stupid prince.'

Leven looked at her from the corner of her eye. 'You don't think I had anything to do with it, do you?'

'You? No.' Epona grabbed her arm and squeezed it briefly. 'Green Man bless you, Leven, but you do not strike me as the sort to revel in conspiracy.'

'I'll try not to be offended by that.'

'But I will tell you what Mersia will think – they will think that my mother sent us here, with the backing of the Druin, and the Imperium, to assassinate Queen Ismere and send Mersia into chaos. To make them easier to conquer. They've always been so rich, and so certain that everyone else wants their riches. And I'll tell you what they'll do now, too – they will send their own soldiers to come for us, and we'll be executed, and they'll declare war against Londus.' She stopped to gnaw nervously at a fingernail. 'And Queen Gwenith was there too, practically close enough to smell the queen's blood. I wouldn't be at all surprised if she dragged Dwffd into this as well. Two kingdoms against Londus has a very good chance of destroying my mother's grip on the throne.'

Leven went to the stream and washed the last of the blood from her hands. Big summer raindrops pattered onto her head, making her scalp sting. *This is all my fault. If I hadn't come here...*

'What will we do?'

Epona glanced up and gave her a brittle smile.

'We hope that Cillian comes back. And we hope that he has good news.'

It was full dark by the time Cillian reached the edge of the Wild Wood, but the people on the slope below him had brought flaming torches, and by that guttering light he could make out who was there quite clearly. There was a large group of men and women further down, most of them standing around a large campfire. These were clearly warriors of some kind. They wore travelling leather and small pieces of well-made armour – a shining pauldron here, a coat of mail there, tiny circles of metal glowing in the firelight. From the way some of them had shaved their heads, and the dark face paint a few had streaked across their eyes and mouths, they looked to be from Dwffd. This was puzzling. There were around fifty of them, which seemed like a lot of warriors for Queen Gwenith to have brought with her simply to see Mersia receive its gift – but then, Cillian reminded himself, the Herald was an unknown factor for them. Perhaps Queen Gwenith was being especially careful, in case Leven had decided to try to massacre them all.

And she's an unknown factor to me too, he thought. *Why am I running with them? For all I know Blessed Eleven could have tampered with the boxes. She could be an assassin.*

Yet in his heart he found he couldn't believe that. She had nearly died getting the three of them out of Wodencaester, and if she were here to cause war on Brittletain, what better way than to leave Queen Broudicca's favourite daughter behind to be slaughtered by the Mersian guard? That was the logical conclusion.

Closer to him, around a hundred yards away from the treeline, was a much more interesting group. Here, Cillian could see Prince Eafen, whom he recognised from their brief talk on the balcony, and Queen Gwenith herself, her pale face severe in the light from the torches. Like her warriors, she had smeared dark paint across her eyes, and she stood at ease in comfortable travelling clothes, a light cloak trimmed with white fur over the top. These two were standing and talking with a group of Druin – there were five of them, a variety of horns amongst them, and in the centre, taking the lead, was Loveday.

'The Atchorn,' Cillian murmured to himself. 'What are they doing here?'

They were just slightly too far to hear clearly, but to go any further beyond the trees would put him in danger of being spotted. In a tree just above him, Inkwort gave one of her sharp *tchawk*s. Tentatively, Cillian reached out with his own awareness towards the bird, but she was still largely closed to him, a warm and friendly presence in the dark, her thoughts neatly cordoned off. She hadn't spoken to him directly since Kornwullis.

'Alright.' He settled back on his haunches, keeping his eyes on the small group of Druin and royalty. 'I will listen as the trees listen.'

Cillian let the tension drain from his body and threw his own awareness out into the woods around him. At night, the trees were at rest; without the sun to lend its energy, their dance of growth and air grew still and watchful. He could feel their restful mood tugging at him, making him tired, but he resisted it. Instead, he travelled along their roots to the edge of the Wild Wood and beyond, seeping out into the open, and when the tree roots ended, he sought out the fungi, the spectacularly intricate network of gossamer-thin threads that travelled almost everywhere across the green spaces of Brittletain. This brought him close enough to the group on the hill that their words finally became clear to him. Very still and very quiet, barely breathing at all, Cillian listened.

'Where will they have gone?' This was Queen Gwenith speaking. Cillian could hear impatience in her voice, and deep beneath it, a very old anger.

'It's difficult to say,' said Loveday. 'Once they are in the Wild Wood, they could technically go anywhere.'

'Can't you track them?' asked Prince Eafen. He sounded cheerful for someone who had just lost two close family members. 'Aren't you wood witches supposed to be good at that sort of thing?'

There were a few mutters from the other Druin at that, but Loveday raised her voice to speak over them.

'Cillian is young, but he will be as skilled at moving through the Wild Wood as any of us – perhaps even better, given that some of us will not have spent the time he has amongst the trees. We shouldn't forget that the Druidahnon himself supposedly picked him for this duty, and he will have had his reasons. It would be sensible to make some educated guesses first.'

'They will go back to Londus, I expect,' said Eafen, as though it barely mattered to him. 'Epona running back to hide behind her mother's chariot.'

'I am not so sure,' said Loveday. 'They will certainly attempt to contact Queen Broudicca, I'm sure of that, but our friends at Dosraiche will intercept anything they try to send through the trees. If they have any sense they will know that travelling straight there will be the most obvious course of action. They might take a strange route there, or perhaps even decide to hide out in the Wild Wood indefinitely. In which case, it's just a matter of time.'

'They've just come from Kornwullis,' said Eafen. 'And by all reports Queen Verla was rather taken with them. Could they go back there?'

Cillian could hear the smile in Loveday's voice. 'I will know if they go back there, Prince Eafen. But I doubt that they will. They have reason to feel they are not welcome there.'

Only because you tried to drop rocks on our heads, thought Cillian.

'Then where—' began Queen Gwenith, but someone spoke over her, a Druin voice Cillian didn't recognise.

'There's someone here,' the man said gruffly. 'I can feel it under my feet.'

The group turned and looked up the hill, into the trees. Cillian blinked rapidly, bringing his awareness back from the deep chill of the soil, and moved very quietly further back into the trees. There were shouts below him, loud enough for him to hear quite clearly, and he heard Loveday calling orders to her Druin.

'We've wasted enough time! Each of us will take a few of Queen Gwenith's men, and we'll get on the Paths after them. I've a feeling they're not so far away after all.'

Moving nearly silently, Cillian opened another Path and stepped through onto it, Inkwort flying close behind him.

53

For some time, Ynis drifted in and out of consciousness. They kept her within the nest-pit she shared with her sister, heaped with so many sheepskins and furs that she felt constantly too hot, although when she complained about it, Witch-seer Frost gave her a sideways look and told her that she had a fever – of course she was too hot. Eventually the heat took hold of her and pulled her down into its depths, and she spent much of her time dreaming, or watching the patch of brittle sunlight that crept in and out of the entrance to their nest as the days passed, faster and faster it seemed to her, and the little trickle of melted ice that flowed down the walls. She was reminded of her earliest childhood, when she had been sick so often, and once she awoke to T'rook telling Frost as much, a mixture of exasperation and pride in her voice.

'My sister was always ill,' said T'rook. 'Everything she ate made her regurgitate. It drove our fathers spare. And then she would be like this for days, so hot I couldn't bear to be in the nest next to her.'

'This is serious,' said Witch-seer Frost, an unusual note of uncertainty in her voice. 'Humans, the shell that hides their brains is quite soft. A knock like that can do a lot of damage.'

T'rook gave an indignant squawk, and Ynis forced her crusted eyes open a crack to look at her sister. The young griffin stood by the door, her sooty wings almost purple in the daylight.

'Like I tell you, she is tough,' she said dismissively. 'A few days more is all she needs.'

'Perhaps.' Witch-seer Frost was somewhere to Ynis's left, and she didn't have the energy to turn her head. 'It's true that seers must walk the narrow path between the living and the dead more often than anyone else. Perhaps this is the path she must walk now to become who she needs to be.'

T'rook's snort this time was openly insulting. 'Keep your Edge Walker ravings. I know my sister.'

Exhausted with the effort of opening her eyes, Ynis let go of the daylight and sank back into a deep and chaotic sleep. While she was there she dreamt of woods greener and thicker than any she'd ever seen in Yelvynia; the trees grew so close together that even a young griffin would have had trouble moving between them, and there was a soggy humidity to the day that felt very far from the icy tundra and mountain of her home. She had the sense that she was being carried, held tight in someone's arms, and the feeling was reassuring even as she recognised it as an echo of the blankets and furs tucked neatly around her sleeping body.

There were people in the woods. Humans, like her; although not like her, really. Their faces were clean, and they wore clothes of woven cloth. They did not have feathers and bones wound through their hair, which was tangled hardly at all. Ynis couldn't see their faces, could only sense their closeness, and that they were furious with each other, garbled words and phrases that were full of anger but no meaning. She felt afraid, and sad.

'Stop it,' she thought, although in the dream she had no way of talking. 'No more fighting.'

And then she heard her sister's voice, cutting through the dream and tattering it into insubstantial pieces. T'rook was angry, and underneath her usual bluster, afraid. Ynis struggled against her covers again, only for a huge pulse of pain to strike her back down again.

'You are not looking after her properly,' T'rook was saying, her voice raised. 'She should be better by now!'

'Edge Walkers know better than anyone how the sick must be cared for.' Witch-seer Frost was by the door now, her elaborate bone headdress catching the last pieces of daylight and lending a faint blue glow to the crown of her head. 'We knew it might take this long.'

'It has been a week,' snapped T'rook, and Ynis felt her stomach turn over sickly. A week? How was that possible? 'What do you all know of healing? You only know death, and that is where you are leading her.'

Her sister reached over and took hold of Ynis's sleeve with her beak, and Ynis felt herself yanked back and forth. Her body moved slackly, and she couldn't raise her arms to hold herself still. She felt as though she had been buried in thick, cloying mud. She wanted T'rook to stop it, and she opened her mouth to tell her so, but the pain from her head swept over her, cutting everything else out.

Some time later, although she couldn't tell how much, the spirit of Brocken returned to her. It was dark in the nest, and the dead griffin appeared as a patch of pearly moonlight on the grey stone wall.

'You're nearly there, Witch-seer.' Brocken's voice was quieter than it had ever been before, but she seemed to speak directly into Ynis's ear. 'You're moving away from us again, Arrow, which means you're returning to the land of the living.'

'My sister was just here,' said Ynis. For some reason she felt it was important to tell Brocken this. 'Did you see her?'

Brocken ignored the question.

'Do you remember, Arrow, when you cut my fate-ties, and let my spirit return to the Bone Fall?'

'Yes.'

'You remember how to see them? The ties that bind us to the griffins who matter most to us?'

'I do.' Ynis tried to sit up, and managed to get one elbow underneath her. Weakly she pushed some of the furs away and felt the clean frosty air of the mountains on her skin again. It was a relief. 'What are you talking about?'

'It's important,' said Brocken. Her voice was growing faint again, and the patch of moonlight on the wall was fading as a cloud passed in front of its bright face. 'You are a witch-seer, Arrow. You can see them, which means you can follow them. Remember.'

And then all at once the soft glow of dawn filled the cave again. Ynis was sitting up, blinking at the light. The skin on the back of her head felt tight, but the thunderous pain was gone, and her limbs no longer felt so heavy. Witch-seer Frost appeared at the entrance. She looked smaller than Ynis remembered, as though she had dwindled in some way. *She's mourning Brocken*, she reminded herself. *They were close.*

'Ah, you are awake.' Frost sounded glad, but there was a reticence to her tone that immediately put Ynis on edge. 'I thought your fever might break today – there's a change on the wind.'

'What is it?' Ynis pushed her hair, still damp with sweat, back from her face. 'What's happened?'

Frost clicked her beak together several times before she replied.

'This is the problem with us witch-seers. We see things, sense things, before they are known.' The old griffin shook her head. 'There is no gentling the blow.'

'*Tell me*.' Ynis took a deep breath, trying to slow the rapid pulse in her throat. 'Tell me what has happened. Frost, *please*.'

'It is your sister, T'rook. She went hunting four days ago and hasn't returned.'

54

While Tyleigh and Belise worked on opening the door to the Undertomb, Kaeto had taken to tracking Felldir around the city. The place was so silent and bare that even the tiniest noise echoed down its streets, and he quickly became adept at telling the difference between the scuttling of beetles and the whirring rush of the Titan's wing. He kept out of sight most of the time, contenting himself with the odd glimpse of his prey, or investigating the spaces where Felldir had been. Frequently he found nooks and hidey-holes in the upper floors of abandoned buildings and towers, which he couldn't help thinking of as nests. There would be the remains of a fire, and usually bones of some animal picked clean – and on one memorable occasion, a pile that Kaeto was fairly sure were human remains. Some of the bones were old, and had odd sigils and curving shapes cut into them, little carvings that could be animals, birds or beetles. A few of these he kept, thinking he would ask Tyleigh if she knew what they meant.

It was after he had found one of these carved bones that he began to realise that Felldir was leaving them deliberately. The Titan knew Kaeto was following him. And he still hadn't killed him.

On the fourth day of this peculiar hunt, Kaeto followed Felldir to a part of the city that was new to him. It was a raised plateau made of flat slabs of the black stone, with tufts of tough jungle grass growing up through the cracks. Sprouting up from the space like huge, unlikely flowers were seven tall edifices that he initially took to be sculptures of some kind. They had long thin stems of black marble, rising thirty feet into the air, and on top of these were balanced vast hollow globes; they had elaborate holes cut into the marble, intricate patterns almost like lace, so that it was possible to see in and through them. Felldir, he could see, was sitting inside one. The tall black stems were entirely smooth, so that there was no way to climb up if you did not have wings, but the structure Felldir had chosen had a rope ladder descending from its globe. Kaeto paused and looked at it. The ropes were sturdy, the slats made of wood. It was a strange invitation, but that's certainly what it was.

He climbed up the ladder swiftly – you could not be much of an Envoy if you couldn't climb a rope ladder – and pulled himself through one of the openings to stand cautiously in the base of the globe. Inside, it was spacious and well-lit, and directly above there was a neat circular hole, more than big enough to admit a winged Othanim. Felldir was sat on the far side of the globe, his back straight, his long white hair falling to either side of his handsome face. On the ground next to him was an elaborate winged helmet, very like the one on the statue, only this one was made of silver and steel rather than gold. Kaeto found his eyes drawn to it, as though it had its own quiet, watchful intelligence.

'What is this place?' asked Kaeto.

'Years ago, before my people fell from grace, we loved music above all things. Do you believe that?'

Kaeto took a few slow steps forward. The floor of the globe was clean and smooth.

'I know practically nothing of your people, Felldir, so I am afraid I am in a position to believe anything.'

Felldir rested his arms on top of his knees; the fingers on his left hand, Kaeto observed, had been bandaged tightly with a rag. One great foot poked out from beneath his tattered robe. It was as perfect a foot as Kaeto had ever seen outside a work of art, and he realised that was what Felldir made him think of: some extraordinary statue brought to life.

'We would give concerts in these arenas.' Felldir gestured briefly at the lace-like globe. 'Our musicians would sit up here, and sing and play their instruments, and when the wind blew through these apertures, it was as though the wind was singing with us.'

'There's hardly even a breeze out there today,' said Kaeto. 'This jungle heat is relentless.'

'And no musicians left to play,' agreed Felldir. 'I wanted you to know what this place was, once. It wasn't always a cursed city. It wasn't always a place of death. Once, a long time ago, your people, the light-boned, would visit us, and trade with the Black City. They even came to our concerts. They stood down there, in the grass, shoulder to shoulder with Titans.'

Light-boned. Kaeto had never heard the term before, but it made sense. To Titans, human bones would seem so light they must be hollow, like a bird's bones.

'That must have been extraordinary,' said Kaeto. He came within ten feet of Felldir and crouched himself, trying to look casual about it. 'When you say we stood shoulder to shoulder with Titans, do you mean just your people? Or were there other Titans, too?'

Felldir lifted his head. His amber eyes, like that of a winter wolf, were steady and calm. Being looked at by Felldir was like being thrown into a shaft of pure starlight – you could hide nothing. Kaeto, whose entire life was about concealment and secrets, found it extremely uncomfortable.

'Others, yes. Before she... There was a time when all Titans would visit this place. The Othanim were the Titans who had built the closest relationship with the light-boned, because our shapes were so similar. They found that fascinating, I think. The wyverns, the griffins, the god-boar, the firebirds, the great bears... they all walked these streets once.'

'You said "before she"... Who were you talking about?'

The Titan narrowed his eyes. 'You do not miss much, light-bones.'

'It's my job to take notice of details like that. Who were you talking about? Another one of your people?'

'Hmm. Her name was Icaraine the Lightbringer, and you have seen her already, human.'

Kaeto could think of only one other Titan in the Black City. 'The statue above the Undertomb. Who was she?'

A tiny beetle, bright green like a jewel and no bigger than Kaeto's thumbnail, flew in through one of the openings and alighted on Felldir's shoulder. Kaeto watched it pick its way through the Titan's ash-coloured feathers.

'She was a leader, a priestess. A mad woman,' Felldir said eventually. 'When the Black City was at the height of its fame, Icaraine led a secret movement, one that eventually boiled up out of the ground and overwhelmed all of our people.'

'And were you there, Felldir? How long have you been here?'

The Titan did not reply. Outside a breeze chased dust across the black stone, and Kaeto heard the faintest of hums as the wind moved through the globes around them.

'Here.' Kaeto removed his pack and put it on the floor in front of him. He pulled out a small parcel and placed it in front of Felldir. 'Some tea. Did you have tea, here? And some cheese. I thought you must be sick of all the... meat. It's not the Imperium's best cheese, not by any stretch, but it is the best cheese that will last a long journey.'

Felldir reached over and picked up the parcel, turning it over in his long-fingered hands. He pulled some of the cheese from its wrapping and sniffed it. He made no move to eat it. Kaeto noted the bandaged fingers again.

'What happened?' he asked, pointing at the injured hand. 'Beetle bite?'

For a long time Felldir said nothing, and when he did speak, he ignored the question. 'Yes. I was there,' he said eventually. 'When the Black City was a glorious place. I have been here so long that time feels broken.'

'Then why haven't you ever gone somewhere else? What ties you to this place? Even if you are the last of your kind, there are places you could go. There are other Titans still living, in Brittletain.'

'Other Titans will not want to see me,' said Felldir, and he smiled crookedly. A cold sensation moved down Kaeto's spine. That smile had made the Titan look almost human. 'Icaraine the Lightbringer began to whisper that it was our destiny to rule Enonah, because the Othanim were clearly superior to the humans that infested every part of the world, and clearly superior to the other Titans – because we built cities, we made music, we traded and created and we were ambitious. Some listened, and believed her. She grew popular with my people, and her calls for war and blood were not dismissed as perhaps they should have been. It began to sound like it was our right, to rule over others. They built that statue, and the other Titans were thrown out of the Black City. It was the beginning of a war.'

A war between Titans. Kaeto could barely imagine it. 'And what about the people? I mean, the humans that came to the Black City? Were they also thrown out?'

'No. The humans were thought of as useful. We kept them in chains forged from our own bones. Chains of Titan ore never rust, and they cannot break.'

Kaeto had been rubbing one finger below his lower lip, trying to picture a Black City thronged with humans and Titans. He stopped.

'You enslaved us?'

'Icaraine created a device,' Felldir continued as if he hadn't spoken. 'It was to be her ultimate weapon, her way of throwing down all the other Titan races and putting every human in a Titan-ore chain.'

'What was it?'

Felldir shook his head. 'She did not get to use it before the rest of the Titans came for us. We did not win the war, light-bones, and what remains of my people lies in the Undertomb.'

Another silence. Kaeto was beginning to get used to them. It was like Felldir could only speak in short bursts, after so many centuries of silence.

'We had wine,' the Titan said eventually, in a different tone of voice. 'Do you have wine?'

'I do,' said Kaeto. 'Not on me, but I could get you some. If you came away with us, away from the Black City, I could get you all the wine you could ever want.' Kaeto felt suddenly that it was important to get Felldir away from the city. And on the back of that impulse, his Envoy mind calculated the details. What a glory it would be for the Imperium to have its own pet Titan! Felldir could live in one of the empress's palaces, their most honoured guest, and prisoner. Tyleigh would be able to learn much more from a living Titan than from their scattered bones. But for the first time in a long while the thoughts felt shameful, and he pushed them aside. Felldir was shaking his head.

'I will take any wine you can give me, human, but I cannot leave the Black City. I am tied here by blood oath and by magic. It is my fate to wait here forever, guarding the Black City from thieves and from trespassers. It's my fate, my duty and my punishment.'

'Yes, I have seen what you do to trespassers.' Kaeto settled on the floor, crossing his legs. He did not feel safe, far from it, but it was becoming clear that Felldir did want to talk. 'Are we not thieves and trespassers to you then? You have known where we are for weeks now, but the three of us remain unslaughtered.' He smiled to let the Titan know this was a kind of joke. 'What is different about us?'

Felldir fixed him with that baleful amber eye again. 'Perhaps I am tired of slaughter. Perhaps my belly has had its fill of human flesh.' He smiled, although his eyes were still cold. 'And perhaps I will change my mind.' He shifted where he sat, and the huge feathered wings that were folded neatly away on his back flexed slightly. Kaeto felt his skin turn cold.

'What are you not telling me?'

For the first time, Felldir laughed.

'So many things, light-bones. You don't have enough years in your short human life to hear what I have to tell. Your woman, she is still trying to get into the Undertomb? You are determined to do so?'

Kaeto grimaced. 'She is not my woman. I don't think Tyleigh is anyone's anything. But yes, she is trying to get into the hidden place beneath the city.'

'Then if you are set on this course of action, you will need this.'

Felldir reached into his robes and then held out his hand. On his palm there was a small piece of Titan bone, its silvery-blue and green hues unmistakable in the dappled light. Kaeto looked at the shape of it, and then looked at the bandaged hand. He felt sick.

'Did you... *Is that yours?* Did you cut your own finger off? Why?'

Felldir stood up, his wings stretching out to fill the curving walls of the globe. He dropped the bone on the floor. 'Take it. Your witch will need it.'

Kaeto picked up the bone. It took all his willpower to sit there, looking up at the Titan. He felt very small, and vulnerable, but he also felt faintly irritated. He had been getting somewhere with his questions, and now he was being dismissed, like a child being ordered to bed.

'Thank you.'

'Do not thank me yet. You don't know what's down there.'

'Will you speak to me again, if I return? With wine?'

'Perhaps.' The wind chose that moment to pick up, and a soft musical sigh moved through the globe. 'Or perhaps I will eat you up.'

55

'Keep moving.'

It was the darkest part of the night. Even the moon overhead had vanished behind some swift-moving clouds, and Leven could barely make out her own hand in front of her face, let alone Cillian ahead of them. He was having no difficulty moving through the dark, but for Leven every step felt like she was chancing a broken ankle. The ground beneath her boots was uneven and tangled, and thin branches caught in her hair and dragged across her skin. She tried to keep her eyes ahead of her, trained on the curve of Cillian's horns, but she kept losing them.

'Easier said than done,' she muttered into her chest. Behind her, Epona laughed breathlessly.

'I suppose it's better to be crashing about out here than languishing in a Mersian dungeon,' she pointed out with some of her more usual cheer. Epona, Leven noticed, wasn't having quite so much trouble in the dark, and as if she had heard her thought somehow, she continued, 'I'm not as tall as you, I'm not catching so much resistance. And I'm trying to step wherever you step.'

'I'm glad I could clear the way for you,' snapped Leven, brushing away a branch intent on tangling in her hair; her head wound was healing rapidly, but every tug made it sore again. Ahead of them, Cillian's footfalls stopped, and Leven narrowly avoided crashing into him.

'You need to be quiet,' he said to them tersely. 'The Atchorn could be close. Can you not make less noise?'

Leven bit down several replies to that. In truth, since she had pulled them both out of the tower she had felt beyond exhausted, and the level of fatigue was beginning to frighten her. It felt as though the Titan strength had ebbed somehow.

'You can't expect us to walk as silently through the Wild Wood as you do, Cillian,' said Epona. 'Let's just keep moving.'

'There's another south-leading Path just ahead here,' said Cillian. They began moving again, Leven trying to step more lightly, when directly to their left the trees burst with light. Several men and women, some with Druin horns, crashed out onto the Path; some of them carried torches, and all those without horns carried weapons. At once the night was full of shouting and movement.

'Shit!' cried Epona.

'There they are! Take them down and bind them!'

Leven couldn't see which woman spoke, but there was something familiar about her voice. Automatically she reached for the Titan strength, willing her blue glass sword to leap to her waiting hand, and instead the forest around her shivered and changed. There was snow under her boots, and the trees around her were older, greyer.

'Not now, not now!'

A great piercing cry rent the air around her, and she looked up to see a vast creature in the sky, an impossible vision of feathers and fur and fury. Between it and her there was a veil of snow and branches, which was no protection at all. Her fear was suffocating and she wanted to run – *you are a tiny mouse to the griffin*, it told her, *a thing to be broken and eaten* – but something else was holding her back.

Cillian. Epona.

She heard their voices then, raised in anger and fear, and it was enough to bring her back. The cold winter forest of her visions faded, casting her into the chaos of the Wild Wood at night.

'Get behind me!' Cillian was shouting. He stepped in front of Leven and Epona and threw up his arms. At his command, a great wall of earth erupted in front of the Atchorn, hiding them from view, but almost immediately huge pale roots burst through it, causing it to break apart. There were more shouts from their pursuers and the ground began to tremble.

Leven summoned her sword, and the trees around them were lit with its eerie blue light.

'I will fly over it,' she said. The fear of the griffin was clinging to her like a spider's web. 'And I'll cut them all in half.'

'You can't!' cried Epona, grabbing her arm. 'If you do that they'll say we are murderers.'

'They are *already* saying that!' Leven tried to shake off the princess's hand. 'Listen, Epona, I won't let them harm you or Cillian – you have to let me fight!'

The more the ground shook, the faster the wall was falling. Already Leven could hear the other warriors running to find the end of it.

'Quickly, follow me.' Cillian took off into the dark again, away from the hectic torch lights. Leven banished her sword so that its light would not lead their attackers to them. There was a shimmer just ahead, barely perceptible in the gloom, and a new Path opened up. The three of them ran through it and emerged into another part of the Wild Wood. Here, they were near the crest of a hill and could see the swaying tops of the trees below them. It was windy, and cold, with an icy drizzle in the air. Cillian was breathing hard, and his skin was faintly green across his cheeks, as it had been when they had been confronted by the forest soul.

'We can pick up our Path south from here, we'll just have to go a little out of our way,' he said. 'It's best if we—'

The night fell apart into flame-lit shards again as another Path opened some distance from them. More soldiers and Druin came through, a tall man with a beard and bull horns in the lead, and Leven heard Epona cursing colourfully next to her.

'It's not even the same group,' she hissed. 'How many of them are there?'

Leven glanced at Cillian. On this more exposed section of the Wild Wood there was more starlight to see by, and she saw quite clearly the expression of dismay that passed over the Druin's face.

'They're running us to ground,' he said. He raised a hand to summon some other piece of Druin magic, and Leven saw that it was trembling slightly. *What is it taking out of him to do all this?*

'That's enough.' Leven raised her hands again. 'I can make short work of them.'

'And what, you will kill every man and woman they send after us? *Shit*, we need time to think.' Epona looked around desperately. 'Cillian, is there anywhere we can go?'

All around them, the green magic of the Druin was making the forest lively; small animals scuttled through the undergrowth, the trees swayed as though caught in a wind. A look of uncertainty passed over Cillian's face, and then he nodded. Once more he stepped up to the treeline and tore a new Path. The three of them sprinted through it with the voices of the Atchorn ringing in their ears, Inkwort a flurry of sooty wings above their heads. Once the doorway closed Cillian fell forward onto his knees, his head down.

'This place again?' Leven looked around. They were back in the swampy section of the Wild Wood that Cillian and Epona had called the Lich-Way. The light here was different, as though dawn were well on its way, and all around she could hear the strange musical croaking of frogs. 'I thought it was dangerous to come here?'

'It is,' said Epona. 'But slightly less immediately dangerous than those maniacs who want to chop our heads off.'

'We can't stay here for long,' Cillian said quietly. With what looked like a lot of effort he lifted his head and looked around.

'Are you alright?' Leven held out a hand. After a moment, he took it and she helped pull him to his feet.

'It's a lot of Druin magic to summon all at once,' he said, not quite meeting her eye. 'And I'm not used to fighting my own people. They have all the same tricks.'

'What's to stop them turning up here?'

'In reality, nothing,' he said. 'But it may take them a little while to figure out that we came here, and aren't on any of the Paths leading from Demdyke Hill. Like I said, we can't stay here for long.' He looked pointedly at Epona. 'What are we going to do?'

'Yes. What *are* we going to do?' Epona held up her hands and began to pace back and forth on the small section of solid land they stood on. In the silvery dawn light, the waters of the swamp stirred and rippled with unseen life. 'So. We were heading south, back to Londus, and they caught us almost immediately. I had hoped we would simply miss them on the way through, but I think we can assume that all the ways south will have a group of Atchorn seeking us out. Cillian, will the rest of the Druin side with them? Will we be hunted by every set of horns in the Wild Wood?'

He looked grim. 'My people have no love for Mersia, but the murder of a queen and a prince is a serious crime regardless of which kingdom they belong to. I would say that we can't count on them to be friendly. And that's not all.' He hesitated. 'From what Loveday said, it seems they have Atchorn agents at the Dosraiche itself. The Mother Oak won't be safe.'

Epona nodded. The blue paint on her face had smudged, giving her an ill, ghostly look. 'Then I say we head directly north.'

'Why?' asked Leven. 'What's up there?'

'Galabroc, my mother's old kingdom, and my sister Ceni. It's about as north as you can get – any further, and you're in griffin territory.'

At the mention of griffins, Leven crossed her arms over her chest. 'And what then?'

Epona lifted her hands up and then dropped them in a gesture of helplessness. For a little while the three of them stood together, not looking at each other, while the noises of frogs and tiny buzzing things went on around them. It was growing dark again, the silvery light on the water dimming to an unpromising lead. Leven frowned slightly. Hadn't it been dawn just now?

'Your sister,' she said, desperate to fill the silence. 'She'll protect us?'

'Yes,' said Epona firmly. 'It's been years since I've been to Galabroc to see her, but when I was up there last, it was a good place to make a stand. There are strong walls lining the border, and its people are loyal to Londus.'

Something about that made Leven feel uneasy. She thought of the Imperium, and the empress. They said she had poisoned her sister to make sure there was no one to question her rule, although if you valued your head you did not repeat the rumours.

'But your sister is a queen in her own right?'

'Of course.' For the first time, Epona sounded slightly irritated. 'What's your point?'

Leven shook her head. 'No, you're right. I don't know anything of this land's politics, and I'm happy to trust your judgement.'

'How gracious of you,' said Epona, back to grinning again. 'And I fear that's exactly what we've stumbled into, the three of us. The politics of Brittletain is a pit of shit-covered vipers, and we've been thrown right in. Who would want Queen Ismere dead? And more to the point, who would want everyone to think that we did?'

'Should it be this dark this fast?' Leven had turned to look out across the swamp. Shadows were bleeding across the water towards them, and there were other things out there in the wet; old, decaying things moving slowly through the murk.

'We've stayed too long,' said Cillian. 'The Lich-Way isn't a place to rest. Come on, before we're in even worse trouble.'

'Alright then.' Leven pushed her hands back through her hair. 'So we head north. And pray to the stars that we manage to give the Atchorn the slip.'

'And what about you?' Epona put her hand on Leven's shoulder, gently for once. 'How is our Herald holding up? When the Atchorn first appeared, it was like you... went away for a moment.'

'It's not the first time either,' said Cillian. Both of them were looking at her closely. 'Our first day in the Wild Wood, and again, at the Mersian palace. Are you ill?'

'I... I don't know.' Leven's throat seemed to close up. She wanted to tell them about all of it: the visions of Brittletain, the sense that somehow she was connected to this place. At some point between Londus and this dark, dead-filled marsh, Epona and Cillian had become people she wanted to confide in. People she cared about. Would it be so bad to admit to a weakness for once? Leven looked away, not meeting the princess's eyes. 'But there's no time for that now. We have to keep moving.'

Cillian opened another Path. Before they passed through it, Leven cast a last look over her shoulder. The shadows of the marsh had coalesced into a huge shambling shape, a shaggy four-legged giant with enormous tusks, and it was watching them from the water with eyes that glowed like embers. There was a deep, echoing sound, like a great bell tolling far under the ocean, and a voice came with it; a dreaming voice.

The child of the chains is coming.

'What?'

Beware the child of the chains.

Inkwort landed on Leven's shoulder and gave a brisk *tchack* directly into her ear, making her jump. The sound of the bells ceased, and Leven turned her back on the watching shape. She followed the others onto the next Path, leaving the stink of the Lich-Way and its monsters behind her.

56

'Arrow, you are not yet healed enough to go anywhere.'

Ynis held her chin up and kept walking. At the bottom of the steps she could see a number of Edge Walker griffins gathering, attracted by the raised voices. Next to her, Witch-seer Frost was watching her closely.

'I am healed more than enough, thank you.' She concentrated on putting one foot in front of the other. Although she felt significantly better than she had, she did feel oddly light, as though her arms and legs were filled with air, and her head was aching faintly. On her back she had her old leather pack, which she had filled with as much dried meat as she could scrounge, and then strapped it across her shoulders. Her claw-knife was tucked securely into her belt. Gathering all her things together had been a stark reminder of how little she had. *It doesn't matter*, she told herself. *Your sister is your home.* 'I have to find T'rook.'

'She could be anywhere, Arrow,' said Frost. Her voice was very gentle, and it was making Ynis furious. 'Be reasonable. Stay here, get stronger. Your sister will likely come back on her own.'

'Hunting? For four days, without telling me?' Ynis snapped. 'Are any of *you* going to look for her?'

Frost looked away and said nothing.

'Then I have to go.'

They had reached the bottom of the slope, and Ynis began to shove her way through the griffins that had gathered there. She recognised a few of them: the young handsome griffin called Festus who had brought his dying father to the Bone Fall, and Scree, his sleek grey feathers lying flat across his chest. His headdress, made from the polished bones of fallen griffins, clattered in the wind.

'What is happening?' one of them piped up.

'This is witch-seer business,' Frost replied gruffly.

'It is not!' said Ynis, furious with the lot of them. 'It's all of our business, because griffins are being killed and butchered, on our very own ice.' She stopped walking and turned to glare around at them all. She pointed at Frost. 'Your own witch-seer was shot with an arrow the day me and my sister arrived here. And then Brocken, a good friend to all of you, was killed and carved up into pieces by humans. And none of you will do anything!'

'It's not our—' began Frost.

'My sister is missing.' Ynis pushed her hair back from her face. She felt lost — even more so than when she and T'rook had been banished from Yelvynia. At least then she had not been alone. T'rook's absence was like a wound. 'If the griffins of the Bone Fall are happy to be gradually picked off by human hunters, that's up to them.' She glared around at them all. 'But I am going to get my sister.'

'How will you even find her?' asked Frost, in an infuriatingly reasonable tone of voice. 'We do not know where she went to hunt.'

Ynis smiled grimly. She was thinking of Brocken's last visit to her cave: the patch of moonlight on the wall, her whispered voice. Brocken's spirit had asked her about the fate-ties, and now she knew why.

'I will follow our fate-tie,' she said. 'There is a bond between us. I will simply follow the thread to wherever it takes me.'

There was a murmur at this from the gathered griffins. Ynis saw Scree glance at Frost, although he was uncharacteristically quiet.

'Arrow, it is not as simple as that,' said Frost sadly. 'To see the fate-ties you must walk close to the Edge — to skirt around the chasm that is death. As witch-seers we bring ourselves to this chasm willingly, but rarely. To stay so close to the fate-ties, for so long... would be very dangerous.'

'What is wrong with you all?' Ynis shook her head. 'It doesn't matter if it's dangerous! T'rook is my *sister*.'

'And how will you get there?' Frost's voice was rising, and Ynis felt a shiver crawl down her back. She had never heard the older griffin get angry. 'You cannot fly, yenlin.'

Ynis felt as though she'd been struck in the chest. To have lost T'rook, and then to be reminded just how weak and useless she was. To the griffins, with her lack of feathers and talons, she would never be more than newly hatched. It was almost too much to bear.

'I will walk across the world if I have to,' she said between gritted teeth.

'And she will not have to,' said Festus. He stepped up towards Ynis and looked down at her with his bright green eyes. 'I will take you, Witch-seer Arrow.'

Ynis blinked with surprise. 'You will?'

Festus shook his head and looked around at them all. 'I don't pretend to understand the ways of the Edge Walkers. Coming here with my father was the hardest thing I've ever had to do, but T'rook was kind to me. And this human helped me to heal. In Yelvynia we do not refuse help when it is asked for.'

'Let them go,' said Scree, barely bothering to conceal the satisfaction in his voice. 'The human has stayed long enough. Sooner or later, Frost, you knew it would end this way. The human yenlin's commitment to being a witch-seer is as thin and breakable as her bones.'

The chatter from the other griffins grew louder at that. Frost spread her wings and stretched them, shaking her head. She looked small and sad, and somehow lost.

'For what it's worth, Arrow, I hope that you find her. And that you bring her back to her new family.'

Family would look for her, thought Ynis furiously. *Family would fight for her.*

She met Festus's bright green eyes with her own, and nodded. She wouldn't look at the rest of them.

'Thank you, Festus. If you could... If you could take me up onto the Bone Fall itself, please. It will be quiet there, and easier for me to see the fate-ties.'

Festus landed amongst the litter of bones lightly, and Ynis climbed down. Being on another griffin's back was unsettling, and she took a moment to brush herself off. Around them the Bone Fall was still under the muted afternoon light. There had been snow recently, and many of the greenish-blue bones were hidden beneath the soft white drifts. The air itself felt thick with the promise of more snow, and Ynis pulled her fur hood up over her head.

'You'd best be quick.' Festus was looking around the Bone Fall uneasily. 'Every moment we waste, your sister could be in even graver danger. Why do you think it'll be easier for you to see these... fate-ties in this place?'

Ynis stepped carefully around a rib cage that was taller than her. 'Frost told me that some places are naturally closer to the Edge than others. The barrier between this living world and the spirit world is thinner, particularly in haunted places. And you can hardly get more haunted than the Bone Fall.'

The wind picked up, threading eerie music through the scattered bones. Festus flattened himself, cat-like, to the wall. Ynis wondered if it was the cold or the ghosts that was troubling him.

'Can a griffin even see their own fate-ties? Can *you*?'

'I don't know for sure.' Ynis found herself unable to meet his eyes. 'But I *had* to do something. I knew none of them would help me.' Finding a relatively clear spot, Ynis knelt on the rocky ground. 'I will look now.'

Ynis forced herself to relax, taking in a big breath, and then letting it slowly out. She thought of how the Bone Fall had looked the first time she had seen the griffin spirits, their shifting luminous forms under the starlight. She tried to concentrate on the way it had felt to be close to the spirit world, how it felt to be in the presence of death: an odd tightness in her chest, the sense that solid, everyday objects had become insubstantial. She thought of Brocken's ghost, floating up from her cooling corpse, and how she had reappeared as a patch of light on the cave wall. The silence, the ghost-light, and the dead...

'Is it working yet?'

'Shit.' Ynis glanced above her head, just in case the fate-ties had appeared, but there was nothing. 'Festus, you need to be quiet.'

The young griffin sniffed, and turned his head to sift his beak through his feathers. 'I thought that as the witch-seer's apprentice you would be good at it.'

'I *am* good at it.' Ynis blinked, realising this was true. These talents were rare amongst griffins, let alone humans. 'But it is also difficult. Wait.'

Stiffly, Ynis got to her feet and reluctantly loosened the ties on her fur cloak, and gathering it up, folded it into a pad to kneel on. Once she was back in position, she immediately began to shiver. She had grown up in the mountains of Yelvynia so she did not feel the cold easily. But the cold up here, in the land of glaciers and snow, was a harder thing, with sharper teeth. Her fingers and ears and nose stung with it. Festus stopped his preening to watch her.

'What are you doing? You'll freeze.'

'As I get colder, the closer I will be to the spirit world. And the easier it will be to see my fate-ties.'

'If you freeze to death, shall I leave your corpse here, or would you prefer we ate it?'

'Let me concentrate.' Ynis took a deep breath. 'I must accept the cold, and the death that walks behind it.'

'Hmph.' Festus went back to preening. 'Humans are very strange.'

Ynis gritted her teeth against the freezing wind as it pushed her hair aside and slipped around her neck. Her fingers were nearly white, now blue. Every part of her skin felt bitten with cold, but that feeling was slowly fading into a dangerous numbness. She pictured her tiny human bones lying amongst the huge bones of the griffins, yellowed and pale. A strangled laugh escaped her throat.

'I'm ready,' she said, her voice faint enough that the wind brushed it away into nothing. The tension went out of her shoulders, and she lifted her chin, no longer feeling the ragged claws of the wind. She let her eyes close halfway, and again she reached out for that feeling of the Edge. This time, the change was almost immediate; whereas before the Bone Fall had seemed desolate and abandoned, now she could sense the teeming spirits all around her. When she opened her eyes again, the world was full of shadows that moved and flew. They looked at her with hollow eyes.

What if I have no fate-ties? What if my yost is not strong enough?

Slowly, almost dreamily, Ynis lifted her head. Above her, twirling up into the yellowing snow clouds, were a number of long red ribbons. They were moving gently to some unseen current.

'Can you see them? Your fate-ties?' Festus's voice was very quiet. Against the maelstrom of spirit, he was little more than a shadow.

Ynis nodded. Frost had spoken of a web, but she could not see anything like that. Instead, there were five fate-ties that she could see clearly, although her eyes were watering and making it difficult to focus. Three of those were wide but faint, as though their blood-red colour had been watered down. The other two were much stronger and more vivid; the largest of them as red as the blood that spurts from a rabbit's neck. Ynis focused on it, following its trail as it slid up and across the sky.

'There are more than I thought there would be.' Her heart fluttered with panic. How was she supposed to know which one was T'rook? 'Frost told me that the boldest lines are for the strongest bonds. Two of them will be for my fathers... I don't know who the other two could be, but the strongest has to be T'rook.' She nodded, trying to convince herself. 'Yes. There is no one I am closer to, so it must be her.'

I will find you, sister.

'She's to the south.' That was unexpected, but the south was where the human territory began. If T'rook had been captured, there was no telling where she might have been taken. Ynis blinked her eyes rapidly, and the ghosts of the Bone Fall fell away. With numb fingers she began to pull her furs back on. 'Let's go.'

57

Brittletain is built on the bones of giants, it is said, and a great skull is buried underneath the kingdom of Galabroc. Beneath the keep there are echoing tunnels of bone, and dark spirits walk there, thinking only of the lost ages of ice. As bright and bustling as Galabroc is, as sturdy and as forthright its people, it is a melancholy place, and such mood seeps into the earth and stones. The ghosts are so old that no one knew their names even in my time. I do not like to go to Galabroc.

Extract from the private letters
of the Druidahnon

'How much further to Galabroc?'

Cillian spared Leven a glance. There was no avoiding how much paler the Herald had become since their flight from Mersia, but there was a determined set to her jaw and her eyes were bright.

'We're close,' he said. 'The next Path will bring us there.'

Leven nodded briskly and increased her pace. Epona had her head down; an uncharacteristic quiet had fallen over her in the last few hours, and Cillian had the curious idea that she was less than enthusiastic to meet up with her older sister, Queen Ceni. Not that they had any choice. Twice since they had left the Lich-Way they had heard or seen the Atchorn and Queen Gwenith's guard, closer and closer on their heels, while the Wild Wood itself... Cillian shivered. It put him in mind of an injured animal, one that was too wounded to attack when you approached, but was willing to strike, despite the pain, if you came any closer. There was anger, and sorrow, and a deep-seated horror he didn't understand. The trees and the earth and the mists were thick with it, like pollen, and as they travelled north, it was getting worse. It pained him to think it, but he would be glad to get behind the walls of Galabroc. They would be safer there.

He opened a new Path and the others followed on close behind. The trees here were tougher, older, mostly evergreens, holding themselves firm against the cycle of the year – pine, spruce, mountain hemlock. The ground beneath their feet was steeper and rockier, and far to the north it was possible to see the distant chilly peaks that marked the beginning of griffin territory. It was sunny and bright, turning the Titans' mountains soft shades of purple and brown. Underfoot there was gorse everywhere, heavy with thick yellow flowers. Inkwort flew up into the trees and was gone. Cillian could feel her joy in the day.

'What can you tell me about your sister, the queen?' asked Leven. She was walking alongside Epona. When the princess didn't immediately reply, she hesitantly touched the woman's arm. 'Are you well?'

'Oh, yes,' said Epona brightly, lifting her head. 'Just gathering my thoughts on Ceni. There's a lot to tell.' She gave a flash of her old grin. 'Ceni is the eldest of my mother's brood. Her father was a northern warlord, who died long before I was born. All the stories Mother ever told us suggested that he was a rogue, but one that she admired, all the same. Ceni was born when my mother was still quite young, and they grew up as close as sisters in many ways. Ceni was brave, and clever. Loyal. She has a keen sense of justice. If there was a fight between us sisters, Ceni was the one who would wade in and break it up, and she'd make sure that we would all say sorry, so we'd go to bed not hating each other.'

'She sounds like a good sister,' said Leven.

'The best,' said Epona firmly. 'When Mother conceived of the plan to take Londus, Ceni was the one who helped her put the whole thing together. They discussed the strategies, drew up the plans. Ceni was her war commander – she made sure their army had everything it needed, spoke to the warriors at the head of each legion. Ceni rode a battle chariot, although she was barely a woman grown.' Epona smiled in obvious pride. 'She rode at the front of the army, just like Mother. They sacked Londus together. Me and Togi and Bronvica all knew Ceni would be a queen.'

'Queen of Galabroc,' said Leven, in a musing tone.

'The ancestral seat,' said Epona. 'It's been a long time since I've been here. A long time since I've seen my sister.'

Cillian found himself looking at Epona again. It could have been that the tension he was feeling throughout the Wild Wood was clouding his judgement, but despite her sunny words Epona seemed uneasy, and her pace was slowing again as they followed the Path.

'You will see it again now,' he said. 'There, see, beyond the trees. The walls of Galabroc's great citadel.'

Rising above the trees ahead of them were walls of pale grey granite, topped with huge swathes of virulent green moss. There were men and women on the tops of the wall, guards dressed in red leathers with powerful longbows slung across their backs, although they were no bigger than sparrows at this distance. As they moved on through the trees, the Path grew wider and the Wild Wood less crowded. They began to pass clusters of homes, solidly built cottages of yellow stone circled by low walls. Eventually the Wild Wood dropped away entirely and they entered a bustling town filled with men and women and children going hurriedly about their days, wagons piled with crates of apples, bales of hay. It was a market day, and the air rang with the sound of merchants shouting their wares to each other and passing customers. Cillian saw more than a few faces turn to follow their small group, and he felt the familiar lurch of discomfort as his ties to the Wild Wood grew taut with distance.

Epona was looking around, her eyes wide. 'There, that's the gate.' She pointed needlessly to the citadel walls, which loomed over the town like a thundercloud. 'Let's get inside. It's making me nervous, being out here in the town. I feel like the Atchorn could turn up at any bloody minute.'

The gate was a vast set of wooden double doors, patterned here and there with the same yellow and green moss that crawled across the battlements and securely banded with iron, but in the lower right half there was a smaller door. This stood open, and it was this that Epona approached. Cillian hung back with Leven as the princess had a hurried whispered conversation with the guard on the door.

'Does she seem nervous to you?' asked Leven.

'Perhaps,' said Cillian. 'It's been a hard few days. I expect we'll all be glad to be behind some sturdy walls.'

The Herald turned to look at him with her unnervingly frank gaze.

'Really? Will you be glad to be out of the Wild Wood for the night? I thought you hated to be away from it.'

The urge to confide in her was surprisingly strong. He made himself look at the glittering ore-lines that traced her face and neck. *Remember who she is.* But looking at her face – her grey eyes, the tiny scar at the edge of her bottom lip – did not repel him as it should.

'The other Druin can find us there,' he said. 'We will need to sort all this mess out before any of us are safe in the Wild Wood again. Including me.'

Epona waved them over, and she spoke to them in a hushed voice.

'They're calling my sister. She is out hunting – she always loved to do that – so they've sent messengers to bring her back to the citadel. Until then we'll wait for her inside.'

They were led through the outer and inner gates into a vast cobbled courtyard. Cillian had never been inside the citadel, and he was reassured to see so many animals around: horses waiting to be stabled, a pen of goats being milked, and everywhere, scurrying chickens. It made him think not of Mersia, with its elegant white towers and clean coloured glass, but of Kornwullis, with its nets and fish and boats. No sign of the sea here, but it was a working place, just the same. The central building of the keep was made from warm brown brick – they had obviously saved the sturdy expensive granite for the outer walls – and there were pennants of red and yellow cloth hanging from windows, with the great skull that was the sigil of Galabroc embroidered in the centre. The guards took them into the keep through a side door, passing servants carrying buckets of milk and water, and led them up to a low-ceilinged but spacious room with leaded windows lining one side. The wooden floors were scuffed and the tapestries on the walls were faded, but the place was clean and there was a table and chairs for them to sit. The guards left swiftly, and very soon the three of them were alone again. Epona plonked herself into a chair with a great sigh.

'I don't mind telling you, it feels good to be back on friendly territory.' There was a bowl of apples on the table. She took one and examined it, before putting it back. 'If Queen Gwenith had caught up with us… It's not easy to get out of her lands at the best of times. If we'd been taken back there I'm not sure Mother would have ever been able to extract us. The Lich-Way is strange, but Dwffd…'

'We're still in serious trouble,' Cillian added quietly. Leven had not sat down. Instead she had gone to the windows and was peering through the thick glass. From somewhere down the corridor Cillian could hear someone shouting in an impatient tone, someone else shouting back. 'We need to get a message to Queen Broudicca and explain what has happened.'

'Yeah. Except we can't explain it.' Leven turned away from the window, her arms crossed over her chest. Behind her, Cillian saw a fluttering movement at the window: Inkwort had found them. The little jackdaw pecked irritably at the window and then flew off again in a blink. 'Epona, it's not possible that your mother would…? She did not expect you to be here with us, after all. I doubt she would put her daughter in direct danger, but a despised member of the Imperium and a Druin?'

The princess laughed, crossing her own arms in a defensive posture. 'Are you serious? My mother is ambitious, but she's not an idiot. Sending a Herald to kill the other rulers of Brittletain isn't the most underhanded gesture, is it? There could hardly be an act more guaranteed to unite the other queens and kings against her.'

'Perhaps that's the point,' said Cillian. He picked up one of the apples and turned it over in his hands. It was old and bruised, the green and red skin starting to wrinkle slightly. For reasons he couldn't pinpoint, he felt afraid. 'Epona, given that your sister isn't here, I think we should leave.'

Epona raised her eyebrows at that. 'What? What are you talking about? This is the only safe place for us.'

Cillian looked up to see Leven staring back at him. Whatever was making him uneasy, he saw that it was affecting the Herald too.

'Listen,' she said, glancing again at the window. 'I think—'

At that moment the doors opened, and a tall woman swept into the room, a guard to either side of her. Cillian had never seen Queen Ceni himself, but there was no doubting who this was. She looked much like Queen Broudicca, only younger and taller; the same dark hair plaited into hundreds of slim braids, the same tanned skin and blue eyes. She was wearing hunting gear and there was mud on her boots, and he felt a small rush of relief at that. They hadn't lied about her being out in the country, at least. Queen Ceni looked around at the three of them, taking her time, taking them in. She nodded slightly to herself.

'Dearest sister,' she said, her eyes finally settling on Epona. 'Welcome back to Galabroc.'

58

The answer to your query is yes, the child is supposed to be here and yes, I will be taking responsibility for her myself. I caught her last week in the Street of Bonesaws, her hand and much of her arm inside one of the leather bags full of clerk supplies. She was a stinking and pitiful creature, grimy from head to foot and so skinny I half believed she would blow away in the wind, but she had already stolen three rolls of the best parchment without our noticing and given that I personally pick all the guards that accompany me on these goods runs, that must have taken some considerable skill. I brought her back to my offices, had Missus Scatterbrook in the kitchens give her the hottest bath possible, and had her fed. She can eat an astonishing amount – as Missus Scatterbrook commented, she 'must have hollow legs'. The girl has no parents, no family she knows of, and no particular attachment to continuing to sleep in narrow smelly alleyways. I think she has potential. I will pay for her keep out of my own coin, and she will be of no bother to anyone else. Thank you for your interest, Imperator.

(For your records, her name is Belise. She appears to have no other.)

A personal note from Envoy Kaeto to
the Imperator, marked with the black
wax seal of the Envoy office

'Fine. You can have her for the afternoon. Well. Three hours. No, two.'

Tyleigh had emerged from the tunnel for a brief break in the sunlight. She was wearing a thick pair of glass goggles over her eyes, giving her an oddly insectoid air. Belise grinned up at Kaeto, wiping her hands on a cloth.

'Thank you,' Kaeto said politely. 'We shouldn't be long. Is the donation from... *our friend* helping?'

Tyleigh rubbed a thumb over the corner of her goggles, wiping away a spot of dirt. 'His entire skeleton would be more use, but yes. It may be exactly what we need. Now let me work.'

When he and Belise were up the street leading away from the Undertomb, Kaeto spoke again.

'You have been making yourself indispensable.' It wasn't quite a question.

'You bet I have.' Belise laughed. 'She's not so bad, you know. No worse than you on a really grumpy day, maybe.'

Kaeto frowned at that. To his surprise, Belise's words made him uncomfortable, although he couldn't have said why exactly.

'What do you do for her?'

'Fetching and carrying mostly.' It was another flat, hot day. Beetles of all colours scuttled away from them as they walked up the street. To either side of them, the dusty black buildings radiated heat. 'She wants a thing, I grab it for her. She wants water, or food from our packs, I fetch it. Once she's got her head in a thing, she doesn't want to move away from it, not even to eat, so it helps if I bring everything directly to her. It was rough going at first, because I didn't know what anything was called and she doesn't bloody label anything, but I learn quickly.'

Kaeto smiled. That was certainly true.

'She's letting me do some of the work too,' the girl continued. She lifted her pale face to the sun, eyes half closed. 'She's shown me how to make rubbings of the carvings. And because my hands are smaller than hers, she's having me do some of the finer work with the Titan ore. Tyleigh thinks we just have to find the right combination and we'll get inside. A lot of it is like the work we do – remember when you had me sneak into the ambassador's office and take impressions of all the official seals?'

'Yes. He was sending coded letters to Unblessed nations. I'm glad you're finding this experience... educational, but I should get you out in the sun more. You're very pale.'

'It's bloody dark in there alright. Being out in the daylight is giving me a headache.' When he looked down at her, she rapidly shook her head. 'I'm fine though, don't send me back. I want to see this Titan!'

They had reached the building. Inside was as empty and dusty as all the others, but this one had a set of stairs that led out onto the roof, and from the top it was possible to see much of the city. The pair of them moved to the edge where there was a waist-high wall, and Kaeto pointed out the globes where he had last spoken to Felldir.

'They played music inside them?' asked Belise.

'Apparently so,' said Kaeto. 'Once this was a city every bit as alive as Stratum. People lived here as well as Titans. It must have been a very famous place.'

'But we knew nothing about it.'

'When no one wishes to talk about a thing, it's remarkable how quickly we can all choose to forget. Do not go to the forbidden city, do not speak of its people, long dead. Erase it from your maps and neatly tear out each relevant page from your history book. When there is no trace left, can it really be said to have existed at all?'

Belise looked up at him but kept her silence for a few minutes. When she did speak again, her voice was soft and careful.

'Like the place where you're from, chief? The place the Imperium destroyed for the empress's observatory?'

Kaeto leaned forward on the wall, looking out across the deserted city.

'Hmm. It's no wonder Tyleigh is finding use for you. You're twice as quick as that miserable creature. Here, look. There's your Titan.'

A pale shape flitted across the rooftops, white and eerie. Belise gasped, a look of wonder on her face that made her look even younger than her years. Felldir was flying down near the globes, swooping and arcing up into the air like some monstrous bird. Seen in action his wings looked even larger, even more remarkable. It shouldn't have worked, thought Kaeto, the human shape is not made for the air, yet there was no denying the grace and beauty of the Titan. He reached into a pocket and passed Belise his compact spyglass, which she opened with a practised snap of her wrist.

'Stars' arses,' she breathed, the glass pressed to her eye. 'A real Titan. Just one, all alone.'

She lowered the glass, her eyes still following the graceful shape.

'I thought Tyleigh would want to see it. Him, I mean. But she'd rather be down in the dark, working on opening that door.'

'You mistake her for a historian, Belise. Tyleigh isn't interested in the Titans as such – not the living ones, anyway. She is interested in what she can make from their bones. And in the Undertomb she expects to find more than enough Titan remains to keep her working on her sticky little projects for decades to come.'

'Look, he's getting closer.'

And he was. Felldir swept up into the flat blue sky, turning so that the sunlight flickered across his grey feathers. Kaeto had the sudden idea that the Titan knew they were watching, and was showing off.

'Well, you've seen a Titan, Belise. Are you ready to talk to one?'

The girl raised her eyebrows. 'He's coming here?'

In a few minutes, Kaeto was proven correct. Felldir landed on the far side of the roof, alighting as quietly as a cat, and he came towards them slowly. In the brilliant daylight, it was possible to see more details; the shabby clothes and armour he wore had clearly been patched and mended many, many times, and his grey wings darkened towards the tips of his flight feathers. His long white hair, in this light, was pearly and strange. He was wearing his spectacular winged helmet, and the smallest finger of his left hand was still tightly bound with a rag.

Even if it weren't for his size, Kaeto thought, *you could never mistake him for a human. He is clearly something more.*

'I brought you wine, as promised,' Kaeto said in way of a greeting. 'This is Belise. She has been very eager to meet you.'

To his surprise, Belise said nothing, and when he looked down at the girl he saw that she was as still as a mouse before a cat. Not frightened, exactly, but rigid with shock and wonder. *He must seem like a giant to her.*

'The child,' said Felldir. He removed his helmet and sat on the edge of the wall, his amber eyes trained on the girl. 'Why would you bring a child to a place like this?'

'She is my assistant. Belise left the world of childhood behind a long time ago.' Kaeto bent to his pack and removed the bottle of wine. He had not expected to, but he felt tense and on edge. Perhaps it had been a mistake to show Belise to Felldir. Perhaps it had been a mistake to bring her at all. He thought again of the shattered body of Riz, reduced to a bloody shout of colour just outside their door. His fingers trembled a little as he pulled the cork from the bottle, and he reminded himself of each hidden weapon. The throwing knife in his boot, the poisoned dagger in his sleeve, the sharpened hook hidden against his belt, the packet of lethal powder sewn into his shirt. If Felldir attempted to harm Belise, the Titan would not survive it.

Belise had unfrozen somewhat, enough to remove three tin cups from her own pack. She placed one nervously on the wall next to Felldir, and then stepped back. Felldir picked it up. In his great white hand it looked like a doll's cup. Kaeto poured the wine for the three of them, and the Titan lifted the cup to his lips.

'Not the best the Imperium has to offer – Envoys are paid well, but not that well, and Tyleigh has no taste for it. Not bad though, I think you'll agree.'

'Any wine after five hundred years of no wine is fine enough,' said Felldir.

'You've not had any wine for five hundred years?' asked Belise, finally finding her voice.

'Five hundred years ago a band of thieves camped within the Black City,' said Felldir. 'They had whole casks with them, although it was very poor stuff. I drank one of the casks, and I left the others for the beetles. The beetles are quite partial to alcohol.'

'You killed them?' asked Belise.

'The thieves? I did,' said Felldir evenly. 'It is my duty. This wine,' he lifted the cup, 'is an improvement. These days, people rarely venture into the Black City, and the locals do what they can to keep the walls intact. They are happy to leave the place well enough alone. But every now and then, someone will get too curious...' He shrugged. 'A human failing.'

'Have you killed all the curious people that have made it inside?' asked Belise. She seemed to have gotten over her initial fright of Felldir, and her natural urge to ask questions had resurfaced. Kaeto drank his wine and watched the Titan carefully, waiting for any move that might indicate an attack.

'Yes,' said Felldir. He placed the cup down on the wall and Belise refilled it from the bottle for him. 'Thank you. Sometimes, people will dare each other to come here. It never ends well for them.'

'You could just chase them off,' said Belise, a slightly obstinate tone to her voice that Kaeto recognised. He almost felt sorry for the Titan. 'You're scary enough.'

'They would come back. Word would spread through the villages and towns that perhaps it wasn't a death sentence to enter the Black City after all, and they would come back, seeking treasure, or answers, and...' He stopped, and took a sip from his cup. He emptied it in one. 'I cannot break my oath, child.'

'But we are here, and we're curious. And you're sitting in the sunshine drinking wine with us.'

The Titan looked away, across the rooftops. His handsome face in profile looked sad, and somehow lost.

Kaeto opened his mouth to ask more – now was the time to push for answers, he could see it in the Titan's face – but there was a sudden chiming of bells from the centre of the city, so loud that he saw Belise visibly jump, spilling her own wine on the dusty roof.

'What was that?'

Felldir pointed. In the centre of the city the huge winged statue with its golden helm was slowly changing colour. The black stone clouded and grew white, curling up the figure's legs and across its waist, turning the whole thing alabaster. And all the while, invisible bells clanged and crashed in a chaotic song of alarm and celebration.

'It seems your witch has made a breakthrough,' said Felldir.

PART THREE

UNDERTOMB TO THE CAUL OF STARS

59

If you look for the wisdom of Great T'vyn the Trickster, look for it in his stories. Tell the yenlin of the time he talked the krakens out of the sea; tell them of the year and a day he spent learning the secrets of the wyverns, or how he challenged and bested the unicorns, those vain and dangerous creatures. He lives on in us, when we pass his tales beak to beak.

The Griffin Creed, as written on the
Silver Death Peak by Fionovar the Red

'You can still see it?'

Ynis nodded and sat back on the cold earth, her head swimming. The red fate-ties flickered in front of her eyes and then vanished. Festus stood some way off, by the fire Ynis had built before she checked on the fate-ties, but he was watching her very closely with his green eyes. He looked worried. Somewhat shakily, Ynis got to her feet and wearily pulled on her furs again. They were stiff with cold, and she knew she would have to sit in front of the fire for at least an hour before she started to feel warm again. She trudged back to their little camp and gratefully knelt in front of the flames. Her eyes watered with the new heat.

'South, it's still south,' she said through chattering teeth. This was the fourth time in their journey so far that she had pushed herself close to a freezing death in order to see the fate-ties. 'And it's still there.

Still strong.' She didn't want to admit it to Festus, but the fate-ties felt like another mystery, one she didn't have time to untangle. If her fathers and T'rook were at the ends of three of her strongest fate-ties, then who did the other two belong to? When she was reunited with her sister, perhaps they could begin to figure it out.

'If they had killed her already, would her fate-tie have changed in some way?' Festus asked. Ynis held her hands out to the fire, holding herself very still. Her eyes were full of tears she was determined that Festus would not see. It took her a few moments to be able to speak without her voice shaking.

'The witch-seer rites cut away the fate-ties at the time the soul travels into the next world. If T'rook is already dead, her fate-tie will continue to be attached to her body. Humans don't know how to cut fate-ties,' *apart from me*, she added silently. 'So even if... even if they have killed her, we should be able to find her.' She tried not to think about what the humans had done to Brocken's body. 'I have to know, one way or the other. So we keep on going, as fast as we can,' she said. 'But I will need to rest first.' The darkness around them had grown complete since she had sat down at the fire. 'A few hours' sleep, and then we'll get going at first light.'

'Yes,' said Festus. 'When you are ready, human, we will go.'

They settled by the fire together. When some of the feeling had come back into her fingers, Ynis got a package of food from her pack and passed some of it to the young griffin, who took it carefully in his powerful beak. It was dried goat's meat, stringy and tough but fatty enough to still be tasty. Festus made short work of it.

'Why are you helping me, Festus?' Ynis asked, when the silence between them had grown too heavy to endure. 'I know what the griffins of Yelvynia think of my kind. I know you'd rather eat me than that leathery old goat meat.'

'Do not tempt me,' Festus said drily. 'I help because I like your sister,' he continued, and despite everything Ynis had to suppress a smile. T'rook no doubt would have been very glad to hear those words. 'She is forthright, and stubborn. Her eyes are like gorse flower in summer.' He snapped his beak together, his crest of blue feathers shivering with embarrassment. 'But also, Witch-seer Arrow, because you helped me. You and Witch-seer Frost gave me a precious gift – time and space to say goodbye to my father.' His tone had become serious, making him sound older than he was. 'We do not forget things like that, not even in Yelvynia.'

Ynis nodded, her eyes on the fire. Again she was fighting not to cry, but for different reasons this time.

'Helping you and your father was a great honour for me,' she said quietly. 'Thank you, Festus. Whatever we find at the end of this fate-tie, I thank you for bringing us there.'

We're coming to get you, T'rook, she said to herself. *Whatever it takes.*

60

Beware the dead who sleep in the bog. The water holds them softly and forever, and in that dark time they can only listen, and think, and gossip among themselves. Their own flesh has turned hard as wood and so they have no sympathy for it. If you go into the Lich-Way, guard your flesh well, because given a chance, they would grind it between their teeth just for something to do.

Extract from a Druin text concerning
the darker places of the Wild Wood

The corridors they were led down initially were bare and rather gloomy. The lead windows let in only a portion of the day's light and even Leven – who had no memory of living in her own home and knew only the army's slapdash approach to accommodation – could see that the floors needed sweeping. But the room Queen Ceni led them to was something different; the double doors were embedded with glass of all colours, and these had been polished to a high shine. The queen paused before she opened them, casting a look over her shoulder at Epona as she did.

'You won't remember this room, little sister, as it's been the work of ten years to put it together. I should go and get changed, but I simply cannot wait to show you.'

They stepped inside, and Queen Ceni nodded at the guards to leave them.

'It's extraordinary,' said Epona, and it sounded like she meant it. 'Where did you get all this stuff?'

The room looked, to Leven, like a small museum. She had been to places like it in Stratum, where the Imperium displayed the vast variety of wares brought back from Unblessed lands, and if it was on a much smaller scale than those in Stratum, it was just as lavish. There were thick embroidered carpets on the floor, and two complicated strings of brightly burning oil lamps hung from the beamed ceiling. The walls were lined with cases of crystal and glass, all polished and dusted, and inside them was a dizzying range of objects. Leven saw elaborate golden crowns, studded with pieces of pink coral, and strings of brightly coloured beads and jewels; there were weapons, swords and daggers in enamelled wooden sheaths, as well as exquisitely carved bows; there were suits of armour, many of which Leven recognised from her eight years travelling across the Unblessed territories; and there were books too, huge volumes bound in leather and open to display illustrations inked in a rainbow of colours. At the far end of the tightly packed room there was a carved wooden throne, very like the one she had seen Queen Broudicca sitting in when she had first arrived at Londus-on-Sea. Queen Ceni went to it and ran one hand fondly over the armrest.

'Our mother's old throne, the one she left behind,' Ceni said. 'Do you recognise it, Epona?'

'Yes,' said Epona. 'It looks smaller than I remember. Why didn't you keep it in the throne room?'

'I wanted to make some changes, little sister,' she said warmly. 'Since I became queen I made it my goal to open Galabroc to the wider world. We have no coast here, no handy river traffic for trade, so it was quite the struggle, but gradually, gradually, I have built something out of this place.' She paused, looking as though she meant to say something else, and then turned back to them, smiling. 'Please, have a look around. I've waited years for you to see this, Epona.' Queen Ceni shifted her gaze to Leven. 'And I'd be very interested to know what a citizen of the Starlight Imperium would think of my little collection. I'm sure it seems very small and paltry to you.'

Leven shook her head. 'Not at all, my queen. I've never seen anything like it.'

Queen Ceni smiled and nodded, as though this response pleased her, and walked over to a nearby cabinet. From within it she took a loose piece of golden fabric embroidered all over with silver threads. 'Here, Epona, I thought you'd like to see this. I remember you reading all those stories about princesses when you were small. This is the bridal veil of Queen Ishta.' Epona made a noise of delight and took the offered fabric from her sister, turning it around in her fingers. Ceni addressed herself to Leven and Cillian. 'Ishta was Epona's hero when she was a little girl. The first warrior queen of Brittletain – the first to ride a war chariot and expand her territory.'

'This is incredible, Ceni,' said Epona. She put the delicate fabric back in its cabinet. 'But we've got some important news, which you won't have heard yet. It's not good I'm afraid.'

'Oh there'll be time for all that.' Ceni waved her off and went to the far side of the room, where she opened another display case. 'When did I last get to show my little sister my favourite toys?' This one held what looked to Leven like a thick golden ring with a small section missing. Delicate fronds of ivy had been engraved in the surface, and it was clearly heavy as Ceni wrestled it out of its padded enclosure. 'My lord Druin, I think this one will be of greatest interest to you. This is the nose ring of Magognin, the...'

'The Druidahnon's mother.' His eyes wide, Cillian reached out to touch the golden circle, then seemed to think better of it. 'That truly is a remarkable artefact, your highness.'

Ceni beamed and nodded. She looked back to the doors, as though checking they were still shut. 'My court will be furious I haven't presented the three of you yet, but there are a few last things I would like you to see. Ah!'

She approached another display cabinet, this one waist-high and narrow. From what Leven could see, it appeared to contain a number of brightly coloured rocks and coins. *Half the nation of Brittletain is after us, and our protector has us looking at her coin collection. What is going on?* She tried to catch Cillian's eye, but he was looking at the door.

'These items are medallions from the very dawn of the Starlight Imperium. Your first empress, Blessed Eleven, would have handled this one in the centre here – it was a medallion given to her firstborn son when he reached manhood. This was when the Imperium was little more than Stratum itself. As you might expect, it's made from Titan bone.'

Leven, feeling it was expected of her, peered into the display case and nodded. The medallion was the same familiar blue-green as the ore-lines that were traced all over her body, and carved in the centre was a star, rays of light reaching out to touch the edge.

'Please,' Queen Ceni gestured to the medallion, 'do pick it up and have a proper look. The inscription on the other side is worth reading.'

Leven hesitated, just for a moment. Epona's sister seemed tense, and the fact that they were spending their time looking around her room of treasures when war was looming on the doorstep seemed increasingly ridiculous, but she reminded herself that she was here representing Queen Broudicca. She had to behave as a diplomat might, and not like a paranoid soldier.

'I know very little about our history,' she said, 'truthfully, I know very little of my own. But to think that something from the beginning of the Imperium made it all the way over here...'

She knew something was wrong the moment she picked it up. The medallion was heavy in her hands, and oddly powdery – not at all the smooth sensation she had been expecting from Titan bone. Her fingers tingled and grew hot, as though she were holding them too close to an open flame. She opened her mouth to say something, and all that came out was a strangled noise.

'Leven?' Cillian was at her side in a moment. He took her arm, and he made to take the medallion from her grasp too, but she moved it out of his reach and dropped it. It made a solid thud on the carpeted floor.

'Poison.' It was the only word she could manage. Her ore-lines were burning, but more worryingly, the strength was seeping rapidly out of her legs. In desperation she tried to summon the Titan magic but she could barely move. She sank to her knees, her vision growing dark at the edges. Epona rounded on her sister.

'*What did you do?*'

Queen Ceni had walked round the three of them and was stood by the door, where she was leaning quite comfortably.

'Do you know how many years it's been since you've been here, Epona? It's been a while, hasn't it? Because you'd rather stay in Londus than travel up to this cold and rocky kingdom. More to the point, how many years since *Mother* dropped this place like the sack of rancid shit it was and carved her way to a more bountiful land?'

'Ceni!'

'Thirty years, little sister. Thirty years I have been left here, at the arse end of the country, to wither and grow stagnant and scratch what little good I could out of Galabroc. After *I* did all the work. Commanded our armies, led the fight. What was I left with?'

Leven tried to lift her arms, but they were made of lead. Cillian was holding her up, his arm slung protectively across her chest, and she tried to concentrate on the warmth of his touch even as the room grew dim and cold around her. She could hear Epona speaking now, her voice sharp with outrage.

'What are you talking about? Mother made you a queen! All of Galabroc...'

'Yes, all of this stony, bleak, constricted little land.' Ceni laughed. 'The Wild Wood to the south, and the griffins to the north. Mother always knew it could never grow as she wanted it to, so she took Londus for herself and left me here to moulder away. But I haven't.'

Leven made a noise in the back of her throat, and Ceni turned her attention to her. 'I wouldn't move, if I were you. The substance on that medallion is lethal – a near instant death for anyone who hasn't had their body augmented with Titan ore, and to be honest we're not at all sure what it will do to a Herald either. Stop you in your tracks, at least. And that's enough for now.'

'This is madness!' Epona sounded close to tears. 'I'm your sister! And Leven is my *friend*. How can you treat us like this?'

Cillian spoke where he crouched, his face very close to Leven's. She could feel his breath on her cheek. 'Because it was all her, Epona. The queen of Mersia, that very public murder. You said yourself: such a thing would turn all of Brittletain against your mother. And that's exactly what your sister wants.'

Ceni grinned widely, and even in her growing agony Leven recognised that this was her *real* smile – everything else had just been for show.

'They say the Druin are wise, don't they?' said Queen Ceni. 'I honestly thought it would be you to figure it out, Epona – Mother always claimed you were the clever one.'

'No,' said Epona. She sounded like a little girl. 'No, you *wouldn't*.'

'I had thought that Prince Eafen would manage to deal with the Herald in Mersia, but I should have known better than to trust such an important job to that little whelp. Your friend here will be taken to the dungeon.' Ceni knocked on the door twice, and the guards that had been waiting there for them all along threw them open. 'I'll be interested to see if your pet Herald lives through the night.'

61

Unblessed Houraki is known across Enonah as the country of a thousand gods, but there are easily more than that, perhaps ten times over. I have never been able to find an official list, which is not surprising as Houraki is particularly secretive and, by all accounts, new gods are added every year. There are gods of trees, of streets, of houses, kitchens, rivers, of new marriages, births, the sunrise, the sunset, twilight, and the deepest part of night. There are even gods of beetles, of bees, and snakes, and scorpions, and everything else that scuttles around that sweaty country. Much of the earth of Houraki is thick with clay, and you will see evidence of it in every building, but its main use has become the depiction of these gods: families will often find a rich vein of clay out amongst the trees and craft household gods with their own hands. It makes you wonder what they are so afraid of.

Notes on Unblessed Houraki
gathered for Envoy Kaeto

The great stone door to the Undertomb stood open, and Tyleigh leaned just inside it, a huge grin splitting the woman's face in two. Kaeto had never seen her look so happy. Above their heads, the cacophony of bells was slowly dying, leaving an unpleasant ringing in the ears.

'How did you do it?'

'I would explain, but you wouldn't understand, and I have no patience for wasting time. I have only waited here for the two of you so that you can carry the lamps.' Tyleigh picked up two already lit oil lamps from the ground at her feet and passed them to Kaeto and Belise. 'Hurry up. I will be taking notes as we go.'

'There could be traps,' said Belise, an uncharacteristically uncertain waver to her voice. 'Or anything really. Should we check it out a bit more slowly?'

'If there are traps, child, you'll find them for me.' Tyleigh stood aside and urged them forward. She pulled a wad of papers from her pocket and the long graphite pencil she had tied to her belt. Belise took a few steps forward, then looked up at Kaeto. She was clearly reluctant. He rested a hand on her shoulder for a moment.

'I'll go first,' he said. 'Be alert for anything potentially hazardous.'

Yet to begin with, the Undertomb was only remarkable in its mundanity. There were more steps, leading downwards in a slow spiral, and the walls were smooth and unmarked by any carvings. The place smelled strongly of dust, as well as the sharp mineral tang of water left without sunlight for a very long time. The echoes of the bells still reverberated down here, but very faintly, so that it sounded like someone calling mournfully from a distant room. The three of them followed the stairs down, the scritch and scratch of Tyleigh's pencil working feverishly across the page while she muttered to herself.

'Steps carved directly from bedrock, appears to be same material as buildings constructed from above ground, no leaf matter or beetle remains in evidence, air is stale and very still, acoustics unusual, may benefit from further study...'

After some minutes of walking, the stone spiral staircase emerged from the ceiling of a vast cavern. The walls fell away, and the staircase circled a huge pillar of black rock, with a steep drop to one side. All around them was a hissing, scratching noise that sounded almost like the sea, or something huge moving on thousands of legs. Kaeto stopped, frozen in place, while Belise sat on her step and shuffled to the side closest to the pillar so she could press herself against it. Tyleigh, meanwhile, had walked right up to the edge and peered over, her long untidy hair hanging down over the precipice.

'Extraordinary,' said Tyleigh. 'Would you look at that? This must spread right underneath the city and beyond.'

The light from their oil lamps spread a faint luminescence that seemed to hide more than it revealed, but it was possible to see a faint grey smudge in the distance; walls carved from bedrock. Beneath them the view was confusing. There was a sense of movement, which put Kaeto again in mind of the sea, but it was a sea that boiled and teemed.

'What is that? What is moving down there?'

'It's moving up here too,' said Belise in a strangled voice. 'Look.'

Kaeto glanced up. Just feet above their heads, thousands and thousands of beetles squirmed and crawled and skittered across the stone, their brilliant carapaces a constantly moving carpet of jewelled colours; reds, golds, greens, blues, yellows and pinks.

'*Yuch*,' said Belise.

'Yes, that is a… lot of beetles. Are you alright?'

Belise was still sitting on the step, her lamp held out awkwardly in front of her. It wasn't like the girl to be frightened of heights or squeamish about insects but then, he reminded himself, this situation was very much outside of her experience. Belise had grown up in the hectic political chess game that was Stratum, and as his assistant she had cut her teeth on more mundane things – the quiet poisoning of diplomats, the staging of crimes, the planting of evidence and the hiding of bodies. She could hardly have expected to end up deep under the earth, exploring the graveyard of the mythical Othanim. And he had noticed that children either loved bugs, or they hated them – and it wasn't so long ago that a beetle bite had almost proved fatal for Belise.

Kaeto crouched next to the girl and lowered his voice. 'Do you want me to carry you down the rest of the way?'

The look she gave him, half wide-eyed with fright and half defiant, made him feel foolish for asking. She stood up, the fingers of one hand resting against the stone wall.

'No, I'm fine, chief. Besides, if you lift me up I'll be closer to *those* things. It's not that I'm scared of them,' she added quickly. 'There's just too many of them.'

'Fascinating,' said Tyleigh, still feverishly taking notes. 'There is a kind of faint light down there, do you see? A great many of these beetles are *ignus koleopteros*, producing a glow from their abdomen.'

His eyes adjusting to the gloom beyond their lamps, Kaeto saw that she was right. There were points of greenish light, soft as moon-glow, moving all over the vast cavern. Together, they made their way slowly down the spiral steps, Kaeto in the front while Belise stayed close to his side, her lamp held up as a kind of protection. When they reached the bottom, they found themselves surrounded by a vast sea of life, beetles of all sizes and colours crawling and skittering, so thick on the ground it was impossible to see what they were walking across. To Kaeto's relief, they didn't seem to be interested in their human visitors at all. Instead, they marched and crawled back and forth, clambering over each other or bursting into short flights. Many of them, he noticed, were carrying materials in their mandibles – pieces of leaf, stone, or even the bodies of other dead beetles.

'It all looks so... industrious.'

'More so than you realise,' said Tyleigh. 'Look.' She pointed out across the teeming masses. 'Watch them, just there, and you will see it. There is order to their movements. Lines. Do you see?'

At first, Kaeto could not. There were just too many of them, thousands of legs and carapaces and antennae creating a shifting carpet of life with no pattern.

'I see it!' said Belise, sounding more like her usual self. 'There, look! There are circles, and spirals, like they're all following each other.'

Kaeto blinked, and then what he was looking at seemed to fall into place. Amongst the teeming mass there were clear lines of movement, beetles following each other in formation. *Like a dance*, he thought, *or many workers all performing the same task together.*

'Fascinating,' Tyleigh said again. 'You see this behaviour in bees, or ants, but beetles? What could make beetles behave with a single purpose? And so many different species working as one. It makes no sense.'

'What are they doing?' asked Belise. She had gone to the edge of the sea of beetles and crouched low, to watch them more closely. 'Ants and bees are builders. They build things.'

Kaeto saw Tyleigh glance at Belise, as though she were impressed.

'Here, open your lamp.' Tyleigh took a balled-up rag from within a pocket and held it to the open flame. Once it had caught she threw it outwards into the teeming sea of beetles, and where it landed they scattered, tumbling over each other to get away from the small fire.

'There!' Tyleigh grabbed Belise and pushed the girl forward. 'Lower your lamp to the ground, let me see it.'

Belise took a few faltering steps forward, and then crouched, placing her lamp on the ground while the beetles cowered away from her. In the buttery light, Kaeto could see very clearly the expression of surprise that passed over her face.

'It's like a honeycomb in the ground,' she said. 'Look!'

The girl was right. Underneath her feet was what looked at first glance like a great sheet of glass, and caught within it were large honeycomb shapes, each one at least three feet across. It was hard to see what the thin walls of the honeycomb were made of – they were fibrous and a greenish-grey – and besides, Kaeto found his attention taken by what the honeycombs contained. A cold feeling settled in the base of his stomach. Tyleigh, though, was ecstatic.

'This is where they are! The last, lost Titans. This is more than I even dared to dream of.'

Standing within the honeycomb, held by something unseen, was a winged man not unlike Felldir. He wore a helm like the golden one on the statue, but not identical. His face was turned up towards them, his eyes open and unmoving. His broad shoulders were clothed in what looked like very fine golden chain mail, and at his back it was just possible to see the tops of his neatly folded wings. In the hexagon next to him there was another, and joined to those two, a woman with wings was held in the same position. Her eyes, Kaeto noted with wonder, were a pale violet, and her hair was black.

'They must be thousands of years old,' Belise said quietly. 'Why do they look like that? They look like they were put down there yesterday. Just... planted and sealed over with glass. Are they alive or dead?'

Kaeto shook his head. He was thinking of the vastness of the cavern. What if the entire floor was covered in these strange pods? Tyleigh had found herself an army. *An army for the Imperium*, he reminded himself. *That is why we are here.*

'Is it glass though?' Tyleigh leaned down and pressed her fingers to the floor. 'We'll soon find out.' She took a dagger from her belt, and passed it to Belise. 'There, child. Make yourself useful – strike the floor, and we'll see how tough it is.'

The girl took the dagger, an expression of pleasure passing over her face – *she is happiest when she is holding a weapon*, thought Kaeto – and then she knelt, and struck the floor with its deadly point. There was a hard, discordant noise that put Kaeto's teeth on edge, and all at once the beetles flooded back in.

'Get back!' Kaeto lurched towards the girl, trying to grab her, but Belise was hit by a vast wave of scuttling creatures. He saw her pale face turn towards him, her eyes full of fear, and then she was gone, knocked to the floor and lost beneath a tide of beetles. 'Belise!'

Drawing his own short sword, Kaeto waded out into the sea of movement, keeping his eyes trained on the spot where Belise had gone down, but when he reached it there was no sign of her. He kicked at the beetles, stabbed at them, thrust them away with his free hand. There was nothing. Behind him, Tyleigh – who had leapt to the spiral staircase the moment Belise had struck the glass – was shouting at him to return. He rounded on her, his heart thundering.

'You knew, didn't you? You *knew* that would happen. It's why you didn't do it yourself!'

'Calm yourself, Envoy. What's one assistant? I lose assistants all the time.' Tyleigh was shoving her papers back into her pocket. Her face was flushed, excited. 'We've learnt something important. The beetles will protect their charges if they sense—'

'Shut up!' Kaeto turned back to the sea of beetles. He was looking for any sign of Belise – a hand clutching at the air, a shout. There was nothing. 'We have to get her back. Get down here and help me look, or I swear on the stars I will cut your throat and leave you—'

At that moment, a great booming voice echoed around the cavern, making all the hairs on the back of Kaeto's neck stand up.

'THERE YOU ARE,' it said. 'I HAVE WAITED FOR SO LONG, LIGHT-BONES.'

62

Leven lay where they had thrown her, against the hard floor of the cell. There was a small window high up in the wall above her, which let in a little light between its thick iron bars, and the sturdy wooden door also had a small porthole, through which a smoky lamplight entered. Normally, such a prison would be no particular problem. At full strength, with the Titan magic running through her limbs, she could have crashed through the wooden door in a matter of moments – could even have yanked free the iron bars across the window. Currently, she could barely lift her head, and the tingling numbness that had started at her fingers had spread to cover her entire body. She lay still, concentrating on her breathing and trying not to panic.

'This is going well,' she said to the empty room. 'Realistically, I'm surprised it took me this long to end up in a prison cell.'

She paused, breathing hard. Outside, there were low voices talking. A face appeared at the hole in the door, peering in cautiously, and then the bolts rattled across and the door opened. Queen Ceni stepped inside and stood over her. Leven attempted to lift her chin a little, to meet the woman's eyes, but her muscles weren't cooperating.

'I wanted a closer look at the Imperium's dog, now that she has no teeth to bite with.' Queen Ceni grinned, and turned back to one of the guards. 'Wait outside. I will be quite safe.'

'Where are the others?' Leven asked. 'What have you done with Cillian and your sister?'

'For all my sister's nonsense, she is still a princess. Do you think I would put her in a dingy little cell like this?' Ceni gestured at the damp walls. 'She is perfectly secure. The Druin is with her. They were anxious not to be parted, which is sweet, isn't it? Do you think she intends to bed him? Or has she already? Epona always did have a rebellious streak.'

'Did you come down here for a gossip?' Leven found herself biting back harsher words. She didn't want the queen to know she was getting to her. 'Nothing better to do, I suppose.'

'That upsets you. How interesting.' Queen Ceni placed her boot on Leven's leg and pushed her a little. Leven rocked back, unable to resist. 'I didn't expect to have you here, in my dungeon, but it is an unexpected treat, I must admit. When we heard that the three of you had fled Mersia, I wasn't too concerned – it didn't matter where you ran to, the news of your crimes travelled faster. But I have always made a point of being prepared for all possibilities. It's one of the reasons I was so good at commanding my mother's armies. So I had this poison prepared, just in case you should arrive in Galabroc.'

She pulled a small bag from her belt. Belatedly Leven saw that she was wearing leather gloves that went up to her elbows. From the bag, she removed the medallion of Titan bone and turned it over in her fingers.

'What do you do with an impervious enemy, one who can summon wings and a sword? On the battlefield I'm sure you've dealt with elite warriors and peasant soldiers alike, but I doubt any of them came armed with something like this.' She held the medallion up to the weak light and turned it back and forth. 'I wasn't lying when I said this stuff is lethal. We lost two apprentice alchemists in the making of it, and another applying it to something you could be convinced to touch. Having seen how quickly it took them, I was convinced that it would take you too, regardless of your Titan magic. But here you are, wheezing on my floor. Perhaps I will keep you. Mother would never let me have a pet. She said it was frivolous.'

Leven took several long, slow breaths before she spoke again.

'Who else is in on this with you? Prince Eafen, obviously. But there has to be someone in Londus too. Someone who could tamper...' She paused to take another breath. 'Who could tamper with the gifts your mother gave us.'

'Look at you, trying to play politics in Brittletain. *Clever* dog.' Ceni crouched down over Leven, close enough that Leven could see the dried mud on the queen's riding boots. 'Why did you come here, Herald? Not that I'm complaining – it was your sudden arrival and my mother's ridiculous scheme that prompted me to put this plan in motion – but I'm fascinated to know what a single Imperial soldier could want here.'

'Obviously it was to experience the legendary Brittletain hospitality.'

Ceni laughed.

'When my guards dragged you away, your Druin tried to summon his own magic. In here, the heart of the keep, where the land has been tamed for generations. He wanted to save you, I think. That's interesting, isn't it? A Druin of the Wild Wood, fighting tooth and nail to save a weapon of the Imperium. Perhaps my sister is barking up the wrong tree with that one after all.' Ceni took hold of Leven's chin and turned her face so that she could look into her eyes. 'What is he to you? If I brought you his head, would it break you?'

Leven gritted her teeth, wishing she could move to bite the woman.

'Do that, and not even Epona could stop me from burning your precious keep to the ground.'

Ceni smiled. And then she reached out with the hand still holding the medallion, and pressed its cold surface to Leven's cheek. Leven tried to jerk away from it with her whole body, but all she managed was a violent twitch. Immediately the numbness in her face increased tenfold, and searing lines of pain travelled down her neck and across her torso. The dim light in the cell grew dimmer, fading and shrinking until darkness rolled up and over her.

'Time to sleep, dog.'

Cillian stood by the window, anxiously scanning the patch of grey sky beyond the courtyard. It was raining in the steady, thorough way of summer rains. Behind him, Epona was pacing the room, her brows furrowed.

'Any sign yet?'

'No.' Cillian laid his hand on the sill outside the window, his last pinch of inkwort seed spread across his palm. He wasn't sure how much he could rely on the little jackdaw, and it never hurt to include food when dealing with animals. 'It will take some time to look around this place.'

'I just can't believe it.' Epona came to a stop, and threw her hands up in the air. Cillian had heard those words from her mouth several times over the last few hours. '*Ceni.* She is supposed to be... She was always Mother's favourite, the golden child. She made her a queen and gave her Galabroc.'

'And then left her here, while she ruled over the prosperous Londus-on-Sea, a kingdom with the largest trade routes. The kingdom that faces the whole world.' When Epona glared at him, he shrugged. 'This is how Ceni sees things, Epona.'

'Well then... she's an idiot!' Epona came over to the window and fiddled once more with the latch; they had already discovered that it didn't open wide enough to fit either of them. The room itself was a fine one, with carpets and a grand bed with a canopy of silk, as well as a smaller adjoining room with rushes on the floor and a narrow cot. There was a large basin of cold water, and more bowls of fruit. But the door was locked and guarded, and the courtyard below them thrummed with more of the queen's guard. It was pleasant, but it was a prison. 'And to use poison against Leven...' She rubbed her hands over her face, smudging the remnants of blue paint into blurred lines. 'The weapon of a coward.'

Cillian said nothing. He had not liked the way Leven had gone limp on the floor of the throne room, or the glassy expression in her eyes as he and Epona had been dragged away from her. He had reached out at the time for anything that might aid him – living wood or stone, the animals of the forest – but they were in the middle of a keep in the middle of a town; the stones under his feet were old and had forgotten their ties to the Wild Wood long ago, and he could only reach Inkwort, who could do no more than call her displeasure from outside. Deep below them, he had felt the chill of the old bones Galabroc was built on.

As if thinking of the bird had summoned her, the jackdaw lighted on the sill, her pale blue eyes focused intently on the seeds in his hand. The rain had beaded on her fine black feathers so that she appeared to have been adorned with diamonds.

'There she is!' cried Epona, who immediately clapped her hands over her mouth. 'Sorry. What does she say? Does she know where Leven is?'

'Here.' Cillian spread his fingers towards Inkwort and she hopped onto his hand. Carefully he reached out for the small bird's mind, wary of alarming or annoying her. At first, there was her usual resistance – a sense that she had little interest in human concerns – and then she seemed to relent. A picture arrived in his mind of a dark cell of weathered stone, as seen from a small barred window. Leven lay on the floor, not moving, her untidy brown hair spread across the stones. She looked very vulnerable.

'She's in a cell. There's a window, so she's not below ground.'

'That's something at least,' said Epona. She had pressed the edge of her thumb to her mouth and was gnawing at a scrap of loose skin there. 'Is she... is she still alive?'

Cillian cleared his throat and tried to focus more clearly on the memory Inkwort had given him. The Herald was so still, it did not look like she was breathing.

No, he thought. *Come on, Leven. You're stronger than this. Please.*

He held the vision as long as he could, too aware of Epona's tense form next to his, and his own quietly desperate need for Leven to be alright; a host of feelings he was keen not to examine too closely.

Come on. Move, Leven, take a breath. Anything.

The image was beginning to shiver and break up – it is not in the nature of birds to sit in one place for long if that place is not a nest or a perch – and then he saw it: one finger on her right hand curled inwards, followed by another. And then her shoulders moved a tiny amount, as though she had gasped or sighed. And then the image was gone. He opened his eyes.

'She's alive, but she's in a bad way.'

Epona let out a huge sigh, and pushed her hands back through her hair, making it stick up wildly. Then to Cillian's surprise, she grabbed his free hand and squeezed it. Inkwort hopped in through the window and began looking around for other things to peck.

'Leven might be a foreign warrior, she might be the Imperium's bloody sword even, but I've never met anyone else like her, and I am not about to let my bloody stupid sister murder her over some stupid fight with our mother.' She nodded, as though coming to an agreement with herself. 'And if I'm right, my lord Druin, I think you like her too? Yes?'

Cillian nodded the tiniest amount, not trusting himself to speak.

'Right. Then we're going to find a way to get her out of this shit hole and stop Ceni's madness.'

Madness.

'I have an idea.' He stood up. 'Do you have any of your blue paint on you?'

63

L even was in the Wild Wood again. Her head was thumping steadily, and she felt as sick as a dog, but at least when she looked down at her arms, she could see the ore-lines there, silver and blue against her skin.

'I am still myself,' she said aloud. Around her, the forest was dark and threatening. The gaps between the branches of the trees revealed a bone-white winter sky, and she was so cold her hands and feet were numb. 'What am I doing here? I was... we were in Galabroc.'

A terrible shrieking cry broke over the forest like a thunderclap and Leven shrank back; it was very easy to imagine what it was like to be a mouse on a night when the owl was out. The cry came over and over, terrible and furious, and Leven moved to stand next to a wide tree trunk, trying to get out of sight of whatever awful thing was in the sky, but a figure appeared to her left, crashing through the bushes.

'There you are!' It was a man, tall and wide across the shoulders. He had a black beard and untidy, slightly wavy hair that he had failed to pull back into a braid, and he looked like a woodsman. There was a small axe at his belt, and he wore a tough leather apron under a fur cloak. At the sight of him, Leven felt something inside her, so hidden and so small, shatter into a thousand pieces. She did not know him. She *did* know him, and he knew her better than anyone. How could both things be true?

'I... I don't...'

The shrieking came again, but this time it was different. Not the war cry of some terrible, flying beast, but the wail of someone small and lost. *It's a baby*, thought Leven in wonder, *a baby crying in the woods.*

The man looked up, his body tense with some new emotion. Then, to Leven's shock, he took her in his arms and embraced her. She could smell the woodsmoke funk of the furs he wore, and some deeper, less identifiable scent that took hold of her heart and squeezed it. *Home*, she thought, *this is what home smells like.* And then he let go of her.

'Come on, little bird,' he said. He smiled at her fondly. 'It's not safe up here, so close to the border. Let's go home.'

Leven made to follow him, but the forest was dark again and getting darker by the second. Shadows seeped out of the undergrowth like smoke, and the winter sky above flickered and grew dim, while the normal sounds of the wood – the birds and the wind and the insects – were replaced with something else: a flat, mechanical *click, click, click.*

'Not this again.' She didn't know what the noise meant, but it felt *bad.* All the saliva in her mouth dried up, and her arms broke out in gooseflesh. *Click, click, click. Clack, clack, clack.* Leven reached out for the bearded man, desperate not to leave him behind after she had finally found him – surely if anyone could keep her safe, it would be him – but the noisy dark rose up and ate her in one hungry bite.

64

If there's one thing that the civil war taught Brittletain, it's that the powers of the Druin can be used to wound, disable and kill. It was a reality that we were reluctant to acknowledge ourselves, and for a time it did appear that we would not be able to step back from what this war had revealed about us; and indeed there were skirmishes for some time after the war ended, between the common folk of Brittletain and the Druin. It was apparent to the Druidahnon that these small conflicts could lead us down the path to war again – something none of us wanted – so each newly horned Druin took an oath not to use certain magics, or not to use them against other men and women. These days, the darker arts of the Druin – the ability to use roots and rocks to form weapons, for example – are very rarely seen.

Extract from the private
writings of a Druin elder

'Guards! Guards, I demand your attention at once!'

Epona banged on the door with both her fists, making an extraordinary racket. Cillian, crouched down by the far wall, imagined she had done similar whenever she was confined to her bedroom as a child. From outside the door, he could hear urgent footsteps and some irritable shouting. She was getting their attention. Then, from beyond the door, a male voice spoke.

'Princess Epona, you have everything you need in there. Such treason would usually land you in the dungeon, but the queen is merciful and kind to her wayward sister.'

'Fucking cheek.' Epona rolled her eyes and then relaunched her dramatics. 'It's the Druin! He's gone thrawn! We're too far from the Wild Wood and... you have to help me!'

With that she threw the clay bowl she had in her hands against the wall, where it shattered, and then kicked over the small wooden table. 'Help!' she cried again. 'He's going to kill me! What are you doing out there, for fuck's sake?'

There was more confused shouting beyond the door. Bolts rattled as someone on the other side pulled them across, and Epona turned to raise her eyebrows at Cillian. This was the difficult bit. Getting the guards into the room while they were confused and perhaps slightly afraid was one thing – actually taking advantage of that was quite another. The door swung open and one guard stepped fully into the room. His face was creased with a combination of disgust and fear. Cillian saw the man look at his horns, which Epona had carefully painted with her powdery blue make-up. For his part, Cillian bared his teeth and growled, tensing all his muscles as if he meant to leap at the guard.

'There you are.' Epona grabbed the guard's arm and shoved him lightly in Cillian's direction. 'You have to remove the Druin and put him in the dungeon before he kills me. Go on! I won't be torn apart by some rabid animal just because you're a coward.'

Another guard, a stocky woman, hung just in the door, and Cillian cursed silently to himself. That made things more difficult.

'Has he really turned?' she called to the other guard. 'I didn't think it could happen so quickly. He looked fine when we brought him in. His horns certainly weren't that colour.'

'I've suspected it for days,' said Epona quickly. 'He hasn't been himself since we left Mersia. Quickly! Don't you know what a thrawn Druin is capable of?'

Cillian got to his feet, and that seemed to galvanise the first guard into action. The man drew the short sword at his belt and walked further into the room, putting himself between Cillian and Epona. Without hesitation, the princess picked up the stone water basin and hurled it at the back of the guard's head. It crashed into his unprotected skull with an unpleasantly meaty thud and the man stumbled to one knee, barking with pain and surprise.

'Hoy!' cried the woman at the door.

Cillian ran forward and snatched the sword from the guard's hand, and levelled it at the female guard, who was already backing into the corridor. If there were more guards waiting out there, then they had already lost.

'Stop!' he shouted, before grabbing hold of the injured guard by his hair. 'Don't move an inch, or I swear by the Green Man I'll cut his throat.' For a strange moment, Cillian felt a wild bubble of laughter constricting his own throat. He had attacked a royal guard and was threatening to kill him. This couldn't be the path the Druidahnon had foreseen for him, could it? Perhaps he really had gone thrawn. The woman in the door had stopped moving, clearly torn over what she should do next. Epona, however, wasted no time.

'In you come, sweetheart.' She yanked the female guard over the threshold and took the woman's sword from her belt. 'You two are going to wait in here for us.'

The female guard, however, was at least a foot taller than Epona and significantly broader, and she knew it, too. The larger woman crashed bodily into the princess, making her drop the sword and fall against the small table. Sensing his chance, the guard Cillian was holding made to stand up despite the sword against his throat – and then a piece of shadow bolted through the window and threw itself at the female guard. The woman called out, flapping her hands madly at her own head. It was Inkwort, pecking and cawing with all her strength.

Epona scrambled up from where she had fallen and lunged for the door.

'Hurry!'

Cillian shoved the guard into the corner of the room and joined Epona on the other side of the door. The princess slammed it and threw the bolt across, breathing hard.

'What about your little bird?'

'Inkwort is clever.' Cillian found himself smiling. 'And the window's open. Come on, we won't have long before we're discovered.'

65

'FREE ME, AND I SHALL RETURN YOUR CHILD TO YOU!'
'Belise!' Kaeto ran through the sea of beetles, kicking the
creatures to all sides as he did so. 'Belise, if you can hear me,
shout!'

No answer. The scuttling hiss of thousands of insectile legs
continued. Behind him, Tyleigh was calling him from the base of the
spiral staircase.

'Envoy, come away, or the beetles will take you too. You'll be
perceived as a threat.'

'Belise!' He kept seeing the startled look on her face as the insects
rose up and swept her away. *I brought her here. This is my fault.* 'Belise!'

'GIVE ME FREEDOM, HUMAN!'

Kaeto cast around. The voice came from no obvious place, instead
seeming to bounce off the surrounding walls and come from
everywhere at once. There was no one to see, and no one to threaten.
No one to bribe or cajole or kill to get Belise back. A hand took hold of
his elbow, startling him, and he saw that Tyleigh had waded through
the beetles to reach him. Her grip was surprisingly strong.

'Come on,' she said tersely. 'We're in danger here. We have to go
back up, above ground, where we can think.'

'I can't leave her.'

Tyleigh opened her mouth to say one thing, then shook her head,
and said something else. 'Shouting at the beetles won't get her back.
Back up the stairs. We need to talk.'

Feeling sick with guilt, Kaeto followed the alchemist back up the spiral staircase and along the tunnel, back out under the sky. Waiting for them at the entrance was Felldir, his expression grave. Tyleigh did not seem surprised to see him, or even especially curious about it. She squinted up at him and scratched her headband where it lay against her forehead.

'I thought you would be here.'

Felldir nodded and his amber eyes settled on Kaeto.

'You entered the Undertomb and found what is hidden there.'

'And we have to go back,' said Kaeto. He pushed his hands through his hair. At some point in his desperate search for Belise, the cord had come loose, letting his black hair fall to either side of his face. 'Belise was taken, Felldir. Just… swept off by beetles. And there's something down there that says we can have her back if we… if we let it out.'

'It is *her*,' said Felldir simply. 'The one who led us all to ruin. Icaraine the Lightbringer has waited so long for someone to free her.'

Their rough camp was by the circular door. Kaeto rifled through the packs until he found a small bottle of rum. He took a swig, savouring the burn as it went down his throat.

'I don't think that would be a very good idea,' Tyleigh was saying. 'Icaraine is, I suspect, exceptionally dangerous.' She turned to Kaeto with her hands on her hips. 'Your assistant is gone, Envoy. Those beetles are acting under a very powerful magic. One I do recognise, as it happens.'

'What?' Kaeto lifted the bottle to his lips and finished it, before throwing it on the ground. 'What are you talking about? Of course she isn't *gone*. She's just lost down there somewhere.'

Tyleigh was paying him no mind. She was addressing the Titan again, and for the first time Kaeto noticed that Felldir looked uncomfortable, as though he were waiting for some terrible truth to be revealed.

'You know what I am, don't you?' Tyleigh was saying. 'Or what I used to be, at least. It's why we were allowed to live, and explore the city.'

Felldir nodded.

'And are they alive? The Titans trapped in the Undertomb?'

'Most of them,' said Felldir. Standing in the strong sunshine, he looked very brittle and old, an ancient statue close to falling into dust. 'Some died of despair over the years. I felt them when they passed. Not *her*, though. She refused to die.'

'What are the two of you talking about?' Kaeto shook his head. 'What do you mean, he knows what you are?'

Tyleigh turned back to him, as though she had almost forgotten he was there. 'The magic controlling the beetles. It took me a moment to place it, because it's been so long since... well, it's been a long time. But there is only one kind of magic that can command other living creatures in that way. The magic of the Druin.'

'The Brittletain wizards? What do they have to do with anything?'

'You know so little about them in the Imperium. Lots of books, lots of writing about Brittletain, but actual knowledge?' Tyleigh rolled her eyes. 'The Druin have a direct link to their Wild Wood, and to all the creatures that live in it – it enables them to tend the wood, and the forest souls, and to open paths through the wilder places. But there is a forbidden form of Druin magic, which they call "going thrawn".' She shook her head. 'They are frightened idiots, too scared to grasp the power they've been given. Being thrawn allows you to force an animal to obey you. With Druin magic you can take hold of another creature's mind and command it to do as you wish.'

'Tyleigh, there are no Druin here.' Kaeto felt exhausted. He could barely follow her words. Felldir continued to watch them both, his amber eyes expressionless. 'How could the Druin be commanding those beetles? And why would they?'

'You're forgetting, Envoy, where the Druin get their power from. Who gave it to them in the first place. And I thought you were supposed to be clever.' She spoke again to Felldir. 'He was here, wasn't he? The Druidahnon? All those years ago?'

The Titan nodded. 'He, and his people, led the war against mine. When the Othanim lost, it was the Druidahnon that sealed them into their tombs, and commanded that the scuttling creatures of the Black City keep them so forever.'

'It's remarkable,' Tyleigh shook her head in wonder, 'for such a command to last thousands of years...'

'He was angry,' Felldir said simply. 'Our war had killed all his brothers and sisters. He was the only one left, at the end.'

Kaeto stood very still. He could feel the rum in his stomach softening the edges of his panic and slowing down his thoughts. It was important that he paid attention. It was important that he understood what was going on. Any piece of knowledge might be the key to saving Belise.

'Alright,' he said, keeping his voice level. 'So Icaraine and these other Titans are trapped with Druin magic. The beetles are controlled by Druin magic. What does this have to do with you, Tyleigh? And why did that spare us from Felldir's attacks?'

The alchemist sighed and rubbed again at her headband. She went to their camp, and pulled a bulky-looking leather bag from inside one of her packs. Kaeto recognised it; the bag was always with Tyleigh's belongings, and it was one of the few things she did not demand he or Belise carry for her. Her clever fingers plucked at the strings holding it shut, and then she reached inside and retrieved two long, curving objects, ridged and roughly splintered at one end. It was a pair of horns, like those you might find on a ram, although they were tinted a faint cornflower blue. Tyleigh weighed them in her hands thoughtfully, one thumb tracing a spiralling crack.

'Once upon a time,' she said, 'in a land very far from this one, my name was Echni.'

66

The empress is a wizened devil. The stories say that she poisoned her own sister – not at once, but slowly, over several years, and when she finally died she had her body buried in the desert and a doll made in her image, which she takes everywhere with her. What sort of queen is this, that uses poison and mocks her own sister's death? Little wonder that the Imperium itself is heartless and cruel.

> The private writings of Queen
> Ceni, ruler of Galabroc and
> daughter of Queen Broudicca

The winter wood that had been haunting her for hours finally edged back into darkness, and Leven saw instead the damp walls of the cell, black mould tracing the brickwork with inky fingers. She attempted to lift her head, but her muscles were still like lead, hard and rigid and numb. Pain flickered down her ore-lines in agonising waves.

'Ah... shit. *Shit.*'

The second dose of poison had paralysed her completely. What if Ceni came back for a third go? Leven doubted she would survive it. Her heart began to beat wildly in her chest, a sour mixture of panic and fury in her blood. To die here, in this miserable place, with no answers to her questions, with no idea what had happened to Cillian and Epona or if they were even still alive. It was unthinkable. A tear crept from the corner of one eye and tracked the curve of her cheek before dropping onto the floor.

And then, something just out of sight moved. A tiny blurry shape pattered across the dirty bricks, furtive and twitching. Leven initially took it to be a rat – perhaps that would be the final indignity, for her corpse to be eaten by rats – but as it came closer she realised she recognised it. A rodenty face and a little blue cap.

'You! What... are you... doing here?'

The pixen ran towards where she lay on the ground and stopped inches from her face, so that he filled her vision. As she watched, he knelt and a tiny blue tongue flicked out, quick as a moth's wing. He was tasting her tears where they had fallen onto the floor.

Leven opened her mouth – to say what, she wasn't sure – but her breath caught in her throat. All she could do was wheeze.

And then another pixen came into sight. This one was a little more bird-like, covered in mismatched feathers. One scaly hand like a chicken's foot held an acorn cup brimming with blood.

Unable to move or protest, Leven lay still as the first creature took hold of her lower lip and yanked it firmly to one side, opening her mouth a little more. The bird-like pixen meanwhile climbed up her face, cold scaly feet pushing against the skin of her jaw and cheek; Leven could feel it very faintly, a whisper of sensation and weight. A moment later, she felt the blood being poured into her mouth, much more than could possibly have been contained in the acorn cup. She twitched once, violently, the taste of blood mineral and thick and obscenely hot, and a moment later she jerked up into a sitting position, her whole body tingling.

The pixen scattered. Leven swallowed compulsively, and warmth spread through her body, followed by a wave of stinging pins and needles.

'Ah, ouch. Thank you.'

For a moment she could see the pixen still, tiny bristling shapes against the brickwork, and then with a noise that sounded suspiciously like laughter they were gone again, vanished into the shadows. Leven sighed and tried to stand up. Her head swam woozily and black stars flickered at the edge of her vision. She fell back against the wall, bracing herself with one hand that still felt faintly numb.

'Alright, I'm getting there. I can do this.'

Half afraid, she tried to summon her sword and wings, but although her ore-lines burned, they would not come. She fought down a new surge of panic.

'You have to give yourself time,' she whispered to herself. 'Don't fly before you can walk.'

For the next few minutes, she concentrated on taking big, deep breaths, until she realised that the silence in the corridor beyond her cell had been broken. Someone was shouting, and then they were cut off.

On the stony floor there were patches of bright green moss and mustard-coloured lichen, and as Leven watched, the patches closest to the door began to grow. The moss grew thick and velvety, sprouting tiny green hairs, and the lichen seeped across the stones like something that had been spilled from a pot. And the door was changing too – the thick wooden slats were bowing and bending inwards, and as she watched they began to split apart into questing wooden tendrils. Green shoots burst out of the woodgrain. Tiny pink and white flowers, like spring blossoms, snapped open. Despite the strangeness of it, the transformation also felt oddly joyful, as though the door had been waiting all its life to reclaim its tree-ness and carry on the rhythms of the natural world.

With the straight lines of the planks that made it gone, the door was a soft, organic shape, roots and branches stretching out across the floor. A second later, Leven realised that this magic was because of Cillian – it *was* him, it couldn't be anyone else. She grinned, her heart skipping in her chest.

'Hey!' she called out. 'They'll probably make you pay for that door!'

The woody tendrils of the door split apart, and Epona stuck her head through, also grinning.

'You're alive! And on your feet – will wonders never cease. Cillian, get this hole wider so we can retrieve our Herald. And keep your voice down, you,' she added, although Leven noted that Epona wasn't exactly being quiet herself. There was a manic, desperate energy about the princess that Leven was both amused and faintly alarmed by. *What's it like to have a sister betray you? To have your sister plot against your mother?*

The roots and branches that had once been a door twisted and flexed, and the hole Epona had been poking her head through grew longer and wider. Finally Leven could see Cillian clearly; he was standing further back in the corridor, an expression of concentration on his face. Epona reached through the door and helped Leven climb over the writhing roots, and they were all together again, in the dungeon corridor.

'Are you alright?' Cillian asked tersely. He let his arms fall to his sides and the life faded from the newly re-formed door. 'Thank the Green Man that actually worked. That door is the first place in this stinking human keep I've been able to influence with my magic. There must be pixen here somewhere.'

'Oh they are definitely here,' said Leven. 'And I'm good, thank you, or at least a lot better than I was.' And she felt good – it felt good to see him, she realised. 'Why are your horns blue?'

He reached up to touch them, and the colour came away on his hands. 'It's Epona's paint,' he said, sounding slightly embarrassed. 'We had to pretend—'

'Yes, we can all talk about how clever we are when we get out of here,' said Epona rapidly. 'Can you run, Herald? Or walk quickly?'

'I think I can,' said Leven. 'But I can't summon the Titan magic. Do you... do you think the poison has destroyed it somehow?'

'We'll worry about it later,' said Epona. She grabbed Leven's arm, and the three of them moved furtively up the corridor. 'We've knocked enough guards on the head by now that it won't be long before the whole keep is looking for us. We have to get out of here.'

'How? If I could summon my sword, I could cut our way out, but...'

'I used to come up here for the summer, when I was small,' said Epona. 'Mother said it was important that I knew Galabroc as well as I knew Londus, but I spent all my time sneaking off and avoiding official duties.'

'You surprise me,' said Leven.

'I wanted to see all the bits of the keep that were off limits, and I got to know the servants' quarters fairly well. Here, at the end of this corridor, there's a door that leads up past the kitchens, and from there we can get to the stables. Hopefully. Unless they've changed things. But I don't believe so.'

Beyond the door there was a brighter, warmer corridor, the stone floor covered in a thin layer of sweet-smelling straw, and there were other good smells too: meat roasting, and bread baking. There were shadows at the far end, and Leven could hear voices – too far away to hear clearly, but they sounded relaxed, even bored. Servants in the kitchen, talking over the tasks of the day.

'What are we going to do?'

'Right,' whispered Epona. 'We're going to assume that news of my apparent treachery hasn't made it to the kitchens yet. They like to gossip down here, but remember, my sister was eager to keep me out of sight. So we're going to walk straight through those kitchens like we have every right to be there, and we're going to go to the stables, get some horses, and then fuck off out of here as fast as we can.'

'That's it? That's your plan?'

'Trust me.' Epona took her hand and squeezed it. 'Even when I was a kid the cook didn't like to tell me off. People are happy for princesses to get on with their own business, and they definitely don't like to question us. Just keep your head up, keep close, and we'll be out of here.'

Impulsively Leven lifted Epona's hand and kissed the back of it before letting go.

'Our lives are in your hands then, Princess.'

Epona looked delighted.

'Come on, heads up. Don't look guilty, and follow my lead.'

The kitchen was a large low-ceilinged room full of steam and chatter. There were servants everywhere, rushing back and forth with trays of buns or big silver pails of milk. Epona walked directly through the middle of it all, where the action was particularly frantic, and men and women in scratchy tunics or dark blue shirts skittered back from her as though she were made of glass. Leven kept close behind her, trying to concentrate on putting one foot in front of the other while her head continued to pound. Cillian walked next to her, his expression pained.

'Thank you,' she said in a low voice. She wanted to tell him how she had known it was him when the door filled with green life, but instead she cleared her throat. 'You didn't have to come find me.'

He looked at her once, his green eyes serious. 'Yes, I did. We did.'

Ahead of them, Epona had paused by a tray of jam tarts. She snatched one up and bit into it with relish.

'*So* good,' she nodded to a nearby cook, who was watching her with a worried expression. 'Galabroc always did make the best pastries, I think it's to do with the butter up here. The cows get better grass, which means you get better cream...'

She continued in this vein, not quite addressing anyone but talking enthusiastically about the quality of Galabroc's baking and dairy products, until they reached the far side of the sprawling room. Here there was a wide set of stone steps leading down into a courtyard. Two guards were standing either side of the steps, facing out towards the stables. There was a maid kneeling on the steps, scrubbing them with a horsehair brush, and she glanced up at the trio as they appeared.

'This is where it gets tricky,' Epona said under her breath. Now that they were outside, Leven could hear shouting again, and somewhere, a bell was being rung, over and over. 'We'll only get one chance at this, so walk as quickly as you can over to the stables and grab a horse. *Don't* look at the guards. If things go arse about face, *run*.'

To give credit to Epona's somewhat chaotic plan, they were halfway across the courtyard before the guards realised who they were and what they were doing. Cillian heard the chorus of shouts go up behind them, and then the three of them were running – or in Leven's case, limping rapidly – towards the stables. There were two horses in the stalls, a big bay-coloured animal with a splash of white at his socks, and a smaller grey horse. Cillian reached out to both of their minds and felt their fright and confusion crackle through him like a summer storm. The sounds in the courtyard were upsetting the animals, and they didn't appreciate three humans running towards them either. He picked the bay and shoved Leven towards it, and then when she failed to leap up onto the creature's back he grabbed her round the waist and helped to lift her up. Epona was facing the guards, her hands held up.

'You know me!' she was shouting. 'I'm Princess Epona, the queen's sister! You'll stand back and let us leave now.'

Cillian climbed up after Leven, sitting behind her, and placed his hand on the horse's flank. The animal was snorting and shaking its head, and crucially, not moving towards the stable doors. He could feel its fright and annoyance radiating out at him in waves, and to make matters worse a stable boy was approaching, a pitchfork held in both hands.

Be calm my friend, he told the horse. *There's nothing to worry about. We're just going for a run. Wouldn't you like that, to be far away from all these noisy humans?*

'Stand down!' Epona was shouting. 'That's an order!'

'Epona!' Leven leaned out over their horse's head. 'Get on the bloody horse! We have to go!'

Epona turned and waved at them frantically. 'Go! I'll follow you. My sister would never do me any real harm!'

At that moment, an arrow sprouted from the wooden wall behind them, and both horses jumped, nearly unseating them. Epona shouted again, and then she leapt backwards herself, another arrow sticking out of her shoulder. Leven yelled and made to scramble down from the horse, but Cillian looped an arm around her waist and yanked her back into place. This was all going so wrong, so quickly. Now the smell of blood was in the stables with them, and the horse's panic was almost out of control.

'Epona!' Leven yelled again, but the princess had gone down onto one knee. The guards were approaching, cautiously but steadily – no doubt they were waiting for the Herald to unleash her wings and deadly sword. Once they realised that wasn't going to happen, nothing would stop them. Cillian pictured them pulling Leven down from the horse, out of his arms, a quick glint of silver as they cut her throat.

No.

With all of his will he reached out towards the horse's mind and surrounded it. The natural panic of the animal railed and crashed against him, and he smothered it.

Obey me, he said. *Do as I say, and you will live.*

The horse went very still. Cillian could feel the limits of its mind and presence, pushing back against his. This was the border he had never crossed – the border it was forbidden to cross.

He pushed it aside and took a hold of the animal's mind.

At once, the bay surged forward, clattering past Epona and out of the stable door like a shooting star. There was a shout of alarm from the guards as the horse headed straight for them, and the archer amongst them even managed to loose another arrow – Cillian felt the wind against his cheek as it passed by – and then they were through, throwing the men and women who had come to capture them aside like skittles. In front of him, Leven gasped and threw her arms around the horse's neck.

'Hold on,' he said.

They were trying to close the gates. He commanded the horse to gallop, and it did, the enormous power of its muscles and its need to flee thrumming through his mind. It was dizzying and glorious and terrifying all at once. Tiny impressions from the horse's being flooded his own senses until it was difficult to know who he was: *the taste of old grass in his mouth, the sickening slickness of wet cobbles under his hooves, awareness of so many other animals in the courtyard, most of them with meat on their tongues and none of them trustworthy.*

But they made it through. The big bay shot through the gates at the last possible moment and they were out in the wider world again. Ahead of them, the Wild Wood waited. There were men and women on the tops of the walls still, and more arrows came, but they were *faster* than the arrows, so much more *powerful* than the arrows, *nothing* could catch them while they ran together.

Beyond the walls of the keep he felt stronger, more alive, and once the branches of trees passed over their heads again, he felt safer too. The horse was not used to being in the Wild Wood and he quickly extinguished the animal's feelings of alarm. *Tread where I tell you*, he told the horse, *and you will be safe.* He opened a Path and once they were through the horse slowed, and Leven half slid, half fell from its back, staggering into the long grass.

'We can't just run away,' she panted, wiping one shaking hand across her brow. Her face was flushed and her untidy hair was stuck to her forehead with sweat. 'We have to go back. Get Epona.'

Cillian climbed down from the horse and relinquished his hold on the animal's mind. He felt electric and strange, as though this new connection had shifted something deep inside him. He looked at Leven and the shape of her seemed to hit him in the pit of his stomach. She was looking at him strangely, her grey eyes wide with alarm.

'Are you alright?'

He nodded stiffly, but she went over to him anyway. Behind them, the horse seemed similarly stunned, and was wandering off into the undergrowth.

'I… I've done something… very wrong.' He pushed his hair back from his face. 'Ah, roots strangle me, I'm a fucking idiot.'

'No, you're not.' She cupped his face in her hands. 'Look at me. You're not.'

The touch of her fingers against his skin was maddeningly cool. He wanted, quite out of nowhere, to take her hand and kiss it, not as she had kissed Epona's hand, dry and chaste and quick – quite suddenly he wanted to do all sorts of things.

'Leven…'

From quite close by, the sound of horns broke through the forest quiet. Leven let go of him and looked around for the horse.

'Let's get to safety before we decide what our next disaster will be.'

67

The whole thing is ludicrous. It was over three hundred years ago! And the benefits of the expansion of arable land are here to see all around us. Would Mersia be the prosperous kingdom it is now without the loss of some largely worthless woodland? Would Wodencaester be the shining jewel of Brittletain without that sacrifice? It would not. And I hardly need remind you that the vast majority of Brittletain is still covered in that bloody forest, wasting useful land feeding trees that are never cut down for timber, and impeding the travel (and trade!) of every normal citizen of Mersia and beyond. But what can you do? You know as well as I that the Druin are as stubborn as the goats they steal their horns from.

Personal letter from one member of the
Mersian royal family to another, unnamed

It was raining steadily, but here in the deep of the Wild Wood the rain was only a noisy neighbour, clattering against the canopy overhead and cooling the air. Cillian had gone off the Path, but only for a moment. Above him, hopping from branch to branch, Inkwort was chastising him, her little squeaks and squawks of outrage muffled by the rainfall.

'I know,' he said. 'But I have to know for sure. It won't take me a moment.'

What he was looking for was just ahead. A small, deep pool in the wood, protected from the rain by a crowd of tall, old trees that crowded their heads together like old women gossiping: oak, alder, pine and holly. A pair of bright blue dragonflies danced and hummed over the pond's surface, which was as clear and as still as a mirror.

Cillian sat by the pool and, dipping his hand into the chilly green water, began to wash Epona's blue paint from his horns. He rubbed until his hands came away clear of the paint, and then he sat and waited for the pool to regain its perfect stillness. He tried not to think about Epona herself, injured and captured by her treacherous sister, or of Leven, who was hidden in another part of the Wild Wood, waiting for him to return from his scouting. He tried, and failed, not to think about what he might see in the pond's surface.

The water is quiet. Time to look, child.

Cillian glanced up, startled. Inkwort was watching him from the lower branches of the oak tree with her pale blue eyes.

'You speak to me so rarely I keep forgetting you're capable of it,' he said softly. The bird pecked at a branch.

You are stalling.

Cillian sighed. 'Fine.'

He leaned forward and was met with his reflection. The pond water was green, and the day was gloomy, but Cillian was used to reading the surfaces of puddles, of lakes, of ponds – even fast-moving rivers could reveal what was above and what was below. He saw his own face, etched with worry, and the curling shape of his horns, spiralling out from his untidy hair. Princess Epona's gaudy blue paint was gone, and underneath... a hint of blue, particularly at the pointed tips, the blue of cornflowers and an early spring sky. Without much hope, Cillian rubbed at the colour with his fingers, but it stayed where it was.

'That is it, then. I am thrawn after all.' He almost felt like laughing, but instead his throat grew thick, and he swallowed heavily. 'Won't Aeden be pleased? It turned out he was right. I'm not to be trusted on the Paths. Or in the Wild Wood.' Inkwort flew down from her perch and alighted on the grass near his feet. 'What will happen to me?'

He hadn't expected an answer, but Inkwort's voice inside his head was thoughtful and not unkind.

The Wild Wood is already disturbed, she said. *It will turn against you. But these are the paths you must walk, Cillianos.*

Cillian blinked. How did she know his full name? Only the Druidahnon called him that.

'What do you mean?'

But if the little bird had any further thoughts on Cillian's fate, she did not share them. She flew up into the darkened canopy and was gone. After a few moments, Cillian left the mirror-pond and headed back towards the Path.

Leven was supposed to be keeping the horse quiet, but it seemed to her that the horse wasn't in any danger of being noisy; since their hectic escape from Galabroc Keep the animal had been exceptionally docile. It simply stood where they left it, its head hanging down from its long muscular neck, its big dark eyes glassy and distant, not even bothering to clip at the grass growing in this particular nook of the Wild Wood. Instead, Leven sat on a tree stump and tried to will the Titan strength back into her ore-lines.

'Come on, you bastard,' she muttered, glaring at the blue-silver patterns that traced across her hands and arms. 'I know you're there. Stop fucking about.'

Cillian was scouting ahead, looking for safe routes through the Paths. The Atchorn; Queen Gwenith's men; soldiers from Galabroc – all were likely looking for them, and no corner of the Wild Wood would be safe for very long. Not that it would matter, if Leven could just be a Herald again... With her wings and her sword she could fly back to Galabroc Keep, drag Queen Ceni out by her hair, and kick the whole place into bloody rubble. If the strength hadn't abandoned her.

She could almost feel it there, a faint buzzing of energy under her skin, a gathering of tightness in her chest. But when she reached for it... nothing.

'Shit.' Leven stood and rubbed her hands down her trousers briskly. The pain and the paralysis caused by Queen Ceni's poison was gone. Was this effect something that would last forever? Or did this have nothing to do with the poison? Perhaps this was simply the final stage of the illness that had begun in Stratum, with visions of snow and griffins. '*Shit.*'

'Do all the creatures of the Imperium curse so much?'

A figure stepped out of the space between the trees. Her hair was a deep red-tinted brown and her horns were a pair of long, narrow spirals that burst from her temples. She was wearing worn travelling gear, and she carried a long wooden staff ringed with green paint. Leven curled her fingers into fists.

'You were the Druin at Kornwullis. You were with the rogue Druin who tried to kill us.'

The woman nodded. She was willowy and beautiful, but the look she trained on Leven was thin-lipped and tense. Leven had the idea that just looking at an Imperial soldier filled the Druin with rage.

'I am Loveday, yes. Where is Cillian? Has he come to his senses and left you here?'

Leven crossed her arms over her chest. She felt naked without the Titan strength at her fingers.

'Cillian has more honour than the rest of you put together. Where is your little gang, anyway?'

The woman came closer, walking with the stick as though she were out for a gentle stroll on a summer morning.

'As if the Imperium knows anything about honour. Butchers, murderers, thieves. That is what the Imperium is.'

'How many times do I have to tell you lot? I am not the Imperium. I am not even a Herald anymore, not really. I was discharged, along with the rest of the soldiers, and I am free to do what I please.' Leven rolled her eyes, keeping her stance as casual as possible. She knew that if she retreated from Loveday's advance, it would be obvious that something was wrong. 'You don't even *know* me. I am more than the magic that's grafted into my skin. Just like you are more than the horns growing out of your head.'

Loveday's lips twisted as though she had tasted something sour.

'How dare you speak of the Druin! You are a poison to the Wild Wood. I can feel it! The wood is furious that you are here, and it is our duty to rid it of your presence.' Leven carefully moved her weight to her back foot, giving herself the possibility of retreat. She was thinking of the things she had seen and heard since arriving in the Wild Wood – it was possible that Loveday was correct. Something did not want her here, that felt true enough. 'You have already poisoned Cillian, and for that alone I will be happy enough to kill you.'

'Poisoned him? What are you talking about?'

'When I shared minds with him—'

'When you shared *what*?'

'—it was clear that you had worked your influence on him. His mind was full of you. I could smell it. Unnatural, foreign.' The Druin wrinkled her nose. 'You are an invasive species, and you need to be eradicated.'

Leven blinked. She didn't know what to make of that. What she had noticed was that Loveday had moved into reaching distance, and she still appeared to be alone; the rest of the Atchorn had failed to appear in the gap of the trees behind her. Without giving herself too long to think about it, she jumped forward and snatched the staff from the Druin's hands, and brought it back in a wide arc, just as she would have done with her own magical glass sword. But before she could bring the staff down across the Druin woman's head, the ground underneath her feet heaved and bucked, throwing her off balance. Loveday laughed.

'You must be desperate, Herald, to try and make use of a simple wooden stick.'

Pale white and brown roots erupted from the soil like snakes, curling around Leven's ankles and shins. She gave a shout of surprise, dropping the staff, and then she was on the ground, the roots twining around her limbs and pinning her in place. It had all happened so quickly she'd barely had time to take a breath. Slowly, with an infuriatingly casual air, Loveday came to stand over her. She picked up her staff from the ground and rolled it between her palms.

'Fuck.'

'I'm no idiot, Herald. If you had access to your filthy Herald powers, I would have been dead the moment you saw me.'

Leven strained against the roots, tensing every muscle in her body, but it was like being encased in wood. The Titan strength remained out of reach, a distant flicker of feeling across her skin. Loveday, meanwhile, had placed the end of the staff against Leven's throat.

'It wouldn't take much to choke you like this,' she said quietly. 'Just a little more pressure.' She leaned on the staff, and the blunt wooden end pressed into Leven's neck. She squirmed and gasped. 'But then the fun is over too quickly.'

'You want to hurry,' said Leven, squeezing the words out with difficulty. 'My powers could return at any moment. Then see... then see how far your root tricks get you.'

Loveday smirked. From somewhere nearby, out of Leven's sight, the horse whickered and shook itself.

'What I should do is take you back to the Atchorn,' said Loveday. 'You're a symbol to them. You've become a sign of *everything* that's wrong with Brittletain today.' She waved a hand at the wider Wild Wood. 'Queens that let monsters do their errands, regardless of the crimes they've committed. Queens who have forgotten how much they owe the Wild Wood.'

'From what Cillian said, it's *you* that's forgotten the Wild Wood.' Leven tensed against the bonds again, but they only drew back tighter. 'He said you've been away too long, lost your connection.'

A spasm of fury passed over Loveday's face and was gone, as quick and as lightless as a cloud passing in front of the moon.

'I should take you back to the others, but it won't matter if I take you back a little broken. It'll make things easier in the long run, and there's always the chance you'll tell me something useful in between your screams.'

Leven forced herself to laugh, although it sounded flat and unconvincing to her own ears.

'Untie me and fight me standing up, you coward.'

Loveday smiled again, as though she were savouring a meal she'd been looking forward to for days.

'Where's the fun in that?'

The roots around Leven's arms and legs began to pulse and twist, drawing the bonds around her tighter, closer, pulling her into agonising shapes. Another looped around her neck and Leven felt the dark taste of panic in the back of her throat as her body sang with agony.

This can't be where I die.

Cillian's first clue that something was wrong was the harsh cries of Inkwort as he appeared back on the Path. The little bird was swooping frantically back and forth in front of him, making enough noise to wake the dead.

'What? What is it?' Falteringly Cillian reached out for the bird's mind, but she had gone back to shielding it from him, and he felt a quick stab of guilt. No doubt Inkwort had learned better than to trust him. 'Inkwort, what is it? Have the Atchorn found us?'

The bird fell silent then, and with a last flutter of her inky feathers, she was gone, back up into the canopy. Cillian, taking that to be a warning in itself, dropped into a crouch and moved into the undergrowth, opening his awareness to the wood around him. The small place where he had left Leven looking after the horse was just ahead. He could taste the horse's mind, still painfully raw and blank, and... something else. Something green and sharp and electric. From ahead came another cry, low and human this time, and on its heels, someone laughing. He shuffled forward until he could see into the clearing, and then held himself very still.

Loveday was there. She was standing over a prone figure on the ground. Leven was bound with vines and roots, and she lay in an unnatural position, as though some great unseen force were trying to snap her in two; an especially thick vine was curled around her throat, pressing tightly enough that Leven was gasping for air. Without thinking, Cillian stood up and blundered out of the undergrowth.

'Let her go.'

Loveday snapped around to face him, her creamy skin flush with pleasure. When she grinned at him, it made him think of how an animal bares its teeth before attacking.

'Oh, this is perfect,' she said. 'You can watch as I break your lover's back into pieces.'

'Cillian.' Leven spoke from between clenched teeth. 'Go. Open a Path and go. The rest of them will be here any minute.' She gasped as the bonds cinched tighter. 'Go!'

'She has done nothing to you.' Cillian met Loveday's eyes calmly enough. 'This isn't how you win back your connection to the Wild Wood, Loveday. Go to the Druidahnon and ask for his mercy. He might let you live. He might not even exile you.'

Loveday made a strangled noise. 'All I've done is protect Brittletain! That's all the Atchorn cares about. If you had any sense, you'd have joined me when I asked you.'

'You've betrayed the order, Loveday. You've tried to kill me, Princess Epona, and Queen Broudicca's guest.' He gestured to Leven on the ground. He was finding it curiously difficult to look at her. 'Do you think that working for Queen Ceni will save you? You're using Druin magic right now, in a way that is strictly forbidden.'

'Says the boy with thrawn-marked horns.' Loveday grinned. 'Do you ever think, Cillian, that they forbid those powers because they make us too powerful? Because if we used everything the Wild Wood gave us, we would finally take our places as the rightful rulers of Brittletain? No more queens, no more kings – just one island, covered in the Wild Wood from coast to coast.' Loveday's smile looked more natural, less of a grimace. *She truly believes this*, thought Cillian. 'I know that you understand. Sometimes we have to use the power we're given.' She nodded to the horse, which still stood facing away from them, its head down. 'You did what you had to do – you pressed your will upon that horse's soul, took control of a lower creature, as is a Druin's right. Join us, Cillian. I won't ask again.'

On the ground, Leven cried out again as the roots twisted and curled around her. They were in her hair, stretching her so that her neck was bared. When Cillian did not reply, the feverish grin dropped from Loveday's face.

'Fine,' she spat. 'Then the Imperial dog will die here, and her blood will nourish the Wild Wood.'

'No,' said Cillian quietly. 'That's not what will happen.'

Beyond the horse and the two humans, the electric green presence had solidified itself into not one Dunohi, but two, their shadowy presences watching from the edge of the trees. Before, he had lived in awe of these beings, revered them as an extension of the Wild Wood's truly alien heart – a thing that ultimately his human mind and body would never be able to completely comprehend. Now though – since he had taken a hold of the horse's mind and forced it to flee – he saw how they, too, could be grasped. You simply had to be open to the heart of the forest. *I'm sorry*, he thought. *I can't let her die. And I am already doomed.*

Feeling along the web of connections that was the Wild Wood – so open to him now, so malleable – he reached out to the forest souls. *This one has wronged you*, he told the Dunohi. *She has used the magic of the Wild Wood for violence. Take her.*

'What are you doing?' demanded Loveday. She looked around frantically. 'What are you... I can feel... Stop it!'

The Dunohi emerged from the wood, their long bone faces blank. Skeletal arms reached from the teeming foliage of their bodies, and in their eye sockets, pale green flames burned. One sported the skull of an elk, its antlers brushing the under-canopy of the trees; the other the skull of a vast wolf, jaws filled with wickedly sharp teeth. But they were hesitating, their minds fizzing with questions. *Is forbidden? We can taste? What harm? The horned one? A poison?*

'No!' cried Loveday. She dropped her staff and leapt away from Leven, but the Dunohi moved as spirits moved, through wood and bracken and earth; they swarmed on her like bees. Their strange appendages, formed of bone and branch, reached out for her tentatively. 'What are you doing?'

Is forbidden? We can taste? What harm?

Cillian sensed their reluctance as a bitter taste on his tongue. He reached out for them as he had with the horse, feeling for the slippery edges of their minds. It made him think of reaching into a pond to retrieve a stone slick with duckweed – you just had to push away your natural horror and... grab it.

Take her, he commanded. *Now.*

Loveday screamed, the shrill high sound of a wounded rabbit, and the Dunohi surged around her, bones and weeds and tendrils moving at speed, jaws snapping, the green lights in the darkness of their skulls flickering to a baleful red. There was a confused noise – bones breaking, flesh tearing perhaps – and then Loveday was lifted up into the air by the Dunohi, even as she screamed for her life, screamed for them to let her be.

'I'm sorry,' said Cillian, uncertain who he was apologising to: Loveday, the Wild Wood, the Druidahnon, or himself. 'You brought this on yourself.'

There was a frantic movement, that of a predator disembowelling its prey, and a light patter of blood against leaves. Loveday ceased her screaming, and the Dunohi took her, vanishing back into the spaces between the trees as if they had never been there at all. On the ground, the roots twisted around Leven's limbs loosened and fell apart as though they had been dead for hundreds of years. The Herald scrambled to her feet, brushing plant matter from her clothes briskly. There were livid red welts around her neck, her forearms, her wrists, and in a few places her skin had broken.

Cillian took a deep breath, disconnecting himself from the Wild Wood. The Dunohi were gone, and Loveday with them, but he could still hear them faintly in his head, like an echo.

'Are you alright?' Leven was peering at him cautiously. Her voice was hoarse. 'You've gone very pale.'

'That's what I should be asking you.' Cillian rubbed a hand over his face. 'Come on, we have to get out of here before the rest of them turn up.'

'Fine with me. But when I get my Titan magic back, I'm going to seek out every one of those Atchorn bastards and find out how they like to be dropped from a great height onto a collection of very pointy stones...' Leven stopped, her eyes growing wide. 'Is it me, or has this place gotten very dark all of a sudden?'

It was true. The shadows between the trees had grown deep and inky, and the constant background noise of the forest – the bees, birdsong, the chattering of squirrels and magpies – all of it had fallen silent. A deep and unfriendly cold was pooling up around their ankles like a sudden winter mist. Somewhere up above them, Inkwort gave several mournful cries.

I knew there would be consequences, thought Cillian. *I have commanded the very heart of the Wild Wood, and it will hate me for it. I've poisoned my home, my own heart. I have lost everything.*

'Come on,' he said again. His voice felt perilously close to breaking. 'We should get moving.'

'What about the horse?'

'Let him go,' said Cillian wearily. 'Let him have his freedom. It's the least I owe him.'

68

They sat down around the small campfire, which Kaeto relit. Tyleigh still had the severed horns in her hands, and she turned them over continually as she spoke. Felldir lurked at the edge of the light, apparently uncertain if he should stay or leave.

'I don't know why I've kept them with me,' she said. By this time the sun had set, and their fire was the only light, blotting out the stars. 'It always felt wrong to leave them behind, somehow. They were a part of my body once, a part of me, one I carried for years. Or maybe it's just because they are technically magical artefacts, and I knew they had to be useful one day. If anything, it's stranger that the Druin let me take them with me when they banished me.'

Kaeto shook his head impatiently. It was taking all of his willpower to sit by the campfire when he could be down in the Undertomb searching for Belise.

'You are from Brittletain, then,' he said tersely. 'How is it I did not know that? I have read the file the empress keeps on you many times.'

Tyleigh shrugged. 'Fabricated. The Imperium found me too useful to look too deeply into where I was really from.' She hesitated a moment, and then reached up and pulled off the headband she habitually wore across her forehead. With it gone, it was possible to see the flat discs of bone that rose just clear of her hairline. She reached up and tapped one with her finger. Kaeto felt a sick kind of laughter brewing in his chest. How could he have been so blind? It seemed it was easy to hide secrets under a veneer of eccentricity. 'I could have told you all so much about the mysterious nation of Brittletain, but it suited me not to.'

Kaeto took note of the use of past tense, but said nothing. Tyleigh continued.

'I was born in one of the poorer regions of the kingdom of Mersia, a place with a, uh, difficult relationship with the Druin. Being a Druin doesn't carry the same weight or respect there as it does across the rest of Brittletain. Not that I ever gave a shit about that. I was drawn to the Wild Wood, and when I heard stories about the horned men and women that acted as its protectors and rangers, I knew that was what I had to do. I don't remember much of my mother and father – they were farmers. Parochial, tedious. Unimaginative. I left for Dosraiche as soon as I was old enough to make the journey.'

'The Druin city.'

'Not a city as the Imperium knows them. At first I was enchanted with it all. The vast living tree where we lived and trained, the secrets we were given charge of. I was even impressed with the Druidahnon.' At this she glanced across the fire at Felldir, but if he had an opinion on his ancient enemy, it didn't show on his face. 'He is quite a sight, and once, very wise. I learned how to open the secret Paths that crisscross the Wild Wood, how to listen and see with the senses of animals and plants, how to tap into the green energy of the place and manipulate it, and how to communicate with the forest souls, which they call the Dunohi. But then, when I knew all this and had mastered it... my education stopped.'

'They stopped teaching you?'

'The elders said there was no more to learn, which was ludicrous.' Tyleigh gave a short laugh, still bitterly amused decades later. 'I could see for myself that there was untapped power everywhere in the Wild Wood. I could feel it in my bones. Once you're joined to the forest, they say that what runs through your veins is more sap than blood, and it infuriated me, to have all that power sitting just out of reach.

They had ridiculous restrictions on the Druin abilities, things that were strictly forbidden even though they were obviously the natural progression of what we could do. I was particularly fascinated with the Dunohi, living projections of the interior life of the wood. Imagine what they could tell us! Imagine what they could unlock. I began to walk the Paths alone, at night. I visited the Lich-Way, and questioned the creatures that called that place home.'

'The what?'

Tyleigh flapped a hand impatiently. 'It doesn't matter, you wouldn't understand. I sought out the Dunohi and tracked them, learned their patterns and learned how to speak to them. Eventually I realised they were just like animals, really. Simple-minded, easy to command if you just pushed hard enough.'

Despite everything else occupying him, Kaeto felt a cold chill work its way down his spine.

'Commanding these Dunohi was one of the things that was strictly forbidden?'

'Yes. Forcing a Dunohi to your will is like... desecrating one of the Imperium's Star Temples. Unthinkable. Which is *stupid*.' Tyleigh rubbed her fingers over the ridges of her severed horns. 'They call it going thrawn. They have a lot of very hysterical lore around the idea. It was risky, but all great things come with an element of risk. And then, one day, my luck ran out.' She lifted her hands and dropped them into her lap. 'I had three of the forest souls under my command, and somehow one of them broke free and went wild, which sent the other two into a frenzy. Annoyingly there were other Druin nearby, and it is true that the Dunohi can be dangerous. A couple of idiots got themselves killed and I was exiled from Dosraiche and the Druin order. They severed my horns and I headed north, until I came to the very edge of the Wild Wood, the area that borders griffin territory. I made a new life for myself, made a couple more mistakes, and then I began to have ideas about the Titans themselves, and how their power might be gained. But what I want to know,' she turned then and raised her chin at Felldir, 'is how you knew what I was. That's why you didn't kill us, isn't it? Because you needed Druin magic.'

The winged figure at the edge of their firelight shifted. It took him a moment to speak, and Kaeto was reminded that Felldir had likely spent centuries in silence.

'I can smell him on you, the Druidahnon,' the Titan said eventually. 'Cutting your horns off doesn't remove his presence in your blood.'

'Hmm,' said Tyleigh. 'How curious.'

'And that's the point, isn't it?' said Kaeto sharply. 'Can you still do the Druin magic? Can you set Icaraine the Lightbringer free?'

'Those are two very different questions, Envoy. If you had asked me yesterday if I could perform Druin magic, I would have thought you were making a poor joke. But if he can smell the magic on me,' she jerked her head at Felldir, 'then it must still be there somewhere. As for setting Icaraine free? That seems to me like an especially idiotic idea. She must have been exceptionally dangerous for the Druidahnon to be moved to use thrawn magic.'

Kaeto chose his words carefully. The urge to grab Tyleigh and shake her was stronger than ever.

'But you heard her down there. If we set her free, she will give us Belise back.'

Tyleigh looked at him like he was mad. 'You would believe that creature? Is it possible, Envoy, that you are even more stupid than you look? No. We must proceed slowly, carefully. I won't let power be taken away from me again because I was impatient. And certainly not because *you* are impatient.'

Kaeto stood up. He couldn't keep still a moment longer. 'And what about you?' He turned to Felldir. 'She has just said she will not release your... priestess, or whatever she is. What are you going to do about it?'

Felldir's face was unreadable. 'Your choices are your own,' he said eventually. 'I was told to kill all who entered the Black City, save for those with the blood of the Druidahnon. That is all I was told to do, and it is all I will do.'

'This is fucking ridiculous!' Kaeto threw his arms up in exasperation even as a cold hand tightened around his heart. 'My – Belise is down there, right now, trapped, and neither of you will help me get her out.'

'You're here to help *me*, Envoy,' Tyleigh said coldly. 'Those are the orders the empress gave you. Perhaps you should have a think about that.'

The wind picked up, pushing their small fire into erratic shapes and casting strange shadows all around. Kaeto felt the reassuring weight of the throwing knife at his wrist, imagined the satisfaction of watching as the blade split Gynid Tyleigh's throat open to the night. But then any chance of finding Belise would be lost entirely.

Instead he took a slow breath in through his nostrils, and sat once more in front of the fire, folding his hands in his lap neatly.

'You are quite correct, Crafter Tyleigh,' he said in a colourless voice. 'Tell me then, how I can best help you with the next part of your endeavour.'

Later, in the deepest part of the night when Tyleigh was sleeping soundly and Felldir had vanished back off to his own haunts, Kaeto went back to the door and down again into the Undertomb. His heart was in his mouth as he made his way down the spiral staircase. He was half convinced he would just look up and see her – Belise wading her way out of the teeming beetles with a faintly disgusted look on her face. She'd lost her footing, that was all, and fallen down inside some unseen nook in the floor of the cavern. But when he reached the bottom, all was as it had been when he'd left it. Hundreds of thousands of beetles busily crawling over the floor, the ceiling, the walls, intent on the strange duty they had been performing for thousands of years. He went to the edge of the beetle sea and stood looking out across them. Points of greenish-blue and yellow light swarmed and dipped in the echoing space.

'I am here,' he called out across the living expanse. 'Tell me what I should do to free you.'

69

Kneeling in the frigid water, Ynis lifted her head to watch the movements of two of the fainter fate-ties as they floated off towards the west. The thickest, strongest fate-tie – blood red against the colourless clouds – still marched away to the south, but for once she could not take her eyes from the others. The ones that ended, somewhere across the mountains, with her fathers, deep in the heart of Yelvynia.

Somewhere, T'vor and Flayn were going about their lives, hunting and flying and resting, while their daughters were lost to them. If T'rook died, and Ynis died trying to reach her, would anyone ever tell them what had happened? No Edge Walker would, and perhaps that was for the best. She didn't like to think of the pain it would cause their fathers, to know that they had both died in such stupid, pointless ways.

'You can see them still?'

Festus's sharp voice by her ear startled her. The wavering fate-ties that looped up into the sky shivered and vanished.

'I can,' she said. 'T'rook's fate-tie still leads to the south. My fathers.' Ynis lifted a trembling hand to point. 'They lie over that mountain. We are truly in the heart of Yelvynia now.'

'Hmm.' Festus hooked his strong beak over the back of her shirt and gave it a sharp yank. 'Out of the water, human. You should dry before we travel further.'

They had long since left behind the ice and snow of the Bone Fall, and were deep into the milder lands of Yelvynia. Snow-covered mountains still loomed over them as they flew, but the land they camped on each night was soft with grass, and the air itself was much milder; in comparison to the Bone Fall, it was practically warm. All of which meant it was difficult for Ynis to reach the state of near-death that allowed her to see the fate-ties clearly. They had taken to seeking out small streams or tarns where she could kneel in the water, letting it seep into her clothes and chill her to the bone.

With Festus's help, Ynis stumbled to her feet, wincing at the wave of pins and needles that spread through her numbed feet and legs. Some distance away she had made a fire, and she shuffled towards it blearily.

'I'm not sure how much longer you can keep this up,' said Festus when she had settled by the little fire, her hands held out towards the warmth. 'You grow weaker by the day.'

'No I don't.' Ynis cuffed a hand across her running nose. She could feel the warmth against her face, but her body would not stop shaking. 'I would like to go and see my fathers. I'd like to see them, in our nest-pit.' She was aware that she was rambling, but for the last few days she had existed in a near constant dream state, and it was impossible to stop. 'They kept me and raised me, despite everything. Can you believe that?'

Festus had settled by the fire too. He was watching her carefully.

'It is certainly difficult to believe that any griffin could be so foolish, but here we are,' he said dryly. 'Whatever possessed them to do such a thing?'

'They said I was a mystery, and Flayn knew that my fate was tied to theirs. He wasn't... he wasn't a witch-seer, or anything like that, but he is claw clan, and they are closer to these things. Aren't you? That's what T'vor has always said. He did not want to believe it either, but when they brought me home to the nest, T'rook took to me straight away. She preened my hair and she... she didn't eat me...'

Ynis shuddered violently, and the bright little fire seemed to dim and shiver in front of her eyes.

'It would likely have been better for all of you if she had,' said Festus. He had turned away from her to preen his long flight feathers, scouring them of dust and dirt with the flat edge of his beak. 'Humans do not belong in Yelvynia.'

'I want to go and see them,' Ynis said softly. 'Our fathers. Just for a little while. To rest in the nest-pit, while they talk over our heads, like they did when we were yenlin. Do you remember, sister? When the winter winds were blowing they would crouch over us, so that it was always warm...'

'Arrow? Arrow, what are you talking about?'

Something hard struck Ynis from one side, and she pitched awkwardly into the grass. Festus was standing over her, the feathers on his neck puffed out with fright.

'You're rambling, talking to those who aren't there.' He shook his head. 'I was an idiot to come with you. Edge Walker business is the business of death, and here I am, following a scent I cannot smell with a human, of all things. I should probably just eat you.'

Ynis got to her feet and brushed herself down. She thought of how Frost had spoken to Festus when they had first gone to help his father pass away.

'You won't eat me,' she said firmly. 'You will help me, because you're a good griffin and because T'rook needs your help too. Am I right?'

A chill wind blew up, rippling the water of the tarn and sending a cold hand down Ynis's back. She felt exhausted and ill, worn away to a tiny sliver of her yost, but Festus was looking at her with a kind of quiet awe and respect, and that alone made her smile.

'I thought so. Let me dry off, and we'll fly again.'

70

On the question of the border between Galabroc and Yelvynia I think we have pushed it as far as we can, your majesty. We've had people out there every year moving the marker stones back, building small settlements as far north as we can, to the point where we have a few scattered in the foothills of the Spine itself, but there does appear to be a limit to it. Push the settlements too far, as we did with the ill-fated Crow's Foot settlement, and the griffins will act swiftly to wipe it out. It was a tiny loss in the grand scheme of things, around seventy men and women who were desperate enough to try and make homes so close to Yelvynia, but it's not the only one. Men and women who scout far enough in that direction don't return, and it's not hard to figure out what's picking them off. It pains me to say it, but Galabroc has expanded as far north as it is able.

Official report from Galabroc's
chief advisor to the queen

'Keep down,' hissed Cillian. 'It's hunting us.'

Leven lay in the undergrowth, the Druin crouched beside her. It was still cold, and much too dark for the time of day, and around them there was a thick, persistent mist, but through the thistles and the foliage she could just about make out one of the forest souls moving between the trees. Its long bony face was sweeping back and forth, the empty eye sockets clearly looking for them as it crept along. Around them the forest itself was silent; no birds sang and even the sound of insects was absent.

'Why?' she whispered back, although she knew why.

'We'll wait for it to pass,' he said, ignoring her question. 'And then we keep heading north.'

Since Cillian had used his magic to command the Dunohi, the Wild Wood had turned against them. The ground underfoot turned to mud, thick and deep and sticking to their boots; mists came and went at random, covering the Paths with a fog so impenetrable that even Cillian struggled to find the way; at night the temperature dropped alarmingly, and every morning they woke stiff with cold, frost rime on their hair, on their clothes, their eyelashes frozen. The creatures of the wood were, as one, unfriendly – twice now they had been attacked by foxes in their sleep, and throughout the day they kept to the shade, to avoid being bombarded by whatever birds might spot them from above. The day before a wolf had slipped out of the shadows, black lips peeling back to reveal sharp yellow teeth, and Leven had felt the loss of her Titan powers keenly. Cillian's wood magic had saved them, but the fear had stayed with the pair of them throughout the rest of that day. It was a miserable and, Leven had to admit, even a frightening experience, and even worse, Cillian was clearly devastated by it. The home he had known and loved all his life had turned him out. They headed north now to get out of the Wild Wood. The trees were no longer safe.

In time, the Dunohi moved off down the Path and vanished. Leven and Cillian stayed where they were for a little longer in case it should come back.

'There,' Cillian said eventually. He stood up and moved cautiously back onto the Path. 'I think it's safe again. Or as safe as it's going to get, anyway.'

Leven followed him out, glancing down at her hands as she did. Her ore-lines no longer felt numb, and she could almost feel the power waiting there to be summoned… yet still, when she called for them, the sword and the wings would not come. Cillian saw where she looked, and gave her a weary smile.

'It'll come back,' he said. 'You're still healing.'

'If it could come back in time for me to be of some use, that would be great.' She turned on the Path, looking around. 'Do you hear something?'

Cillian grabbed her arm. 'Quick, back into the trees—'

At that moment, a pair of horses leapt out onto the Path ahead of them, ridden by two soldiers dressed in the livery of Galabroc and accompanied by a member of the Atchorn, who was on foot. Instinctively, Leven summoned the Herald magic and just for the barest second her sword was there, flickering and ice-like in the gloom of the woods... and then it was gone again.

'Fuck. I lit us up like a comet.'

'There they are!' The two riders were urging their horses towards them. 'Stop, in the name of Queen Ceni!'

'Queen Ceni is a traitor!' Leven shook her hands, willing the ore-lines to come to life. 'And frankly, a terrible host.'

'Get back.' Cillian moved to stand in front of her. 'Let us go.'

'Or you'll do what, Blue Horn?' jeered the Druin. He was a tall, fearsome-looking man with the antlers of a buck deer, wide and sharp. His neck and shoulders were thick with muscle. 'Give yourselves up and perhaps you'll be granted the mercy of a swift execution.'

'I don't want to do this,' said Cillian. There was sweat standing out on his forehead. '*Please*. Don't make me.'

'We take them here,' snapped the Druin to the soldiers. 'Don't let them move away or he'll open another Path.'

The horses surged forward, and Cillian raised his hands again. For a moment, there was a blankness behind his eyes that was frightening, and then the horses were rearing up, screaming and rolling their own eyes up to the whites. The soldiers cried out, and then one of the horses charged wildly to the side, colliding with the Druin and trampling him underfoot. There was a ragged scream as hoof met flesh, and Cillian dropped his arms, an expression of despair on his face.

'Come on!' Leven grabbed his hand where it lay at his side and squeezed it. 'Don't let that be for nothing. Let's get out of here.'

His green eyes met hers, and some light that had been missing came back into them. Together they ran back down the Path, and as they did the space ahead of them shifted and twisted. Behind them the soldiers were shouting, trying to get their horses back under control, and then they were gone into some other part of the day.

'I can't go back.'

It was night time, and they had left the edge of the Wild Wood behind them. They sat together on the slope of a foothill, thickly covered in deep green moss and a lush kind of grass Leven had never seen before. Below them, the Wild Wood was a great dark sea, a mass that shifted and whispered with the wind.

'You'll go back eventually,' said Leven. 'When all this is sorted out. We'll get Epona back, and Queen Ceni will be exposed for the viper she is, and...' Her voice trailed off.

'It doesn't seem very likely, does it?' said Cillian drily. 'And that's only half the problem. I have used thrawn magic. Even if I could go back to Dosraiche, even if I could make it back to the Mother Oak without the forest killing me, I would be exiled. The Wild Wood has simply saved them time by exiling me itself.'

'Stars' arses, what a mess.' Leven lifted her face to the night sky, and her breath stopped. It was a clear night, the deep indigo of the sky scattered thickly with stars, and far above them was a shimmering curtain of blue and green light. It flickered and flowed like some ethereal piece of silk caught in the wind. 'What is that?' she asked, hardly daring to breathe. Next to her, Cillian smiled.

'The Northern Lights,' he said. 'We, that is, the Druin, call it the Caul of Stars.'

'It's beautiful,' she said. 'It *looks* like how Herald magic *feels*. Is it magic? Is it linked to the Titans in some way?'

'I don't know,' Cillian said quietly. 'We're technically in griffin territory now, so it could be.' He looked at her then. 'It certainly looks like magic to me.'

'Amazing.' She grinned. 'You know, despite everything, I'm glad I came here. I'm glad I am here, to see this incredible thing. With you.' She pushed her hand through her hair, uncertain what she was talking about. 'Listen. You're right, my Herald powers are coming back – slowly, but I can feel the difference. I think, in a few days perhaps, I will be strong enough to fly again, and I will go to Broudicca and explain what has happened. I think I can make it, you know, flying in short bursts, only stopping in the Wild Wood when I have to. You can stay here, in hiding, until I've got it all sorted out. I know you think you've got no way back, but it's me they hate. Me they don't trust. I will tell them that you are innocent of all of it, and I think they will forget, and take you back. You're one of their own, after all. And I'm the evil Imperial agent. They will blame me. With Broudicca's help, we can get Epona back. And...' Leven paused. She wasn't at all sure she would be allowed to leave the island alive, with everything that had happened, but she didn't want to talk about that. 'And we'll see what happens from there.'

For a long moment, Cillian said nothing at all. Next to him on the downy moss, Leven fidgeted.

'Well? What do you think? It's a better plan than anything else we've got.'

'It won't work,' said Cillian.

'Why not?'

'Because, despite everything, I'm glad you came here too. Because...' He paused and laughed a little. 'Loveday thought that you had poisoned my mind, do you know that?'

'She mentioned something about it while she was strangling me.'

'There is a thing that Druin can do, a kind of sharing of minds. When we were in Kornwullis, Loveday came to me and asked for it.

From me.' Cillian cleared his throat. It was dark and Leven couldn't be sure, but she thought he was blushing.

'I'm guessing this is… an intimate thing?' Leven felt her own cheeks grow hot.

'It can be,' he said. 'We share our impressions and memories of the Wild Wood. It deepens the bonds between Druin, and between us and the wood. I showed her only a little of what we had seen and experienced, and when I didn't want to… share any further, she claimed that all my memories and impressions were tainted with you. That you were a constant in the background of my mind. All my thoughts leading back to you, as all the Paths lead back to the Mother Oak.'

'What are you talking about?'

'Loveday was many things, but she wasn't wrong about that. I can't let you go back to Londus alone, Leven. I can't let you do this heroic sacrifice nonsense you're clearly planning. Because… I need you. Like rain in the wood.'

Leven swallowed. Her heart was beating very fast. She felt how she had felt jumping from the cliff in Unblessed Lamabet, the air too quick to fill her lungs and something huge coming to lift her up.

Cillian stood up and turned away from her, shaking his head slightly. He laughed again. 'I half think I'm going mad – it surely has to be madness to tell you – but that is one thing I'm pretty sure about. Roots curse me, I've lost my home and I've poisoned my magic, but I'm still glad to be here in the arse end of nowhere with you.'

Leven got to her feet and turned him to face her. His skin was lit with the eldritch glow of the Northern Lights, and he looked uncertain, almost afraid. Suddenly it seemed to her that the mystery that had been growing inside her for the last few weeks had an answer. She had never been so certain.

'You idiot,' she said, and kissed him.

He tasted how the trees felt, and the warmth of his mouth and his body was the purest joy she had known in a long time. They lay together in the long grass, abruptly feverish with desire. When he pulled her shirt off, he paused to trace the ore-lines that ran down her arms and across her chest and stomach, first with his fingers and then with his mouth. It seemed to her that it took an age to get all his clothes off – the cloak and the leather and the belts and the shirt – and then when finally she could run her own hands over his skin she was delighted to find it tanned and supple, crisscrossed here and there with a constellation of scars. It was cold under the Caul of Stars, but they hardly felt it. Once or twice, particularly when she eventually lay beneath him, as vulnerable as she had ever been, she wondered if what they were doing was wise – there had to be a hundred people out for their blood, after all. But his mouth and hands chased all thought away, and when he hesitated, just for a moment, his green eyes seeking permission, she slid her hands down his gloriously naked back and pulled him flush with the centre of her.

'I think I love you,' she murmured into his ear. 'Pair of idiots that we are.'

71

Leven and Cillian headed further north, and the further they went the colder it got, and the more barren the landscape. There was grass, and rocks covered in moss and lichen, and looming over them were purple mountains topped with snow, but the trees fell away almost entirely, and Leven began to notice a lack of wildlife too. Whereas the Wild Wood had teemed with foxes, rabbits, squirrels, stoats and more, here, in the far north beyond Galabroc, they saw only the odd bird flying high in the changeable skies and the occasional hare, slender and fleetfooted. Cillian's jackdaw kept pace with them, but even she seemed skittish, as though she were afraid of the open country and lack of cover. On the second day in that cold place, Cillian paused by a yellow rock, which he nudged gently with his boot.

'Look at that,' he said. 'We're truly in griffin territory now.'

Leven did look, and then she grimaced. It wasn't a rock at all, but a human skull, peering blindly up at the blue sky. A few feet away there was another one, its lower jaw missing.

'Where's the rest of the body?'

'Ground up between beaks as hard as mountains, I imagine.' Cillian smiled lopsidedly at the look on her face. 'They eat the juicy parts, and then they like to drop the skulls along the border of Yelvynia, or so I've heard. A warning to us to keep out.'

Leven stood up straight and scanned the tops of the mountains.

'Yet here we are, marching right across their decorative skull borders. Epona would love this.' She smiled, thinking of their friend, and then her smile faded. 'I hope she's giving Ceni trouble, at least.'

'We just need to go far enough that we can be sure the queen's forces won't follow us,' said Cillian. 'It's dangerous, but...'

He did not need to say it. Yelvynia was dangerous, but so, now, was the Wild Wood.

'Do you think we'll see any? Griffins, I mean?' Leven was thinking again of the scraps of memory she had regained walking the paths of Brittletain. They had contained the flying Titans too.

'Maybe.' Cillian brushed some dirt from the face of the skull and stood up. 'Let's hope not. Keep an eye out.'

When the griffin came, though, it took them both unawares.

It was the time of day that Cillian referred to as 'owl-light', when the sun was just dipping below the horizon and everything had become still and eerily quiet. Shadows were beginning to creep across the foothills, and as the light dropped away it grew colder quickly, so that Leven was starting to think quite seriously about a campfire, a bed roll, and perhaps other things too – when a movement off to her left caught her eye. She turned, assuming it was simply Inkwort making her last circuits of the night and saw instead a vision of avian lethality dropping out of the sky towards them.

'Cillian!'

It moved so quickly and so silently it was like a thing from a nightmare. Cillian, who had been walking just ahead of Leven with his head bent in thought, threw himself out of the way a fraction of a second before the griffin's talons smashed into the earth, digging up great dark furrows in the dirt and stone. Leven ran towards him and was pushed bodily back by the wind from the creature as it swept back up into the air again. Finally, the griffin broke its silence with a deafening screech.

'Fuck.' She reached Cillian and grabbed him, dragging him up from the ground. 'There's no cover.'

'Can you summon your sword?'

'I... *fuck.*' Leven held out her hands, and the ore-lines were tingling, but still she couldn't summon the blade. 'What about you? Can you tell it to piss off? *Command* it to piss off?' She crouched next to Cillian, watching as the Titan turned around in the sky, preparing to make another pass.

'No!' Cillian sounded horrified by the idea. 'I can't influence a Titan's mind, and there's no animal around here big enough to—'

The griffin dove a second time and, on this strike, connected with the pair of them, knocking them both to the ground like skittles. Leven rolled, gasping to get her breath back, and scrambled up just in time to see the griffin, all four feet on the ground, turning to snap at Cillian where he lay. Cillian raised an arm to ward off the blow and Leven could only watch as the griffin's beak slashed neatly through the tough leather of his vambrace. He looked so small, beneath the thing, and the griffin's copper-coloured eyes were glassy with fury. Leven felt an entirely new fear reach up and close around her heart.

'No,' she murmured. '*Not him.*'

Leven ran, arms wide and screaming at the top of her lungs, with no thought in her head but to get between the griffin and Cillian, and the Titan looked up, startled by her approach. Dimly, Leven was aware of a surge of electricity through her ore-lines and then she was flying, a missile catapulted from the ground directly into the flank of the huge beast. She and the griffin went rolling across the dirt together, Leven's mouth and nose full of the creature's musky stink – somehow, she was still screaming – and then the creature threw her off, spinning into the air.

'Ground-stuck stone-licker!' shrieked the griffin. 'You dare?'

'I absolutely bloody dare,' cried Leven, half laughing. She spread her glassy blue wings, exalting in the feeling of being in the air again, and summoned the blade to her hand. But as fast as she was, and as powerful as she felt, the griffin was faster. Before she could even bring the sword around she was slammed near out of the sky. Spinning madly in a flurry of feathers as long as her arm, Leven crashed into the ground and rolled several feet before she came to a stop.

'Leven!'

She caught one glimpse of Cillian's face, white with shock and smeared with mud, and the griffin was on her again. This time she managed to get her blade between her and its talons, and she was pushed back through the dirt, her heels kicking up ridges in the hard ground.

'Get off me, you bastard!'

'I will eat your guts, tiny trespassing human, and I will shit on your bones! And then I will feed your mate to my yenlin!'

The griffin lunged, its beak clapping shut inches from Leven's ear, and she felt her knees beginning to quake under the sheer weight of the thing.

Perhaps this is what I saw in the end, she thought wildly. *Not my past, but my future. Torn to bits by a griffin in the arse end of nowhere.*

Leven began to laugh, which only infuriated the griffin more.

'What is so funny, prey creature? Do you—?'

A brown and blue blur collided with the griffin, moving at such a speed that Leven was thrown ten feet across the foothill. When she'd figured out which way was up again, she looked up to see another griffin fighting with the first one – a powerful beast with bright feathers and eyes as green as grass. Incredibly, there was a small human figure clinging to its back, screaming her own oaths at their opponent. Leven stood, mouth hanging open. Cillian grabbed her hand and kissed it fiercely.

'Are you alright?'

'I'm great,' she said, still watching the fight. 'But what is happening up there?'

The new griffin was winning. As they watched, it cuffed the smaller griffin with a huge paw, and then snapped at its legs with its powerful beak. The lesser griffin dipped and fell away, before hovering in the air, clearly considering whether the meal of scrawny humans was worth the effort. The blue and brown griffin – and, incredibly, the human figure on its back – screeched with fury at the creature until, finally, it turned tail and fled. In moments it was lost over the hills and in the growing darkness.

'So,' Leven nodded as the new griffin dropped to the ground, wings folding away neatly along its back, 'did we just win the opportunity to be eaten by a different griffin? What do you think?'

'I do not know,' Cillian said in a low voice. 'None of this makes any sense to me.'

The human passenger climbed down from the griffin's back and made her way towards them. She looked to be around sixteen or seventeen years old, dark hair pulled back from her face in braids woven with feathers and tiny bones. Her skin was the tawny brown of someone who had spent almost their entire life outside, and she had sharp grey eyes, which she narrowed at them as she grew closer. She was wearing a strange patchy outfit of fur and leather, and on a leather cord around her neck hung a long dark arrowhead that was instantly familiar to Leven. In her hand she carried a lethal-looking curved dagger, clearly made from a griffin's claw.

And her face... Leven had rarely seen such an expression of combined fury and anguish. The girl walked right up to her and brandished the dagger, tears standing out as clear as diamonds in her eyes.

'Who are you?' demanded the girl. 'And why does my fate-tie lead to you?'

72

The order of the Druin have lost their way. Forgive me, but our lord the Druidahnon has lost his way. Tell me truthfully – what do your rangers and path-walkers spend most of their days doing, Elder Kirka? I know well enough, because I have seen it myself every day: the Druin are shepherds for merchants who need to travel through the Wild Wood, for travellers and common people and jumped-up nobility. None of them really know the importance of the Wild Wood, none of them comprehend the powers that are at the Druin's fingertips. Instead they regard us as servants, slaves even, maids to scamper back and forth at their command, when in truth we are the true lords of the Wild Wood. The true lords of Brittletain. The Druidahnon is old beyond reckoning, and he has forgotten the days of his own glory – and so he expects us to fade into obscurity too. Brittletain has too many queens, and not enough trees. Let us return to the wild.

A letter to Elder Kirka, signed
only with 'The Atchorn'

Outside the walls of the Black City the busy life of the jungle continued. Beetles and other insects crawled and buzzed, birds called from tree to tree, their voices liquid and strange. From some distance away the call of something like a wild cat came over and over, low and unsettling, while a breeze that barely troubled the lightest leaves drowsily moved the thick air around. Kaeto paused in his work to glare at it all.

Finding the right plant had been easy, but extracting the thick bulb at the bottom of the slender stem was less so. He could follow the plant down to where it met the black soil, and he could dig down into the ground with his knife, but every time the roots snapped before he found the bulb. He knew he was being impatient and not taking the care he normally would, but he didn't have time to be annoyed with himself. He found another plant and tried again.

He became aware of Felldir's presence when the section of jungle behind him grew oddly silent – no insects buzzed, no birds sang. Even the wind seemed to die down. Kaeto sighed and slipped the extracted bulb into an interior pocket.

'What do you want?'

'I thought I should speak to you,' said Felldir. Outside of the Black City his pale form looked even more like an extravagant statue brought to life. 'To explain.'

Kaeto stood up. 'You don't have to explain anything to me.'

'No. You are right. I do not understand why I feel like I should. A human is nothing, beneath notice...' His voice grew quiet. 'But you brought me wine and cheese. Kindness, after hundreds of years of feral solitude. You were the first person I had spoken to in an age.'

'Belise brought you the wine,' said Kaeto, unable to keep the chill from his voice. 'She poured it for you.'

'Yes,' Felldir agreed, simply enough. For some time neither of them spoke. Kaeto, with his main task complete, began picking fruit from a nearby bush – whatever was happening in the Black City, they still needed to eat. Eventually, Felldir cleared his throat.

'When the Druidahnon cast his spell over the Black City, I was the only one to escape. So I waited, with Icaraine's orders, for hundreds and hundreds of years.'

'I know that already,' Kaeto said. The fruits were staining his fingers purple.

'I have been isolated. That long alone… turns you in on yourself. You have a lot of time to think, and then eventually it becomes easier not to think at all. But I suspect that underneath, your soul keeps turning over the same questions regardless.' He faltered. 'Am I making sense?'

'No.'

'I have yearned for them, for my people to return, for so long. For so long I'm not sure I know how to feel another way. You can't know what it's like, to be so entirely alone without another person that looks or thinks like you.'

'Hmm.' There were more fruits on the next bush, so Kaeto moved along. When Belise returned, she'd be hungry, upset. She would need to eat.

'I knew what I had to do. I had simply to wait, until someone capable of the magic I needed came to this place, and then I would capture them, and get them to release all of my people, including Icaraine. And then when it finally happened… I just watched you from a distance. I watched you move around the city, and I did nothing. It was as though after a thousand years of waiting, I had turned into a statue myself, unable to act.'

'I wouldn't say that you did nothing.' Kaeto turned to face the Titan finally. Clearly he wasn't going to leave. 'You killed Riz.'

Felldir nodded. 'He was not who I needed, so I let my instincts take over.'

'Instincts.' Kaeto felt strange, light-headed. He knew that provoking the Titan was stupid, even lethal behaviour, and he knew also that if anyone had the moral authority to make judgements on the taking of lives, it certainly wasn't him. But he was angry and frightened, and those feelings had nowhere else to go. 'Are all your people so bloodthirsty? It sounds as though the Druidahnon was right to wipe you from the face of Enonah. Tyleigh, you realise, has no intention of letting your high priestess out of her prison, despite what… what has happened to Belise. What do you think of that, then? Will you kill her too?'

'She is the last person I can kill.'

'Torture her then. In my profession, we have whole books on the correct and most efficient way to extract information from a prisoner. Slowly pushing iron pins under the fingernails. Burning the soles of the feet. Putting out one eye. There is an elegant process where you lay a cloth over the prisoner's face, and then pour water over it. Sounds like nothing, but it's quite horrific, I promise you.' He rubbed a hand across his forehead, wiping away sweat dotted with plant matter. 'There was an Envoy a century ago who devised a variety of tortures all involving ants and honey. He was quite fixated on them, if you ask me. The problem with that, as I have explained to the Imperator several times, is finding the ants, or cultivating them. Who has the time, when a wet cloth over the face is so effective?' He met Felldir's eye. 'I could assist you, if you would like.'

'For the sake of your little girl.'

The phrase almost seemed to stop his heart in his chest, but Kaeto swallowed past it and forced himself to smile grimly.

'For her, yes. But you won't, will you? Won't kill Tyleigh, won't force her to do anything. Why?'

Felldir took a moment to answer. The Titan didn't sweat, Kaeto noticed, and did not seem at all discomforted by the relentless sun, despite his pale skin and white hair. *A person so fair in Stratum would get sunstroke*, he thought.

'For the same reason that I wouldn't have stopped you if you'd tried to leave the Black City once you'd arrived. I believe I have chosen to let fate decide if Icaraine gets her freedom. I gave you my own bones to open the door, but what comes after will have to be performed by your witch. Icaraine was not... You have not seen what I have. The bodies she strung up in every high place, the ground slick with blood, human and Titan alike. Perhaps our time is over, and I should let it go into history where it belongs. I've seen enough blood.'

Kaeto found himself intrigued by that, despite everything.

'And what about you? If you don't help your priestess from her prison, what will you do?'

'Die, finally,' said Felldir without a hint of hesitation. 'The Black City can become a proper ruin. A tomb. I will lie down in some corner, where I can see the sky, and simply wait.' When he spoke of his own death, Felldir sounded almost wistful. Uncomfortable, Kaeto turned away from the Titan and began making his way back up the path towards the rent in the city wall. After a moment, Felldir followed.

'Can you make Icaraine give Belise back?' Kaeto asked tersely.

'No,' said Felldir. 'Certainly not while she believes the child to be the key to her freedom, and she was never one for granting requests in any case.'

'Then what use are you?' Kaeto growled. He shook his head. 'Why do I even talk to you? Useless.'

'The girl is your family,' Felldir said quietly. 'I remember what those were, at least.'

Kaeto paused at the broken wall, his hand on the hot stones. He kept thinking of how unnerved Belise had been at the thousands of beetles crawling all over the Undertomb, and how she must have felt when they reached up as a wave and pulled her down.

'You had a family here?'

'A small one,' Felldir replied. 'My partner and I, we flew together for many years. But he was quite taken with Icaraine and her stories of how we were the true overlords of Enonah.' He spoke quietly, his chin tucked towards his chest so that his pale hair half covered his face. 'I can't believe he truly had hatred in his heart for the light-boned, or our Titan cousins, but she offered something he felt we were missing. A purpose, perhaps. Glory.'

'There are always those who believe they are deserving of what others have,' said Kaeto. He was thinking of the Imperium.

'In any case,' Felldir continued, 'my lover was at her side when the Druidahnon and his brothers and sisters led the first attack on the City, and he did not survive it.'

'I had family, once,' said Kaeto. His voice barely seemed to travel beyond his lips in the hot flat heat of the jungle. 'We weren't rich and we weren't poor. My father had a shop that had belonged to his father, and sometimes it was difficult to keep our heads above water. We all worked in that shop. My first memories are of learning to count the coins, of sweeping the floor. It was hard work, but at the end of the day we would sit in the room above the shop together and we'd eat and laugh about the customers and all their problems. Father had a clay pipe, and Mother would make him smoke it by the window... And then one year, when I was still very small, the Imperium came and claimed the town as the personal property of the empress, who required the land for one of her observatories. We were turfed out and set on the road to Stratum, and our little shop – the place I knew best in all the world – was broken down and flattened like every other building. My mother and father never recovered from that loss. Now, Belise is my only family. A child in my care.'

'Yet you still serve the Imperium,' Felldir said quietly. 'Despite what they did.'

Kaeto's hand tightened on the black stone. 'My mother and father couldn't survive in Stratum, but I did. I built something new. Belise is part of that.'

'So what will you do now?'

Kaeto turned to face the Titan, keeping his face expressionless.

'I will continue to serve. What else is there? You of all people should understand that.'

73

The cave they had found to shelter in was well hidden, the entrance so obscured with thistle and creeping vine that Leven was sure they would never have found it alone, even with Cillian's uncanny sense of the landscape. Inside it was dry and, once the fire was going, almost suffocatingly warm. The thin line of black smoke trailed off into the ceiling, flowing out through some unseen natural chimney. The griffin, who was too big to fit comfortably in the cave with the rest of them, sprawled outside, his head close to the entrance so that he could listen, while the girl sat on the far side of the fire, her posture so tense that her shoulders were almost up by her ears. Leven would have found it amusing if the girl wasn't so obviously distressed.

'I don't understand this at all,' she said again. 'You say you can see these... invisible lines that lead from one person to another. And that one of these cords binds us. What are they? Can I touch them? What does it mean?' She glanced at Cillian. 'Have you heard anything like it?'

'No,' said Cillian. 'But we know that the griffins have their own kinds of magic, ways of seeing and knowing that we don't have. And we also know that they don't share them with humans. As far as I know, the only interactions humans have ever had with the griffins are the sort that end with our guts spread across the snow. As we almost experienced just now.'

The girl, who had said her name was Ynis, shook her head violently. 'I have told you! Ground-stuck fools. My fathers found me as yenlin and took me to their nest-pit to be a fledgling with my sister. I've known nothing else. I am not *human.*' She practically spat the word. 'Not like you.'

'It is true,' rumbled the griffin, who had told them his name was Festus. 'She was raised in Yelvynia amongst my people, and then, she came north to the Bone Fall. This is where she was taught Edge Walker magics. She helped my father to die well.'

Die well? Leven shifted slightly, so she could keep half an eye on the entrance. Having such a beast – a living Titan – sitting at their backs was making her very uneasy.

'Fine. Let's say I believe that,' she continued. 'Then how can our "fates be tied", as you put it?'

'That is what you must tell me!' Ynis sprang up, her fists clenched. In the firelight Leven could see the wiry strength in her skinny arms, and the hectic pattern of old scars across much of her skin. There was such an energy to the girl, like a pot about to boil over. She pointed her claw-knife at Leven. 'Explain! There must be a thing, something that ties you to me. Where were you hatched? How were you raised? Where are you from?'

Leven leaned back from the fire, a cold sensation freezing her stomach.

'There's no need for us to fight,' Cillian was saying, his eyes on the knife. 'We want to help.'

'You help by telling me what links us,' Ynis shouted back. She jabbed at something in the air Leven couldn't see. 'This tie, it is the strongest, and it should lead to my sister! Instead it leads to prey animals. There must be a reason we are linked. The fate-tie cannot have brought me to you for nothing.'

'Perhaps the human is meant to help us find T'rook,' added Festus.

'The problem is,' said Leven, '*I don't know.* Ynis, if I knew I would tell you, I promise you that, but the reality is I only remember the last eight or nine years of my life. Everything before that...' She shrugged. 'It's gone. I don't know where I was, uh, hatched. I don't know where I come from.'

'Why?' demanded Ynis.

'It was the process that made me a Herald.' Leven held out her hands, palms down, so that the girl could see the intricate ore-lines that crossed her skin. 'The magic that was grafted onto my skin obliterated all my memories from before.'

'A Herald. This is the thing that makes you fly?' asked Ynis, and there was a hunger in her voice that Leven hadn't heard before. 'How do you do this? This grafting? If I could fly, I could fly myself to T'rook.'

'It's not something I did to myself, and believe me, you're better off without it. The point is, I don't have any answers for you. If there's information in my memories, I'm afraid they're lost to us.'

Ynis gave a sharp cry then, a noise between the disgusted shout of a teenager and the angry squawk of a bird. It made Leven jump.

'Then you are wasting my time!'

Their group fell silent. Outside the cave, the wind picked up, throwing pebbles from the top of the hill in a sound like rain. Over the crackling of the fire, Leven could hear Ynis's ragged breathing and knew that the girl was trying not to cry. For reasons she didn't quite understand, Leven experienced a sudden surge of feeling for her, a need to make things better. She opened her mouth to say something – although she had no clue what – and the griffin spoke before she could.

'Witch-seer Arrow, what of the ritual of Death's Remembrance? Even if her memories are lost to her, I think it is possible they are still in there somewhere, in that tiny, thin egg-skull. If there is a clue to what this fate-tie means, you may be able to find it.'

Ynis's grey eyes grew very wide.

'The Death's Remembrance is sacred,' she said, sounding uncertain. 'Witch-seer Frost said so. She said that it is sacred to griffins. I cannot use it on this human.'

'Witch-seer Frost did not think it so sacred it could not be *taught* to a human, did she?' Festus glared around at them, and then bowed his head briefly to Ynis. 'Forgive me. But there could be answers here. Will you not even try to take them?'

'Hold on,' Cillian leaned forward, 'I don't like the sound of this "death's remembrance". Is it dangerous? What will you be doing to Leven?'

'It's a ritual.' The girl looked around at them, turning her wicked little dagger over and over in her hands. 'When a griffin has died, we use it to help loved ones with their grief – we walk together through their memories, so that they know nothing is lost.'

'It sounds dangerous,' Cillian said obstinately. Leven glanced at the stubborn set of his jaw and had an overwhelming urge to kiss him. 'How dangerous is it?'

'I don't even know if it will work on a human,' Ynis said. 'If it does…'

'You mean to say I could see everything I've forgotten?' Leven's heartbeat thundered in her chest. This could be it, the answer to all her questions – something that could finally make sense of the visions.

'It could work,' said Ynis, clearly reluctant.

'I'll do it,' Leven said quickly. 'Whatever information is stored in my lost memories, I think I need it as much as Ynis does. If it helps, then I'll do it.'

74

One of the more fanciful legends of Brittletain concerns a so-called Titan 'legion of the dead' in the very far north of the island. This supposed cult comprises a group of griffins who choose to live far away from the main griffin habitat and spend their lives tending to some vast griffin graveyard. I suppose it is feasible that they might have elaborate rituals for dealing with their dead, yet I feel instinctively that the idea that a whole group spend their lives living among the bones of their ancestors is the product of a Briton with an overly active imagination. After all, no one has ever laid eyes on such a griffin, and I have quite thoroughly searched the Imperium archives and found nothing to verify such a claim. The small amount of griffin history we have gleaned from the griffins themselves does not mention them at all.

Excerpt from *The Lore of the Deep Forest: An Examination of the Myths and Facts of Brittletain*

'I don't like it.'

The horned man who claimed his name was Cillian was scowling, his arms crossed over his chest. Ynis knew vaguely of the Druin as a kind of human Edge Walker, men and women that had their own weak magic, but she had never seen one up close; they were generally thought to be at least wise enough to keep far from the borders of Yelvynia. He had been pacing around the space they had made in the old grass, looking at the woman lying there from different angles as though he could find one that reassured him. The woman – whose name was Leven – kept propping herself up on her elbows to watch what was going on. Ynis could hardly drag her eyes from her. Not only because her fate-tie – her strongest fate-tie! – led to this human, but because her skin was laced with the same strange lines as the golden woman who had attacked them on the northern coast. She could fly, too.

'Stop fussing, Cillian,' she said. 'I'm sure it will be fine. The stuff is made from ground-up griffin bones, right?'

Ynis nodded. She had put a pinch of the bone powder into a small cup of melted ice water and was mixing it with her finger.

'And rabbit's blood.'

'See?' Leven smiled up at the horned man. She looked a little queasy. 'That's not likely to do me any harm, is it? Because...' She glanced at Ynis and Festus, then looked away. 'Well, I think it's worth the gamble.'

Festus was standing over them, watching Ynis as she cut the throat of the rabbit he had fetched for them. Steam rose from the quick spurt of blood, which she deftly aimed into the cup.

'The bones of my ancestors,' Festus said importantly. 'Be sure you know what an honour this is, human.'

'I do. So, what happens?'

Ynis passed the cup to Leven. For a long second she found herself uncertain what to say; there was a chance the bone powder, even in such a tiny amount, could kill the human at the first sip, and if that happened she would never know how the woman had received her magical blue wings. *There is a secret here*, she reminded herself. *One that has hung over my head since I was yenlin. If T'rook were here, she would want these answers too. It is worth the risk of one human death.*

'You drink it. It will make you sleep, and dream very vividly. I will

detach my spirit from my own body and walk into your sleeping mind.'
Ynis cleared her throat. The idea of being inside a human's mind was
deeply unappealing. 'From there, together we find a door that leads
to your memories. Even the memories you hide from yourself.'

'You can do that?' asked Cillian. 'Detach your spirit and just...
wander around?'

'Despite her human frailty Ynis is quite skilled,' said Festus. Ynis
glanced at him, surprised by this mild praise, but he had his lively
green eyes trained on the human. 'She will be able to enter a weak
human mind easily enough.'

Leven made an amused noise, and then lifted the cup to her lips.
For a split second, her steady grey eyes met Ynis's, and she gave her a
lopsided smile.

'Bottoms up.'

She drank the cup back and lay down in the grass, folding her
hands a little self-consciously across her chest. Within seconds, her
eyelids flickered and her head sagged to one side. Anxiously the man
Cillian pressed his hand to her throat.

'It hasn't killed her at least.'

'What did she mean about bottoms?' asked Ynis.

Cillian shook his head. 'I don't know. It is some Imperial thing.
It's not important. What happens now?'

'I go and join her.'

Ynis sat cross-legged next to the human woman and let herself
relax. After so many days and nights following the fate-tie across the
sky, the spirit state came to her almost as easily as closing her eyes.

I am good at this, she thought fiercely, allowing herself a small
moment of pride. *Frost was right to make me a witch-seer, whatever
Scree might think.*

Around her the world had dimmed, the early dawn light unfocused
and strained, as though seen through a thick sheet of old ice, but there
was a bright arc of light shining from the sleeping woman's forehead.
Different from a griffin, then, but not as much as she had expected.

Ynis reached out with her spirit fingers and placed her hand on Leven's forehead. There was a sense of movement, and rushing, and—

—she was in the middle of a vast open space, no safe mountains or trees to shield her. The ground underneath her feet was soft and untrustworthy, the pale golden colour of an autumn leaf. The sky was blue, but it was a blue deeper than any she had ever seen. And the sun!

'There you are!'

Ynis turned. The human woman was with a group of other humans, their skins similarly patterned, but she came jogging lightly over the soft earth towards her. She was smiling. Beyond them, Ynis saw, there was a dizzying number of people gathered in the distance. They wore so many pieces of metal that the hot sun glinted and danced off them like a stream in springtime. There were other things there, huge four-legged grey animals with large flat ears, and something, some kind of flexible tail hanging from the front of their faces.

'What is this place?' Ynis grabbed hold of the woman's arm, and then just as quickly dropped it. 'What are those things?'

'Those?' Leven glanced over her shoulder. 'They're quite a sight, aren't they? Loxodonta, the Unblessed tribe of Karpathia called them. Karpathia is this place.' She gestured around at the strange, eerily flat land. 'They would ride the Loxos into battle. And we killed them all.' Leven grew quiet. 'I dream about this place, and this time, quite often.'

'You killed them?' Despite herself, Ynis was curious. 'To eat? Surely one of those things would have lasted an entire year.'

Leven laughed, although it sounded false to Ynis's ears. 'Not to eat, no. To be honest with you, Ynis, I'm not sure why we did it at all. Not anymore.'

In the distance, the Loxodonta were falling slowly to the ground, a great wave that made the ground shake under their feet. As they watched, their grey skins began to peel away from their flesh, and that was melting too, so that only the enormous skeletons were left, their huge curving tusks lifted to the sky.

'What's happening?' asked Leven, a slight note of alarm to her voice. 'What's happening to the Loxos?'

'This is a dream, remember?' said Ynis. 'There are no rules in dreams. We have to go deeper to find your memories.'

'That's what we were,' said Leven, still watching the skeletal remains of the giant animals. Her grey eyes looked hard as flint. 'Just a wave of death, a natural disaster – only worse, because a natural disaster can't think or make its own decisions. We could make our own choices but we still chose the slaughter.'

'There's no time for this.' Ynis took the older woman's arm again, and tugged on it. 'We have to look for a portal. Through it we will be able to move back through your memories. Since I have never met you, we should go back at least sixteen years – the secret to our fate-tie must be in there somewhere.'

Leven tore herself away from the sight of the skeletal Loxodonta. She rubbed the back of her hand across her face and seemed to find new focus.

'Right. So what does the portal look like?'

'I don't know.' Ynis cast about desperately. The strange flat land with its unfriendly sun was beginning to make her panic. She had never felt quite so profoundly ground-stuck. What if they were attacked from the sky? They were so vulnerable here. 'It is… an entrance, a way through. A tunnel, an opening in a cave, or a cavern.'

'Like… a door?'

When Ynis looked at her blankly, Leven smiled and pointed to a boxy structure of fabric off to one side of the gathered humans.

'The only door I can see is the entrance to that tent. Could that be it?'

Ynis nodded. She didn't know what a tent was, but it looked like a shelter of some sort, and the idea of being hidden from the baleful sun was very attractive. The two of them walked over to the tent, and a few of the humans called out to them. Leven called back cheerfully, holding out her hand in greeting, and Ynis saw that one of them was the golden woman – her yellow hair impossibly bright under the sun. She opened her mouth to ask who she was, and what she might be doing on the northern coast of Yelvynia, but Leven was pushing aside the curtain to the tent, and a cold familiar light filtered through, calling them home. Ynis grabbed the woman's hand – and how strange that was, to feel a hand so like her own curled around her fingers – and they stepped through together.

75

I t was the Wild Wood, and it was winter.

Leven could tell that much by the bare branches and the thick crust of frost underfoot. The tent and the desert of Unblessed Karpathia was gone, as vanished as completely as things vanish in dreams.

'Where is this place?' asked Ynis. The girl had hurriedly let go of her hand, and was peering around the forest as though she expected to be attacked.

'I've no idea, I've...' Leven stopped. Ahead of them, half hidden by a thick covering of moss and grass and snow, was a small wooden house. It was so well hidden she had almost missed it, but now that she looked she could see a thin line of grey smoke twisting up from its lumpy roof. 'That's where we have to go.' She swallowed hard. 'Come on.'

The door was stiff and Leven had to shove it with her shoulder to open it. Inside was a cosy mixture of living room and kitchen; a short fat iron stove sat in the corner, a hearth in the other. A roughly hewn table stood in the centre, covered with tools and cutlery, and there were people in the room. A tall, broad-shouldered man sat with a baby in his arms, and a skinny girl of around thirteen or fourteen leaned against the table. A woman with a lot of reddish-brown hair held back by a band of fabric across her forehead stood by the hearth...

'Hold on,' said Leven. The world seemed to be dipping and swirling around her crazily, as though she'd just been hit on the head. 'That can't be right...'

'That is you, I think,' Ynis was saying, pointing at the teenage girl. She had a strange expression on her face, as though some terrible truth was gradually dawning on her. 'It must be. Your face, your eyes, your hair.'

'Yeah,' Leven said, barely giving the teenage version of herself a glance. 'But who the fuck is *that*?' She jabbed a finger at the older woman with the headband.

Ynis shrugged. 'How should I know? These are your memories.'

'No, I mean, I *know* who that is.' Leven took a few steps into the room. 'I saw her every time the Heralds came back to Stratum. She insisted that only *she* could check us over, and we all hated her because she treated us like weapons, like things she had made and discarded, instead of people...' Her voice trailed off. 'What the fuck is Gynid Tyleigh doing here? In Brittletain, in my memories?'

'Shhh,' said Ynis. 'They are speaking.'

'Are you excited, lass?' The man was speaking to the older girl, but he was smiling down at the baby in his arms, who kept trying to grab his beard with her tiny hands. 'A whole week in the woods with your mother, learning secret things.'

'Owain, please,' said the woman Leven knew as Gynid Tyleigh. Her voice was softer than Leven remembered it being, but there was still that impatient undertone. 'You make it sound like some silly, girly thing. Deryn has to learn to take the Wild Wood seriously.'

'I do, Ma,' the girl said. Reluctantly, Leven let her eyes be drawn to the shrimpy teenage girl leaning against the table. She was all lanky legs and elbows, and there were scabs on her knuckles. *That's my real name*, Leven thought in wonder. *Deryn is my name. Before I was a number, I was Deryn.* 'I keep to the Paths just like you say. And I'm ready to learn the other stuff too. I promise.'

'Yes. Well. It's more than overdue.' Tyleigh crossed her arms over her chest in a stance Leven recognised: Gynid Tyleigh had no time for nonsense. 'They might have taken the Druin magic away from me, but that's not to say that there's not plenty of magic still out there for the taking.'

'Druin magic? Tyleigh was a Druin?' Leven bit her lip. *More to the point, Tyleigh was my mother?*

'Well, I'll miss you both.' The man called Owain rested the baby on his knee and jostled her up and down until she giggled. 'But I'll get to spend some time with this little squirrel, and that won't be so bad, will it, Alaw? My silly little squirrel.' The baby laughed again, and Gynid Tyleigh grimaced.

'Owain, you spoil that baby. Deryn, take your sister off your father before she starts thinking she has a bushy tail.'

Owain laughed. 'Echni! Don't you think a tail would suit her?'

'This is too much.' Leven began backing away towards the door. She had had a family once, a mother, a father, a baby sister, and she had known about none of it. She hadn't even known her real name. What else had she lost? 'I have to go back.'

She crashed through the cabin door and, in the way of dreams, they were somewhere else again – still the Wild Wood, and still winter, but the trees were sparser, and they were in the middle of a circle of tall standing stones. In the centre was a vast slab of granite supported by two smaller rocks, and the girl Deryn lay on top of it, looking very small against the dark grey stone. Tyleigh was standing nearby, pulling a length of rope through her hands.

'What is this place, Ma?' asked Deryn. It was cold, a strong taste of snow in the air, and the light grey clouds above them were an eerie blank canvas. The girl, Leven noticed, had bare arms despite the weather, and a cold worm of dread began to curl in her stomach.

'A place sacred to the Druin,' said Tyleigh, her tone brisk, business-like. 'Sacred to them, but largely forgotten. Idiots. They have all this magic and power at their fingertips and they're happy to just let it go to ruin.' She brought the rope over to the granite slab and began looping it around the girl's waist, tying her to the stone.

'What is she doing to you?' asked Ynis.

'I… I don't know,' said Leven, although she had a terrible suspicion she did know, after all. 'I told you, I don't remember any of this.'

Ynis was walking around the stone circle when she stopped dead. On the ground, in a wooden crate, were bones – the unmistakable blue-black bones of griffins. She bent down and ran her hands over them, frowning.

'And where did these come from?'

'I *told* you,' Leven said, unable to drag her eyes away from the small shape of her teenage self. 'This is all news to me.'

'Ma,' Deryn was saying, 'Ma, I don't think I like this. I'm cold.'

Tyleigh leaned over her daughter, tightening the ropes. She smiled, a thin-lipped thing as icy as the stones around them.

'You trust me, don't you, Deryn?'

'Yes...'

'Don't you want to know all the secrets of the Titans? Don't you want to know all the magic of the Wild Wood? I just need you to keep still, and keep quiet. I'm doing this to make you better, Deryn. I'm doing this for all of us.'

When Tyleigh brought out the ore-line device, Leven found herself moving without thinking, leaping forward to try and dash the awful thing from her mother's hands. But, just like in a dream, her desperate action had no effect, and Tyleigh continued with her terrible work. From another box she pulled out a thin glass bottle filled with a shifting, silvery-blue liquid that shone oddly under the winter light. She fitted it into the ore-line device and shook it briskly.

'What is it?' Ynis asked. Alarmed by Leven's distress, she was half crouching, ready to flee or fight at a moment's notice. 'What is she doing?'

Leven laughed past the sob that was rising in her throat. 'It's how she makes these.' She touched the ore-lines that ran up and down her forearm. 'It's how she crafted us into Heralds, except, apparently, I was the first. She did this to a *child*.'

Deryn was trying to sit up, straining against the ropes, her eyes trained on the ore-line device. It looked a little like a great metal insect, clamped onto the end of Tyleigh's arm. A set of three needles pointed out of its mandibles, and with her free hand Tyleigh began to turn a crank on the side of the contraption. There was a loud clicking and clacking noise, and Leven felt all the hairs on the back of her neck stand up. *I know that sound,* she thought. *I know what it means.*

'You have to keep still, Deryn,' Tyleigh was saying. Back in the cabin, her voice had been warmer – the voice of a mother with too much on her mind, perhaps, but still, there had been something akin to kindness in it. Now her voice was cold and distant, the voice that Leven recognised from every visit to the Imperium's most celebrated alchemist. This was the voice of the woman who knew that the Heralds were useful weapons, and nothing more. 'You mustn't move an inch because these patterns must be exactly right.'

'But, Ma, what has this got to do with the Druin?'

'It's *better* than the Druin. You'll see.'

Deryn was crying, in the silent, restrained way of someone who knew that crying usually didn't help.

'Please, Ma, can we just go home?' Her face crumpled. 'I want Daddy.'

Something tiny and hidden inside of Leven compressed, and shattered. She turned away from the stone altar.

'I can't see any more of this,' she said. 'Let's go.'

Ynis joined her. Her eyes looked very wide in her dirty face. 'But what does any of it mean? What has this got to do with me?'

Leven opened her mouth to reply, and then from behind them came a wail of pain that very quickly grew into a scream. The ore-line device chittered and clicked and thrummed, and the girl screamed, and all around them the birds took off from the trees in fright.

Click. Click. Click. Clack. Clack. Clack.

Leven closed her eyes and ran away from the memory.

76

On my return I will want my workshop thoroughly cleansed and organised. I will want fresh supplies of all of the following (fresh, mind you – if you try to reuse the stuff I already have I will know, and I'll have your lackeys strung up in the square for it)

> *Powdered snake bones*
> *Oil from the scorpion leaf*
> *Salves and bandages*
> *Blue slipper mushrooms*
> *Dried inkwort leaves*
> *(all the usual amounts)*

You will also provide a new set of the sharpest possible knives, and I will need the beds in the workshop fitted with new leather restraints. And lastly, this should go without saying, I will need at least twenty to thirty new subjects to work on. I don't care where you find them, but they must be young and relatively healthy or they won't survive even the beginning of the process. Send me any old duffers and I will simply cut their throats, leaving you to deal with the mess.

With regards to the other 'materials' – I understand the limitations well enough, and I suppose I will do what I can with what can be provided. But if it is at any point possible to bring back a live specimen, even a juvenile, I will personally see that the empress rewards those responsible.

Note from Gynid Tyleigh left for Imperator Justinia

'You have found a way to use this Druin magic again?'

Tyleigh looked up from where she sat. She was back in the daylight at the entrance to the Undertomb, her various tools laid out around a steadily burning fire. Before her lay the remains of one of her horns, which she had carefully sawn into pieces and then ground into dust. Her own arm was held out before her, covered with blood. She bared her teeth at Kaeto in a mixture of satisfaction and pain.

'I believe I have,' she said. 'I always wondered if it were possible, but never had a chance to try it out. The magic of the Titan ore was enough at the time, after all. But as it turns out, the Titan ore is also the key in this case, or at least, the method I used.' She picked up a wet cloth and swiftly rubbed it down her bleeding arm; livid red lines were revealed, scored into her skin. They were not unlike the stripes of Titan ore Kaeto had seen on the Heralds, but the shapes were different; curls and loops instead of hard geometric lines. 'You see?' continued Tyleigh. 'The horns contain the essence of the Wild Wood, and turned to powder, they can be mixed with my blood, and written into my skin.' She laughed then, even as the blood began to seep again from the new lines she had tattooed into her arm. 'I never thought I'd feel this again. This... connection to living things. I can feel it buzzing all around me. All those bloody beetles.'

Kaeto crouched by the fire. In his hands he held a small clay teapot. Steam curled from the lip of the spout and then was lost in the heat of the day.

'And you think with this you can gain access to the Titan remains?'

'It is a certainty.' She laughed again, and he noticed that her face was flushed, feverish. 'Gods, I can't believe I left this behind. This *power*. I...' She took a deep breath and rubbed a bloody palm across her forehead. 'The process is exhausting though. I have a better understanding now of why so many of the initial Herald volunteers died under the needle.'

'Here, I brought you tea.' Kaeto picked up a spare clay cup and poured some of the steaming liquid. 'It's my own mixture, for long nights of surveillance. It will give you some of your energy back.'

Tyleigh took the cup from him and, after blowing on the surface, took several sips.

'Yes, that's better. I will have to make sure that each of the Titans is dead before we extract them from their pods. If I open a small section, I was thinking we could use one of your weapons to cut their throats. Or a simple lobotomy perhaps? That can be done with a pick and hammer easily enough.'

'You still intend to take back only remains?'

Tyleigh rolled her eyes at him over the top of her cup and took another sip of tea before replying. 'I keep forgetting how idiotic you can be. They are much too dangerous to live. But *whole* Titan bodies, barely touched by decay? The knowledge, the power gained, it will be... Stars' arses, it will be...' She coughed, and frowned. 'I'm not sure the flavour of this tea agrees with me. I...' Her hand dropped the cup as she spasmed in pain and fell over onto her side. She jerked and flopped in the dust like a fish plucked from water. Kaeto watched her, unmoving. *'What have you done?'*

'It's an interesting poison,' he said, then paused as Tyleigh writhed and reached out for him, hands clasping. Her face, previously so flushed, had drained of all colour. 'The plant it's made from only grows here. Or at least, so Icaraine says. They called it the Black City Orchid, or the Dead Man's Heart. Right now, the tea is reacting with the natural fluids in your stomach to create an intensely corrosive acid that will break down your internal organs.'

'You... *fucker*,' Tyleigh gasped between gritted teeth.

'Eventually the reaction will work its way into your saliva too, dissolving the inside of your throat and mouth. It sounds like an especially unpleasant way to die, and you should bear in mind that I have spent much of my life studying poisons and their effects.'

Tyleigh was pawing at her own belt, trying to reach a short knife.

Kaeto reached over and slapped her hand away, before removing the knife himself and throwing it into the dust behind him.

'Hurk... ghgh... why?'

'Why do you think?' Kaeto stood up and reached inside his shirt to reveal a slim glass vial filled with a chalky mauve liquid. 'There is an antidote. The longer you leave it the more damage is done, of course, but if we're quick you may only suffer enormous pain every time you eat something for the rest of your life. If we're not quick, you'll die here in the dirt, expelling the liquified remains of your digestive system.' Holding the vial between his thumb and forefinger, he shook it gently. 'You can have the antidote once you have freed Icaraine. Simple enough that even I can understand it. Yes?'

Tyleigh glared up at him through streaming eyes. A thin line of blood was already creeping from the corner of her mouth. After a moment she nodded her head sharply, once.

'Good. I knew you would see reason.' Kaeto reached down and grabbed her by the back of her shirt, yanking her to her feet. 'Let's get moving.'

Getting Tyleigh down the spiral stairs to the Undertomb was not easy. Not because she resisted Kaeto, but because her body was wracked with cramps, and every few steps she would gasp and twist, hissing through gritted teeth. What little breath she had she used to curse him, promising him all manner of punishments and tortures once she could get her hands on a weapon. Kaeto endured it all, keeping one hand bunched in the back of her shirt and the other clamped around an upper arm – whatever happened, she had to make it to the bottom of the steps without falling and breaking her neck.

Once at the bottom, they paused, the great teeming sea of beetles chittering and rushing around them.

'Well?' he demanded. 'You can command them now, can't you?'

Tyleigh spat a wad of red spit onto the ground at her feet. 'I don't know where she is, idiot.'

Kaeto pointed to the north of the tomb. When Icaraine had spoken to him, she had described her location exactly. *It won't be long now*, he told himself. A few more steps and Belise would be back, Tyleigh could take her antidote and they could leave the Black City forever. Any further complications could be considered later. Tyleigh raised her bloody arms, and after several agonisingly long seconds, the beetles began to fall back, uncovering an uneven stone path that led to the back of the cavern. Together, they began to make their way across, Tyleigh sweating from the effort. To either side, Kaeto could see large numbers of the strange hexagonal seals over the heads of the sleeping Othanim. There had to be thousands of them.

'This is madness,' Tyleigh wheezed. As they walked, fat drops of blood were running down her chin and hitting the stone. 'She'll kill you. Even Felldir knows it. She'll kill all of us.'

'If I were you I'd be less worried about Icaraine the Lightbringer and more worried about my insides turning into soup.' Kaeto increased his grip on her arm. 'Come on. I can see her tomb just ahead.'

Unlike the other Titans, Icaraine had been interred separately, above ground. Perhaps, Kaeto mused, the Druidahnon had not wanted to lose her amongst her followers. Her sarcophagus, when they reached it, was a long horizontal protuberance from the ground, made of a strange gritty substance that almost looked like soil, except that it was as hard as stone. It made Kaeto think of the tall towers built by colonies of ants, in the deserts outside Stratum. In the surface of this strangely textured stone were hundreds of curving organic lines, similar to the ones Tyleigh had carved into the skin of her arm. The alchemist placed her shaking hand on top of the stone. She was breathing hard and talking was clearly difficult.

'Are you… sure about this?' The beetles were creeping in at the edges, soft blue and green lights encasing the sarcophagus in a strange underwater glow. 'Give... give me the antidote and... we'll go. Just go now.'

'Tyleigh, all these delays are only damaging yourself.' Kaeto stood back and drew his short sword, ready in case any of the beetles got too curious. 'Release her, or die.'

'Be it... on your head, then.' Tyleigh raised her bloodied arms and after a moment, the gritty rock of the coffin itself began to crumble. The lines that had been cut into the rock began to glow with a soft white light, and then that flickered, and vanished. Around them, the beetles moved with sudden urgency, in a chaotic, panicked tumble. A deep vibration bled up through the ground, a rumble that coalesced into a frantic *thump-thump-thump*, like a monstrous heartbeat. Dust and small stones began to fall from the ceiling.

'The whole place will come down. What is happening?'

'Only what you commanded, Envoy.' Tyleigh had fallen to her knees, but her voice was full of a new energy, and when she tipped her head back to look at him she was grinning. 'Gods, I had forgotten... how it feels... to be thrawn.'

All at once the sarcophagus split down the middle as though it had been struck by lightning. Pieces of stone fell away, and Tyleigh slumped back as *something* began to climb out of the hole left behind. It was much bigger than Felldir, and as if the thought had summoned him, Kaeto heard a voice shouting from the spiral stairs behind them. Felldir was at the top of them, his face hidden within his elaborate helmet.

'Run!' he was shouting. '*Run!*'

But Kaeto couldn't. If anything, he felt as though he were rooted to the spot. Instead, he watched as the huge form shouldered its way out of its tomb, breaking the structure apart as easily as if it were made of straw. The beetles had moved back and away, a tide drawing swiftly out, so that the wide expanse of glassy hexagons on the floor were exposed.

The figure that climbed from the rubble was humanoid, but only just. She wore elaborate armour of blue-green metal – in his shocked state Kaeto still recognised it as Titan ore – and a vast pair of white feathered wings flexed at her back. Long black hair fell down to her waist, and she wore a Titan-ore helm framed with a fan of golden feathers. From a thin slot near the middle of the helmet Kaeto could just make out a pair of eyes, wild and yellow.

'At last!' The voice was painfully loud. The figure raised one hand and pointed at Felldir. 'Don't think I don't see you, worm!' Icaraine stepped out of the tomb fully, scattering stone and beetles. She was carrying something cradled in one arm. Kaeto glanced back towards the steps, but the other Titan had vanished. Tyleigh, meanwhile, he had lost sight of. He forced himself to step up to the huge figure, craning his neck to keep her head in sight.

'Icaraine Lightbringer!' His voice felt pitifully small. 'I have freed you, as you asked.'

Icaraine looked around, and then twisted her head back and forth, rolled her shoulders. She did not look at him.

'Thousands of years they've cost me, the bastards.' She brushed dirt from the bundle in her arm. 'And you, my sweet, have hardly had a chance to grow. No matter. I will go there now, to their stinking island, and find every last bear and griffin, and I shall eat their flesh and their hearts, and I will take their bones, my sweet, and you—'

'My lady Icaraine!' This time, finally, she did look down at him, the features of the Titan-ore mask appearing to move in the shifting light. 'Please! I have freed you as you asked, and now I ask for my... You said you would return Belise to me. The child. Please.'

A great knot of panic was building in Kaeto's chest, a chilling rush that told him he'd made a terrible error, but there was nothing to do but hold on. He'd have Belise back, and he would figure things out from there. That was all he could do.

'Light-bones.' Icaraine's voice was full of silky menace. 'Yes. I remember our bargain. You have done well.' The huge figure turned away from him and bent back to the space where her tomb had shattered into pieces. She turned back with something held in her free hand, which she lowered down towards Kaeto, her palm held flat.

'Your child, returned to you, as promised,' she said, her voice warm with amusement. 'The beetles were hungry, I'm afraid.'

Resting on her hand was a small, delicate skeleton, the skeleton of a child, the flesh picked clean save for the untidy clusters of ropey tendon between each joint. The eyes were gone but there were a few strands of brown hair still adhering to some ragged pieces of scalp.

'What...' Kaeto reached out a shaking hand. 'What did you...'

Icaraine dropped the bones in front of him and wiped her hand on her breastplate, her attention elsewhere. He barely noticed as she leapt away from the ground and crashed headlong into the ceiling, bringing half of it down. Instead he leaned over the bones, protecting them with his own body.

'Belise?'

Chunks of stone the size of apples rained down against his back and he barely noticed it. He laid his fingers against the child's skull. It was cold. And then a sharp pain under his rib brought him back to himself. Tyleigh was there, her mouth and chin slick with blood and her teeth bared. One of her hands slipped inside his shirt and removed the vial of antidote, which she uncorked with one flick of her thumb. Kaeto was surprised she was still standing.

'Die down here, you fucker,' she spat, before putting the vial to her lips and drinking the contents. The knife she had stabbed him with was still protruding from his side. 'I've got better things to do.'

With that, she was gone. There was a shuddering crash, and another part of the ceiling fell, scattering beetles in all directions. Kaeto looked up to see the sky, high and blue and utterly blank. From somewhere above, he could hear the buildings of the Black City falling.

'What have I done?'

77

They were back at the remote, half-hidden cabin, all the more hidden now because it had been snowing heavily, and it was the dead of night. The crook of forest where it crouched was filled with the eerie dead-light of moonlight on snow, and a tiny orange light glowed at one frost-thick window. From within, they could hear voices. They could hear shouting.

'What is happening now?' asked Ynis. She was rubbing at her temples. 'Your memories have such sharp edges to them.'

'Probably because they are all broken,' said Leven, simply enough. 'I think we're coming to the end of it. I know I don't want to go back inside there.'

'But you have to,' said Ynis. Leven turned to look at the girl. She looked like a creature born in a nest, it was true; her skin was crusted with ground-in dirt, and the feathers woven into her matted braids were old and new – picked not because they were striking or beautiful, as any other child might collect feathers, but picked because they might make her look more like the thing she desperately wanted to be, but wasn't. Ynis the griffin child had not been hatched from an egg, and the longer Leven looked at her, the more she saw the truth. She turned her head away.

'Come on then.'

Inside, the cabin was hot. The hearth was blazing, and the fury of the man and the woman seemed only to heat it further. The girl – *Deryn*, Leven reminded herself, *that girl's name is Deryn* – was sitting on one of the wooden chairs. Her arms were crusted with dried blood, and she sat with her shoulders slumped, her arms hanging loose at her sides. Her left side was covered with the silvery-blue tracings of ore-lines. Deryn's eyes stared at nothing in particular, and her face was entirely blank. In a crib near the hearth, the baby was weeping quietly to herself.

'What have you done to her? What have you done to my girl?' Owain gestured fiercely at Deryn, then grabbed the girl's shoulder and shook it briskly. She didn't react. 'Look at her, Echni! She doesn't know who we are!'

Echni, the woman Leven knew as Tyleigh, folded her arms across her chest. She didn't quite look as confident as she had done when she was tying her daughter to the stone – there was perhaps too much blood still drying on her clothes for that – but her brow was furrowed and there was a set look about her jaw.

'An unexpected side effect. An unfortunate one.' At an incredulous noise from her husband, she shook her head. 'Really, Owain, how much has she lost? Fourteen years of living in the woods? Much of her memories will be the same things, over and over.'

'What has she lost?' asked Owain, his voice hoarse. 'She's lost *us*, Echni. And we've lost her.'

'But think of the power, Owain!' Some animation came back into Echni's face, a kind of joy that was horrible to look at. 'This is far beyond anything the Druin have dreamt up. This is the power of the Titans themselves, distilled and threaded through our daughter's skin and blood. You haven't seen yet what she can do! So she has lost her memories – she will make new ones. Eventually it will be like it was before, but Deryn will be... she will be a god!'

'You remember her name then,' said Owain. 'Or do you have names for all your tools?' Owain knelt in front of Deryn and took the girl's limp hand. He kissed it, rubbed at it with his own big hands, all the while searching her eyes for something. 'Deryn, honey? Do you know me, sweetheart? It's your pa.' The girl blinked at him slowly. 'Speak to me, my little bird. You know your pa, don't you?'

'It's possible I could find a way to avoid this side effect in the future,' Echni said in a musing tone. She had moved over to the crib, and was looking down at Alaw. The baby was looking up at her mother, her face red and bleary. 'A different configuration of lines, or a sleeping brew of some kind. Yes. I think when I try again, I will use a strong sleeping brew, something from the blue slipper mushroom, perhaps.'

Owain appeared next to her, shouldering her away from the crib and snatching the baby up from where she lay.

'What are you doing?'

'You are never laying another hand on our daughters,' said Owain. His cheeks were wet with tears, but his eyes were a hard, stormy grey. *Grey like mine*, thought Leven. 'I'm getting them out of here. Deryn, come with me now, sweetheart.'

The girl did not move from her place. Echni laughed.

'What are you going to do? We're miles from anywhere. It's snowing.'

'Deryn! Come with me please, I can't carry you both through the snow.' The girl lifted her chin slightly, as if she had heard a strange noise, very far away, but did not move otherwise. Owain stood for a second, clearly torn with indecision, before picking up a shawl from off the table and wrapping it hurriedly around the baby.

'Deryn, honey, I will come back for you, I swear.'

Still carrying the baby in his arms, Owain shouldered the door open and stepped through into the night. The snow had picked up again, and in moments his bulky form was lost to the blizzard. Echni watched him go, and for a few seconds she trembled all over, as though she were trying to keep a strong emotion in check. And then she went and placed a hand on the back of Deryn's chair.

'Deryn. I need you to do something for me.'

They stood together and watched the man carry the baby along the treeline. Ynis risked a glance at the human woman's face. Leven's eyes were dark, and her mouth was a thin, grim line. The cold was a deep biting cold, winter at its hungriest.

'He's heading into Yelvynia,' Ynis said quietly. 'Just a little further north, and he'll be in griffin territory.'

'She was right,' Leven said. 'He shouldn't have gone out into the night.'

'Why?' asked Ynis, but Leven just shook her head, and they followed the stumbling figure north. After a while, he stopped, breathing hard, and held the baby up, pulling the blanket she was wrapped in closer around her face.

'I'm sorry, Alaw,' he said, and he kissed the baby on her nose. 'There will be shelter around here somewhere, and in the morning, we'll head for Dosraiche. If we're lucky, we'll find Druin patrolling the Paths, and they can get us there faster.'

At that moment, a slim figure stepped out of the shadows. Her face was lit with an eerie blue light, and when Owain saw it, he took an involuntary step backwards. Deryn watched him, saying nothing. In her hands she held something like a sword, made of crackling blue light. It moved and shifted, as if it wasn't yet quite sure of its shape.

'Deryn? What is that? Did you come after us?' Owain made to walk towards the girl, and Deryn brought the sword up. He stopped. 'What are you doing?'

Ynis had seen the golden woman with the blue wings fight, she knew how fast these augmented humans could move. Even so, it seemed to her that one moment the human man was whole and standing, and the next he was short a head, and his body was pitching forward into the snow. Next to her, Leven gave a low moan of misery, almost hidden beneath the sudden shrieking of the baby. The girl Deryn stood looking down at her father, his blood running from her blade, steaming in the cold.

'Have you done it?'

The woman called Echni emerged from the trees behind them cautiously. She went over to the man's body and nudged it with her foot. His grip on Alaw had loosened as he fell, so that she was only pressed into the snow under his arm. Echni extracted the baby, who was now screaming at the very top of her lungs. Deryn watched blankly, the blue blade vanishing from her hand.

'There, Alaw, that's enough.' Echni attempted to jostle the baby into silence, but Alaw was having none of it. Grimacing, Echni passed the baby to Deryn. 'See if you can get her to shut up. I'm sorry you had to do that, Deryn, but he would never have understood – not my work, or how important you will be to it. How important you will both be. When we return...' A great harsh cry sounded from somewhere above their heads, drowning out even the sound of Alaw's shrieks. There was a thunder of wings, and Echni looked around wildly, fear etched into every line of her body. 'Shut that baby up!'

'It is a griffin,' Ynis said, scanning the night's sky beyond the tops of the trees. 'Hunting. These humans are too close to Yelvynia.'

Alaw, though, went on crying, and Deryn just held her as she was told. Echni grabbed her eldest daughter and tried to drag her deeper into the trees, but above them the screeching of the griffin was getting louder, the thunder of the wings almost on top of them.

'Damn the roots,' hissed Echni. 'That screaming will lead them straight to us. Smother it, or leave it behind – I don't care which!' And with that she left both her daughters, running deeper into the woods. Deryn looked down at her sister, who was wailing at an ear-splitting volume, her small round face red with the exertion of it. Ynis, though, found her eyes drawn to Deryn; the girl was blinking slowly, as though she were coming out of a very deep sleep. A spasm of some emotion passed over her face – horror, fear, sorrow – and then was gone again as fast as a falling star. She held the baby close to her face, and whispered a single word.

'*Sister.*'

And then she laid the baby down on the packed snow and dirt, and she walked away after her mother.

'What happens now?'

The forest and the snow had faded until the two of them were alone in a dark place. Ynis could feel the strange crumbling earth under her feet again, but this time the tiny grains were black. The only light came from a creamy expanse of stars over their heads.

'We go back,' Ynis said. She found herself peering at the face of the woman standing opposite her with a new interest. Now that she knew who she was, it seemed obvious; she had seen a face very like that looking out of every pond and tarn.

Leven, though, did not move. Instead she looked away across the darkness and said nothing.

'You are my sister,' Ynis tried, and Leven turned back.

'Yes,' she said. 'And I'm sorry. To just leave you like that... is unforgivable. How could I have ever done it? A baby left in the woods to die.'

'I didn't die,' said Ynis. 'And I became me. I am not sorry.'

Leven rubbed a forearm across her eyes once. Something like a smile played across her lips and was gone.

'Ha. Yeah. You became someone pretty remarkable, little sister. And I won't leave you alone again. Alright?'

Ynis did not know what to say to that. She had not expected, or ever looked for, a human family, and she wasn't sure she wanted one in her life. Yet despite all the stark honesty of her griffin upbringing, she sensed it wouldn't be helpful to point that out. Instead, she held out her hand.

'It's time to go, Deryn.'

On their journey back through Leven's dreaming mind they saw glimpses of other times that had been erased from her memory, pieces of a larger puzzle she suspected she would never grasp in its entirety.

Here they were in a tiny, crowded cabin, the sea visible through a smeared porthole. Gynid Tyleigh was bent over her ore-line device, while the girl Deryn lay on a tiny cot, her skin covered in feverish sweat. The child appeared to be unconscious, but as she worked, drilling more silvery lines into her daughter's skin, Tyleigh was muttering to herself.

'It's not quite there yet, my girl, not quite, but it's within sight all the same.' She paused to wipe away some of the blood with a wet rag. 'A fresh start, that's what we need. The power you will wield when I'm done…'

And then they were somewhere else entirely, and the girl Deryn was a young woman, carrying a heavy crate on her shoulders through a town filled with sunshine. It was hot enough that heat haze warped the sandy streets, but Deryn wore a long-sleeved shirt of thick wool, and a pair of fingerless gloves. The townsfolk glanced at her as she passed, clearly curious, but Deryn paid them no mind at all. In the girl's grey eyes Leven could see their father, and along her jawline she could see Tyleigh's stubborn expression; both hurt her in different ways.

The next memory brought them to a room that was half familiar. The Imperium's complex at the heart of Stratum, a room of men and women standing around nervously while Gynid Tyleigh looked them over, a handful of assistants flocking after her. Deryn stood in the corner, wearing a hood now as well as her long sleeves.

'These are the best the Imperator could send me?' Tyleigh grabbed one man by the chin and yanked his mouth open. She peered at his teeth. 'Criminals and cut-throats. No, send him back.'

She walked on to the next man, who eyed her warily. With a start, Leven realised she knew him: it was Foro, looking impossibly young, his dark hair shaved so close to his scalp it was a shadow. And on the heels of that, she realised she knew most of the people in that room. These were the recruits that would eventually make up the first Herald unit, their skins yet to be marked with the Titan ore.

'Yes, he'll do.' Tyleigh turned to one of her assistants. 'Take him to my workshop and get him prepared. Quickly, I haven't got all day.'

When the recruits had been divided into those that would become Heralds and those who would go back to their prison cells, Tyleigh went to Deryn. With one hand she pushed the young woman's hood back, and Leven could see that half of her face was already traced with ore-lines.

'It's finally time, Deryn,' Tyleigh said. She sounded proud, and Leven felt her heart ache for the girl she had once been. 'You will finally be complete, and the Imperium will see what I am capable of.'

Deryn nodded absently.

'I was already complete,' said Leven. 'I was *always* complete.' Next to her, Ynis took her hand again. 'Tyleigh is a monster. I'm not sure I can take much more of this, you know.'

'We're close now. Come on.'

78

The natural resources of Stratum were depleted decades ago, your Luminance. I do not need to tell you of the many core applications of the Titan ore, or the unlimited potential of its magics, and the vital quest we have undergone to make sure that the Imperium remains rich in the substance. With each newly Blessed land we expand our chances of coming across a new vein of Titan ore, and with each new batch of Heralds our ability to conquer the Unblessed increases. However, we cannot pretend that these new lands are relinquishing anything close to the amounts that Stratum did back in the reigns of your ancestors, and increasingly we are left with a difficult truth: Brittletain, with its living Titans, remains the last great source of Titan ore, and if we hope to maintain our dominance, it must, finally, be conquered.

Notes from the Imperial
concordance on the future
of Titan magics

The hole was small and shallow, but then it hardly needed to be big. Kaeto had dug it as best he could with his bare hands, and it had still taken him a very long time. It was hot, and his own blood was still trickling steadily from the wound in his side. He did not want to bury her here – Unblessed Houraki was no place for a child of Stratum to rest, and there were too many beetles, which she would not have liked – but more than anything he wanted the child to rest. The thought of carrying her small bones back with him, packed away in his bags like the Titan remains they were supposed to be returning with... it was too painful.

Carefully, he placed her into the hole, arranging her with the thoughtless skill of a man who had long been familiar with the anatomy of skeletal remains, and then sat, looking down into it. Her bones were so pale and fragile against the black dirt, like a bird's bones.

'I failed you, Belise,' he said. Unconsciously, he pressed one hand to the wound in his side. 'Not just here, on this piss poor excuse for a mission, but when I took you off the streets and made you into my creature. I could have simply been kind that day. I could have given you to a loving family, overseen your future and kept you safe from a distance, but instead I couldn't resist the idea that you were *like* me, that you had a potential you hadn't realised yet. I brought you into this dangerous life, gave you weapons and knowledge that no child should have, and then I let you die in this miserable place, in a miserable way. Because I was lonely. I failed you.'

'You didn't fail her.'

Kaeto looked up to see Felldir standing over him.

'What are you still doing here?' Kaeto made to stand up and found that he couldn't. Not that it mattered. 'Did you not follow Icaraine? I'm sure she has a use for her most loyal subject.'

Felldir gave him a curious look, then shook his head.

'I am going to pick you up,' he said. 'And see to that wound. It needs tending.'

'You'll do no such thing.' Kaeto pulled a knife from his sleeve, but it came slowly, and when Felldir reached down for him, he found he barely had the strength to lift it, let alone strike the Titan. His last impression was of a pair of strong arms lifting him up, and then a veil of grey passed over his vision, casting him into the black.

When he woke up, he was lying on the floor of a room somewhere in the Black City. There was a small fire burning in the fireplace, and his shirt had been removed; there was a bandage tight around his side, and his shirt was neatly folded next to him, each of his hidden weapons laid out on top of it. Felldir was crouched opposite him, and through the hole that was the window Kaeto could see the colours of early evening lying peacefully against the sky, a few streaks of cloud soaking up the last oranges and pinks of the sunset.

He sat up, wincing.

'You took me from her grave,' he said, his voice low with anguish. 'Even this last thing I could not do properly for her.'

Felldir shook his head. 'If I had left you there, you would have died too. What use would that be? And I have something I would like you to see, light-bones.'

'What? What could you possibly have that I would care about?' Kaeto shifted, grunting with the effort. 'There is nothing for me here, now.'

'Titans have an unusual relationship with death, and the dead,' said Felldir. Despite himself, Kaeto found he could not look away from the man's face. There was something there that he hadn't seen before, a kind of lightness. 'The griffins called it "walking the edge", this sense of being close to the lands of the spirit. I have been walking there for a long time, Kaeto. For these hundreds of years I have been imprisoned in the Black City, the dead have been my only company.'

Kaeto did not move. He was sure that the Titan had not used his name before.

'I went walking in the Undertomb again. What is left of it. And... I saw the spirit of your child. I saw Belise.'

'How dare you.' Kaeto shook his head. He could barely get the words out. 'How can you mock me with this. What sort of heartless creature are you?'

For a long moment Felldir said nothing at all. And then he stood.

'Get some sleep, light-bones. You need rest in order to heal.'

A couple of days later, Felldir insisted that Kaeto walk with him to the Undertomb, although he would not explain why. The place was a ruin now, a great hole in the centre of the city, open to the sky, and it took them some time to get down to the floor of the cavern. Kaeto was still moving slowly, and he refused to let Felldir help him. By the time they reached the bottommost part, strewn with debris and dead beetles, Kaeto was sweating heavily and the pain from his wound was a constant nauseating throb.

'We are here,' he said, leaning on a chunk of black rock for support. 'What was so important that we had to come back to this cursed place?'

Beneath their feet, the honeycomb that had held the imprisoned Othanim was largely empty, making their path across the cavern floor a treacherous one. Here and there, a Titan body remained, either because they had died long ago, or they had died in the destruction of the Undertomb itself.

'I told you that I saw your child's spirit,' said Felldir. 'She was wandering down here, looking for you. She was lost. And so I spoke to her.'

Kaeto bared his teeth in something like a grin. 'Ha. Good. Did you sustain a head injury when the Undertomb fell? Or have you always been a madman?'

That at least seemed to provoke some anger from the Titan. 'You know so little about us, light-bones, but you are happy enough to grind up our remains to fuel your own bastard magics. Will you listen to one of us for once, instead of using our mortal remains?' Felldir paused, took a breath. 'I spoke to the spirit of your child, here. She was confused, and annoyed that she couldn't find her way back to you. She had been searching for her own body, for a way up into the daylight, and couldn't find it.'

'Ah.' Kaeto rubbed the back of his sleeve over his eyes. Even if it was all a lie, every word seemed to stab him in the heart. 'Belise.'

'So I brought her to a new one.' Felldir began to walk across the cavern floor, taking huge strides, balancing perfectly on the remains of the honeycomb. 'Follow me.'

'You did what?'

Kaeto stumbled on behind, trying to keep up with the Titan, until Felldir stopped. Beneath them was one of the still occupied pods. Within it, a Titan appeared to sleep, her face clear and serene. The transparent seal was cracked where debris had hit it.

'Here. An intact vessel. We might not ever know why she was left behind, but lucky for us she was.' Felldir kneeled and pushed his fingers into the crack, taking hold of it and pulling it up until the seal splintered and came away. A dust of crystal shards fell on the Titan's face, and to Kaeto's surprise, she twitched, like a cat dreaming in its sleep. 'It took some persuading, but your child, she is wily, and persistent.'

'My child… What did you do, Felldir?'

At the sound of his voice, the Titan's eyes flickered and opened. A moment later and she was climbing up and out of the pod that had sealed her in for thousands of years. Her hair was long and black, her eyes were violet like the dusk, and her wings were covered in soft grey feathers. Kaeto shrank back, sure that she would butcher them there, or lay waste to the rest of the Black City, but instead she turned and sat on the edge of the pod, her legs kicking against the crystal interior like a child sitting on the edge of a wall.

'Hey, chief,' she said, grinning at him in a very familiar way. 'You'll never guess what I've been up to.'

79

Leven

I'm sorry our last meeting ended badly. You know me, I've never been good at talking – fighting, drinking, all that other coarse stuff, sure, but communication? Boss always did say that without her shouting orders I'd be lost. And maybe The Lip is just too noisy, I don't know. Listen, all I really needed you to know was that I'm worried, and that you should be careful. But more than that, I hope you can find something better than the Heralds. I hope you get far away from Stratum, and find a new life. And I hope you find something better to fight for.

Your friend,

Foro

Unsent letter from Herald Forty
to Herald Eleven, filed in
the Envoy Archive

'I can hardly believe it.'

'Imagine how we feel.'

Leven threw another small stick on the campfire. It was the morning, and they had moved outside of the cave to eat their breakfast. Cillian had listened to their account silently, only interrupting once when Echni the banished Druin had entered the story. Now he was looking at Ynis in wonder.

'A child, raised by griffins her whole life,' he said, shaking his head. 'How did you even survive?'

'My fathers found me, and they were kind,' said Ynis. 'It was hard for them, raising human yenlin in the nest-pit, but they knew that it was my fate to be there.'

'Strange choices were made in Yelvynia,' said Festus. The griffin was sat at the edge of the fire's warmth, preening his long blue flight feathers as they spoke. 'But I have other questions of you, humans. Why was this Echni in possession of my people's remains?'

Leven held up her arms so that the metallic lines caught the early-morning sunshine. If she was going to get eaten by a griffin, now was as good a time as ever. 'This magic that my mother grafted onto my skin? It is made from the bones of Titans. Echni made it here, in Brittletain first, and then she took her magic to the Imperium, where I imagine they perfected it. These ore-lines give us the ability to fly, like you, and to summon a magical blade.'

The griffin had stopped preening his feathers. His body was still, and he watched them like a hawk watching a mouse.

'You steal our bones, and you steal our magic?'

Ynis though had stood up and was pacing by the fire. Her face looked washed out and pale beneath the dirt.

'The Imperium are the humans that have been hunting us. They wounded Frost, and killed Brocken. They are the ones who have taken T'rook!'

'I recognised the arrowhead that hangs around your neck,' Leven said quietly. 'I've seen enough Imperial arrows over the last eight years. It's them alright. I imagine they've run out of ancient bones in Stratum and have decided to speed up the process.' Her mouth felt sour, as though the words she spoke were poisoning her. 'I've always known they were capable of nearly anything, but this?'

Cillian shook his head. 'It is an abomination.'

'And I've left her to them,' said Ynis, as though the others hadn't spoken. 'I've come to the border of Brittletain when I should have been running to T'rook. What if she's... What if she's already...'

'We'll find her.' Leven stood up. 'I doubt there's anything I can do to make up for what happened when we were children, Ynis, but I can swear this to you at least – I will take you to T'rook, and I will make the Imperium pay for every drop of griffin blood they have spilled. And when I've done that, I will seek out our sweet mother.' Leven smiled grimly. 'And she will pay for you, me, and our father. What a family reunion that will be.'

They agreed to set out as soon as fresh supplies had been gathered. Leven had walked down to a nearby stream and was rubbing ice-cold water on her face when Cillian put a hand on her shoulder.

'Leven,' he said, his voice grave. 'I think we should talk.'

She faced him, feeling a cold hand close around her heart. She had been expecting something like this, ever since she and Ynis had spun their long, awful story by the campfire.

'It's alright,' she said. 'I know. And I don't blame you. I am a creature of the Imperium, and worse than that even, an instrument of an evil woman – a murderer.' She forced herself to smile but it turned into a grimace. 'You would never have touched me if you'd known... if you'd known the extent of it. I killed my own father and left my baby sister to die.'

'No, Leven.' He smiled, although it still looked full of sorrow. 'I came to tell you that it wasn't your fault. I can see you, so intent on blaming yourself, but you were a *child*. All those terrible things that happened in the woods, they were Echni's doing, not yours. Look at your sister.' He nodded to the campfire behind them up the hill, where Ynis was talking to the griffin. 'Would you blame *her* if she were forced to do the same things? And you were younger even than her.'

'I...' Leven swallowed hard. There was a tightness in her throat and chest, and her eyes were full of tears.

'Fool.' Cillian put his arms around her and put his lips next to her ear. 'Perhaps we are both monsters, or perhaps we are both fools,' he whispered. 'It changes nothing for me.'

She reached up to hold his face, and kissed him, so that he wouldn't see her cry. When they came apart, his cheeks had a healthy pink flush to them, and she found herself wondering when they next might get some time alone together.

'Listen.' He cleared his throat. 'We should also talk about Epona. We can't leave her where she is.'

'Epona is safe where she is for now,' Leven said, hoping she was right. 'Remember, Queen Ceni was happy enough to murder me, but she kept her sister in a pleasant room far from the dungeons. I don't think she'll harm her sister – it's Queen Broudicca she wants to hurt. We'll find T'rook, and then we'll go back for Epona. She's the smartest person I know. She'll survive until we come for her, I'm sure of it.'

From further up the hill, Festus was stretching his wings, huge blue feathers like paint strokes against the frosty hill. Next to him, Ynis looked like a tiny thing, a girl made of matchsticks and dirt.

'The other thing I wanted to tell you,' said Cillian, 'is that Deryn is an old Druin word. It means bird. And Alaw – it means song.'

Leven wiped the last of the tears from her cheeks and laughed. 'Yeah,' she said, 'that sounds about right, doesn't it?'

80

S omeone had run ahead to tell the crowds they were coming.

Epona lifted her head. From her vantage point, she could see the roofs of the little village on the coast; tied to her post in the back of a wagon, she could see over the soldiers' heads even as they rode on their tall horses. The people of the village had gathered at the side of the road to watch Queen Ceni as she came past, but mostly, Epona was sure, they had come to see the infamous Murder Princess: Princess Epona, the diabolical schemer and killer of queens, the willing accomplice of the bloodthirsty queen of Londus. Despite everything, the thought made her smile. There was no doubt it was all a gratifying part of Ceni's plan – to hold her sister up as a monster and herself as the hero – but Epona suspected that it had annoyed her considerably to have made her younger sister quite so famous.

It was a gusty, windy day with a smattering of salty rain in the air, and as the procession drew closer to the waiting crowds she could hear the people shouting. 'Queen Ceni!' yes, but also 'Show us the killer!' and 'Epona must die!' If she had to bet on it, Epona would have said that the calls for her death were more enthusiastic than the greetings for Ceni.

'What are you grinning about?'

Ceni rode a horse just to the left of the wagon, between Epona and the jagged cliff edge. *As if she expects me to magic myself out of these ropes and make a run for the sea*, thought Epona.

'Oh, just enjoying the view,' Epona called to her sister. 'I've spent weeks in the Wild Wood, so it's quite the relief to see the sea, you know. What a lovely idea it was of yours, Ceni, to accompany me back to Londus.'

'You always did think you were so clever,' said Ceni. The guard that rode with her had fallen back a few feet for the sake of privacy. 'So clever, and so funny. You won't find it so funny when we reach the gates of Londus, Epona.'

'Why? What are you going to do? Chop my head off and throw it in the moat, like the barbarians did of old?'

Epona chuckled at the image, but when she met her sister's eye she saw that she was smiling, and her stomach boiled like a nest of snakes.

'Mother used to say that it was possible to have too many daughters,' Ceni said. 'It seems to me it's certainly possible to have too many sisters.'

They had reached the edge of the crowd. The shouting became a roar, and Epona did her best to face it with a nonchalant look on her face, but when the first potato hit her – striking her hard on the thigh, as painful as any rock – she found herself gritting her teeth. Her shoulder was bandaged but still painful, and she felt bruised all over. Yesterday, when they passed through one of the larger northern towns, someone had thrown a tomato so rotten she was surprised it had kept its shape in the air, and when it had struck her forehead its juice and seeds had run into her eyes, making them sting for hours. And someone had thrown a piece of flint, and that had opened a cut that bled and bled. She would rather die than admit it to Ceni, but she thought it likely she would be beaten to bits long before they reached the borders of Londus. *She'll be lucky if there's still a head to chop off,* she thought grimly.

Ceni, meanwhile, was shouting to the crowd, urging them on.

'This is the woman who plotted against the queens of Brittletain! This is the woman who walked arm in arm with an Imperial assassin!

We are taking her to Londus to see justice done and the warmonger Broudicca removed from the throne!'

More objects crashed against the wagon. Epona could hear some of the horses whinnying, nervous about the violence. Another potato, bigger than the first one, struck her on the collarbone and for a few seconds she sagged against the ropes tying her in place.

'Fuck.'

As she had done many times over the last few days, Epona turned away from the howling crowds and lifted her gaze to the skies, hoping to see a winged shape there: Leven coming to save her; Leven coming to cut her stupid sister down where she stood.

And for the first time, she saw something.

The pain and the projectiles forgotten, Epona straightened up, squinting at the tiny moving object pinned against the clouds. It was coming in over the sea, which was curious – what would Leven be doing so far out there – and then as she watched she saw that there was not just one figure in the sky, but several. And they were getting bigger all the time. The roar of the crowd changed, becoming less angry and more confused. Whatever it was, they had spotted it too.

'Our justice will be done, I promise you that!' Ceni was still shouting. 'Queen Broudicca will pay for her conspiracy, for her use of corrupted Druin magic, and for her greed!' This time the crowd did not react. They were all looking beyond Ceni and Epona, staring in shock at what was approaching them over the iron-grey sea. Ceni, finally realising she no longer had their attention, turned to see what they were all looking at. She sat up in her saddle, her arms falling to her sides.

'What is *that*?' she asked, her voice hushed. 'More Heralds?'

'Oh no, sister.' Epona, who had spent plenty of time in close quarters with a Herald, and who had been watching the movements of these new flying creatures closely since the moment they appeared, shook her head. 'I've a feeling this is something much worse.'

ACKNOWLEDGEMENTS

I had to delve deep into my document folders to find out exactly when I started writing this book, and to my surprise it began in early 2019, which is a good chunk of time earlier than I was expecting. The last few years have had some good things (writing crime novels) and some totally shite things (Covid, the health problems of my nearest and dearest), and apparently *Talonsister* has always been in the background, popping up when I needed somewhere else to be – which was quite often – and then receding again when I had to work on other books. People often use the term escapism like it's a dirty word, but who doesn't want and need to escape every now and then? Where would we be if freedom from pain was never an option? *Talonsister* began in early 2019, but the catalyst that started it all was the image of a child and a griffin, inseparable; an image that's been with me since the very beginning of my writing career. I'm glad I finally got to write Ynis's story.

As ever there are lots of people without whom *Talonsister* would never have made it off the ground. I am forever grateful for the wisdom and wit of Juliet Mushens, who has been my agent for over ten years at this point and remains an undisputed superstar, capable of banging out karaoke hits and delivering spot on editorial advice (probably at the same time). My editors Davi Lancett and latterly Sophie Robinson and Katie Dent at Titan took to Brittletain and all its chaotic history wholeheartedly, and their comments and advice were like a shot of Titan ore in the arm (without the morally dubious implications). I'd also like to thank Hayley Shepherd for a clear-eyed and sensitive copy edit that has undoubtedly saved me from a menagerie of whopping cock ups.

For moral support/bitching sessions/visits to cat cafes/company down the pub I'd like to thank Andrew Reid, Den Patrick, Adam Christopher, Michaela Gray and the Onesies, as well as all the staff at Clapham Books and Herne Hill Books. Thanks as ever to my family, who periodically remind me to do things like leave my desk and go for a walk around the woods.

I'd also like to send huge dollops of gratitude to Petrik Leo, Elliot Brooks and The Broken Binding, who together brought a whole new audience to the Winnowing Flame trilogy. Publishing can be a hard business, often crushing entire authors underfoot, so it's incredibly uplifting to witness the power of people who just love books and reading and want to share their passion. Bravo!

Lastly, love and thanks to my partner and best friend Marty – who keeps me laughing every day, believes that I can do these things, and doesn't judge me for the number of Skeletor action figures on my desk. You're the best, cariad!

ABOUT THE AUTHOR

JEN WILLIAMS lives in London with her partner and their small ridiculous cat. Having been a fan of grisly fairy tales from a young age, these days Jen writes dark unsettling thrillers with strong female leads, as well as character-driven fantasy novels with plenty of adventure and magic. She has twice won the British Fantasy Award for her Winnowing Flame trilogy, and when she's not writing books she works as a bookseller and a freelance copywriter.

Find out more at www.sennydreadful.co.uk or follow her on Twitter @sennydreadful

For more fantastic fiction, author events,
exclusive excerpts, competitions, limited editions and more

VISIT OUR WEBSITE
titanbooks.com

LIKE US ON FACEBOOK
facebook.com/titanbooks

FOLLOW US ON TWITTER AND INSTAGRAM
@TitanBooks

EMAIL US
readerfeedback@titanemail.com